THE SAMURAI

THE
SAMURAI

SHUSAKU ENDO

Translated by Van C. Gessel

KODANSHA INTERNATIONAL
Tokyo · New York · London

Originally published in English by Peter Owen Ltd, London, 1982.

Published and distributed in Japan by Kodansha International Ltd.,
17-14 Otowa 1-chome, Bunkyo-ku, Tokyo 112-8652. Copyright ©
1980 by Shusaku Endo. English translation copyright © 1982 by
Van C. Gessel. All rights reserved. Printed in Japan.
ISBN 4-7700-1996-3
First KI paperback edition, 1996

03 04 05   5 4 3

www.thejapanpage.com

TRANSLATOR'S NOTE

The process of dismantling a work of foreign literature brick by brick and rebuilding it on one's native soil is seldom a thoroughly satisfying experience. At times the foundation itself will not conform to the unfamiliar terrain; occasionally it is only that the sun-porch looks somewhat ludicrous in a region of incessant rains. In an essay many years back, Mr Endō very properly referred to literary translation as a task of 'transformation', for a piece of literature that is forcibly uprooted from its natural environment and thrust into strange surroundings will of necessity go through some painful but necessary changes.

These transformation pains are much like the throes of 'culture shock', familiar to anyone who has spent considerable time abroad. I wonder sometimes whether the part of a novel that has life in itself does not go through similar trauma when it is translated into a foreign idiom. Remembering the days of physical and spiritual agony during my first sojourn in Japan, I have struggled to make the transition of *The Samurai* to English a gentle one. My foremost concern has been to preserve the integrity of Mr Endō's original work. That is why, for instance, I have insisted that the protagonist remain 'the samurai' throughout, for it is a term connoting 'service to one's master', a central theme in the novel. I have also maintained such terms as 'Nueva España', even when slightly unwieldy, since the more concise 'Mexico' is historically inaccurate for this period. Footnotes have been added to clarify items which only a Japanese reader should be expected to know. All names in the text are given in normal Japanese order, surname first.

In a few instances, however, it has been the consensus between myself and those who have been good enough to read my manuscript that a few minor concessions to Western tastes and preferences were essential. With Mr Endō's permission, I have made a very small number of excisions in the text. These cuts have never been deep enough to draw blood, and if the reader could examine each wound

5

carefully he would, I think, be grateful rather than incensed that minor elective surgery was performed. The cuts were made for two reasons: first, because the Japanese language allows for more elasticity than we are accustomed to in English; second, because the technique of repetition which Mr Endō has employed in his text, though a familiar and acceptable literary device in Japan, would doubtless only irritate and alienate the Western reader. What I have done in the first instance is to tighten the prose ever so slightly; in the latter case, I have blinked for an instant and allowed myself to pass over the redundancies. Only those who can read the original will be able to verify that I have done no perceptible harm to the novel; all others will have to accept my assurance that I have had only the best interests of my friend Shūsaku Endō in mind.

I have drawn on the knowledge and wisdom of many in making this translation. I am grateful to a host of teachers and colleagues at Columbia University and the University of Notre Dame. Special thanks go to Professor Donald Keene of Columbia who, with customary gentility and meticulousness, read and commented on my manuscript; to Mr Dan Franklin, a patient and perceptive editor; and to my wife Elizabeth.

Van C. Gessel
University of Notre Dame
Autumn 1981

PREFACE

The Samurai is set in Japan at the beginning of the seventeenth century. For the benefit of Western readers who might not be familiar with Japanese history, it might be well to explain the general situation in Japan during that period.

Although situated at the furthest reaches of the Orient, in the early 1600s Japan was on the verge of being swallowed up into the extremely complex and perilous maelstrom of international politics. The nations of Europe – primarily Protestant England and Holland and Catholic Portugal and Spain – were struggling to extend their influence into Asia. These European nations established colonies in every corner of south-east Asia, built ships to increase their trade and wealth, and battled with one another on the Asian seas. Such battles were not restricted to political and commercial conflicts, but also included religious disputes between Catholics and Protestants.

Caught up in the middle of this vortex, Japan sensed the need to protect herself. The Japanese ruler, Tokugawa Ieyasu, was careful not to repeat the reckless errors of his predecessor, Toyotomi Hideyoshi, who had attempted to subjugate Korea. Ieyasu set out to crush the forces who supported Hideyoshi's son and ultimately to unify Japan. At the same time, in his foreign policy Ieyasu sought means to shield Japan from invasions by the various nations of Europe. In his day Hideyoshi had ostensibly banned proselytization by Christian missionaries in Japan, but for the sake of commerce he had tolerated their activities. Ieyasu, however, was a devout Buddhist and, persuaded that they were the vanguard for the conquest of Japan, in a series of stages he suppressed the Christian missionaries.

As a result, a severe blow was dealt to the evangelizing efforts of the European missionaries, who had been pursuing their labours with vigour. At about the same time, missionary work in Japan, which had earlier been restricted to the Society of Jesus, was opened up to the Augustinians, the Dominicans, the Franciscans and several other

7

monastic orders. The result was considerable discord between the Jesuits and the newly-admitted societies over the conduct of missionary work in Japan.

Ieyasu's tactics, however, were not confined to the elimination of the danger within. In order to create a Japan capable of resisting the encroaching European powers, he decided to enter the conflict being waged on the waters of the Pacific Ocean. His plan, which showed enormous political skill, involved the unwitting participation of four low-ranking samurai – vassals of the most powerful *daimyō* in the north-eastern provinces of Japan – and an ambitious Spanish priest.

Of course my purpose in writing *The Samurai* was not to depict the condition of Japan in the seventeenth century. But the setting of the novel will doubtless be more vivid for the reader who has some knowledge of the historical background.

Shūsaku Endō
Tokyo, summer 1981

Chapter 1

It began to snow.

Until nightfall a faint sunlight had bathed the gravel-covered river bed through breaks in the clouds. When the sky turned dark, an abrupt silence ensued. Two, then three flakes of snow fluttered down from the sky.

As the samurai and his men cut wood, snow grazed their rustic outfits, brushed against their faces and hands, then melted away as if to underscore the brevity of life. But when the men continued to ply their hatchets without a word, the snow snubbed them and scurried on to the surrounding areas. The evening haze spread and blended with the snow, turning their field of vision grey.

At length the samurai and his men finished their labours and shouldered the faggots of wood. They were chopping firewood in preparation for the imminent onset of winter. Snow pelted their foreheads as they set out, like ants in single file, and retraced their steps along the river bed back to the marshland.

Three villages lay deep within the marshland, encircled by hills of withered foliage. Each house was so positioned that the hills lay to its rear and the fields in front; that way the villagers could watch for strangers entering the marshland. The straw-thatched houses were lined up tightly one beside another, as if they had been squashed together. Racks woven from bamboo were fixed to the ceilings, and on these firewood and cogon grass were dried. The houses were foul-smelling and dark, like cattle sheds.

The samurai knew every detail of these villages. His Lordship had granted the villages and lands to the samurai's family as an inheritance in his father's generation. As the eldest son, the samurai had the responsibility of assembling groups of peasants when orders for corvée labourers were sent down, and in the event of battle he would be required to lead his troops to the fortress of his Patron,

Lord Ishida.

The samurai's house was more impressive than those of the peasants, though it was actually nothing more than several thatched buildings clustered together. It differed from the peasants' houses in that it had several barns and a large stable, and was surrounded by earthworks. Despite these earthworks, the house was not of course designed as a place to do battle. On a mountain to the north of the marshland were the ruins of a fortress which had belonged to a local samurai who had controlled this district until he was annihilated by His Lordship. But now warfare had ceased throughout Japan and His Lordship had become the most powerful *daimyō** in the northern provinces, so the samurai's family had no further need of such bastions. In fact, although distinctions of rank between superior and inferior continued to be observed here, the samurai still laboured in the fields and burned charcoal in the mountains alongside his servants. His wife helped the other women tend the horses and cattle. A total of sixty-five *kan* in land taxes had to be paid annually to His Lordship from the three villages – sixty *kan* from the rice fields and five *kan* from the cultivated land.

At intervals the snow was driven by a strong wind. The footprints of the samurai and his men left smudges here and there down the long road. They walked along like docile cattle, no one uttering an unnecessary word. When they came to a small wooden bridge called Nihonsugi, the samurai caught sight of Yozō, his hair also streaked white with snow, standing like a statue of the Buddha in the wilderness.

'Your uncle has come.'

The samurai nodded, and removing the faggot of wood from his shoulder, he placed it at Yozō's feet. Like the peasants who worked this land, the samurai's eyes were sunken, his cheekbones protruded, and he smelled of the earth. Like the peasants, he was a man of few words who seldom let his emotions rise to the surface, but his heart sank at this news. Although, as the eldest son, the samurai had inherited control of the main branch of the Hasekura family at his father's death, he still consulted his uncle before making any decision. His uncle had fought at his father's side in many of His Lordship's military campaigns. When the samurai was a child, his uncle often sat beside the sunken hearth, his face flushed crimson with liquor. He would call, 'Look at this, Roku,' and show his nephew the pale brown scars on his thigh. Received when His Lordship fought against the Ashina clan at Suriagehara, these battle scars were a

* A feudal lord, one of a class of military warlords who came to power in the sixteenth century. In 1614, there were almost two hundred *daimyōs* in Japan.

source of pride to his uncle. But over the last four or five years the old man had grown feeble, and now when he visited the samurai's home, he sat around drinking liquor and voicing blustery complaints. Once he had registered his grievances, he would return home, dragging his wounded leg behind him like a lame dog.

Leaving his men behind, the samurai climbed the slope to his house alone. Snowflakes swirled across the wide grey sky, and the main building and its sheds rose up before him like a black fortress. As he passed by the stable, the stench of straw mingled with horse dung assaulted his nose. At the sound of their master's footsteps, the horses pawed the ground. When he reached the house, the samurai paused and carefully brushed the snow from his working clothes before entering. His uncle was seated at the sunken hearth by the main entrance with his crippled right leg thrust out, warming his hands over the fire. The samurai's eldest son, a twelve-year-old boy, sat deferentially beside him.

'Is that you, Roku?' his uncle called, pressing his hand against his mouth and coughing as though he had choked on the smoke from the hearth. When Kanzaburō saw his father, he bowed as though he had been rescued from the old man and rushed off to the kitchen. Smoke from the hearth spiralled up the pot hanger and floated towards the soot-stained ceiling. In his father's generation, and now in the samurai's day, this blackened hearth had been the scene of many conferences where a variety of decisions had been made, as well as the spot where disputes among the villagers had been settled.

'I went to Nunozawa and saw Lord Ishida.' The old man coughed again. 'He says there is still no answer from the castle about the lands at Kurokawa.'

Without a word of reply, the samurai took some dried branches from the pile beside him and broke them for the hearth. As he listened to the dull snap of the branches, he tried his best to endure these familiar complaints from his uncle. He was mute not from any lack of thought or feeling. It was simply that he was not accustomed to allowing his emotions to show on his face, and that he did not like to disagree with anyone. Even more than that, however, it oppressed him to have to listen to his uncle's incessant talk about events from the past which he refused to let rest.

Eleven years earlier, when His Lordship had built a new castle and town and reapportioned the fiefdoms, this section of marshland with its three villages had been given to the samurai's family in place of the lands at Kurokawa where their ancestors had lived for generations. His Lordship's explicit aim in moving the family from their ancient domain to an impoverished wilderness was to develop the desolate region, but the samurai's father had his own ideas about the reason for the move. When the *Kampaku* Lord Hideyoshi subjugated His Lordship, a group of warriors led by the families of Kasai and Ōzaki rebelled, and several men distantly related to the samurai's family had participated in the uprising. And because the samurai's father had harboured the defeated rebels and helped them to escape, he was convinced that His Lordship must have taken note of that and in retribution given them this wilderness in place of their lands at Kurokawa.

The dead branches which the samurai had tossed into the fire crackled like the mutterings and grumblings of his father and uncle at the treatment they had received. The samurai's wife, Riku, opened the door from the kitchen and quietly placed before the two men cups of *sake* and *miso* soup in bowls fashioned from dried magnolia leaves. A glance at the faces of the two men was enough to tell her what the topic of conversation was again this evening.

'You know, Riku,' her uncle turned towards her, 'it looks as if we're going to have to go on living in this prairie.'

In the local dialect, a 'prairie' referred to a forsaken wilderness. Fields watered by rock-bound streams, producing nothing but a paltry crop of rice along with some buckwheat, millet and *daikon*. Winter came earlier here than it had in their native lands, and the cold was intense. Before long the marshland, the hills and the forests would be buried deep beneath the pure white snow, and the inhabitants would huddle in their dark houses with bated breath, listening throughout the long nights to the discordant winds and awaiting the arrival of spring.

'If only we had a battle to fight. If we had a war, we could show them what we can do and get even more lands as a reward.'

Vigorously massaging his lean knees, the samurai's uncle repeated the familiar complaint. But the times when His Lordship spent each day and night waging battles had long since passed. Though the western provinces were still unsettled, the eastern domains had now submitted to the hegemony of Lord Tokugawa, and not even His Lordship, the most powerful *daimyō* in the north-east, could manipulate troops at his own will and whim.

The samurai and his wife snapped twigs and listened patiently as their uncle sought to divert his thoughts from his pent-up discontent by drinking *sake*, muttering to himself and concocting tales of his own prowess. They had heard these boastful stories time and time again, until they had come to seem like mouldy food which the old man ate in solitude to stay alive.

Just before midnight the samurai sent two of his servants to escort his uncle home, When they opened the door to leave, a break in the clouds was uncannily rimmed with moonlight, and the snow had ceased. A dog barked until the samurai's uncle had disappeared from view.

In the marshland, famine was more feared than war. Some of the older people still remembered vividly the damage done by the cold that had swept over the area many years before.

They told how the winter that year had been unusually warm, with continuous spells of springlike weather, and how the mountain to the north-west had been wrapped in a constant haze and only faintly visible. But when spring ended and the rainy season set in, the rains were incessant, and even after summer arrived, the mornings and nights were so chilly that it was impossible to remove one's clothing. The sprouts in the fields showed no signs of maturing, and many of them withered away.

Food supplies dwindled to nothing. The villagers gathered arrowroot from the mountains and even ate the rice bran, hay and beanstalks that were intended as feed for the horses. When those provisions were exhausted, they killed their precious horses and dogs and even ate tree bark and weeds to stave off starvation. When they had eaten everything that they could find, parents and children, husbands and wives went their separate ways, leaving their villages in search of food. Some dropped along the road from starvation, but their relatives could do nothing for them and abandoned them where they lay. Eventually wild dogs and crows devoured the corpses.

Fortunately, there had not been another famine since the samurai's family had taken control of the fief, but his father had ordered every household in the villages to fill straw bags with chestnuts, acorns, and millet plucked fresh from the ear, and to store them above the beams of their houses. Whenever the samurai saw these bags, thoughts of his monotonous uncle fled from his mind, and it was the gentle face of his wiser father that he recalled.

Yet even his father had treasured up memories of the fertile lands of his ancestors. 'If we were in Kurokawa', he had remarked, 'we could get by even if we had a bad harvest. . . .' There were rich plains in Kurokawa which were capable of yielding abundant crops of wheat with very little care. But in this desolate wilderness, the principal crops were buckwheat, millet and *daikon*, foodstuffs that could not be eaten every day since annual taxes in kind had to be paid to His Lordship. Even in the samurai's home there were days when all they had to eat were *daikon* leaves with wheat or millet. The peasants often subsisted on wild onions or chives.

Yet in spite of the grumblings of his father and his uncle, the samurai felt no hatred for this unproductive land. This was the first land he had governed himself as the eldest son in the family after his father's death. The peasants, with hollow eyes and jutting cheekbones like his own, worked silently like cattle from daybreak to nightfall, never quarrelling or bickering. They cultivated the barren fields and never failed to pay their taxes even if it meant cutting back on their own food supplies. When he talked to the peasants, the samurai forgot their differences in rank, sensing something that bound him to these people. He considered perseverance his only redeeming personal trait, and yet these peasants were infinitely more obedient and long-suffering than he.

Sometimes the samurai would take Kanzaburō and climb the hill that stood to the north of their home. The ruins of the stronghold built by the rural samurai who had once ruled this region still remained, buried under clumps of weeds, and occasionally, in the dry moat hidden beneath the tangled undergrowth, or on the earthwork covered with withered leaves, they would find charred grains of rice or shattered bowls. From the top of the windblown mountain they could look down on the marshland and the villages. A pitiful stretch of land, almost pathetic. Villages that seemed to be squashed together.

'This . . . this is my land,' the samurai muttered to himself. If there were no more wars, then he would remain here for the rest of his life, just as his father had done. When he was dead, his eldest son would inherit the land and no doubt lead the same sort of life. For as long as they lived, he and his son would never be separated from this land.

Sometimes he went fishing with Yozō in the tiny marsh at the foot of that same mountain. In late autumn, in the thick dark reeds of the marsh, he had seen three or four long-necked white birds flapping their wings amidst the brown waterfowl. These white swans had crossed the ocean from a distant land where the cold was intense. When spring returned they would open their great wings, soar across the sky above the marshland and disappear. Each time he saw the swans, the samurai thought, 'They know lands I will never visit in my entire life.' But he felt little envy of them.

A summons came from Lord Ishida. The samurai was ordered to come to Nunozawa, as his Patron had a matter he wished to discuss.

In former days Lord Ishida's family had often risen up against the ancestors of His Lordship, but now Lord Ishida was a wealthy vassal with the rank of general.

The samurai took Yozō with him and left the marshland early in the morning, arriving in Nunozawa around noon. A freezing rain was falling, and on the surface of the moat that surrounded the walled fortress countless droplets dissolved as quickly as they fell. The samurai waited briefly in the antechamber before he was shown in for an audience with his Patron.

Lord Ishida, a plump man wearing *haori*,* seated himself and smiled at the samurai, who bowed deeply, pressing both his hands against the dark, polished floorboards. Lord Ishida enquired after the samurai's uncle and remarked with a smile, 'He was here again a few days ago with more complaints.'

The samurai bowed deeply in apology. Each time his father or his uncle had begged to have their fief in Kurokawa returned to them, Lord Ishida had forwarded their petition to the castle. Some time later, however, the samurai had learned from Lord Ishida that such petitions from landholders had poured in to the castle and were piled up for consideration by the Council of Elders. Unless there were some compelling reason, it was unlikely that His Lordship would respond to such requests.

'I understand how the old man feels.' Lord Ishida suddenly grew serious. 'But there will be no more wars. The Naifu† wants to concentrate his energies on Osaka, and His Lordship supports him in that decision,' he said forcefully.

Was I summoned all the way to Nunozawa to hear this? the samurai wondered. Does Lord Ishida want to let me know that it is useless to present any more petitions?

Sorrow washed through his breast like water overflowing. Although he was attached to the marshland, not for a single day had he forgotten the lands that were saturated with the sweat and the memories of his ancestors. Now, as Lord Ishida bluntly ordered him to abandon all hope, the solitary face of his father floated up before the samurai's eyes. He could also see the peeved expression on his uncle's face.

'I know it won't be easy, but you must make the old man understand. The old fellow just can't bring himself to accept the changes that happen in the world.'

---

*A short half-coat worn over a long kimono on formal occasions.
†Tokugawa Ieyasu (1542–1616), the last of the 'three great unifiers' of Japan, established the shōgunate which bore his name and ruled an isolated Japan for over 250 years. Ieyasu gave the title of Shōgun to his son Hidetada in 1605, holding actual power himself until his death under such court titles as Naifu.

Lord Ishida looked with real sympathy at the samurai, whose eyes were fixed on the floor.

'The Council of Elders isn't just singling out your family. Many other lance-corporals have asked to have their old lands returned to them. That has caused the elder statesmen a great deal of concern. If they have to listen to the selfish demands of each individual, the entire system of allotments will collapse.'

The samurai rested both hands on his knees and stared at the floor.

'But I asked you here today for another reason. New orders for labour service will be coming soon. There may be some special instructions for you. I want you to remember this.'

The samurai had no idea what his Patron meant or why he had suddenly given him this piece of information. Soon he bowed his head and moved to retire, but Lord Ishida instructed him to stay, and went on to speak of the lively state of affairs in Edo.* The previous year the various *daimyōs* had taken upon themselves the task of reconstructing Edo Castle for the Shōgun. His Lordship had received a share of that responsibility, and recently Lord Ishida, Lord Watari, Lord Shiraishi, and other generals were taking turns to serve in Edo.

'They've launched quite a hunt for the Christians there. On my way back, I saw many of them being paraded through the streets.'

The samurai was aware that this year the Naifu, the father of the present Shōgun, had proscribed the teachings of Christianity in the domains directly administered by the shōgunate. As a result, exiled Christians had migrated to the western provinces or to the north-east, where no proscription was enforced. The samurai had heard frequently of Christians labouring in the gold mines and in other areas within the borders of His Lordship's lands.

The prisoners Lord Ishida had observed had been put on work horses draped with tiny paper flags and paraded along the main thoroughfares of the villages on the way to the execution grounds. The prisoners spoke to acquaintances in the crowds as they passed, and seemed unafraid of death.

'There were some foreign padres among them. Have you ever seen a Christian or a padre?'

'No.'

Listening to Lord Ishida's tale, the samurai could muster not the slightest interest in the Christian prisoners. Christianity itself meant nothing to him. It bore no relation to the snow-laden wilderness where he lived. The people in the marshland would live their whole

---

* Edo is the present-day Tokyo.

lives without ever seeing the Christians who had fled from Edo.

'I'm sorry you have to go back in all this rain.' Lord Ishida's farewell was kindly and paternal. Outside the mansion Yozō, wrapped in a straw raincoat that had been drenched by the freezing rain, was waiting like an obedient dog. Three years older than his master, he had grown up in the same house, and had laboured all his days for the Hasekura family. As the samurai mounted his horse, he thought of the moonlit marshland to which they would return. The snow from several days before would now be frozen ice glimmering in the darkness, and the houses of the peasants would be as silent as death. Only his wife Riku and three or four others would still be awake, awaiting his return beside the sunken hearth. Hearing footsteps, the dog would bark, and in the stable that smelled of musty straw the horses would awaken and stamp their hooves.

The smell of musty straw also permeated the prison cell in which the missionary was sitting. It blended with the body odours and the stench of urine from the Christians who had been incarcerated here before, and this mixture of foul odours constantly assailed his nostrils.

He had been in this cell since the previous day, weighing the odds that he would be executed against those that he would be released. He considered the alternatives dispassionately, like a merchant who coldly scrutinizes two saucers of gold dust to determine which is the heavier. If his life were spared, it would be because the statesmen of this country still had need of him. Up until now, they had used him as a translator whenever emissaries had come from Manila, and in fact there were no other missionaries left in Edo who had his fluent command of Japanese. If the covetous Japanese wished to continue their profitable trade relationship with Manila or with Nueva España far across the Pacific Ocean, they could not afford to dispense with him, since he could serve as a bridge for their negotiations. 'I am willing to die if it be Thy will,' the missionary thought, lifting his head proudly like a hawk. 'But Thou knowest how much the Church in Japan needs me.'

Yes. Just as the rulers of this nation require my services, the Lord also has need of me. An exultant smile crept across his face. The missionary was confident of his own abilities. As Provincial of Edo for the Franciscan Order,* he had always felt that up to now the

---

*In the final printed version of *The Samurai*, Endō refers to the two rival Orders as the Societies of Peter and Paul. At Mr Endō's encouragement, I have restored the names used in the original manuscript – the Jesuits and Franciscans, respectively.

failure of the missionary effort in Japan was a result of the blunders
made by the Society of Jesus, which had continually opposed his
Order in all things. Though the Jesuits strove endlessly to be political
in the most trivial of matters, in reality they knew nothing of politics.
After sixty years of proselytizing they had built up churches in
Nagasaki with independent administrative and judicial authority,
thereby planting seeds of distrust and anxiety in the minds of the
Japanese authorities.

'Had I been Bishop, I would not have countenanced such
stupidity. Had I but been Bishop of Japan. . . .'

As these words formed in his mind, he blushed like a young girl.
He realized that a measure of worldly ambition and vanity lingered in
a distorted form within him. There was still an element of self-
seeking in his desire to become a bishop and receive full responsibility
from the Vatican for the missionary work in Japan.

The missionary's father had been a member of the influential
municipal assembly in Sevilla, and his ancestors included a viceroy of
Panama. Another had been a director of the Inquisition. And his
grandfather had participated in the subjugation of the West Indies. It
was only after coming to Japan that he had recognized that the blood
of politicians in his veins had given him talents not possessed by
common priests. He could present himself before the Naifu or the
Shōgun without a trace of subservience and read the thoughts of the
Shōgun's wily councillors and win them over to his side.

But because of pressure from the Society of Jesus, he had so far
been denied a great stage upon which to display these inherited
talents. He knew that the Jesuits, unable to manipulate Hideyoshi* or
the Naifu adroitly and even failing to appease the Buddhist prelates
who had established a strong foothold in Edo Castle, had instead
sown seeds of antipathy and mistrust among these powerful
individuals. For that reason, although he was ashamed of his own
ambitions, he could not repress his desire to become Bishop.

'The spreading of the gospel in this land is a battle. When there are
incompetent commanders on the battlefield, the blood of warriors is
shed needlessly.'

He therefore had to stay alive in this country. While still in hiding,
he had learned that five Christians had been apprehended, but his
sense of mission had impelled him to avoid a similar fate.

'Yet if Thou hast need of me no longer,' he muttered, rubbing his

* Before the Tokugawa family solidified control over Japan, Toyotomi Hideyoshi
(1536–1598), known as the Taikō or 'Regent', was in effect the ruler of Japan. After
Hideyoshi's death, his family continued to exert influence until the Tokugawas
annihilated them in 1615.

numb legs, 'Thou mayest summon me at any time. Thou knowest better than anyone else that I am not at all attached to this life.'

Something soft and black brushed past the leg he was massaging. It was one of the rats that nested in the prison. The previous night, as he had slept, the rats had been gnawing softly at some corner of this tiny room. Each time the noise woke him, he intoned the Lord's Prayer for the sake of those five Christians, who doubtless had already been killed at the execution ground. By reciting the prayer, he tried to soothe the pangs of conscience that tormented him for abandoning them.

At the sound of footsteps in the distance, the missionary hurriedly drew in his outstretched legs and sat upright. He did not want the guard who brought his food to see him in a slovenly posture. Even in prison, he could not allow himself to behave in a manner that would invite mockery from the Japanese.

The footsteps drew nearer. He decided he must try to smile, so as he listened to the dull clatter of the key being thrust into the lock, the missionary curled his cheeks. He had always wanted to wear a smile even as death approached.

The door opened with a creak and a light like molten tin bathed the dark earthen floor. He blinked his eyes and smiled in the direction of the door, then saw that it was not the usual guard who had come for him. Two officials in black kimonos were peering in at him.

'Come out!' one of them squawked. The word 'release', mingled with a surge of joy, darted about in the missionary's head.

'Where are we going?' Still smiling, the missionary spoke off-handedly, but his legs wobbled unsteadily. Gloweringly silent, the officials led the way from the cell, swaying their shoulders as they walked. This affected manner of walking, peculiar to the Japanese, reminded him of the ridiculous movements of a child and, confident now that he would be released, he could not help smiling at them.

'Look out there.' One of the officials abruptly halted and glanced back over his shoulder, gesturing with his chin towards the courtyard that was visible through a window in the hallway. Outside, the sun was beginning to fade. Straw mats had been spread on the ground, buckets of water had been set out, and two stools stood one beside the other.

'Do you know what that is?' The second official laughed contemptuously and, with one finger extended, pretended to slit his own throat.

'That's what it is!' He watched gleefully as the missionary's body stiffened. 'The foreigner is trembling!'

The missionary clenched both his hands, struggling to stifle the shame and anger that welled up inside him. For two days now he had been humiliated by the intimidations of these petty officials, and, for someone of such overwhelming pride, it was unbearable to think that he had let these men see fear on his face for even a moment. His knees went on shaking until he was led out of the prison and into the building across the way.

It was nightfall and the building was empty, without a trace of another human being. Before they departed, the officials made him sit in formal posture on the cold, polished floor of the room to which they had escorted him. The missionary, like a child eating in secret, gorged himself on the cheerful assurance that release was at hand.

'You see! It's just as I thought!' he muttered, and the shame he had felt so recently melted away, to be replaced by the characteristic self-assurance that his perceptions had not been in error.

'It's such a simple matter to work out what a Japanese is thinking.'

He knew that whether they liked him or not, the Japanese would spare the life of someone who could be useful to them, and his talents as an interpreter were still indispensable to the leaders of this country, who were dazzled by the prospect of trade profits. That was why the Naifu and the Shōgun, even though they despised Christians, continued to allow missionaries to reside in the city. The Naifu wanted another port the equal of Nagasaki from which to trade with distant lands. He was particularly keen to open trade relations with Nueva España, far across the sea, and to that purpose he had sent a number of letters to the Spanish Viceroy in Manila. The missionary had often been summoned to Edo Castle to translate those letters and the replies received from Manila.

Only once had he seen the Naifu. Accompanying an emissary from Manila to the castle, in the dark audience chamber he had seen an old man sitting listlessly in a chair upholstered in velvet. He spoke not a word but, without expression, listened to the conversation between the Councillors and the emissary and glanced at the queer gifts the latter had brought. Yet, many times thereafter that expressionless face and those expressionless eyes resurfaced in the missionary's mind, arousing within him an emotion something like fear. That old man had been the Naifu, and his face was the face of a politician, he thought.

Footsteps sounded in the corridor. The missionary, who was sitting with his head bowed, heard the dry rustle of robes.

'Lord Velasco.'

The missionary looked up. Gotō Shōzaburō, the government Trade Adviser (called the 'Currency Inspector' by the Japanese), was seated on the raised dais, and the two officials were sitting beside him on the wooden floor. For a few moments Lord Gotō stared at the missionary with the grave expression unique to the Japanese. Then he sighed and said, 'You are free to go. This has all been a mistake on the part of the officials.'

'I see.'

The missionary was elated. He cast a look of satisfaction at the two officials who had humiliated him. It was much the sort of look he gave the faithful when he forgave their sins.

'But, Lord Velasco. . . .' The robes rustled again as Lord Gotō stood up, and his face turned bitter as he spat out, 'You know that you are not living in Edo as a Christian padre. If someone of influence had not interceded for you again, there is no telling what might have become of you!'

The intimation was that the missionary was making secret visits to the Christians. Whatever might be allowed in the domains of other *daimyōs*, this year the building of churches and the practice of Christianity had been strictly prohibited in the areas under the direct control of the Naifu. They let him live in this great city as an interpreter, not as a priest.

After Lord Gotō had withdrawn, the two officials, their faces showing open displeasure, motioned with their chins towards a separate exit for the missionary. Night had already settled in upon the city.

The missionary returned by palanquin to his lodgings in Asakusa. A clump of trees silhouetted against the night sky was the landmark that led him to his home. A group of outcast lepers had built up a colony in this area and, until two years before, the Order of Franciscans had operated a tiny clinic here for their benefit. The clinic had been razed, but the missionary had been allowed to stay on with a Korean and a younger priest named Diego in a tiny hut that survived from the former structure.

Diego and the Korean welcomed him back with looks of astonishment and huddled around him as he gobbled up some rice and dried fish. A bird shrieked in the nearby grove.

'The Japanese wouldn't have set anyone else free so quickly, would they?' said Father Diego as he waited on the missionary. His colleague merely smiled, although inwardly he was savouring feelings of satisfaction and triumph. 'The Japanese did not release me,' he instructed Diego with a look that could have been either humility or pride. 'The Lord desires something of me. And the Lord released me to accomplish that work.'

As he ate, the missionary prayed silently. 'O Lord, Thy works are never brought to naught. For this reason Thou hast preserved my life.'

His prayers included a touch of pride unbecoming a priest, but he was not aware of it.

Three days later, the missionary took the Korean with him and set out to the Trade Adviser's residence to express gratitude for his release. Knowing that Japanese officials enjoyed wine, he brought with him several bottles intended for use in the Mass.

Although the Trade Adviser had a visitor when they arrived, they were ushered into his room without having to wait in a separate chamber. Lord Gotō nodded slightly when the missionary came in, but continued with his conversation. He obviously wanted the missionary to hear what was being said.

The place names Tsukinoura and Shiogama came up again and again in the conversation. The Adviser and a plump, ageing samurai spoke deliberately, remarking that Tsukinoura would make a better port than Nagasaki.

Although the missionary gazed casually at the garden that opened out before the chamber, he was listening intently to the conversation. With the store of knowledge he had accumulated in his three years as an interpreter, he felt he had some idea, though admittedly a vague one, of the background to this discussion.

For several years now, the Naifu had been searching for a port in the eastern part of Japan which could rival Nagasaki. In domestic terms, Nagasaki lay too far beyond the eastern sector that was under the Naifu's control, and if a powerful Kyushu *daimyō* rose up in rebellion, the port could easily be seized. Furthermore, some of the powerful Kyushu *daimyōs* like Lord Shimazu and Lord Katō still supported the Toyotomi clan in Osaka, which as yet lay beyond the Naifu's clutches. From the standpoint of foreign affairs, the Naifu was not pleased that ships from Manila and Macao docked only in Nagasaki. He was keen to establish trade ties directly with the source of commerce, Nueva España, instead of dealing through Manila. Thus he was searching in the eastern provinces for a good port that could handle trade with Nueva España. There was one in Kantō called Uraga, but because of the swiftness of the currents, ships that tried to approach Uraga had invariably been wrecked. For that reason, the Naifu had ordered an influential *daimyō*, whose domain in the North-East lay closest of any area in Japan to the Black Current, to search out a port. Tsukinoura and Shiogama were perhaps locations under consideration.

'But why does the Adviser want me to hear this conversation?' the missionary wondered. He glanced furtively at the faces of the two Japanese.

Lord Gotō turned towards him, as though he had sensed the missionary's eyes upon him. 'Do you know Lord Ishida? This is Lord Velasco, who has been permitted to remain in Edo as an interpreter.' The plump samurai smiled and made a shallow bow.

'Have you ever been to the North-East?'

The missionary kept his hands on his knees and shook his head. From years of experience, he knew the proper etiquette on such occasions.

'Lord Ishida's domain is not like Edo,' the Adviser said with a touch of irony. 'I am told that the Christians are not punished there. You could strut about there with nothing at all to fear, Lord Velasco.'

The missionary was of course aware of that fact. The Naifu had proscribed Christianity in the domains under his direct control, but he had not pressed the other *daimyōs* to follow his lead, fearing that the Christian faithful and warriors might rise up in rebellion. He quietly tolerated the many Christians who fled to the western provinces or to the North-East once they had been driven from Edo.

'Lord Velasco, have you ever heard the names Shiogama or Tsukinoura? They are especially fine harbours in the North-East.'

'Do you intend to make them into ports like Uraga?'

'That is part of our plan. But in those harbours we might also build great ships like the ones you Europeans have.'

For a moment the missionary was speechless. To his knowledge, at that time the Japanese had only shōgunate-licensed vessels modelled on Siamese and Chinese sailing boats. They possessed neither the shipyards nor the expertise to produce galleons capable of crossing the wide oceans at will. Even if they were able to build such a ship, there was little likelihood that they would have the skill to sail it.

'Would they be built by Japanese?'

'Perhaps. Shiogama and Tsukinoura face the ocean, and large quantities of good lumber can be cut there.'

The missionary wondered why the Adviser was discussing such secret matters so openly in his presence. Quickly he studied the expressions on both men's faces and groped for a response.

That must mean they will use the crew from that ship. . . .

The previous year, the ship carrying the Spanish emissary from Manila for whom Velasco had interpreted at Edo Castle had encountered a storm on its return voyage and been driven ashore in

Kishū. Repairs were out of the question, so the boat had been detained at Uraga. The emissary and the ship's crew were still in Edo, waiting patiently for another ship to come for them. Perhaps the Japanese were planning to use the sailors to help them build a galleon just like their own.

'Has all this already been decided?'

'No, no. It is just one idea that has been mentioned.'

The Adviser turned his gaze towards the garden. The missionary knew that this was a sign for him to retire, so after uttering a few words of gratitude for his release, he left the room.

As he stooped and bowed to the retainers in the antechambers, he thought, 'So at last the Japanese plan to cross the Pacific on their own and make their way to Nueva España?'

These people are like ants. They will try anything! When ants are faced with a puddle of water, some of their number will sacrifice their own lives to form a bridge for their comrades. The Japanese were a swarm of black ants with those very instincts.

For several years the Naifu had earnestly sought trade relations with Nueva España, but the Viceroy of Manila had evaded each request. The Spanish wanted to hold on to their trading monopoly on the wide Pacific Ocean.

But if the Japanese were to employ the Spanish sailors detained on their shores to build a ship of their own, they would no doubt need the missionary to interpret for them. Gradually, he began to understand why Gotō had arranged for his release from prison. Gotō had intimated that the release had been worked out through the good offices of a certain individual. Perhaps that 'certain individual' had been the Senior Councillor responsible for this entire plan. Or perhaps it had been that old man Ishida who had just been speaking with Gotō. God had use for all men, but the Japanese used only those who could be of benefit to them. They had intimidated and then spared the missionary precisely because he could be useful to them. This was a technique they were fond of employing.

He gave Diego or the Korean no details of that day's conversation. Diego was a clergyman like Velasco, though somewhat younger, and he too had come to Japan as a member of the Order of Franciscans. Inwardly, however, the missionary mocked his companion, with his red eyes like a rabbit's. In their years at the seminary he had not been able to repress the feelings of scorn that flooded his heart each time he encountered his sincere but ineffectual friend. He knew that this was a flaw in his character, but it lay utterly beyond his control.

'There's a letter from Osaka.'

Diego reached into the pocket of his worn habit and pulled out his rosary and an opened letter. Then, looking at the missionary with moist eyes, he said, 'The Jesuits are denouncing us once again.'

The missionary spread out the letter beneath the candle flame, which flickered like the wings of a moth. Yellow drops of rain had stained the paper, causing the ink to run. Written nearly twenty days before by his superior in Osaka, Father Muñoz, the letter said that hatred of the Edo Naifu was intensifying in Osaka and that one after another the retainers of the *daimyō* who had been defeated by the Naifu at the Battle of Sekigahara were being taken into the service of the ruler of Osaka.

After these introductory remarks, Father Muñoz reported that the Provincial of the Society of Jesus in Kinki had dispatched a letter to Rome filled with complaints about the proselytizing methods of the Franciscans.

'The Jesuits protest that we needlessly arouse the wrath of the Naifu and the Shōgun by staying in contact with the Japanese flock in spite of the prohibition on missionary work in Edo, and that as a result the persecutions will soon be extended to include the regions where we are still allowed to preach.'

The missionary suppressed his mounting anger and thrust the letter back at Diego.

'The arrogant fools!' Whenever his emotions were aroused, the missionary's neck and cheeks flushed a bright crimson. Censure from the Jesuits was nothing new. They lurked constantly in the shadows, writing to Rome with slanders against the Franciscans. The sole cause was jealousy. Since Francis Xavier had first set foot in Japan sixty-three years before, the Jesuit order which Xavier organized had monopolized the missionary endeavour there. When a papal brief from Pope Clement VIII had authorized proselytization in Japan by other orders, in desperation the Jesuits had begun backbiting against the other brotherhoods.

'The Jesuits forget that they themselves are the reason that Christians are persecuted here. They ought to consider who it was that aroused the anger of the late Taikō.'

Diego glanced up timidly with his swollen red eyes. The missionary looked into those eyes and concluded that there was no point in discussing anything with his inept compatriot. Three years had passed since their arrival in Japan, yet Diego still did not have an acceptable command of the language. He spent his days like an obedient sheep doing only what his superiors told him to do.

Several decades earlier the Jesuits had procured tracts of land in Nagasaki that were essentially autonomous colonies, and the profits they reaped from the land provided the funds for their proselytizing efforts. Although they did not have military capabilities of their own, they exercised rights of taxation and adjudication over their fiefs. It was common knowledge that when the Taikō, who occupied Kyushu, learned of this situation, he burst into a rage, insisting that this was simply an invasion under the pretext of missionary work, and he had promulgated a ban on Christianity. Such activities had provided the impetus for the persecution which darkened the prospects of missionary labour in Japan, yet the Jesuits had conveniently chosen to forget their role in the whole affair.

'But what kind of reply can we send to Osaka. . . .?' Diego was at a loss.

'We can tell the Jesuits that they no longer need worry about me,' the missionary spluttered, shrugging his shoulders. 'I shall soon be leaving Edo to go to the North-East.'

'To the North-East?'

The missionary turned his back on his dumbfounded comrade and left the room without replying. He entered the storeroom they called their 'Sanctuary', blew out the flame of the candle, and knelt on the hard wooden floor. Since his days in the seminary at Sevilla, he had assumed this penitent posture whenever his pride was wounded or he wished to subdue the anger that boiled within him. The smell of the scorched candle wick pierced his nostrils, and in the darkness he heard the faint rustle of a cockroach.

'No matter who may reproach me, Thou knowest my abilities,' he muttered, supporting his forehead with his hands. 'Thou hast need of me, and for that reason rescued me from prison. As Thou didst not wince under the slanders and calumnies of the Sadducees and Pharisees, so I shall ignore the slurs that the Jesuits fling at me.'

The cockroach crawled boldly across his bare feet, which were caked with mud. In the grove, a bird called out again with a piercing cry; he heard the Korean closing the door of their hut.

'The Japanese are going to build a galleon.'

Once again the image of a great swarm of black ants crossing a puddle of water in search of food flashed before his eyes. In pursuit of profits from trade with Nueva España, the Japanese were at last on the verge of crossing the Pacific like black ants. The missionary sensed that he could use their greed to benefit the missionary cause.

'We can give them their profits, and in return be granted freedom to proselytize.'

The Jesuits did not have the skill to carry out such a transaction. Nor did the Dominicans or the Augustinians. Inept monks like Diego couldn't manage it. The missionary was confident that he alone could arrange such an exchange. To do so, he would have to erase the prejudices harboured by the Japanese. He must not repeat the blunders committed by the Jesuits.

'If only I were Bishop of Japan. . . .'

The stirrings of worldly ambition which caused him constant embarrassment reverberated once more in his ears. 'If I were installed as Bishop, with absolute control over the planning and execution of missionary work in Japan, I could make up for the errors that the Jesuits have committed for so many years.'

In the hills of the brown, withered marshland, the smoke of burning charcoal billowed up into the sky on clear days. With the long winter ahead of them, the peasants worked from dawn to dusk. Once the rice and millet were harvested from the barren fields, the women and children pounded and threshed the husks. The rice went for taxes, not as food for themselves. The withered grass they had mowed between chores was laid out to dry where it had been cut, to be used as straw for the stables. Here fresh straw provided sustenance in time of famine. It was chopped up, then ground into a powder in a stone mortar.

The samurai, wearing the same *hangiri* working clothes as the peasants, looked across the marshland. Sometimes he would call out to the peasants and chat with them; at other times he would work with them stacking up firewood like a fence around his house.

The peasants had their joys and sorrows, too. This autumn two elderly men from the village had died, but their impoverished families could do no better than to bury their dead in the fields near the mountains. Simple stones marked their graves. It was also the custom in the marshland to implant the handle of the old scythe which the deceased had used in his lifetime into the ground above the grave, and to place his rice bowls beside the gravestone. The samurai had often seen children drop flowers into these chipped bowls. But such burials were limited to times free of famine. The samurai had heard from his father that in years when the harvest was bad, old people would suddenly disappear, and no one would enquire after them. In autumn too, there was a festival called *Daishiko*, when the people ate dumplings of unsalted red beans wrapped in cogon grass and boiled in a pot. On the day of the festival, the peasants, hunched from long hours of toil, would come to pay their respects at the samurai's house, eat the dumplings offered them, and return home.

One clear day, the order for corvée labourers to which Lord Ishida had alluded, arrived. Two men were to be sent from the marshland.

When he received the order, the samurai took Yozō and paid a visit to his uncle's village.

'I've heard about it. I've heard!'

His uncle was beaming.

'I've heard rumours that they're cutting down cedars in the mountains of Ogatsu to build a warship. Maybe a battle with Osaka is close at hand!'

'A warship?'

'Yes!'

The samurai had not yet told his uncle what Lord Ishida had said. It had depressed him to think of having to listen yet again to the incessant complaints of the despondent old man. But why would His Lordship be building a warship if the time for battles was over? The samurai was puzzled. Perhaps some secret plans to which someone of his status was not privy had been laid in the Council of Elders at the castle.

'Roku, you must go to Ogatsu and find out what's going on!' His uncle's voice quavered with excitement, as though a battle had already begun. The samurai hardly felt like making the day-and-a-half journey to Ogatsu, but since he had always been obedient to his father and uncle, he nodded silently. Perhaps, if he could see what was happening with his own eyes, it would be easier to persuade this old man, who had such difficulty accepting the way the world had changed, to abandon his futile dreams.

The following day, after selecting two young men from the village to perform the corvée service, the samurai once again mounted his horse. Ogatsu was an inlet on the coastline of Rikuzen province; it bit into the land like the tooth of a saw. They set out from the marshland in the early morning, and when they neared the sea at nightfall, snow from the overcast sky was slapping at their cheeks. They took lodgings at a desolate fishing village called Mizuhama. Throughout the night they could hear the pounding of the sea, and the two young men the samurai had brought with him looked at him forlornly. According to the fishermen, the other corvée labourers had already arrived and had begun cutting down trees in the hills near Ogatsu.

The group set out from Mizuhama the following morning. The sky was clear, but there was a strong wind, and in the icy offing the waves surged and foamed. The young men shivered as they walked behind the horse. When at length their view of the sea was obstructed by islands, they caught a glimpse of the calm harbour. On a hill to the side, several huts had already been built for the labourers, and the dull sound of trees being felled could be heard in the distance. Unlike the rough open sea, the waters of the harbour were sheltered from the wind by islands and hills, and many rafts were already afloat there.

The group reported to the guardhouse, and as the officers were registering the names of the two young men, a servant scurried up to announce that the elder statesman Lord Shiraishi would be arriving shortly. There was a moment of turmoil in the guardhouse before the officers set out for the beach with great solemnity to receive Lord Shiraishi.

The samurai accompanied them to await the arrival of the entourage. Soon he caught sight of a score of mounted men advancing slowly towards him. To his surprise, four or five foreigners were riding with the procession. The samurai had never seen a foreigner before. He stared fixedly at the strange-looking men, forgetting even to bow his head.

The foreigners were all wearing travel robes like his own, clothing they must have been given in Japan. Their faces were flushed as if they had been drinking *sake*, and they sported chestnut-coloured beards. They gazed around curiously at the hills, which reverberated with the sound of toppling trees. One of the foreigners spoke Japanese, and was talking to the retainers on either side of him.

'Isn't that Gorozaemon's son?' Someone called out the name of the samurai's father as the procession passed in front of the row of officers. It was Lord Shiraishi who had spoken. The samurai bowed his head deferentially. 'I have heard a lot about you from Lord Ishida. I fought alongside your father in the battles at Kōriyama and Kubota.'

The samurai listened to Lord Shiraishi's words in deep humility. Half the officers joined the procession and soon disappeared behind the mountains. Those who remained talked enviously of the samurai, who had been paid special notice by Lord Shiraishi, one of His Lordship's housemen.

As he prepared for the journey home, the samurai relished the unmerited commendation he had received. Now that he was here, he realized that the great ship which was being built in the harbour was not a warship, but rather a licensed shōgunal vessel which would return the foreign sailors shipwrecked the previous year off Kishū to their native land. That's who those foreigners were, and the shōgunal ship was being constructed under their direction.

He spent another night in Mizuhama and returned to the marshland the following day. His uncle had eagerly awaited his return, but when he heard his nephew's story, a tinge of disappointment coloured his lean face. But news that Lord Shiraishi had shown the samurai special favour seemed to revive his hopes, and he made his nephew repeat that part of the story over and over again.

The autumn came to a close, and winter arrived. Every night the winds blew across the snow that cloaked the marshland. During the day the servants sat around the hearth braiding straw ropes. These ropes, called *motozu*, were passed through the packsaddles to strap bundles to the horses, or used to make girths and halter ropes. Sometimes Riku told stories to their younger son, Gonshirō, beside the hearth. They were the same stories about exorcizing fox demons, or about men who had been deceived by foxes, that the samurai had heard as a child from his mother and grandmother.

New Year's Day arrived. Offerings of rice cakes were made to the gods of the new year, and red bean rice cakes which were not a part of their usual diet were baked. Though snow did not fall that New Year's Day, at night the wind blew across the marshes with the same plaintive wail as it always did.

His Lordship's elder statesmen were seated in a row on the raised dais in the dimly-lit hall. Their sombre, expressionless faces reminded the missionary of statues of the Buddha he had seen in a Kyoto temple some years earlier. Yet, having lived in this country for many years, he was well aware that this inscrutable surface did not mean that their minds were blank, but rather that it concealed the cunning schemes that lay beneath.

Seated on a stool beside him was the Spanish chief engineer, whom he had brought with him from Edo by special permission. Unlike the missionary, the engineer was unable to sit in the Japanese manner. Some distance from the two, the clerk of the castle sat motionless with both hands on his knees, staring at a point directly ahead of him.

Lengthy greetings were exchanged between the two parties; when the missionary had finished translating these, the conversation turned at once to the matter at hand.

'First, the length of the ship will be eighteen *ken*. The width will be five and a half *ken*, the depth fourteen *ken*, one *shaku*, five *sun*.'*

The elder statesmen were most interested in learning the shape of the galleon that was about to be constructed.

'There will be two masts: the main mast will be fifteen fathoms, the secondary mast thirteen fathoms. The hull will be varnished.'

As he interpreted the chief engineer's description word for word, the missionary wondered exactly what purpose the Japanese had in mind for such a ship. Then the elder statesmen asked how this galleon would differ from a shōgunal vessel. The ratio between the length

*Approximately 108 feet long, 33 feet wide, and 85 feet deep.

and breadth of the galleon was 3.3 to 1, which served to increase its sailing speed. In addition the ship used triangular sails, enabling it to change direction swiftly as the direction of the wind shifted. While the missionary interpreted this reply from the chief engineer, the elder statesmen – in particular Lord Shiraishi, who sat directly in the middle – listened with intense curiosity. But once the explanation ended, their faces once again became blank, like deep marshes.

To construct this great ship His Lordship had already brought two hundred carpenters and one hundred and fifty blacksmiths to Ogatsu from every corner of his domain. But nearly twice that number of artisans was necessary to hasten its completion. The chief engineer complained that the number of labourers was still grossly insufficient.

'He says there are many storms at sea in autumn, and that it would be best to set sail at the beginning of the summer, considering the two months required for the journey from here to Nueva España.'

His Lordship's elder statesmen could not conceive how vast the ocean was. For many years, the Japanese had regarded the ocean as no more than a great moat that protected them from the barbarians. They did not even have any idea where Nueva España was situated. Only now were they beginning to realize that a rich expanse of land inhabited by a variety of peoples lay far across the sea.

'We will discuss it at length with His Lordship,' said Lord Shiraishi. 'You need not worry about manpower.'

The engineer expressed his gratitude.

'There is nothing to thank me for. As I have told you before, now that we are building a great ship of our own, we have something to ask of you.' Lord Shiraishi smiled sardonically.

Their request was that the Spanish sailors extract a promise from the Viceroy of Nueva España to send ships to His Lordship's domain for many years to come. His Lordship intended to obtain permission from the Naifu to build a commercial port that could rival Nagasaki in Kyushu. All they asked of the returning crew members was that they consent to convey His Lordship's wishes to the Viceroy of Nueva España.

The chief engineer replied that they would be happy to serve as mediators. He went so far as to flatter his hosts by asserting that Nueva España would be delighted with Japanese goods, in particular copper and silver and the gold dust that could be obtained from this province, and that Japanese shōgunal vessels laden with such cargo would be welcomed by his country. The only problem, he explained, would be to build a good port where galleons could dock, but happily any one of the inlets they had surveyed over the past week – Kesennuma, Shiogama or Tsukinoura – would be perfectly suitable. Lord Shiraishi and the other elder statesmen nodded to one another, greatly pleased at this report, and the conversation turned to the climate and inhabitants of Nueva España.

When this idle chatter was over, the engineer begged to be excused and, rising from his stool, bowed his head deeply in the Japanese manner. A young attendant who had been waiting in the hallway opened the sliding door for him.

'Lord Velasco, remain here for a few moments,' one of the elder statesmen called.

After the attendant had led the engineer out of the great hall, Lord Shiraishi thanked the missionary for interpreting, then displayed an indulgent smile, quite unlike the expressions he had worn in the presence of the engineer.

'Do you think he was telling the truth?'

Not knowing what Lord Shiraishi had in mind, the missionary was at a loss how to answer.

'He said that Nueva España was looking forward to the arrival of ships from Japan.' The smile disappeared abruptly from Shiraishi's face, and he repeated the question. 'Do you think that is true?'

'What does Lord Shiraishi think?' the missionary responded, hoping to discover the true intent of the enquiry.

'We do not believe it.'

'Why not?' With a deliberately dubious look, the missionary glanced up at the elder statesman.

'It is only natural. It is because your country is the only nation which has ships that can cross these wide seas and the skill to sail them that you have come here and acquired a monopoly on the vast profits we have to offer. You certainly have no desire to share those profits with men from other nations. Nueva España will not be pleased to see Japanese ships cross the ocean.'

Although they had seen through the chief engineer's insincere flatteries, the elder statesmen had deliberately pretended to be satisfied with his replies. That was how the Japanese dealt with others.

The missionary could not prevent a wry smile. 'If you have realized that, there is nothing left for me to say. But if you know all this, why are you going ahead and building the galleon?'

'Lord Velasco. We actually do wish to trade with Nueva España. The ships which come from Luzon and Macao and the nations of Europe all congregate in Nagasaki. Not one of them comes to the Naifu's domain in Edo, much less here to Rikuzen. Though there are many fine ports here in His Lordship's domain, ships from Nueva

España must pass through Luzon before they reach Japan. And we understand that once those ships reach Luzon, the currents invariably take them to Kyushu.'

'That is true.'

'Then what are we to do?' Lord Shiraishi slowly tapped his left hand with the fingers of his right, as though he were in great turmoil. 'Do you have any ideas on how we can establish trade between Rikuzen and Nueva España, Padre?'

The missionary instinctively averted his eyes at the unexpected word 'padre'. He did not wish to betray the tumult in his heart to these men. In Edo he was never called 'padre'.

Outside snow fell, and all was silent.

The senior statesmen stared at him, and they too were silent. Painfully conscious of their eyes upon him, he answered, 'I have nothing to suggest. Here, as in Edo, I am . . . nothing more than an interpreter.'

'I do not know about Edo. But here you are not only an interpreter, but also a padre,' Lord Shiraishi answered softly. 'Christianity is not prohibited in His Lordship's domain.'

It was just as he said. In this domain, priests did not have to hide as they did in Edo. And the faithful did not have to perjure themselves.

'Come, Lord Velasco. Wouldn't you like to summon many more padres from Nueva España?' Lord Shiraishi's voice was gentle, alluring. The missionary clenched his hands until they were bathed in sweat, struggling not to surrender to that gentle voice. With his strong sense of pride, it upset him to be toyed with in this manner by the Japanese.

'Are you making fun of me? I do not believe you.'

'Oh? Why not?'

'Sooner or later the Naifu will ban Christianity in this domain too.'

At the missionary's angry voice, Lord Shiraishi exchanged a self-satisfied smile with the other statesmen.

'You have nothing to worry about. In our domain alone, the Naifu has permitted the worship of Christianity forever. These are also the sentiments of the Naifu and of His Lordship.'

'They will recognize Christianity in this domain and permit more padres to come? In exchange for that, they want Nueva España to agree to a trade arrangement? Are those their sentiments?'

An even more intense anger welled up inside the missionary, and he drew himself up stiffly. His irritation was directed not at these Japanese, but at his own carelessness. It mortified him to be drawn further and further into the traps laid by Lord Shiraishi's adroit words.

'Don't you think Nueva España will consent to such an arrangement?'

'I do not know.' The missionary shook his head deliberately, hoping to arouse a twinge of anxiety in the eyes of the elder statesmen, to cause them even a moment of consternation. 'I think it's . . . probably hopeless.'

As the missionary studied the reactions of the senior ministers, lined up like Buddhist statues in a dark temple sanctuary, he revelled in their inner agitation.

'The Jesuits have already reported to Luzon, Macao and as far as Nueva España that Christians have been executed in Edo. Even if you tell them that Christianity will be allowed in your domain alone, I cannot imagine that they will be quick to believe you.'

The missionary did not miss an opportunity to speak ill of the Jesuits. He had struck at a vulnerable spot, and the Japanese once again sank into silence. The earlier silence had been a part of their strategy, but the missionary was certain that this one was that of men who had received an unexpected jolt.

'There is one possibility. . . .' As if to give his reeling opponents a chance to recover from the blow, he added, 'The only person who could persuade the King of España to consent to this agreement is the Pope in Rome. . . .'

Lord Shiraishi's face hardened suddenly. This subject was too far removed for elder statesmen whose lives had been spent in a domain in north-eastern Japan. Isolated from the Christian world, they knew virtually nothing of the existence of a Roman Pope or of his absolute authority. The missionary had to explain that the relationship between the Pope and the Kings of Europe was similar to that between the Emperor in Kyoto and the feudal lords.

'But we have considerably more reverence for the Pope than you have for the Emperor in Kyoto.'

As he listened to this explanation, Lord Shiraishi closed his eyes and began tapping his left hand with the fingers of his right. The snow outside deepened the silence within the great hall. The elder statesmen coughed occasionally, quietly awaiting Lord Shiraishi's decision.

The missionary secretly relished the discomfiture of the Japanese. These men who had tried to twist him around their fingers were now writhing in uncertainty. He must take advantage of their confusion and play a forceful trump card.

'Our Order,' the missionary announced confidently, 'enjoys a position of special confidence with the present Pope.'

'And?'

'And it would be well for you to send a member of our Order to the Pope with a letter from His Lordship. A letter pledging that his Lordship's domain alone will treat the Christians cordially, that you welcome the arrival of more padres, and that you will permit the building of many cathedrals. . . .'

. . . And a humble request that you make me the Bishop of Japan, the missionary caught himself about to add. For a moment he was ashamed of his pride, yet at the same time he told himself, 'I do not seek advancement out of selfish interest. I wish to have the position of Bishop so that I may set up a last sturdy line of defence in this country that seeks to proscribe Christianity. I alone can do battle with these cunning, heathen Japanese. . . .'

Chapter 2

Third Month, Twentieth Day

Bad weather. Rain. Armaments were tested. Gunpowder was stored away in the hawk coops.

Third Month, Twenty-first Day

Some rain. Three buildings were constructed in the palace grounds.

Third Month, Twenty-second Day

Bad weather. Lord Shiraishi, Lord Fujita and Lord Harada Sabanosuke came. Discussed sending the ship to a foreign land.

Third Month, Twenty-third Day

Conference between Lord Shiraishi, Lord Fujita, and the foreigner Berasuko in the Great Hall. Berasuko is a tall, red-faced, large-nosed man over forty. Frequently wiped the corners of his mouth with a white crêpe cloth.

Third Month, Twenty-fifth Day

Good weather. A bath in the morning. Then a conference. Lord Shiraishi and Lord Ishida attended.

Third Month, Twenty-sixth Day

Good weather. Lord Ishida departed.

(from the castle diary)

Word came suddenly that Lord Ishida, who had participated in the conference at the castle, would be stopping in the marshland the next day in order to rest on his way back to his domain. When this news arrived, the villagers came out in force and energetically sprinkled earth on top of the frozen snow, filled in the quagmires, and raked the snow off the samurai's house. Riku supervised the women, who scurried about in confusion cleaning room after room.

The next day, the sky was mercifully clear as the samurai and his uncle set out for the entrance to the marshland to greet Lord Ishida and his retainers. Not once since the days of the samurai's father had Lord Ishida passed through the samurai's fief on his way home from the castle. For that reason alone, the samurai was vaguely apprehensive, wondering what might have transpired. He resented the buoyant spirits of his uncle, who had not forgotten the kind words Lord Shiraishi had spoken to his nephew at Ogatsu, and who was convinced that his petition had been granted.

When the two parties met at the mouth of the marshland, Lord Ishida called out jovially to the samurai and his uncle, then proceeded to the samurai's house with the welcoming party in the lead. Instead of going directly to the room that had been prepared for him, however, Lord Ishida asked to sit beside the sunken hearth.

'A fire is the warmest hospitality,' he joked, perhaps trying to put his hosts at ease. He ate with relish the boiled rice Riku brought him, and asked various questions about conditions in the marshland. Then, between gulps of the warm water left in his bowl, he said abruptly, 'I've brought you a fine present today!' But, seeing the eyes of the samurai's uncle sparkle at these words, he added, 'It is not news of a battle. Don't think there will be any battles. You had best give up your dream of returning to Kurokawa by distinguishing yourself in battle.'

Having made his point, he continued, 'But there is other service you can render. I have come with news of something that will bring you far more merit than a battle.' His eyes were fixed on the samurai.

'I'm sure you know that His Lordship is constructing a great ship in the inlet at Ogatsu. That ship will carry the foreigners who were cast ashore at Kishū and sail to a distant land called Nueva España. Yesterday at the castle, Lord Shiraishi suggested your name, and you have been ordered to travel to Nueva España as an envoy of His Lordship.'

The samurai could not understand what Lord Ishida was saying. He stared blankly into his Patron's face. He felt as though he had suddenly been caught up in an unexpected event, and he could not catch his breath or speak a single word. All he knew for certain was that his dazed uncle's kneecaps had begun to quiver.

'Do you understand? You are going to a country called Nueva España!'

Nueves Panya. The samurai had never heard the name before, and he tried repeating it to himself. NU-E-VA ES-PA-ÑA. It felt as though each syllable was being boldly inscribed within his head with a thick writing brush.

'I understand that Lord Shiraishi spoke to you at Ogatsu some time ago. And at the Council of Elders he said that things would not go badly with you. So if you distinguish yourself in this mission, he just might consider giving back your fief in Kurokawa upon your return.'

The samurai's uncle was trembling. His kneecaps were visibly shaking. The samurai placed his hands on his own knees and sat with his head bowed. When his uncle's knees ceased their trembling, Lord Ishida laughed, 'I suppose this seems like a dream to you.' But the smile suddenly faded from his face. 'It is no dream,' he said determinedly.

And yet to the samurai, as it spoke of the great ship and Nueva España, Lord Ishida's voice seemed to come from very far away. All that stuck in his memory was that at least thirty foreign sailors, four Japanese emissaries and their retainers, a number of Japanese deckhands, and more than a hundred Japanese merchants would be boarding the ship. The ship itself was bigger than the largest junk, and the journey to Nueva España would take two months. In addition, a foreign padre would join the group as translator and to make all the necessary arrangements for the emissaries when they reached their destination. Nueva España was a territory of España, and with the Naifu's consent, His Lordship was opening trade with that country, with the intent of turning Shiogama and Kesennuma into ports that could rival Sakai and Nagasaki.

The samurai had no way of telling how much of this information his aged uncle was able to grasp. Even to himself, it all sounded like a dream. He lived in this tiny, narrow marshland, and he intended to die here. Never had he thought that he would board a great ship and make a long voyage to a foreign land. Somehow it did not seem real to him.

At last Lord Ishida stood up to take his leave. His retainers scurried to fetch the horses. As they accompanied the entourage back to the mouth of the marshland, neither the samurai nor his uncle had much to say, but followed numbly behind. Even after the entourage had disappeared from sight, the two men did not speak as they returned to the house. Riku, who had listened to the conversation from the kitchen, fled with a sallow face. It was as though Lord Ishida were still seated beside the hearth. The samurai's uncle sat down near the fire with his legs crossed. For a long while he was silent; then finally something, either a sigh or a gasp, escaped from his lips.

'What does this mean? I can't understand it!' he spluttered.

The samurai could not understand it either. If His Lordship was looking for a special emissary to dispatch to a distant land, there were many retainers of status to be found within the walls of the castle. The hierarchy of His Lordship's retainers consisted of generals and colonels at the head, followed by ranks such as sergeant, corporal, and lance-corporal. The samurai's family was only of lance-corporal rank. He could not understand why such a low-ranking vassal as himself had been deliberately plucked out and included among His Lordship's emissaries.

'Did Lord Shiraishi arrange this just for my benefit?'

If that were the case, it must have been because Lord Shiraishi had remembered the service which his father had rendered in the battles of Kōriyama and Kubota. Once again the samurai saw his father's face before him.

Riku reappeared, pale-faced, from the kitchen and sat down on one side of the hearth. She stared at the faces of her uncle and her husband.

'Roku is going . . . to a faraway foreign land,' her uncle said, not so much to Riku as to himself. 'It is an honour. It is a great honour.' Then as if to drive away his own apprehensions, he suddenly muttered, 'If Roku carries out this important mission, we might be able to get back our lands in Kurokawa. . . . That's what Lord Ishida said!'

Riku stood up and disappeared into the kitchen. The samurai knew that she was struggling to hold back the tears.

The samurai opened his eyes in the darkness. Riku and Gonshirō were sleeping quietly. Images of the dream he had just had still lingered on his eyelids. He dreamed he had been out hunting rabbits one winter's day. The report from Yozō's gun ripped through the chilly air over the snowy fields, then widened slowly out like the waves of the sea. A flock of migratory birds danced across the blue sky. Against the blue of the sky the wings of the birds were white. Each winter the samurai had seen these white birds that came to his domain, but where they came from he did not know.

All he knew was that these birds came from a distant land, a distant country. Perhaps they even came from Nueva España, the country he was now to visit.

But why had he been chosen as one of the emissaries? In the darkness doubts floated up in his head like bubbles of water. His family was of the rural samurai rank of lance-corporal, having served since the days of His Lordship's father, yet they had not rendered any exceptional service. There was no apparent reason why the head of such a family should be selected over many others. His naïve uncle attributed everything to Lord Shiraishi's intercession on their behalf, but Lord Ishida should be able to judge whether a tongue-tied, talentless man like the samurai was truly suited for this important responsibility.

'The only thing good about me,' the samurai thought absently, 'is that I have been obedient to my father and my uncle. My only talent is the ability to endure as the peasants do, never going against the current. Perhaps Lord Ishida has thought well of that perseverance.'

His son shifted in his sleep. The samurai hated to leave his family and his home. At some point, the marshland had come to seem like the shell of a snail to him. Now he was being forcibly pried from his shell. And perhaps . . . perhaps in the course of this long journey I will die and never return to this marshland. Suddenly the fear that he might never see his wife and children again clouded his heart.

The gentle waves of the harbour, on which numerous rafts were floating, reflected the silhouettes of the hills. Great quantities of lumber had been piled up on the shore. The neighing of horses was audible from every direction. Zelkova wood from Mount Kenjō, which towered over the harbour, had been used for the rafts and lumber, and cedar had been brought by boat from the Ojika Peninsula. The Zelkova wood was to be used for the keel of the great ship. *Hinoki* cypress for the mainmast had been transported here from Esashi and Kesennuma.

The sound of nails being hammered in and the echo of timber being cut resounded ceaselessly from the three sides of the harbour. Several ox-carts laden with kegs of varnish to be applied to the hull of the ship creaked as they passed in front of the missionary.

In the shallows, diligently labouring workmen clustered like ants on the framework of the ship, which resembled the weathered skeleton of a wild beast.

The missionary had just come from translating another of the endless debates between the Spanish sailors and the Japanese boatswain. The Spaniards ridiculed the boatswain and paid not the least attention to his opinions. The Japanese insisted that a sloping platform should be used to launch the ship, and that it should be pushed into the sea by manpower. Although the missionary spoke fluent Japanese, he was at a loss for words when it came to the specialized jargon required in such debates.

When an agreement was finally reached, the exhausted missionary left the hut alone. It was nearly midday. The others would be searching out a shady spot to rest, but the missionary had to make use of this time to visit each of the work camps.

Nearly a dozen Christians had been hired as manual labourers. The missionary recited the Mass, gave them communion, and listened to their confessions during the noon break. All the Christians had originally lived in Edo, but when the practice of Christianity was prohibited there and the persecutions began, they had fled here to the North-East. They had been labouring in the gold mines, without a single relative nearby. Then, just as ants recognize the smell of food from a distance, they had caught wind of the rumour that a missionary had come, and had gathered here in Ogatsu.

The sky was clear, but the breeze was chilly. In Edo the willow trees would already be sprouting green shoots, but here lingering snow still blanketed the distant hills, and the colours of the hills and forests were lifeless. Spring had not yet arrived.

The missionary stood in one of the work camps, waiting patiently for one of the Christian workers to complete his labours. At length the man approached. A towel was wound around his head and wood shavings clung to his ragged clothes.

'Padre!' the man called. Yes, the missionary thought. Here, now, I am not an interpreter for the Japanese. I am the pastor of this poor flock of believers.

'Padre, please hear my confession.'

The stacks of timber sheltered them from the wind. The man knelt while the missionary intoned the confessional prayer in Latin and then closed his eyes to listen to the words that poured from the labourer's foul-smelling mouth.

'I sat and listened when my gentile friends made fun of the Christian faith. I didn't say anything back to them. I let them ridicule Deus and our Christian faith. I didn't want to lose them as my friends.'

'Where did you come from?'

'From Edo,' the man replied timidly. 'In Edo they won't let us believe any more.'

The missionary set out to teach this man that each and every Christian must stand as a witness of God to all men. But the man gazed sorrowfully at the sea as he listened to the words.

'Let your heart be at ease.' The missionary sought to encourage the man, placing his hand on the rough clothing that was covered with wood shavings. 'Soon the day will come when no one will laugh at your beliefs.'

Then he recited the prayer of forgiveness and stood up from

behind the stacks of timber. The labourer muttered his thanks and
departed diffidently. The missionary knew that this man would
commit the same sort of sin again. Although these faithful Christians
had taken refuge in this region, they were still looked upon with
scorn by their fellow workers. The days when warriors and
merchants vied to be the first baptized had long since vanished from
this land. He was certain it was all the fault of the Jesuits. If the Jesuits
had not been puffed up with pride and had not defied the rulers
of Japan with their actions, the climate would surely still be favourable. . . .

'If I were the Bishop of Japan. . . .'

The missionary sat down on a rock that overlooked the harbour
and once again savoured his dream. He was like a young boy lying in
bed and slowly relishing some food he had concealed. 'If I were the
Bishop of Japan, I would not anger the Japanese rulers the way the
Jesuits have. I would offer them the kind of benefits that would please
them, and in exchange I would obtain enough freedom to spread the
gospel. Missionary work in this country is not the simple task it is in
Goa or Manila. It requires strategy and diplomacy. If strategy and
diplomacy would work to build the self-respect of these poor
believers, then I would be the first to employ such tactics.' He
thought with pride of his uncle and his relatives who had served as
diplomats and cardinals of the Church. Not once had he been
ashamed to have the blood of that family flowing through his own
body.

'With these cunning Japanese. . . .'

In order to deal with the Japanese, the methods of spreading the
gospel also had to be cunning. Over the harbour, which was clogged
with rafts and timber, a seagull soared with a shrill cry, then skimmed
across the surface of the water. The missionary imagined himself
wearing the mitre and red robes of a bishop. He tried to persuade
himself that his dream of becoming Bishop was not the product of
worldly ambition, but rather a responsibility he had to spread the
teachings of God here in Japan.

'O Lord,' he prayed, inhaling the salty breeze and closing his eyes,
'if it be to Thy glory. . . .'

The hut which the officers at Ogatsu had provided for the missionary
was located at the tip of the inlet, a considerable distance from the
temporary shacks of the carpenters and labourers. Like all the other
huts, it was built of rough-hewn logs piled one on top of another.
The single shed-like room served both as his bedroom and as the

place where he could be alone to pray. Since his days at the seminary, he had been in the habit of binding his wrists together before he lay down to sleep. It was a practice which helped him resist the violent sexual drives which swept over his robust body. These lusts, which he should by rights have renounced for his lifetime, no longer tortured him as fiercely as they had in his youth. But just as one ties up a horse which might try to bolt at any moment, so the missionary, after finishing his evening prayers, continued to bind his wrists with cord before stretching out stiffly upon his bed.

That night the roar of the sea was fiercer than usual. Only a short time before, the missionary had heard that roar as he made his way along the dark beach to his hut, carrying the letter from Father Diego in Edo which the officers had handed to him in their guardhouse. Now he struck a flint and lit a candle. The flame flickered and sent up a single black thread of smoke, throwing his large shadow against the logs of the hut. By the light of the flame, he tore Diego's letter open with his bound hands. The face of his incompetent young compatriot flashed before him.

'One month has passed since you left Edo. The situation here has not worsened, neither has it in the least improved.' Diego's handwriting was as clumsy as a child's, but these scribblings crammed onto the paper seemed an adequate reflection of his simple personality.

'They still won't let us proselytize freely and they ignore the fact that we live here only because the magistrate's office knows there is no one else to look after the lepers. Doubtless someday we too will be driven from here and have to flee to the North-East like you.

'I must again be the bearer of some very unpleasant news. The Society of Jesus in Nagasaki has sent another letter to Manila and Macao criticizing you. They say that, although you are fully aware of the Christian persecutions in Japan, you are trying to persuade our Holy Father in Rome to promote trade between Japan and Nueva España. They claim that your activities are a rash experiment which puts the missionary effort in Japan in the gravest jeopardy, and that if you carry this too far, and stir up a great many young priests in Macao and Manila who know nothing about this country and bring them over to Japan, you will arouse the anger of the Naifu and the Shōgun. The Jesuits have already sent a request for your censure to Macao. I pray you will bear this in mind and proceed about your activities with the utmost caution. . . .'

The missionary's twisted face appeared uglier still in the light from the candle. He had been able to suppress his carnal lusts, but he was still unable to cure his innately volatile temperament. At times the fierce pride of his ancestors was torture to him. His face seemed younger than his forty-two years, but now it flushed red with anger.

'The Jesuits are jealous of me because they've fallen out with the Naifu and the Shōgun and can't regain their favour,' he told himself. 'They cannot bear the thought that we are seizing control of the missionary effort in this country.'

Although they were clerics who believed in the same God and served the same Church, the Jesuits nursed an ugly jealousy and spewed out slanders and calumnies against him simply because he belonged to a different monastic order. The missionary could not countenance such behaviour. The posture which the Jesuits had adopted towards him and the Order of Saint Francis was not the stance of a warrior fighting a dignified, manly battle. Their methods were more like the slanders and intrigues of the eunuchs at the Chinese court.

As if to fan his rage, the roar of the ocean grew even louder. The missionary brought the candle up to the edge of Diego's letter. The flame lapped at the paper crowded with clumsy characters and dyed it brown, then consumed it with a flutter like moth's wings. Yet even after he had destroyed the cause of his anger, his heart refused to settle. He clasped his hands and knelt to pray. 'O Lord,' he murmured. 'O Lord. Thou knowest whether I or they can be of greater service to Thee in this land. Make me a rock for these wretched Japanese saints. As Thou didst call one of Thy disciples a rock. . . .' The missionary did not realize that this was not a prayer, but rather a curse upon those who had wounded his pride.

'Padre. . . .'

In the darkness someone had called to him, and the missionary opened his eyes. A man stood like a shadow in the doorway of his hut. The missionary recognized his coarse clothing. It was the labourer whose sins he had forgiven that very afternoon, sheltered from the wind behind the stacks of timber. He stared at the missionary with the same plaintive face.

'Come in.'

The missionary brushed the ashes of the letter from his lap and stood up. This fellow's forlorn look reminded him of Diego's red, tearful eyes. Leaning against the doorpost, in halting phrases the man asked that if Japanese were to be allowed to sail on the great ship, he and his friends might be taken on to do odd jobs. He had come to this region after being expelled from Edo, but he complained that everyone made sport of him because he was a Christian, and there were few places where he was even allowed to work.

'We all feel the same way.'

The missionary shook his head.

'You cannot board the ship. If you and your friends desert this country, who will assist the priests who will soon be coming? Who will look after those priests?'

'The padres have not come here for many years.'

'No, but very soon many Fathers will come here to His Lordship's domain from Nueva España. You wouldn't know anything about it yet, but I'm sure His Lordship will allow it.'

One day I will return here, bringing many priests with me – for your benefit and for mine, the missionary murmured to himself. On that day, I will be appointed Bishop to preside over those priests.

The man rubbed the door frame with one hand, his face growing sadder as he listened to the missionary's words. The candle shrank and its flame grew brighter, lighting up the man's back as he turned away.

'Go back to your hut. Go back and tell the others what I have said. Soon there will be no need for patience. I promise you that.'

Wood shavings from his work still clung to the man's shoulders. When he had been swallowed up by the darkness, the missionary collected himself and tightened the cords around his wrists so that his bound hands would not respond even if the Adversary tried to inflame his carnal lusts. . . .

A group of peasants waited in the earthen entranceway for the samurai to emerge. They were representatives of the three villages of the marshland. They crouched patiently, coughing and sniffling from time to time.

Soon there was a rustling from within, and the coughing and sniffling ceased at once as the samurai, his uncle and Yozō came out.

The samurai sat at the seat of honour beside the hearth and looked out at the peasants. Their faces resembled his own – the sunken eyes, the protruding cheekbones, the pervasive smell of the soil. These were faces that had endured many long years of wind and snow, famines, and backbreaking labour. These were faces thoroughly accustomed to endurance and resignation. From among faces like these the samurai must choose attendants to accompany him across the great ocean to Nueva España, a land none of them had seen even in their dreams. Orders from the castle allowed each emissary to take a maximum of four men.

'We have good news for you.'

Before the samurai could say anything, his uncle spoke up with an air of satisfaction.

'I'm sure you've all heard a little something about the great ship at

Ogatsu. At His Lordship's command, this great ship is going to travel far off to a foreign land.' Then he turned proudly towards his nephew. 'Rokuemon will be on that ship. As an emissary of His Lordship.'

But the peasants looked up with dull eyes that expressed neither excitement nor surprise. They were like old dogs who regarded all the affairs of men with apathy.

'As attendants for Rokuemon,' the samurai's uncle gestured with his chin towards Yozō, who, unlike the peasants in the entrance-way, had been allowed to sit in a corner of the hearth room, 'we have already spoken with Yozō. Three other men – one from each village – will accompany Rokuemon.'

The faces of the crouching peasants tightened for a moment, as though the stiffness of death had set in. Today was not the first time this had happened. Each year, when individuals had to be chosen to perform corvée labour, the peasants gathered here had stiffened momentarily as the samurai read out the names of those selected.

'The journey will be long, so it would be a great inconvenience for men with wives and children. Bear that in mind and make the decisions among yourselves.'

Seated beside his uncle, the samurai thought of the trials facing the three men who would be chosen from the three villages. Like himself, those men would have strong ties to this marshland, like the bond between a snail and its shell. Yet doubtless they would accept this order with resignation, much as they lowered their faces and endured the snow-laden winds.

The peasants thrust their heads together and conferred softly, like a bevy of quail in a cage. Their discussion, in low, suppressed voices, continued for some time. During this interval, the samurai and his uncle said nothing, staring blankly at the peasants. From the three villages, Seihachi, Ichisuke and Daisuke – each without wife or children – were the young men chosen. The samurai's uncle nodded his approval.

'Remember now. We shall all take special care of these men's relatives until Rokuemon returns.'

The remaining peasants seemed relieved that they had not been picked. Once again they sniffled and coughed, then bowing their heads they went out of the entranceway. The smell of soil and sweat that clung to their working clothes lingered persistently in the room.

'Good! Good!' Straining to seem cheerful, the samurai's uncle pounded his shoulders with his fist. 'I hate giving orders like that. But this is just like a battle! The outcome will determine whether or not we recover the Kurokawa lands. Riku will be busy packing and preparing for the journey now. When do the emissaries assemble at His Lordship's castle?'

'After the tenth. We'll receive our instructions then.'

'Now, Roku,' his uncle's voice was suddenly subdued, 'you take care of your health on this journey.'

The samurai lowered his eyes, but he felt a twinge of bitterness. His uncle could think of nothing but the lost lands of his ancestors. The old man's only reason for living was to see those lands returned to them while he was still alive. But the samurai, like the peasants who had just left, had little desire to obtain new lands and move away. He wanted to go on living as he was in this marshland, and to die here.

'I will attend to the horses.' The samurai exchanged glances with Yozō and went out through the earthen entranceway. The horses in the stable sensed the approach of their master; he could hear them pawing the ground. As he inhaled the smell of dank straw, the samurai leaned back against the shelf and turned towards his chief retainer.

'Thank you,' he said softly to Yozō. 'So you will go with me?'

Yozō twirled a single shaft of straw between his fingertips and nodded slowly. He was three years older than the samurai, and streaks of white had already begun to lace his hair. As the samurai gazed at Yozō's hair, his thoughts suddenly went back to his youth, when Yozō had taught him how to handle horses and how to set traps for rabbits. In fact, this servant had instructed him how to care for his gun in battle and had given him his first swimming lessons. Like the other peasants, Yozō smelled of the soil, and he had the same sunken eyes and pointed cheekbones. In their youth, when together they had mowed weeds and cut wood from the forest to prepare for the winter, Yozō had always been with the samurai to teach him one thing or another.

'I still don't understand why I was chosen to be an emissary,' the samurai muttered as he patted the muzzle of a horse that had thrust its head out. He spoke more to himself than to Yozō.

'And I don't know how dangerous the journey will be, or even what kind of country we will be going to. . . . That's why it will help to have you with me.'

The samurai smiled as though ashamed of his own forthrightness. Yozō turned his face away to fight against the emotions that surged within him, and stepping into the stable he made himself busy, silently gathering soiled straw into a corner and spreading dry straw onto the earth, as if by so doing he could forget his anxieties and fears about the journey.

Ten days later, the samurai and Yozō set out on horseback for His

Lordship's castle. Lord Shiraishi had instructions to give to each of those who had been chosen as emissaries. It was a day and a half's journey from the marshland to His Lordship's castle, and the two men passed through many villages as impoverished as their own before they emerged onto a wide plain. Signs of spring had already arrived there – a warm sun was shining overhead, in the forests the magnolia trees were dotted with white flowers, and in the yet-unploughed fields a group of children were playing with a garland of lotus flowers. As the samurai looked out at the scene before him, the realization that he was going to a distant, unfamiliar country clutched at his heart as if for the first time.

Beyond the plain His Lordship's castle rose up like a warship – black, lofty, piercing. At the base of the hill on which the castle was built, the castle town sprawled beneath a hazy veil of spring sunlight. A market-place had been set up just inside the entrance to the town, and merchants, who had spread out on the ground everything from pans and cauldrons to oil, salt, cotton cloth and earthenware, cried out boisterously to the passers-by. The samurai and his companion, accustomed to the quiet life of the marshland, could only stare in amazement at the throng. They forded a river where white herons hovered overhead and ascended the hill to the castle. The thick steel gate was guarded by a foot-soldier holding a spear, and the two men had to dismount before proceeding further.

As a mere lance-corporal, the samurai was not allowed to enter the donjon without permission. When he reached the building within the castle grounds to which he had been directed, the other emissaries had already arrived in the inner court. The three men seated on stools, Matsuki Chūsaku, Tanaka Tarozaemon and Nishi Kyūsuke, were all of the same rank as the samurai. They exchanged greetings, but could not conceal their tension and anxiety.

Another six stools were lined up in the courtyard. The envoys waited for a short while, then there was the sound of footsteps and an officer escorted three foreigners in peculiar garb into the courtyard. Their angular faces reminded the Japanese of crows. They sat on the stools, facing the envoys. At this point Lord Shiraishi and two retainers appeared from inside the building and seated themselves.

Before sitting down, Lord Shiraishi glanced briefly at the samurai's lowered face and nodded with satisfaction. With great solemnity he introduced the foreigners to the assembled group as the chief crewmen of the Spanish ship that had drifted into Kishū two years before. The foreigner who was seated on one side the samurai recognized as the interpreter who had been part of Lord Shiraishi's entourage on the beach at Ogatsu that day.

'You will take along sufficient spears, banners and even clothing for your attendants to ensure that you do not bring disgrace upon His Lordship or appear unseemly in Nueva España. After you arrive there,' Lord Shiraishi shifted his eyes towards the interpreter, 'follow Lord Velasco's instructions in all matters.'

The foreigner called Velasco smiled with self-satisfaction as he gazed at the group of samurai. That smile seemed to be telling the Japanese that without him their envoys would be unable to do anything in Nueva España.

The envoys and their attendants were ordered to assemble at Tsukinoura two days before the fifth day of the fifth month, the date of departure. The great ship would be towed to Tsukinoura and would set sail from there.

After receiving their detailed instructions, the envoys were offered *sake* in a separate chamber. As the group started to leave the courtyard, Lord Shiraishi called, 'Rokuemon,' and ordered the samurai to remain behind.

'Rokuemon, this journey will not be an easy one, but you must carry out your mission to the best of your ability. It was the idea of Lord Ishida and me to select you as one of the envoys. In part, because of the lands in Kurokawa. If you perform your function as an envoy well, after your return the Council of Elders may reconsider their position. But do not mention this to your uncle.'

The samurai listened deferentially. His heart swelled with gratitude for Lord Shiraishi's kindness, and he felt an impulse to press his hands upon the ground and bow his head in thankfulness.

'In the land of the foreigners,' Lord Shiraishi added abruptly, 'the ways of life will probably be different from those here in Japan. You must not cling to Japanese customs if they stand in the way of your mission. If that which is white in Japan is black in the foreign lands, consider it black. Even if you remain unconvinced in your heart, you must wear a look of acquiescence on your face.' His words puzzled the samurai.

Later that day he left the castle and made a leisurely tour of the castle town with Yozō. The mansions of high-ranking vassals lined the streets near the castle, the houses of merchants were clustered on Ō-machi, Minami-machi, Sakana-machi and Ara-machi, and numerous temples dotted every quarter of the town. Yozō pressed his hands together in fervent prayer at each temple they visited. The samurai could well understand how his servant felt.

He bought toy horses for his children and a comb for Riku. As he purchased the comb, his wife's face suddenly appeared vividly before his eyes and, in spite of himself, he blushed in front of Yozō.

As the days passed, one after another, the samurai's heart grew heavier, as if it were being weighed down with stones. He was about to embark on a long sea voyage to an unknown land, and that inescapable realization was suffocating. Like the peasants here, he hated the thought of having to leave the marshland. Each time this thought came to him, however, he recalled Lord Shiraishi's words and stifled his timidity.

Signs of spring began to appear. Horsetails sent spearlike shoots up through the ground, and butterbur stalks cropped up here and there. Since his childhood the marshland had been a part of his life, and the samurai knew that on the voyage he would miss every part of it. He would not see such scenes again for a long time.

The same thoughts filled his mind at night as he sat by the hearth and studied the faces of his wife and children. Once he held Gonshirō on his lap and said, 'Father is going to a distant country,' but the young boy could understand nothing.

'Father is going to a distant country, and he will bring back gifts for Kanzaburō and for Gonshirō, too.'

As Gonshirō sat on his lap, the samurai told him a story he had heard from his mother many years before.

'Once upon a time,' he began, rocking his knees back and forth and speaking as if to himself, 'there was a frog from a village in this region and a frog from the region of San'in. In the spring after the snow melted, they decided to go on a picnic, and they climbed up to the top of a mountain. All the way up to the top of the mountain.'

Gonshirō was almost asleep, but the samurai went on. 'Once upon a time, a frog from a certain place decided to travel to Kamigata. He followed along behind a horse trader. . . .'

The chamber known as the Falcon Hall was dark and cold. The only objects in the hall that caught his eye were the four-panelled sliding doors decorated with drawings of sharp-eyed falcons. In Edo Castle and in the residences of other powerful men, the missionary had often been brought to cold, gloomy chambers like this one. He always had the feeling that the intrigues of the Japanese lurked like shadows in the darkness of such rooms.

'We humbly come before the great Lord of all the earth, His Holiness Paulus V, Pope of Rome. . . .'

An old man serving as a clerk to the castle was reading from a draft of His Lordship's letter. Unlike the elder statesmen, who were seated on a raised dais with Lord Shiraishi once again in the centre, this old man had a shaven head and wore the black robes of a Buddhist prelate.

'Velasco, a monk of the Order of Saint Francis, has come to our land and expounded Christianity. He has visited our domain and taught me the mysteries of the Christian faith. As a result, I have been able to understand the purport of those teachings for the first time, and I have decided to embrace them without hesitation.'

The clerk stumbled occasionally as he read the letter which he had drafted himself.

'Therefore, in consequence of my love and respect for the monks of this Church, I wish to erect cathedrals for them, and to exert all my efforts in the propagation of goodness. If there be anything which Your Holiness might consider necessary for the spreading of the holy laws of God, I will gladly make provision for it in my kingdom. I myself will furnish whatever funds and lands are required for cathedrals, so Your Holiness need have no apprehensions in that respect.'

As he listened to this hoarse recitation, the missionary studied the faces of Lord Shiraishi and the elder statesmen, but their expressions were stern and he was unable to tell what they were thinking.

'Although Nueva España is very distant from our land, I earnestly desire to enter into relations with that land, and I therefore beseech the influence of Your Holiness to assist me in attaining that ambition.'

The clerk slowly placed the draft of the letter on his knees and lifted his head like a prisoner awaiting judgement. Lord Shiraishi put his hand up to his mouth and coughed two or three times, then he said, 'Lord Velasco, do you have any objections?'

'It is acceptable. I will mention just two things. First, I would ask that when you address the Pope, you add one traditional phrase. Add "We humbly kiss the feet of His Holiness the Pope."'

'You wish us to write that His Lordship kisses the feet of the Pope?'

'It is customary,' the missionary said in a firm, unrelenting voice. The statesmen looked up in irritation, but Lord Shiraishi's cheeks curled into a wry smile.

'The next has to do with the part about dispatching padres to His Lordship's domain,' the missionary pressed on, encouraged by the momentary sign of weakness on Lord Shiraishi's face. 'I would ask that you add "only padres of the Franciscan Order." Without that addition, our Order will not be able to convey this letter to the Pope.'

He wanted to add, 'Shut the Jesuits out of Japan, and let only the Order of Saint Francis have the right to proselytize this country.' But of course he could not speak so candidly.

'This is crucial.'

'We shall add it,' Shiraishi nodded. To him, like other Japanese, the Jesuits and the Franciscans were all Christian padres, and the differences between them did not interest him in the least.

'Are you certain this letter will reach the Pope?' Lord Shiraishi asked in an attempt to mollify the missionary. He was fully aware that without this missionary the elder statesmen were powerless to achieve their purposes. After the great ship reached Nueva España, the emissaries, knowing neither the language nor the customs, would be totally unable to do anything for themselves. The missionary was the only one who could help them.

'It will reach him. If needs be, I will go to Rome and give it to His Holiness myself.'

'You would go alone?'

'I would take one of your envoys with me.'

'From Nueva España?'

'Yes. I am sure that would make you feel more secure.' Earlier on, the missionary had realized that, rather than sending this letter to the Vatican by way of his Order, it would be more effective for him to parade into Rome with it himself, accompanied by a Japanese. Having now given voice to these private thoughts, he felt as though his mind had been made up. Yes, I will take a Japanese with me to Rome. The citizens of Rome will surely stare in amazement at these visitors from a distant land. That will prove to the clerics at the Vatican how diligently I have laboured here.

'I see.' Lord Shiraishi covered his mouth with his fist and coughed again. As he did so, he seemed to be deep in thought. 'If that happens . . . you had best take along Hasekura Rokuemon.'

'Lord Hasekura?'

The missionary recalled the face of one of the envoys he had met in the courtyard of the castle a short time before. It was a face with sunken eyes and slightly protruding cheekbones like a peasant's, a stoic face ready to abandon everything and accept its fate. For some reason, the missionary felt that such a face belonged to Hasekura Rokuemon.

Lord Shiraishi proceeded to praise the fine workmanship of the great ship that was nearing completion, as if thereby to curry favour with the missionary. He laughed and said that, if he were younger, he would like to board the ship himself and have a look around Nueva España.

The discussion ended. Thin smiles surfaced on the faces of the elder statesmen as they watched the missionary leave with the servant who had been waiting in the hallway. When the footsteps had receded, Lord Shiraishi glanced sardonically at the clerk.

'The bodies of those foreigners stink, don't they?'

'I suppose it must be what they eat.'

'No, that's the smell of a man who has stifled his lust for women. How many years has he lived here in Japan?'

'Ten years, I understand,' the clerk answered respectfully.

'Ten years? And does he think he has us in the palm of his hand?'

Then he was silent, stroking away at his left palm with his right hand.

The day of departure approached. For several days already the marshland had been filled with bustling activity, just as in the days when the samurai's father and uncle had set out for battle. Since the samurai was the family head, even relatives who lived in villages outside the marshland streamed into his house to bid him farewell, and the peasants appeared one after another to offer assistance. A number of parcels had been tied up and piled in the entranceway.

Since early morning, a clamour had filled the courtyard. Horses had been led from the stables and parcels were strapped to their backs. Pine branches adorned the stable and the gateways, just as on New Year's Day, and dried chestnuts* had been placed in the rooms. With all the preparations completed, the samurai sat beside the hearth and drank down in three gulps the sacred wine sprinkled with cogon leaves that Riku had poured for him, then passed the cup to his uncle. After the cup had been passed from his uncle to Riku, and from Riku to Kanzaburō, the old man smashed it on the floor of the entranceway. This was the custom in the samurai's family on the morning the men set out for battle.

Outside the horses whinnied. The samurai bowed to his uncle, then peered deeply into Riku's eyes. As he looked at her, he placed his hands lightly on the heads of his two children. In the yard, Yozō, who was already prepared to leave, was holding the samurai's spear. Seihachi, Ichisuke and Daisuke, the three young men selected by the village elders, were standing beside three pack-laden horses, and along the road outside the gate the peasants had gathered to see the party leave.

When the samurai mounted his horse, he bowed once more to his

*Literally 'victory chestnuts': good omens placed in homes on New Year's Day or in preparation for battle.

uncle. Behind the old man stood Riku, her face pinched to hold back her emotions. A servant girl held Gonshirō in her arms, and Kanzaburō stood by their side. The samurai nodded broadly to them, forcing a smile. At that moment, he suddenly wondered how much his two children would have changed when he returned home. 'Look after yourself!' his uncle shouted. The samurai tugged at the reins.

The skies were clear. Spring had now arrived in the marshland. In the woods white flowers had blossomed, and skylarks chirped in the fields. From his saddle the samurai gazed around, hoping he would not forget this landscape; he would not see it again for a long while.

They followed the same road they had taken previously to Ogatsu. News of the great ship's departure had already spread throughout the domain, and the group was greeted by people all along the way. Some offered them hot water to drink, others words of gratitude for their service. Winter landscapes had greeted the samurai here before, but now flowers bloomed in profusion, and in the fields peasants lazily prodded their oxen. The following day, they saw the sea in the distance. A warm spring sun was shining on the waves, and the clouds floating in the sky were soft as cotton.

At length the samurai and his company glimpsed the great ship floating on the horizon.

'Oh! Oh!' they cried, instinctively coming to a halt on the beach. The galleon reminded them of a great brown fortress. On the two tall masts, grey sails were puffed out by the wind. The bowsprit stabbed at the blue sky like a sharp spear, and waves churned about the boat.

The group stood silently on the shore for a long while, gazing at the galleon. It was a powerful, manly ship, more awesome than any of His Lordship's war vessels. The realization that in two days they would board this ship, and that this ship would determine the fate of each of them, swept painfully over the samurai. He felt his quiet life in the marshland being stripped violently from him. His heart surged with a mixture of excitement and fear, as though he was a warrior setting out to do battle.

'His Lordship has built a fine ship!'

As a lance-corporal, the samurai had glimpsed His Lordship, who dwelt within the castle donjon, only a few times from a distance. His Lordship had always been remote and inaccessible. But the moment he set eyes on this great ship, the word 'duty' seemed to surface vividly within his head. To the samurai the ship *was* His Lordship, and His Lordship's authority. The obedient samurai was filled with the joy of serving His Lordship.

The bay of Tsukinoura was crowded with people, as Ogatsu had been. The beach, surrounded on three sides by hills, seemed like the bottom of a ravine. Workmen were loading huge piles of cargo onto tiny boats and several officials carrying walking-sticks were shouting instructions. When the samurai and his group threaded their way through this throng, the officials greeted them with words of congratulation.

Foot-soldiers had been set to guard the temple which was to be the samurai's lodging. He learned from the soldiers that the other envoys, Matsuki Chūsaku, Nishi Kyūsuke and Tanaka Tarozaemon, had already arrived, and that the Spanish sailors were staying at a temple in a nearby village. The bay was directly below the room which had been provided for the envoys, but the great ship was hidden by a hill and could not be seen. Tiny boats laden with cargo proceeded one after another towards the point of the cape that concealed the galleon.

'I've never seen so much cargo!' sighed Nishi Kyūsuke, the youngest of the group.

'I've heard there will be over a hundred merchants and miners and artisans on board.'

The samurai and Tanaka Tarozaemon listened diffidently as Nishi spoke of the true purpose of this great undertaking. Some distance from the others, his arms folded, Matsuki Chūsaku stood gazing down at the bay. With a triumphant look, Nishi announced that the merchants were being given passage in order to sell Japanese goods and implements abroad and to make arrangements for future trade, and that the miners and metalworkers and casters were being sent to learn foreign techniques. The samurai was of course aware that there were gold mines and mineral deposits in the domain, but this was the first he had heard of such people boarding the ship. When he went to bed that night, however, he reminded himself that his own mission had nothing to do with such people, that his assignment was to deliver letters from His Lordship to the Governor of Nueva España, to the Roman Pope, and to other foreign dignitaries. He had trouble sleeping because of the roar of the waves and the pounding of his heart.

On the morning of departure, the heraldic bunting stretched along the bay flapped noisily in the breeze. Before boarding the skiff, the envoys paid obeisance to Lord Shiraishi and two other elder statesmen who had come from Shiogama on a military ship. Seated on a stool, Lord Shiraishi spoke words of encouragement to each of the envoys. When the samurai, accompanied by Yozō and his other three attendants, appeared last and bowed his head, Lord Shiraishi said, 'Rokuemon.' He rose from his stool and held out with both hands a box wrapped in gold brocade. 'Here are His Lordship's letters,' he said forcefully, and handed the box to the samurai. The samurai felt his body quiver as he accepted the ponderously heavy box.

The skiff carrying the envoys slowly set out from the shore. It followed the line of the sharp cliffs before advancing silently into the offing. Clutching the box that had been entrusted to them, the samurai and his four retainers gazed speechlessly at the white bunting and at the row of officials and foot-soldiers assembled on either side of the flagposts. Several years from now, when they returned to Japan and again entered this bay, would there be so many people to welcome them back? The thought suddenly crossed the samurai's mind.

The moment the skiff left the bay, the samurai caught sight of the great ship he had first seen two days before. It was unlike any Japanese vessel he had ever seen. The prow, which was like the stone wall of a fortress, towered majestically before his eyes, and from its stem the bowsprit thrust into the blue sky like a spear. The huge sails were furled around the cross-shaped mainmast, lashed down with countless halyards. The foreign sailors were already aboard, watching from the deck as the skiff approached.

One after another the Japanese climbed up the rope ladder and onto the deck. The ship had three decks. On the top deck the Japanese sailors scurried about like ants. The entrance into the hull was on the second deck.

From there the Japanese climbed down to the cabins they had been assigned. The envoys had been given a tiny cabin near the prow, painted with Shunkei lacquer. The room was filled with the smell of it. Their attendants had to go to the large cabin where the merchants were to sleep; it had bare rafters and was stacked high with cargo.

When the envoys entered their cabin, they were silent for a few moments, listening to the noises on deck. The merchants, who had stayed in Ojika the previous night, were noisily boarding the ship. Out of the cabin's little window, the tiny islands of Tashiro and Aji were visible, but from here they could not see the bay.

'I wonder if the elder statesmen have already left?' said Nishi, his face pressed against the window. When Nishi set out for the deck, his fellow envoys followed hurriedly behind. Everything on the ship was new to them, and they were afraid to be left alone.

The samurai, jostling among the crowd of merchants, made his way over to his attendants and gazed back at the shore. The hills of Ojika were blanketed by trees, a deep green in this fifth month. It was the last Japanese landscape he would see for some time. Suddenly the hillocks of the marshland, the villages, then his own house, the stable, and the face of Riku appeared one after another before his eyes. With a spasm of pain he wondered what his children were doing at that moment. There was a great clamour on the upper deck. The Spanish crew were singing something with a strange melody. Several Japanese deckhands scrambled up the mainmast, and at orders from the Spanish sailors they let down the sails, which looked like enormous flags. The halyards creaked, and white seagulls howled like cats. Before anyone realized what was happening, the great ship slowly got under way. At the sound of waves lapping against the hull, the samurai felt that a new destiny was just beginning for him.

Chapter 3

Our ship set sail from Tsukinoura, a tiny port on the Ojika Peninsula, on the fifth day of the fifth month. The Japanese have named this galleon the *Mutsu Maru*, while the Spanish sailors call it the *San Juan Baptista*. The ship pitches as we proceed in a north-easterly direction across the cold Pacific Ocean. The puffed-out sails are like an archer's bow. On the morning of our departure, I stood on deck and stared fixedly at the islands of Japan which have been my home for ten years.

Ten years – it grieves me to say this, but the word of God has yet to bury roots in Japan. To my knowledge, the Japanese are blessed with an intelligence and curiosity that is in no way inferior to that of the various peoples of Europe. But when it comes to our God, they close their eyes and stuff their fingers into their ears. At times this country has even seemed to me to be an isolated, ill-fated island.

But I have not lost heart. I believe the seeds of God's teachings have been planted in Japan, but the methods of nurturing them have been poor. The Jesuits gave no thought to the nature of the soil here, and they did not select the right fertilizers. I have learned from the mistakes of the Jesuits, and above all else I know the Japanese people. If I am appointed Bishop, I shall not repeat their mistakes.

Three days ago we had our last glimpse of the Japanese islands. Yet, strangely, seagulls have flown here from somewhere, skimming over the waves and perching on the mast. Our ship is bearing towards latitude forty degrees north, but most likely we are still not far from the Japanese island of Ezo. The direction of the winds is favourable, and the current aids the *San Juan Baptista* on her journey.

The swell in fact became rather rough when we reached the open sea. Still, this is nothing at all compared to the fury of the Indian Ocean and the storms that assaulted us as I journeyed towards Asia thirteen years ago. But all the Japanese in the cabins are suffering from seasickness; the poor souls cannot even swallow down a meal. Although their country is surrounded by the sea, the Japanese have

58

always lived as people of the land. The only sea they know is the narrow strip of home waters close to shore.

Some of the envoys are also tortured by seasickness. For both Hasekura Rokuemon and Tanaka Tarozaemon, this seems to be their first sea voyage, and when I visited their cabin it was all they could do to force a pained smile.

The envoys are middle-ranking *caballeros* among His Lordship's retainers, but each is also the holder of a tiny fief in the mountain regions. Perhaps instead of choosing from among the powerful elder statesmen of his castle, His Lordship selected these middle-class warriors for this mission because the Japanese aristocracy tends to put little weight on the role of an envoy. Whatever the case, I prefer such an arrangement. There is no need for me to look to them for instructions, and I can act in accordance with my own will. The Jesuit Provincial Valignano once took a group of young men no better than beggars and, pretending they were the children of aristocrats, sent them as emissaries to Rome. Yet in Rome no one was the least bit suspicious. Later many were critical of him for that move, but I rather admired Valignano's flair.

I should record the names of the four envoys who will have to rely on me for everything from now on. Nishi Kyūsuke, Tanaka Tarozaemon, Matsuki Chūsaku and Hasekura Rokuemon.

With the exception of Nishi Kyūsuke, not one of them has tried to get to know me since we set sail. I suppose that is because of the unique caution and shyness the Japanese feel towards foreigners. Young Nishi Kyūsuke alone has demonstrated an almost childlike curiosity, and because he is in high spirits on his first sea voyage, he has questioned me about the construction of the ship and the operation of a compass, and he has asked me to teach him Spanish. The oldest among the envoys, Tanaka Tarozaemon, frowns upon young Nishi's lack of reserve, but this plump fellow Tanaka seems determined to appear sober whatever happens and not to let the dignity of the Japanese slip in front of the Spaniards.

Matsuki Chūsaku is a slender man whose face is clouded with dark shadows. I have spoken to him only three or four times, but it is obvious that he is the most intelligent of the four envoys. Sometimes he goes out onto the deck and appears to be deep in thought. Unlike the other envoys, he does not seem to consider it an honour to have been chosen for this mission. Hasekura Rokuemon appears to be more a peasant than a samurai, and is the least impressive of all the envoys. It has not yet been decided whether we shall go to Rome, but I haven't the slightest idea why Lord Shiraishi encouraged me to take along Hasekura if we do. The fellow cuts a sorry figure, and he lacks

Matsuki's intelligence.

Some distance from the envoys' room there is a large cabin which the Japanese merchants all share. Their heads are filled solely with thoughts of trade and profits. Their greed is marvellous to behold. Just after we boarded the ship, several of the merchants plied me with questions about what Japanese goods I thought could be sold in Nueva España. When I suggested silk, folding screens, armaments and swords, they nodded to each other with satisfaction and proceeded to ask whether they would be able to purchase raw silk thread, velvet and ivory cheaper than in China.

'But in Nueva España,' I replied with obvious irony, 'only Christians are trusted. Only a believer is considered worthy of trust in matters of commerce.'

As the Japanese often do when they are uncomfortable, they crinkled up the corners of their mouths in faint smiles.

Monotonous days follow one after another, each new day indistinguishable from the previous one. The sea never changes, nor do the clouds which float on the horizon, and the creaking of the sails is ever the same. The *San Juan Baptista* proceeds smoothly on her voyage. Each time I conduct morning Mass, I realize anew that the Lord has miraculously granted us such an uneventful voyage in order to assist me in achieving my purposes. The mind of the Lord is hard to fathom, but I believe that with me as an instrument, the Lord wishes the stubbornly resistant Japan to become a nation that follows His teachings.

Captain Montaño and First Mate Contreras, however, do not think kindly of my intentions. They have not said as much openly, but there is no doubt that they are opposed to my plan. That is because during their detention in Japan, the two men did not receive a single good impression of Japan and the Japanese. They make no attempt to associate with the envoys or the other Japanese any more than is necessary, and they do not like the Spanish sailors to converse with the Japanese crewmen. Twice I suggested to the Captain that we invite the envoys to our dinner table, but he refused.

'While I was detained in Japan, I couldn't put up with the arrogance and the short tempers of the Japanese,' the Captain told me at dinner two days ago. 'I've never met a group of people more lacking in frankness, people who think it's a virtue not to let anybody else know what they're thinking.'

I argued that their political system is so refined that it is hard to believe they are a heathen nation.

'That's exactly what makes a country like that hard to deal with,' the First Mate insisted. 'It won't be long before they try to control the Pacific. If you want to convert them to Christianity, it would be easier to subdue them with weapons than with words.'

'With weapons?' I cried impulsively. 'You both underestimate Japan. It is not like Nueva España or the Philippines. The Japanese are familiar with war, and they are fierce in battle. Are you aware that the Jesuits failed in the past because they had that very idea?'

Neither of them looked interested, but I proceeded to enumerate the blunders in the Jesuits' proselytizing strategy one by one. For instance, Father Coelho and Father Frois of the Society of Jesus planned to make Japan into a Spanish colony in order to promulgate Christianity; the Japanese rulers were infuriated when they learned of those plans. I seem to lose all restraint when I start discussing the Jesuits.

'And so in order to spread God's teachings in Japan,' I concluded, carried away in a fit of passion, 'there is only one possible method. We must cajole them into it. España must offer to share the profits from trade on the Pacific with the Japanese in return for sweeping proselytizing privileges. The Japanese will sacrifice everything else for the sake of profits. If I were Bishop. . . .'

At those words, the Captain and the First Mate glanced at each other and abruptly lapsed into silence. It was not a silence of approbation, but seemed rather to result from the impression that my scheming was unbecoming in a man of the cloth. Although I am well aware of the need for discretion in such remarks in the presence of worldly people, I had been careless.

'The padre seems more interested in the proselytizing of Japan,' the Captain said ironically, 'than in the national interest of España.'

He said no more. It was obvious that these two men had taken my words 'If I were Bishop . . .' as the expression of a base lust for promotion. But only the Lord knows the hearts of men and judges them. 'Thou knowest well that I did not speak those words from vain personal ambition. I have chosen Japan as the place where I shall die. It is merely that I feel that I am necessary to Thee so that voices singing Thy praises may echo throughout Japan.'

Something interesting happened. As I was walking on the deck reciting the breviary, one of the Japanese merchants sidled up to me. He studied me curiously as I muttered my prayers, and then, as if observing some strange creature, he asked, 'Lord Interpreter, what are you doing?' Foolishly, I thought perhaps this fellow had some interest in prayer, but that was not the case. He gave me a fawning smile and, suddenly lowering his voice, commenced to urge me to see to it that he alone was granted trading privileges in Nueva España. I averted my face to listen to him, as though he had spewed out foul breath upon me, but he went on smiling and muttered, 'When the time comes, I'll be generous in my gratitude. I'll make money, and there'll be something in it for you too.'

I let my contempt show openly on my face and told him in no uncertain terms that although I was an interpreter, I was also a priest who had renounced the secular world. At that I sent him back to his cabin.

I fear lest the two months which this voyage will require pass in idleness for me as a priest. I say Mass every day in the dining-room for the Spanish sailors, but not one of the Japanese comes even to have a look. To them, happiness seems to mean nothing but the reaping of temporal profits. If a religion promises all the benefits of this life – the amassing of wealth, victory in battle, the healing of disease – the Japanese snatch it up, but they seem totally insensitive to the supernatural and the eternal. Even so, during our voyage I will be derelict if I do not preach the word of God to the more than a hundred Japanese on this ship.

The envoys suffered cruelly from seasickness. Nishi Kyūsuke and Matsuki Chūsaku were not so badly afflicted, but for several days after the ship left Tsukinoura, Tanaka Tarozaemon and the samurai sprawled on their beds like dead men, hearing only the melancholy creak of the rigging and the masts. They had no idea where they were now, and they no longer cared. The ship lurched constantly, and even when they closed their eyes, they could not escape the feeling that some tremendous force was slowly lifting them up, then slowly forcing them down. The samurai experienced nausea, revulsion and helplessness all at the same time. He slept occasionally and sometimes thought dimly of Riku's face, of his children, and of his uncle seated beside the hearth.

The envoys' attendants were responsible for bringing them their meals. When Yozō staggered into the cabin with a tray for the samurai, his face too was pale and drawn from seasickness. The samurai had no appetite no matter what was set before him, but he forced himself to eat in the interest of his vital mission.

'There's nothing to be concerned about.' Velasco came to their cabin and, with a look of sympathy at the samurai and Tanaka, tried to console them. 'Seasickness is just a matter of conditioning. In four or five more days, you'll find that not even large waves or storms will bother you.'

The samurai could not bring himself to believe this. But he envied young Nishi Kyūsuke, who could wander all over the ship expressing his admiration and asking Velasco to teach him foreign phrases.

Strangely, though, when three or four days had passed the agonies of seasickness began to subside, just as Velasco had said. On the morning of the fifth day, the samurai for the first time left the cabin that reeked of lacquer and fish oil and climbed up to the deck. When he stepped out onto the deserted deck, without warning a strong wind slapped his forehead. He caught his breath, and suddenly before his eyes the bounding waves stretched out in every direction.

He was seeing the great ocean for the first time. There was not a trace of land, not even the silhouette of an island. Waves collided, jostled, and sent up war cries like a mêlée of countless warriors. The prow of the ship thrust like a spear into the grey sky, and the hull, shooting up a tall spout of water, seemed about to plunge into a valley in the ocean, then lurched up once again.

The samurai's eyes swam. He could scarcely catch his breath in the gusts of wind that pounded his brow. To the east, an ocean of billowing waves. To the west, an ocean of clamouring waves. To the south and to the north, ocean as far as he could see. For the first time in his life the samurai understood the vastness of the sea. Compared to this ocean, his own marshland was little more than a single tiny speck. He groaned at the immensity of it all.

He heard footsteps. Matsuki Chūsaku joined him on deck. This thin, cheerless man also gazed in wonder at the vast spectacle before them.

'The world truly is enormous.'

But the wind snatched up the samurai's words and carried them far out to sea like a scrap of paper.

'I can't believe that an ocean like this stretches all the way to Nueva España.'

Matsuki seemed not to hear. He stood motionless, his back to the samurai. For a long while he stared at the sea, then turned to his companion. The mast threw shadows across his face.

'It will take us two months to cross this ocean,' Matsuki said. But the wind whisked his words away too, and the samurai had to ask what he had said. 'Lord Hasekura. What do you think about our mission?'

'Our mission? It is a greater honour than I deserve.'

'That's not what I mean,' Matsuki shook his head angrily. 'What do you think about lance-corporals like us being ordered to carry out such an important mission? That's all I've been thinking about since the ship left Japan.'

The samurai said nothing. Since their departure he had struggled with the same problem.

'Lord Matsuki? What do you . . .?'

'We're nothing but pawns,' Matsuki muttered self-derisively, his eyes fixed on the sea. 'We're pawns for the Council of Elders to sacrifice.'

'Pawns?'

'By rights one of the senior statesmen should have assumed this important mission, and yet we were chosen. Why? Because a low-ranking lance-corporal can drown on the way or collapse from disease in some unknown land, and it won't make the slightest difference to His Lordship or the Council.'

Matsuki savoured the effect of his words as he watched the samurai's face turn pale.

'What sort of envoys will we make if nobody can understand what we say? We're nothing more than messengers who have to depend on that Velasco to deliver His Lordship's letters. So long as trade with Nueva España is established and it's decided that foreign ships will visit the ports of Shiogama and Kesennuma, we could rot away in any part of the world and it wouldn't matter a bit to His Lordship or the elder statesmen.'

A burst of spray carried by the wind dampened the feet of the two men. The rigging creaked overhead.

'That . . . that isn't what Lord Shiraishi said,' the samurai protested, almost in a moan. It irritated him that he was too clumsy in his speech to refute Matsuki's claims eloquently. If they really were pawns, why would Lord Shiraishi and Lord Ishida have urged him to look after his health until his return? Why would they have said that they would consider returning the lands at Kurokawa when he got home?

'Lord Shiraishi could hardly tell you something like that,' Matsuki jeered. 'When His Lordship divided up the fiefs twelve years ago, many rural samurai were stripped of their old hereditary fiefs and given barren, desolate lands selected by the Council of Elders. We've petitioned for our former lands to be returned, but we haven't had a satisfactory answer, and the lance-corporals seethe with discontent. You and me, Tanaka and Nishi, we're all the same. So they've chosen the four of us from among the malcontents and ordered us on this miserable journey, and if we die somewhere along the way, our families will be disinherited. If we don't complete our mission successfully, we'll be punished. This is a warning to all the discontented lance-corporals. No matter what happens, the Council comes out ahead.'

'I don't believe you.'

'You don't have to believe me. But did you know that the Council of Elders had split into two opposing camps before this ship was sent out?' Matsuki asked cryptically, placing his foot on a rung of the ladder that led down into the hull. 'Never mind. It's all just conjecture on my part.'

After Matsuki had gone below, the samurai stood alone on the deck, facing the raging sea.

'This mission is like a battle,' he thought. 'On the battlefield, a lance-corporal has to lead the common warriors and foot-soldiers through the hail of arrows and bullets. But the elder statesmen remain in the rear and direct the combined forces.' To dispel the gloom in his heart, the samurai had to believe that the elder statesmen had not become envoys themselves for the same reasons they did not participate in battle, but Matsuki's words curdled in the pit of his stomach.

When he went below, the fierce swirl of the wind and the thunderous echo of the waves died suddenly away. The samurai did not want to go back to the envoys' cabin. The smell of lacquer on the exposed pillars in the hull was stifling. He peered into the large cabin where the merchants were quartered. He knew that his attendants Yozō, Seihachi, Daisuke and Ichisuke had found a place in a corner.

The smell of the straw matting wrapped around the cargo mingled with the odours of sweat and human bodies. Some of the hundred or more merchants were sprawled on the floor or seated in circles playing dice. Yozō and the others were lying down beside the cargo, still apparently in agony, but when they sensed the presence of their master by their pillows, they hurriedly tried to sit up.

'It's all right. Don't get up,' he consoled the four men as they bowed to him. 'Seasickness is dreadful, isn't it? The ocean is even more miserable for those of us brought up in the marshland.'

He suggested that when they finally returned to Japan, they should say nothing about the unsightly figures they had cut under the influence of seasickness. That brought the first smile to his attendants' faces. As he studied those haggard faces, the samurai was very conscious that these four men would be his only inseparable companions on this long, painful voyage. If he returned to Japan, some sort of reward should await him. But for these men, there would be only the same bitter lives of hard labour.

'It must be the rainy season in the marshland about now.'

During this season the rains fell incessantly every day. The peasants, naked and caked with mud, laboured beneath the down-

pour. Yet even that bitter scene now evoked wistful memories in the
samurai and his attendants. . . .

' "*Somos Japoneses.*" That means "We are Japanese." ' Nishi returned
to the cabin speaking strange words to Tanaka and the samurai, who
sat in different positions writing their journals of the voyage. The
samurai glanced up with a dubious look.

'Why don't you come? Lord Velasco the interpreter is teaching the
foreign language to the merchants.'

'Nishi, if the envoys mix with the merchants, we'll be inviting the
contempt of the Spaniards,' Tanaka grumbled bitterly. Nishi blushed
slightly at the rebuke.

'But if we can't understand a single word when we reach our
destination . . .'

'We've got an interpreter, you know. An interpreter.'

As he watched the crestfallen Nishi, inwardly the samurai envied
the fellow's ability to warm to anyone, to blend in anywhere. Having
been brought up in the marshland, he himself was shy and reserved,
like Tanaka. Yet each day this young man strolled through every
corner of the ship, displaying boundless curiosity about its construction and operation. He copied down words used by the Spanish
sailors on pieces of paper, and it was he who informed everyone else
that the ship's captain was called '*Capitan*', the deck officers '*Cubierta*',
and the sail '*vela*'.

'But even Lord Matsuki,' Nishi protested, his cheeks still flushed,
'is in there learning right beside the merchants.'

Tanaka scowled. The oldest of the envoys, he lived in constant
dread that their dignity might be compromised. So in the presence of
foreigners he did his best to show no surprise at any of the new and
varied occurrences aboard the ship.

'Even Lord Matsuki?' the samurai asked in surprise.

'Yes.'

The samurai could not imagine what that pale, gloomy man had
in mind. Earlier, as if spitting out the words, he had claimed that
they were the sacrificial pawns of His Lordship and the Council of
Elders, that the Council had sent them on this perilous journey in
order to stifle the discontent of the lance-corporals over their new
fiefdoms. The samurai had not related his conversation with
Matsuki to Tanaka or Nishi. Somehow he had been afraid to do
so.

The samurai stood up, hoping to drive Matsuki's words from his
head. The passageway which extended through the hull was long,

with one side curved like a bow to form the freight area. On the opposite side were rooms stacked high with cargo, the large cabin of the merchants, then the storeroom and the kitchen used by the Japanese. The cargo rooms smelled of dust and straw matting, the kitchen of *miso*.

'Lord Hasekura.' Nishi ran up behind him and grinned boyishly. 'Wouldn't you like to come and learn some Spanish?' The samurai nodded solemnly. They peered into the large cabin. The merchants were sitting in four rows in front of the stacks of cargo, each holding a brush and paper and intently copying down the foreign words which the interpreter was teaching them.

' "How much is it?" is "*Cuanto cuesta?*" ' Every last one of the merchants earnestly copied the words down. The envoys' attendants were watching this peculiar scene with faint smiles.

'I will say it once more. *Cuanto cuesta?*'

Beside the samurai, Nishi softly repeated the phrase. A world totally unlike any the samurai had known in the marshland was opening up before him here. Amid the black, bent heads of the merchants he noticed the slender head of Matsuki, who was sitting with folded arms.

'Keep in mind, though, that simply learning the language won't enable you to do business in Nueva España,' said Velasco, taking out a cloth and wiping his mouth. 'As I've told you before, you won't be successful there unless you have an understanding of Christianity. Look around you. Even on this ship the Spanish sailors give all their signals to the music of prayers. Those chants you hear every day are songs of praise to the Christian God. Did you realize that those chants were work signals?'

It was true. The day they set sail, the foreign sailors had called to one another in songs with peculiar tunes. Those calls were repeated every day on deck.

'I am not saying you must study the Christian teachings. But I have here a book that tells of the life of Lord Jesus.'

Whispers spread among the merchants like tiny waves, but soon subsided. Matsuki stood up and left the group. He noticed the samurai and Nishi and approached them.

'Look at them. The merchants are going to listen to this. I suppose they would even become Christians themselves if it would bring them more money. Velasco can fill their heads with the Christian teachings because he knows their greed. He's a clever one, this interpreter of ours.'

With a shrug of his shoulder, Matsuki returned to his cabin. The artless samurai actually sensed something unpleasant in Matsuki's

slender back. Matsuki looked at everything with malice, and to the
samurai he seemed an impertinent man.

For half a month now the *San Juan Baptista* has been proceeding ever
eastward across the great ocean. We have not seen a single island.
Fortunately we have experienced no calms, and no great storms have
come our way. Of course lulls are not as common along this northern
route as around the equator, but storms are frequently encountered.
Thus Captain Montaño has commented how unusual it is to have
such a smooth voyage. I recall now that when I first travelled to
Japan, the sailors detested anyone who whistled during a lull. They
have a superstition that whistling intensifies the agony. Each
morning on the *San Juan Baptista* begins with the washing of the
decks. The Japanese deckhands have to perform all the menial tasks –
washing the decks, inspecting the halyards throughout the day,
beating the rust from the chain cables and preparing the rigging. The
Spanish sailors handle the look-out stations, the manning of the helm,
the transmission of orders from the Captain and the First Mate, and
the work in the steering room.
    Every day, the ocean changes colour – or rather, it passes through a
variety of hues between the morning, noon and night of a single day.
The subtle shapes of the clouds, the glittering light of the sun, and the
shifts in atmospheric pressure tint the sea with deep tones, cheerful
tones and plaintive tones that would cause any painter to pause in
wonder. When I look upon such an array of colours, surely I am not
the only one moved to praise the wisdom of the Creator who made
this ocean? The seagulls have long since ceased to pursue us on our
journey, but in their place schools of silver flying fish leap from one
wave to the next to delight our eyes.
    To my amazement, several Japanese merchants stole in to have a
look at Mass this morning. It was just at the point when I was saying
Communion. I was holding the chalice and placing the holy wafer in
the mouths of the kneeling Spanish sailors when I realized that a
group of Japanese were watching the scene; they were hesitant but
full of curiosity. Did they come to look at Mass because they were
tired of the daily tedium aboard ship? Or had they been moved by
the brief portions from the Bible that I have been translating
into Japanese for the past six days after their Spanish lessons? Or
had they in fact believed my taunting suggestion that, unless they
become Christians, they will not be trusted as traders in Nueva
España?
    In any case, I was pleased with the result. When Mass was over, I

placed my vestments and the chalice on a shelf and hurriedly went out into the hall to speak to the Japanese who were still loitering there.

'What did you think? Wouldn't you like to learn the profound meaning of the Mass?'

The yellow-toothed man who had once begged me to give him exclusive trading privileges was among the group. He smiled thinly and replied, 'Lord Interpreter. Japanese merchants will accept anything if it is to their advantage. So it isn't going to hurt our business if we learn something about the Christian teachings on this voyage.'

I couldn't help smiling at this frank reply. It was such a typically Japanese answer, but even so it was a bit *too* forthright. As if to flatter me further, they asked me to tell them more about the blessed life of Christ in the days ahead.

'It isn't going to hurt our business if we learn something about Christianity.' I think this reply from the yellow-toothed man says a great deal about the Japanese attitude towards religion. During my many years in Japan, I have seen with my own eyes how fervently the Japanese seek the benefits of this life even in religion. I could even go as far as to say that their so-called faiths exist solely for the purpose of providing as many worldly benefits as possible. They worship their gods and buddhas in order to escape illness and calamity. The feudal lords promise donations to shrines and temples so that they may gain victory in battle. The Buddhist bonzes are aware of this, and they make their followers worship the image of the devil Yakushi Nyorai,* who is purported to possess greater healing power than any medicine. There is no Buddhist image more revered among the Japanese than this Nyorai. And their cults are not limited to those that offer escape from disease and calamity. There are numerous heathen sects which promise to increase the wealth and protect the property of their followers, and many flock to join them.

When I look at the Japanese, I sometimes wonder whether a true religion – one that seeks after eternity and the salvation of the soul as we understand them – can develop in that country. There is too great a gap between their form of godliness and that which we Christians know as faith. And so I must fight fire with fire. If the Japanese are going to seek worldly benefit from religion, then it is essential for me to discover how to channel their carnal ambitions towards God's teachings. For a time the Jesuits managed it skilfully. They showed the feudal rulers new weapons like firearms and all manner of strange articles from the South Seas, and in exchange for those items they got

* Bhêchadjaguru, the 'Physician of souls' in the Buddhist pantheon.

permission to preach the gospel. But, after that, they did too many things to invoke the wrath of the Japanese. They tore down the temples and shrines where the Japanese worshipped and, taking advantage of the weakness of the feudal lords absorbed in internecine warfare, they created little colonial settlements to protect their own special privileges.

Before we left Japan, I wrote letters to my uncle Don Diego Caballero Molina, to Father Don Diego de Cabrera, and to the Father Superior of the Franciscan monastery in Sevilla. I informed them that I might possibly come to Sevilla from Nueva España, bringing some Japanese with me. I asked that in such an event they arrange as elaborate and extravagant a production as possible to demonstrate to the people of España that the glory of God had extended even to a tiny nation in the Orient. Nothing could be more remarkable for the people of Sevilla than the opportunity to see a group of Japanese, and of course it could be expected that great numbers of them would come to have a look, but we have to ensure that the impact will be even greater. This impact, of course, would all be to the glory of God and would, I wrote, further the spreading of His word in Japan. I intend to send these letters by special carriage from Acapulco to Veracruz, and by the fastest possible means from there to Sevilla.

Yesterday, after teaching them the same essential phrases and simple vocabulary, I once again told the Japanese in the large cabin a little about the life of Jesus. 'Thy faith hath made thee whole.' Fervently I related to them how one after another the Lord had healed the infirm in Galilee. Loudly I told them how the lame were made to walk, the blind to see, and how the bodies of the lepers were cleansed. The Japanese listened intently, with looks of deep emotion of their faces. I deliberately emphasized these stories of miracles, knowing that the healing of the sick was one of the things they always looked for in a religion.

'But the power of the Lord is not restricted to afflictions of the body. It can also heal afflictions of the soul.'

With those words I concluded my remarks for the day. I think I chose exactly the right topic to relate to the Japanese. Yet, in all honesty, my most important work still lies ahead. The road is still very long. For I know from long experience that while the Japanese may be attracted by stories of miracles or talk of their own hopeless sins, when one speaks of the resurrection – the crux of all Christianity – or of a love that requires the sacrifice of one's entire being, at that moment a look of uncomprehending disappointment steals across their faces.

During the evening meal, Captain Montaño told us that the barometric pressure had dropped, and that the storm we dreaded was slowly approaching from the south. I had in fact noticed that afternoon that the waves had swelled considerably. The beautiful deep blue of the sea had gradually turned to a cold black, and, their white fangs bared, the clamouring waves spewed spray from the prow and began to wash across the deck. The Captain said he would be tacking the sails full to starboard in an attempt to move out of range of the storm.

Just before midnight, the storm was almost upon us. At first the vibration was not severe, so I wrote my diary in this cabin which I share with First Mate Contreras. Contreras and all the sailors, Spanish and Japanese, were on emergency alert, wearing life-ropes as they waited on deck for the storm to arrive. Then the pitching of the ship became violent. The candle on my desk crashed to the floor and my books slipped from the shelf. I fled in fear from my cabin and tried to climb up onto the deck, but as I stepped onto the companionway, the ship lurched from a fierce jolt. I nearly tumbled down the stairs. The first great wave had assaulted the ship.

A torrent of water came surging down the staircase. I tried to steady myself, but the rushing waters slammed into me and I ended up on the floor. My rosary was torn from about my waist as I scrambled through the water and braced myself against the wall, where I was barely able to keep from being swept away. The ship began to roll violently. Water had evidently rushed into the large cabin too, for I could hear the cries of the Japanese, and about ten of them elbowed their way out of the cabin. In the darkness I shouted to them not to go up on deck. If they went up on deck without life-ropes, they would surely be swept into the sea by the waves crashing over the side of the ship.

At my cry, Tanaka Tarozaemon rushed into the hall, clutching at his sword. I screamed to him to restrain the merchants. Tanaka drew his sword and barked at the men who were scrambling for the stairs. The merchants hesitated and then shrank back.

The ship began to pitch as well as roll, and it took all my strength to remain upright against the wall. From the deck the fierce crashing of waves echoed like a cannon, and the sound of objects falling and breaking reverberated throughout the ship. And all the time, the cries of men continued without a break. I tried to return to our cabin, but I could not even walk. Eventually I crawled down the flooded passageway on all fours like a dog. When at last I got the cabin door

open, objects that had fallen from the shelves lay in a jumble at my
feet. I sank onto the bed, supporting myself by clinging to a handle
fastened to the wall. Each time the boat pitched, objects on my
shelves slid back and forth. These sounds continued until morning.
Near daybreak, the commotion below deck finally subsided, and the
tossing of the ship abated for a while.

When the white light of dawn seeped through the window, I
realized that our books and wicker baskets were scattered across the
floor. Fortunately, thanks to the grace of God, our cabin, which lies
one level below that of the Japanese, was not flooded. The large cabin
of the merchants had suffered the most damage – the sleeping area
near the cargo was inundated and could no longer be used. I am told
that water also got into the room where provisions are stored.

I took some of my own clothing and bedding and gave them to a
man who was standing dazed outside the large cabin. He was not a
merchant, but rather the servant of one of the envoys. He had a
peasant's face that smelled of the earth, like Hasekura Rokuemon's.

'Use these,' I told him, but he stared at me as though he could not
believe what I had said. 'When your own things have dried, you can
return them to me.'

I asked his name. Timidly he told me it was Yozō, and that he was
one of Hasekura Rokuemon's servants.

In the afternoon I caught hold of Contreras, who was coming
down off the deck in a flurry. He said that an auxiliary mast had been
broken, and that two Japanese sailors had been swept into the sea and
lost during the previous night's storm. Of course we were still not
allowed to go up on deck.

The waves were as high as ever, but in the afternoon the ship
finally passed out of range of the storm. I was unable to endure the
smell of filth and vomit from the seasick Japanese below deck, so with
Contreras' permission I climbed up to the hatch leading onto the
deck. The waves were snarling and spitting spray, and the sea was
still black. On deck Japanese seamen were struggling frantically to
untangle the halyards and repair the snapped mast.

At the evening meal I was at last able to talk at length with
Montaña and Contreras. Both men had gone virtually without rest
for a full day. Dark rings circled their eyes, and the shadows of
weariness were etched deep on their faces. They told me there was no
hope of rescuing the Japanese sailors who had been hurled into the
ocean. I felt sorrow for the two crewmen, but it is the fate which God
has bestowed upon them.

As I was reciting my breviary on the now steady deck, the man to whom I had lent some clothes after the storm four days ago appeared. He vanished again and then returned with his master. Hasekura bowed to me and thanked me for taking pity on his servant. He apologized for being unable to express his gratitude adequately aboard ship, then offered me some Japanese paper and several writing brushes. The tongue-tied fellow tried his hardest to express his thanks. As I studied his face, I felt something akin to pity for this man who was being forced to go to a distant land, even if at the command of his Lord. Yozō stood slightly apart from his master and bowed his head earnestly. This servant reminded me of the simple country yeomen of España, and the thought made me smile.

They had not been gone long before Matsuki Chūsaku appeared on deck and stood staring intently at the sea. This has become a habit with him. Normally when we meet each other there, he merely nods to me and makes no attempt to speak, but today he watched me from a distance while I paced the deck reciting my breviary. As the strong sun beat down upon us, I sensed in his gaze a deep hatred and hostility.

'I won't be able to rest easily until the embassy has arrived safely in Nueva España,' I ventured.

Matsuki remained as quiet as a stone, so I began to murmur my breviary again.

'Lord Velasco.' There was accusation in his voice. 'I would like to ask you something. Did you actually come on this ship to be our interpreter? Or do you have some other purpose?'

'To assist you as an interpreter, of course.' I was puzzled. 'Why do you ask?'

'Then is it part of your function as interpreter to tell Christian stories to the merchants on the ship?'

'It's for their own good. In Nueva España, even people from foreign lands are welcomed as brothers if they are Christians. But if they aren't Christian, they can make little headway in their business negotiations.'

'Then I assume,' Matsuki taunted, 'that it would make no difference to you, if the Japanese merchants were converted to Christianity, that their only motive was to benefit their business.'

'It would make no difference to me,' I nodded. 'There is more than one road leading to the top of the mountain. There are roads from the east and west as well as paths from the north and south. One will reach the top no matter which one climbs. The roads that lead to God are surely the same.'

'You're quite a schemer, Lord Velasco. You play upon their greed and make them into Christians. I understand you used the same strategy on the statesmen in the Council of Elders. They tell me you made a bargain to assist in opening up trade with Nueva España in exchange for permission to convert people to Christianity.'

I peered into his eyes. His eyes were unlike those of Nishi, full of childish curiosity. Nor did they resemble the stubborn eyes of Tanaka or the submissive eyes of Hasekura. I realized this Japanese envoy was no fool.

'If that is true, Lord Matsuki,' I replied calmly, 'what will you do? Will you resign your mission?'

'Of course not. But let me tell you this. If the merchants on this ship are able to make money in Nueva España, they will probably become Christians. But if they find out there is no profit in it, they will abandon your religion in an instant. By the same token, the Council of Elders will authorize the preaching of Christianity only so long as trade with Nueva España continues. If trade comes to a halt and foreign ships no longer call at the ports of our domain, Christianity will be prohibited. Are you aware of all this, Lord Velasco?'

'Of course I am. That being the case, if everything goes well, and the merchants prosper and trade continues, then there will be no problems, right?' I tried to laugh the matter off with a joke. 'Still, even if the trade relationship with Nueva España is severed, a seed once sown will begin to sprout. We men cannot fathom the mind of God.'

'Lord Velasco.' Matsuki spoke earnestly now, abandoning his tone of cross-examination. 'I don't know anything about that. To me you seem to be a clever schemer who has crossed many oceans to come to Japan and bring misery upon himself for the sake of some God. Do you really believe there is a God, Lord Velasco? Why do you think there is a God?'

'I can't explain the existence of God logically. For God manifests His existence in the lives of each individual. In the life of every man there is something which bears witness that God lives. If I appear to you to be a schemer, then perhaps God is manifesting His existence even in the life of a schemer like me.'

I was surprised myself at the words that forced their way from my lips. It was almost as though some force had moved me to say that God witnesses His existence through the lives of each and every individual.

'You think so?' The look of mockery reappeared on Matsuki's face. 'Your God cannot demonstrate His existence in the lives of those Japanese merchants.'

'Why not?'

'It makes no difference to them whether there is a God or not. And they are not alone. Most Japanese feel the same way.'

'And what about you, Lord Matsuki?' I pressed him. 'Is that lukewarm sort of life what you want for yourself? I came to Japan because I believe that being alive means living fervently. That it is like the relationship between a man and a woman. Just as a woman seeks fervent passion from a man, so God seeks passion in us. A man cannot live twice. To be neither hot nor cold, but merely lukewarm . . . is that what you want, Lord Matsuki?'

For the first time Matsuki wavered before my sharp voice and piercing gaze. He stammered, as though embarrassed by his own look of consternation.

'What can I do about it? I was brought up in Japan. . . . Extremes are not well thought of in Japan. You and your sort seem very strange to me.'

For an instant I saw a look of inexpressible exasperation flicker across Matsuki's face. It didn't seem to be exasperation with me for forgetting that I was a mere interpreter and for arguing obstinately with him, but rather exasperation with himself. Perhaps, even as he hated me, this man was attracted to something within me.

One quiet afternoon, a school of whales was sighted. All the Japanese on board were taking a nap. Only the regular creaking of the rigging and the clanging of the ship's bell to announce the hour broke the languid silence.

'I've spotted some whales!' cried a sailor keeping watch from the mast. Some who faintly heard the call woke the others. Everyone aboard the ship clustered on deck.

Several whales were diving and surfacing between the dark waves, swimming unswervingly out into the open sea. They disappeared for an instant as they plunged into a valley between the waves, but soon their black bodies, which seemed to glisten with a coat of oil, reappeared and spouted jets of water high into the air. As one whale disappeared, the back of another surfaced with a geyser of vapour. They frolicked together, utterly oblivious of the ship. Each time the whales came into view, the onlooking Spaniards and Japanese emitted a cry of amazement.

Beside the samurai, Nishi smiled with delight. 'Everything we see is new and different.'

The samurai watched motionlessly until at length the whales disappeared on the horizon. Rays of sunlight seeped through the clouds like sheaves of arrows, markedly tinging the edge of the now-deserted ocean with silver. It had never occurred to the samurai that there were so many new and different things to experience. He had not realized the world was so vast. His Lordship's domain had been the only world of which he could conceive. But now a subtle transformation was taking place in his heart, and with it came a vague uneasiness and a formless fear. He was setting foot in a new world. And he feared that cracks were beginning to form in the wall that had supported his heart until now, and that it would eventually crumble into dust.

When the school of whales passed from view, the Japanese who had assembled on the deck started making their way back to the large cabin. The ship's bell clanged. Siesta time was over, and hours of listless idleness lay before them until evening.

'Won't you come down to the large cabin,' Nishi invited the samurai as they descended the stairs, 'and learn some Spanish?'

Velasco entered the noisy cabin beaming his customary smile. It was a confident smile like that of an adult looking at young children who are unable to do anything for themselves.

'*Más barato por favor.*' As Velasco, his hand resting on a cargo crate, pronounced the words, the merchants recorded them faithfully on paper with their brushes.

'*No quiero comprarlo.*'

This queer but earnest class went on for an hour. When it was nearly over, Velasco once again began to recite from the life of Christ.

'Once there was a woman. For many long years she had suffered from a disease of the blood, and had spent all that she had and visited many physicians, but all to no avail; rather she grew worse. At this time, Jesus passed over the lake by ship, and many people gathered around him. When the woman heard of Jesus, she came in the press behind him and hesitantly touched his garment with her finger. For she thought, If I may but touch his clothes, I shall be whole. Jesus turned about and said, Woman, be of good comfort. And the woman was made whole.'

The samurai paid little attention to Velasco's words. The Christian teachings had always been alien to him, and there seemed no point in listening to such talk now.

Then suddenly the pitiful woman in Velasco's story reminded him of the women in the marshland. The huddled villages of the marshland, where there lived scores of people more wretched, more pathetic than this afflicted woman. His father had often told him of the old women and girls who had been abandoned on the roadside in times of famine.

The merchants did their best to refrain from smiling at Velasco's story. They looked up at the priest with wonder on their faces, but the samurai knew that they were not listening in earnest. As Matsuki Chūsaku had said, the merchants merely felt that it would be expedient for their future business in Nueva España to know something about the Christian tales.

Velasco closed his Bible, and with his usual smile looked around at the merchants to determine what effect his recitation had made. Among the wondering faces, he discovered one that glared at him as if in anger. It was the face of the samurai's servant, Yozō.

When Velasco left the large cabin, the merchants put their brushes back into their writing cases, then yawned and pounded their tired shoulders with their fists. The expressions of serious intent had vanished completely, and the large cabin was filled with the air of laxity that comes after one has fulfilled a duty. Some began to play dice beside the stacks of cargo where Velasco had stood.

As he walked out of the cabin with the samurai, Nishi volunteered one of his youthful dreams. 'When foreign ships finally begin to call at the ports in our domain, His Lordship and the senior statesmen will certainly need interpreters. I would like to do that kind of work. I'm hoping to learn a sufficient amount of Spanish during our voyage.'

The samurai felt the familiar envy and mild jealousy towards this young man. As for himself, he was much too old and dull in the head to learn a foreign language.

As the envoys ate the breakfast which their servants brought to their cabin, Tanaka Tarozaemon berated Nishi Kyūsuke again. Nishi had been reporting enthusiastically how, with Velasco as interpreter, he had learned from the First Mate how to use a compass, when Tanaka unexpectedly lashed out at him.

'Can't you be a little more serious? If we appear frivolous to the foreigners, it will damage our reputation as envoys.'

For a moment Nishi was speechless with surprise. Then he retorted, 'Why? Even if they are foreigners, there are many things we can learn from them. It was the foreigners who brought us guns and powder when we were still using only bows and arrows. As envoys, what's wrong with us learning the good points of their country and acquiring useful knowledge from them?'

'I'm not saying there's anything wrong with it.' Tanaka's disgruntled expression made it evident that he had not expected a younger man to argue with him. 'I'm saying you're behaving frivolously by strutting around the ship and gaping in amazement at all the foreign gadgets.'

'Of course I'm amazed when I see something new. And I think how useful the foreign ship fittings and such would be if we took them back to our domain.'

'It's up to the government whether to adopt new implements or not. The Council of Elders will decide. When did an upstart like you begin telling the government what to do? It's just because you're young that you think anything is good as long as it's new.'

Tanaka's livid profile made the samurai think of his uncle. It was typical of the rural samurai of their domain to prize honour above all else, to consider an insult from another the ultimate shame, and to disdain new ways and make no attempt to revise old-fashioned habits. Both Tanaka and his uncle possessed these traits in large measure. The samurai himself shared similar attitudes. Yet, on board this ship, he had at times felt a loathing for the rustic part of himself, and envious of Nishi's incessantly curious mind.

'Nishi.' Seated across from the samurai, Matsuki placed the lid on his lunch box and spoke abruptly. 'Have you been in the inner cabin where the foreigners are staying?'

'Yes.'

'What do you think of the way those foreigners smell?'

'The way they smell?'

'Ever since we got on this ship, that rotten stink has been more than I can bear. Every time Velasco comes into our cabin, he brings that foul foreigner's stink with him.'

Since their conversation on deck, the samurai had been disturbed by Matsuki's all-knowing manner. Personally he had no interest in Christianity or the Christian missionaries, but he felt a twinge of shame whenever he saw Velasco, who had loaned his own paltry clothing and bedding to Yozō. In his own mind Yozō was after all a menial, a servant. But Velasco seemed to make no such distinctions.

'What good does it do you to think badly of everything?' the samurai interjected. 'I don't like him either, but . . .'

'Velasco's smell is the vehemence of the foreigners,' Matsuki went on. 'It's because of that stink in his body that he travelled all the way to Japan. And it isn't just Velasco. The foreigners have built great ships and roamed the nations of the earth because of that passion. Nishi, it's nothing more than blind imitation to steal what the foreigners have created without being aware of their passion. And remember that that passion is a poison to us.'

'But . . .,' Nishi muttered in consternation, 'Lord Velasco seems like a very gentle man . . .'

'Velasco pretends to be gentle to conceal the passions raging inside him. I can't help feeling that his faith in Christianity is also an attempt to stifle his own cravings. When I see him up pacing in the sun all day by himself, I sense something frightening about him.'

Matsuki realized how loudly he was speaking and smiled sourly. 'Velasco did not come along with us to be our interpreter out of a sense of duty to the Council of Elders. He boarded this ship to gratify his own impassioned heart.'

'What are you suggesting he plans to do?' Tanaka asked.

'I don't know yet. It will become clear in time. But whatever happens, we must be careful not to be lured into his schemes.'

'If he does anything to interfere with our mission,' said Tanaka, shifting his eyes to his sword, 'I'll kill him, even if he is our interpreter.'

'Idiot!' Matsuki laughed. 'If you kill our interpreter, how do you expect us to carry out our mission in Nueva España!'

Several days ago our ship entered a fog. It is that thick fog which envelops all the ships which pass along the northern route of the great ocean. The boundless expanse of waves is now concealed in the grey mist, and when you stand on the deck, everything before you is obscured, as if a thin veil had been stretched across it. The crew appear to move about like ghosts. Every two minutes I hear the sound of the bell that the watchman strikes. Below deck, all is quiet, and in the large cabin and the envoys' cabin, the bedding and clothing and even the paper on which I write my daily record of the voyage are unpleasantly damp from the fog that rolls down the stairway.

The daily ration of water had been reduced several days earlier. The four envoys, who had been receiving two scoops from a wooden pail, were now given only one. Fortunately they encountered no further storms or lulls, and the ship advanced eastward without incident through the fog.

Then the monotony was shattered by an unexpected incident. A Spanish sailor stole a watch and several pieces of gold from Captain Montaño's cabin. The Captain took Velasco and went to the envoys' cabin, where with a flushed face he explained that the thief would have to be punished.

Montaño told the envoys that there were strict regulations for punishment on board ship and that it was his duty as captain to carry them out. If, for example, the sailor on watch were discovered sleeping, his hands were bound and water was poured over them. If he still did not mend his ways, he was flogged. This was a long-standing nautical custom, the captain explained. The present offender must be punished in the presence of everyone on the ship, including the Japanese.

The punishment was carried out on the fog-shrouded deck. The Japanese deckhands and merchants all assembled, and the Spanish sailors watched from another part of the deck as their comrade was dragged out and bound with halyards. A rag was stuffed into the prisoner's mouth to prevent him from biting his tongue. He knelt and was stripped bare. The fog stirred occasionally in the wind, thinning out, then growing thick again. Velasco stood beside the Captain, watching the punishment in silence. The two men were like great black statues.

In the murk, the whip cracked and a voice groaned. The whip lashed out again and again, and when at length the wind whisked the fog away, the prisoner lay crumpled on the deck like a scrap of cloth. As the others watched, Velasco rushed to the man's side, lifted him up, and wiped away his blood with his own robes. Then, supporting the man's body, Velasco helped him down into the hold.

The samurai felt an indescribable revulsion. The feeling was not a result of the flogging. He could still see the immobile figure of Velasco on the deck, watching with composure as the whip lashed out through the fog. As Matsuki had said, there had been something unpleasant about this foreigner's face as he dabbed at the blood of the semi-conscious man with his own garment and carried him into the hold. The samurai could not bring himself to believe that this Velasco and the Velasco who had shared his clothing with Yozō were one and the same man.

Five, then six days passed, but still the fog did not lift. The sails and the deck began to give off a foul, rotten smell from the dampness, and every two minutes the sound of the bell could be heard through that milky curtain. Sometimes the sun peeked like a white dish through a crack in the fog, but the next dense cloud quickly blotted it out. Each time the sun shone through, the Spanish sailors hurriedly set up their sextants and tried to fix the ship's position.

A week after the ship entered the fog blanket, the swell of the waves from the north-east gradually mounted. As she tacked leeward, the pitching of the ship intensified. Another storm was approaching. The crew scurried about the deck, unfurling the studding-sails fore and aft.

The barometric pressure began to plummet. As the mist cleared, surging black waves appeared on all sides. The wind lapped at the sails, and slanting rain began to beat down on the men as they worked. Learning their lesson from the previous storm, the merchants in the large cabin and the envoys took down all the trunks from their shelves and placed them on top of the cargo crates. They lashed their bedding and clothing tightly on top of the stacks of cargo to keep them from being swamped.

At length the spewing waves began to swamp the deck. They smashed angrily against the prow of the listing ship, rattling her ribs. The envoys, preparing for every possible eventuality, stretched a life-rope between the pillars of their cabin, and the samurai strapped the box containing His Lordship's letters to his back and secured his sword firmly to his side. All the oil lamps had been extinguished to prevent fires, and, though night had not yet fallen, their cabin was gloomy.

The pitch and roll of the ship became fierce. Even the heavy crates of cargo began to shift little by little. Water had evidently got into the large cabin, for the merchants shrank back with a cry. Here and there men clung to the cargo ropes and prayed softly to the Dragon God. Each time the ship lurched, the envoys clutched at the life-rope to keep from being hurled across the cabin. It grew steadily darker. The murmured prayers ceased for a time, then suddenly a shout that was either a cry of anguish or a howl of rage echoed from the large cabin. The forward porthole had burst and water was streaming in. The waves knocked aside two men who had been standing beside the porthole and pounded against the stacks of cargo. The men engulfed by the waves groped frantically for a hand-hold, but just as they were about to clutch the cargo, the water in the cabin shifted with the tilt of the ship and washed out into the passageway. Men collided with one another, slammed into crates, or went flying across the cabin. A thundering noise echoed from the end of the corridor.

The men could no longer hear the orders from the Captain or the First Mate. The waves shot up like mountains and broke over the ship.

The torrent swept away everything on deck, beat against the masts, formed swirls and poured madly down the stairway to the ship's bottom. One sailor, swallowed up by the waves, pulled himself back to his feet with the life-rope, but at that moment the next wave assaulted him. His head disappeared into the swell.

In the cabins of the Japanese the water lapped at their knees and they stumbled, crawled and staggered to their feet, crying out in terror. The heavy crates swung back and forth as though possessed by a demon. Some, forgetting the Captain's orders, rushed to the stairway to seek refuge on deck, but were instantly swept back by the cascades of water surging down the stairs.

At last, after four hours, the ship passed beyond the range of the storm. The waves were still rough, but they no longer broke over the deck. The deck was strewn with the irreclaimable remains of fittings that had been torn away by the waves, and a cruelly snapped mast. Several sailors had been lost overboard, and moans seeped from various corners of the hold. The large cabin would be uninhabitable until it was bailed, so the exhausted merchants, like so many drowned rats, collapsed in heaps in the lower baggage compartment used by the Spanish sailors, in the dining-room and in the passageways, where they lay until dawn. No one had the strength to assist a comrade. Only Velasco walked among the near-corpses leaning against walls or prone on the floor, binding the wounds of the injured.

At last morning came. Once the storm had passed, the horizon miraculously changed from gold to pink. As the colours of the sky gradually stretched across the horizon, the surface of the sea began to glow. There was no sound other than the splash of waves against the hull of the ship. In the light of dawn, the *San Juan Baptista*, bereft of one of its sails, drifted on the still choppy sea like a ghost ship – not a soul could be seen on deck, and the bell was silent. Drained to the depths of their souls, the sailors sprawled about the ship, fast asleep.

At midmorning, the samurai mustered what little strength he had left and stumbled out of his sodden cabin to search for Yozō and his other attendants. The envoys' cabin, unlike the large one, was some distance from the stairway and was built higher than the corridor, so although it had been flooded, the water had soon drained out, and they had suffered little damage. And thanks to the providence of Heaven, His Lordship's letters had not been soaked. The samurai walked down the corridor, where the water was still ankle-deep, and went down to the lower level. Merchants clogged the floor, scarcely leaving room to walk past. Even those who noticed the samurai lacked the energy to sit up and bow to him. Some were fast asleep; others stared groggily at some indistinct point through heavy eyes.

The cargo room was also crammed with men. Among them the samurai discovered his attendants sprawled on the floor. Straddling heads and bodies, he called out to them. Yozō, Ichisuke and Daisuke sat up painfully, but Seihachi, who was lying on his face, did not move. A heavy cargo crate had fallen on his chest the previous night, and he had passed out for a time amid the murky deluge. The other three had pulled him out from beneath the crate.

'Lord Velasco cared for him.' Yozō lowered his eyes, as though such a thing was inexcusable to his master. 'He stayed with Seihachi until dawn.'

The samurai recalled how Velasco had lent Yozō clothing after the earlier storm. Once again Yozō seemed to be moved by the compassion shown to someone of his status by a foreigner he had not even known before. And once again the samurai felt ashamed. The consideration with which Velasco had treated his attendants should by rights have been shown by him, their master.

Beside Yozō lay a tiny string of beads. He explained that they were Christian beads which Velasco had left behind.

'Lord Velasco,' Yozō stammered, as though he had been caught in some forbidden act, 'used these to pray for Seihachi and the others.'

'Listen to me,' said the samurai, raising his voice slightly. 'I am grateful to Lord Velasco, but you are not to listen to the Christian teachings.'

His attendants said nothing. The samurai lowered his voice so that the merchants sleeping nearby would not hear. 'The merchants listen to the Christian tales so that they can do business in Nueva España. But you are not merchants. So long as you are retainers of Hasekura, you are not to become familiar with the Christian teachings.'

As he spoke, he suddenly remembered what Matsuki Chūsaku had said to him. Matsuki had spoken of an intensity within Velasco that was somehow frightening. He had said that Velasco tried to appear meek to mask that intensity. And he had cautioned against becoming entangled by the foreigner. The samurai had not understood precisely what Matsuki meant, but he feared that his own attendants might be influenced by the man.

'Do whatever you have to for Seihachi. Don't worry about me.'

After speaking a few words of encouragement to Seihachi, who seemed unable to reply, the samurai picked his way past more bodies and stepped out into the corridor. Then he climbed up onto the deck where the sun was beating mercilessly down.

The sea was calm now. The masts cast black shadows. A gentle breeze stroked his face. The breeze felt good against his languid body. The Japanese deckhands, stirred at last by orders from the Spanish sailors, were repairing the severed halyards and replacing the torn sails. The sparkling waves were dazzling, broken occasionally by the leap of a flying fish. As the samurai sat in the shadow of the mast, he realized he had unintentionally brought the rosary with him. The row of beads was made from seeds, and a crucifix dangled from one end of the string. The naked figure of an emaciated man had been carved on the crucifix. The samurai gazed at this man, whose arms were outstretched, and whose head drooped lifelessly. He could not understand why Velasco and all the other foreigners called such a man 'Lord'. To the samurai, only His Lordship could be called 'Lord', but His Lordship was not a wretched, emasculated figure like this. If the Christians really worshipped this emaciated man, then their religion seemed an incredibly bizarre sort of heresy.

The samurai had an embarrassing dream. In a damp, dark room in the marshland, he was making love to his wife, trying not to disturb the sleeping children. 'I must go now.' He was ashamed that though tomorrow was the day appointed by the Council of Elders for the ship to set sail, he alone of the envoys was still at home, unable to tear himself away from his wife's naked body. 'I have to go.' He repeated the same words over and over again. But beneath him Riku pressed her damp face against his. 'Even if you go,' she muttered, panting heavily, 'it will come to nothing. They will not give back the lands in Kurokawa.' He pulled away from his wife and spluttered, 'Does Uncle know that too?' He watched as Riku nodded, then stood up in confusion. He awoke.

He had defiled himself. From a corner of the cabin, still damp from the storm waters, he could hear the snores of one of his companions, first loud, then soft. It was Tanaka. So it was a dream? he sighed. He realized that he had had such a dream because somewhere in the depths of his consciousness he had been disturbed by Matsuki's words. The samurai had not related his conversation with Matsuki to Tanaka, now snoring so peacefully, or to Nishi. It was as if by telling them he would somehow be acquiescing in what Matsuki had said. 'Lord Shiraishi and Lord Ishida would never do such a thing to us,' he reassured himself as he changed his soiled loincloth.

He closed his eyes again, but could not sleep. He had a vivid picture of his children playing in the garden and Riku's profile as she hung the washing out to dry. He could visualize each separate room in his house. In an attempt to fall asleep, he tried to recall one scene after another from the marshland. The hills and fields blanketed with spring snow. . . .

The *San Juan Baptista* sustained considerable damage in the second storm. She lost a mast, one sail and a lifeboat, a tremendous amount of water flooded the interior of the ship, and fittings demolished by the storm are scattered all about the deck. I received a gash in my forehead, but it is of no consequence. The crew toil ceaselessly to bail water from the ship. Yet compared to the agonies which Captain Ferdinand Magellan and his ship endured on this same Pacific Ocean ninety-three years ago, our discomforts amount to but little. Magellan's crew were without provisions, their water spoiled, and I am told they ate even rats from the hold and chips of wood. Fortunately we still have our water tanks, and there is no lack of foodstuffs. In last night's storm, however, we did lose a number of Japanese crewmen overboard, and there are several injured and afflicted in the large cabin. Until morning I walked among the moaning Japanese, ministering to them not as an interpreter, but as a priest.

The most seriously injured are an old merchant named Yahei, and Seihachi, one of Hasekura's attendants. Both were struck in the chest by cargo crates. Yahei has spit up blood. I'm certain that Seihachi has broken some ribs. I gave both of them wine and placed compresses on them, but they are scarcely able to speak and grow weaker every day. It concerns me that they might not live to see Nueva España.

Although only a month has passed since we left Japan, I feel as though our voyage has lasted several months already. Life aboard ship is little different from when I first came to the Orient thirteen years ago – perhaps my mind is unsettled because I am impatient for my plan to become a reality at the earliest possible juncture.

Tonight, after finishing my prayers on deck, I asked myself once again, Why do I want to return to Japan? Why am I so attracted to that land? It was almost as if I was gazing into the unfathomable mind of a stranger. It is not that the Japanese are more fervently religious or more capable of grasping the truth than the other peoples of Asia. Indeed, while the Japanese do in fact possess superior mental faculties and curiosity, surely there can be no people in the world who have so consistently rejected things which do not bring them worldly benefits? Though they pretend for a time to give a listening ear to the teachings of our Lord, they do so only because they want to increase their fighting power and their wealth, not because they desire the word of God. How often I have tasted of despair in that country! The Japanese touch for acquiring worldly wealth is almost too sensitively attuned, but they have not the slightest feeling for things eternal. Yet somehow Japan and the Japanese intensify my yearning to preach the word. I feel it my mission to return to Japan because I want, just as one tames an obdurate beast, to subdue each of the adversities which rears its head there. Through my veins courses the blood of my grandfather, who helped to conquer the West Indies and thereby found favour with King Don Carlos. I am also descended from Vasco Balboa, a great-uncle on my mother's side who became

Viceroy of the Panamas. My ancestors, the pride of my family, governed those islands with ships and with swords, but I want to try to subdue Japan with the word of God.

The moon is bright. At night the ocean shimmers. All unnecessary lamps are to be extinguished at ten pm. In the moonlight, each fitting on the deck appears sharply defined. 'O Lord, make of me an indispensable commander for the benefit of that nation. Use my blood for the sake of Japan, as Thy blood was used for the sake of mankind.'

During the night, the condition of the two injured men worsened. Half of the inundated cabin was finally drained and made habitable, so many of the Japanese who had been sleeping in the central passageway returned to their quarters. But we could not move the two injured men.

Just after noon the merchant Yahei died. Then, close on his heels, Hasekura Rokuemon's attendant Seihachi also breathed his last. The Japanese gathered round the two men, intoning the name of Buddha and filling the ears of the dying men with descriptions of the Gokuraku, which corresponds to our Paradise. Such is their custom. Seihachi's comrades were pitifully downcast. Their master, Hasekura, with tears welling in his eyes, covered the dead man's body with a cotton garment and continually intoned the Buddhist sutras. This samurai, the least imposing of the four envoys, seems to be a gentle master to his attendants.

Orders came from the Captain that the two corpses were to be buried at sea. The Japanese all gathered on deck, as they had done for the flogging some time ago, and the Spanish sailors also assembled in a row. The sea that afternoon was smooth, almost gloomily so. Normally the Captain or a priest aboard ship would recite a prayer, but since none of the Japanese are Christians, Montaño and I left the ceremony to them.

One of the merchants seemed to have some knowledge of Buddhism. He chanted some sutras, an incantation which was gibberish to me. The other Japanese chimed in after him, and the two bodies were cast into the sea. The corpses were swallowed up by the waves and disappeared. The melancholy ocean was silent, as though nothing at all had transpired. After all the others had deserted the deck, Hasekura and his attendants stood motionless at the edge of the ship for a long while. Finally they disappeared into the bowels of the ship, leaving Yozō alone on deck. As I watched curiously from a distance, he approached me.

'Would you offer a prayer for Seihachi?' he whispered, almost as if afraid.

'Christian prayers are for the benefit of Christians. Such prayers could only be an annoyance to you.'

Yozō stared at me sadly. I realized he was trying to say something that could not be spoken, and I began to recite the Latin prayer for the dead. Yozō clasped his hands, staring into the sea and moving his lips.

> *Requiescant in pace*
> *Dominus vobiscum et cum Spiritu tuo*
> *Requiem aeternam dona eis.*

The ocean which had swallowed up the dead men was silent, and flying fish leapt between the waves. The rigging creaked monotonously, and clouds laced with gold floated beyond the horizon.

'I. . . .' Yozō muttered, 'I would like to hear about Christianity.'

Surprised, I peered into his face.

Today our ship finally passed the half-way point of its voyage.

Chapter 4

The battered ship was now scarcely more than a hulk, and the Japanese were exhausted. A water shortage developed, and some came down with scurvy because of the lack of vegetables.

Some time after the sixtieth day of their voyage, two birds which looked like snipe flew towards the ship and alighted on the mast. The sailors sent up a cheer. The birds, with yellow beaks and brown-and-white wings, swooped over the edge of the ship and disappeared, but their presence made it obvious that land was near.

At dusk the horizon to port was dotted with the silhouettes of mountains. It was Cape Mendocino. There was no harbour in the cape, so the galleon weighed anchor far out into the offing. Five Spanish sailors and five Japanese crewmen boarded a skiff and went ashore to replenish the supplies of water and food.

Captain Montaño, citing the possibility of danger, would not allow any other Japanese to go ashore.

The following day the ship proceeded south. With new stores of water and vegetables, the men on board revived as though restored to life and were once again able to enjoy their voyage upon the calm waves. On the morning of the tenth day after leaving Cape Mendocino, they caught sight of a tree-covered shoreline extending far into the distance. It was the first stretch of land in Nueva España that the Japanese had seen. Those who had gathered on deck cried out; some even wept. Though little over two and a half months had passed since they left Japan, the feeling that they had journeyed for close to an eternity swept over them. They slapped one another on the back, delighted that somehow they had managed to survive the voyage.

The following day the ship approached the shore. The heat was oppressive. The blazing sun lit up the broad white beach, and orderly rows of unfamiliar trees lined the hills beyond. From the Spanish sailors the Japanese learned that these were called olive trees, and that their fruit provided oil and food. Native men and women, tanned and naked to the waist, raised a clamour and came running from the grove.

A tiny island came into view. As they drew nearer, they could see the waves beating and breaking against the cliffs of the densely forested island. Seagulls flew near the ship. As the boat slowly circled the island, a promontory, thickly blanketed with olive trees, appeared beyond it.

'Acapulco!' an ecstatic voice bellowed from the mast. A Spanish sailor was pointing towards the inlet. At the same moment, the Spaniards and Japanese assembled on deck sent up a cheer. Startled by the shouts, the flock of seagulls soared in the sky. The envoys stood in a row, intently studying the inlet and the surrounding cape. It was the first foreign port they had ever laid eyes on, and this would be the first foreign soil on which they would set foot. The faces of Tanaka and the samurai stiffened with tension, Nishi's eyes flashed, and Matsuki stood with folded arms, the look on his face somehow angry.

The inlet was calm. Not a single wave. The harbour was wider than that at Tsukinoura, but for some reason they could see no other ships. At the far side of the inlet was a yellow beach with a single white building at its furthest edge. A wall with gunports surrounded the building, but not a soul could be seen there. The ship came to a stop.

The Spanish sailors knelt. Velasco climbed to the top deck and made the sign of a cross over them. Even some of the Japanese merchants followed suit and clasped their hands together.

'Hosanna. Blessed be they who come in the name of the Lord.'

The sharp cries of the seagulls blended with the sound of Velasco's voice. The ocean breezes blew invigoratingly against the men's cheeks. When the prayer was concluded, the Captain, the First Mate and Velasco boarded a skiff and set out for the shore to obtain a landing permit.

The men on board stared absently at the dense, hot scene before them as they waited for the three men to return. The rays of the sun beat down on the inlet and the beach. The profound silence filled the Japanese with a gnawing uneasiness. For no reason, they began to feel that they were not welcome here.

A long time passed, and still the three men did not return to the beach. Two sailors boarded another skiff and went to find out what had happened. The sun scorched the deck, and the impatient Japanese returned to their cabins. Three hours later word came that only the Spanish sailors would be permitted to come ashore. Apparently the commander of the Acapulco fortress did not have the authority to grant landing privileges to this unexpected Japanese ship, and he had sent a messenger to the Viceroy of Nueva España in Mexico City.

Voices of displeasure rose in a chorus. During the voyage the envoys and merchants had come to believe that when they arrived in this country everything would be ready for them, that they would be warmly welcomed, and that all matters would proceed smoothly. They could not understand why only the Japanese were being detained on board ship.

In the evening, when the hot sun had set and a faint breeze at last blew across the deck, with a flock of tiny birds hovering about the ship, the three men returned. The envoys, as representatives of all the Japanese, went to seek an explanation from Velasco.

'There is no cause for concern,' said Velasco confidently, flashing his customary smile. (He was in the habit of saying, 'There is no cause for concern.') 'I'm certain you will all be able to go ashore tomorrow.'

Tanaka Tarozaemon would not be mollified. 'His Lordship built this great ship for the Spaniards and sent it all the way here. You realize of course that by treating us rudely you are insulting His Lordship and the Council of Elders.'

'But I also know,' Velasco kept his smile, 'that His Lordship and the Council of Elders told you to follow my instructions in all things after we arrived in Nueva España.'

The following day the Spanish sailors went ashore. It was not until the afternoon that the fortress commander sent a boat manned by Indians to fetch the Japanese and their cargo. Armed soldiers from the fortress lined the beach, staring apprehensively as the strangely-garbed merchants and emissaries disembarked.

The four envoys, accompanied by Velasco and the ship's officers, solemnly set out for the fortress, which was surrounded by hills covered with olive trees. The fortress was built of plaster and encircled by a wall dotted with gunports. Flowerpots holding plants of various shapes rested in niches in the wall, and flowers red as flame blossomed in profusion.

They passed through a guarded gate and entered the courtyard. It was enclosed on all sides by buildings, and two guards were stationed at each strategic position. The envoys walked in silence along the stone path. The scent of flowers drifted their way from somewhere, and they could hear the buzzing of bees. The stronghold was of course meagre in comparison to His Lordship's castle, and seemed more like a stockade than a castle.

The fortress commander, who came out of his office to welcome the envoys, was an elderly man. He greeted the Japanese with a lengthy speech they could not understand, then gawked at them rudely while Velasco interpreted his words. His welcome was full of exaggerated appreciation, but from the man's discomfited gaze the samurai realized that they were not being greeted with open arms.

When the greetings were over, the envoys were invited to supper. The commander's wife and several officers were already waiting in the dining-hall. As the Japanese entered with the Captain and Velasco, the company stared as if at some outlandish creatures, then cast furtive glances at one another. Determined not to be shamed in front of these people, Tanaka drew up his shoulders in an angry gesture. Using a knife and fork for the first time, Nishi managed to drop both onto the floor. At the dinner table the commander and his wife, with Velasco as interpreter, politely asked the four emissaries about the distant land of Japan, but they soon became involved in their own conversations, and the four Japanese were left to themselves, not understanding a word that was said.

They returned to the ship exhausted. There were no inns or monasteries in Acapulco which could accommodate the Japanese, so the merchants also returned to the large cabin. The envoys were out of sorts, their pride wounded. The twilight sun shone brightly through the window, and the room was hot. The moment they entered the cabin, Tanaka first upbraided Nishi for behaving frivolously, then insisted for a second time that they were being treated rudely by the foreigners, and ended up by denouncing Velasco and blaming him for their reception.

'I don't think Velasco even told them what the Council of Elders intends, or of His Lordship's feelings.'

'There's no point railing against Velasco,' Matsuki interjected, a typically knowing look on his face. 'I knew right from the beginning.'

'Knew what?'

'How Velasco felt. Think about it. If everything proceeds smoothly, it won't be to his advantage. That would leave him little to do as interpreter. But if we run into problems, that of itself will increase the role Velasco plays. If it turns out that the envoys' mission is successful all because of Velasco, the Council will not be able to refuse his demands outright. The man is a schemer.'

Tanaka's burst of rage sprang from an indefinable uneasiness. The samurai shared that uneasiness. He recognized that the fortress commander here did not have the authority to accept His Lordship's letter or to grant permission for trade with the Japanese merchants, but he could infer from the atmosphere of the few hours he had spent there that Nueva España was by no means pleased that the Japanese had crossed the ocean. If that was the case, then it was quite possible that they would receive the same reception even if they set out for Mexico City to meet the Viceroy. Perhaps His Lordship's letters would be flung back in their faces, and the merchants would have to load their goods back onto the ship and return to Japan. Were that to happen the envoys would lose face, and any hope that their old domains would be returned to them would be dashed. Or perhaps, as Matsuki said, the failure of their mission would be taken as an excuse to punish all the lance-corporals severely.

A day passed. The next morning Velasco, the Captain, the First Mate and the emissaries mounted horses provided by the fortress commander and set out from Acapulco. The envoys' attendants, carrying spears and banners, were followed by the company of merchants on foot and wagons laden with their goods. The peculiar entourage set off amid shots fired into the air by soldiers of the fortress.

The landscape of Nueva España, which they were seeing for the first time, was blinding, hot and white. Ahead of them gaped an endless wilderness studded with giant cacti, and in the far distance stretched mountains spotted with granite, looking as though they had been sprinkled with salt. They could see shabby huts, the homes of the native Indians, their roofs fashioned from mud and leaves and twigs. A boy, nearly naked, caught sight of the procession and hurriedly hid himself in one of the huts. The Japanese were startled by the herd of black, long-haired animals the boy had been leading. They had never seen such creatures, or indeed even cactus, before.

The granite mountains went on for ever. The sun beat down ceaselessly. As he swayed back and forth atop his horse, the samurai thought of the marshland. His own fief was impoverished, but the poverty here was different. In the marshland there were greenery, fields and streams. Here there was no water, and the only vegetation these spiny, gnarled plants.

Beside the samurai, Nishi spoke up. 'I've never seen scenery like this before.'

The samurai nodded. He had crossed a limitless ocean. Now he was travelling through an unfamiliar desert. It was like a hallucination. Had he really come to a country unknown to his father, unknown to his uncle, unknown to his wife? For a moment he felt that it might all be a dream.

Just before noon on the tenth day they sighted a village ahead. Grey adobe huts dotted the slope of the mountain like shoots of rice, and a church steeple thrust up from the centre of the village.

'That village,' Velasco pointed from his horse, 'is one that is pleasing to God.' The village, he explained, had recently been built for the Indians who were native to this region. Here they studied the teachings of Christianity under a Spanish priest, and shared not only the land but all their possessions in common. Such a village, Velasco said, was called a *reducción*, and many were now being built in various parts of the country.

'The inhabitants themselves choose the village headman. There is no forced labour or military duty. The padres pay frequent visits, not only to preach the word of God, but to teach the villagers how to raise cattle and horses, how to weave on looms, and how to speak Spanish.'

He glanced around, trying to assess the reaction of the Japanese. This sort of village was one of the things he wanted them to see in Nueva España. A place where the people had to perform no labour service for their rulers and no military duty, where the people lived lives of genteel poverty and honest labour by keeping the laws of God – one day Velasco hoped to create such a village in Japan. But the merchants had been travelling since dawn, and they merely glanced at the white buildings with eyes devoid of interest or curiosity. When at length they entered the village, the people, who wore their hair in pigtails down to their shoulders, stood fearfully at the edge of the stone road and stared at the encroachers. Dogs barked and flocks of mountain goats scattered with a bellow. As the Japanese slaked their thirst at the well in the public square and wiped away the sweat of the journey, Velasco brought an old man to introduce to them.

'This is the village headman.'

Velasco nudged the old Indian's shoulder and pushed him in front of the Japanese. Unlike the villagers, he was wearing a broad-brimmed straw hat; he stood stiffly before them like a nervous child.

Velasco questioned him like a priest hearing a child's catechism.

'Are all of the people who live here Christians?'

'*Si*, Padre.'

'Are your people happy that you have abandoned the mistaken beliefs of your ancestors and heard the teachings of the true God?'

'*Si*, Padre.'

'What have you people learned from the padres who come here?'

'*Si*, Padre. We have learned to read and write. And to speak Spanish.' The headman stared at the ground; his replies were mechanical, as though he were muttering memorized phrases. 'And how to sow seeds and cultivate a field. And how to tan leather.'

'Are all your people pleased with this?'

'*Si*, Padre.'

Somewhere in the village a cock crowed, and from a corner of the square a throng of naked children stiffly observed this facsimile of a trial.

Velasco turned triumphantly towards the Japanese. As he did so, a strong, sweet-and-sour odour rose from his armpit, but Velasco was oblivious to it. 'We have built up these villages of God in Nueva España. I am sure that all the Indians who have become Christians are happy.'

Then he placed his hand upon the old man's shoulder as if to demonstrate the brotherly love and compassion they shared for one another.

'This must be the first time you have seen a Japanese, eh?'

'No, Padre.'

A commotion ensued. The Japanese could understand 'No, Padre' even without waiting for Velasco's translation. They could not believe that any of their countrymen had come to this distant land before them. Those sponging off their bodies and those drinking water all turned an ear to the discordant exchange between Velasco and the old man.

'The headman doesn't know the difference between a Japanese and a Chinese. It must have been a Chinese.' Velasco shrugged his shoulders. 'But he says that two years ago a Spanish padre and a Japanese brother came to this village. And that the Japanese taught them how to plant rice.'

'Ask him the man's name,' someone called. 'If you ask the man's name, we can tell whether he was Japanese or Chinese.'

The headman shook his head like a scolded child. There was no point in questioning him further. The old man could not remember what order the Japanese brother belonged to, or even if he had come from Mexico City.

The party had to leave before sunset. The headman treated the Japanese to a food called tortillas. These were made from cornbread fashioned into a shape like rice crackers and wrapped around a cheese that resembled bean curd. They smelled suspicious, and the Japanese struggled to choke them down.

The company regrouped and descended the mountain. They were greeted by the same monotonous scenery as before. Maguey and cactus stood stiffly like abandoned tombstones on the parched earth. Bald mountains shimmered hazily in the distance. Bird lice swarmed noisily over their perspiring faces.

Swatting at the insects with his hands, Nishi turned to the samurai and Tanaka. 'Do you really think that another Japanese is around here somewhere?'

'I'd like to meet him,' the samurai answered, gazing round at the wide plateaux. 'But this journey isn't a sightseeing excursion. We mustn't make any diversions.'

The group had been travelling for two hours when suddenly a pillar of black smoke shot up from one of the nearest mountains. The Captain and Velasco raised their hands and stopped the procession, staring for a few moments at the smoke. Then a similar stream of smoke rose from another quarter. In the distance they saw a single Indian, pigtailed and naked to the waist, fleeing from one crag to another.

Sluggishly, the procession started up again. When they rounded the opposite side of the bald mountain a row of huts appeared, their roofs burned, and only the adobe walls still standing. The walls were scorched, as though a fire had broken out, and the burned, denuded trees that remained were blackened. There was not a soul in sight.

'I was planning to take us to a village called Taxco,' Velasco said to the Japanese after examining the barren scene. 'But I think we had better stay in the next *reducción* tonight.' Then he gave his usual confident smile. 'I think that smoke back there was a signal from the Indians who are still hostile towards the Spaniards. We should reach Mexico City in another seven days.'

Because of the Indian smoke signals we saw in the mountains along the way, we spent one night in the village of Iguala. These Indians are a savage tribe who hate us Spaniards and know nothing of God. On guard against any eventualities we avoided Taxco, and a week later we entered Mexico City in the wake of a rainstorm.

When we caught our first glimpse of Mexico City from the top of a hill, the Japanese suddenly fell silent. Not even the inquisitive merchants made a stir. The cool reception they received in Acapulco had thoroughly drained their spirits, and I sensed a feeling of discontent spreading among them. Even so, the envoys regrouped their entourage, equipping their attendants with spears and banners.

When we passed through the city gate, a market had been set up in the rain-swept plaza within, and people had congregated there to shop. The crowd were so startled by their first sight of the Japanese that they forgot their work and their shopping and trailed along behind us.

We were met at the gate by brethren from our monastery who had come out to welcome us. They led us to the San Francisco Monastery. The climb from the hot lowlands to this high elevation had totally exhausted the Japanese. Some complained of difficulty breathing because of the thin oxygen in the atmosphere of Mexico City, while others suffered from dizzy spells. Immediately after supper (Spanish cuisine did not seem to appeal to them; they avoided meats, which are prohibited by Buddhism, and ate only fish and vegetables), they all retreated to their bedrooms. The shadows of weariness were also etched deep into the faces of the envoys, and when they had eaten they bowed their heads in gratitude to the Father Superior, Guadalcázar, and our other brethen, and retired to their rooms.

The moment the Japanese had gone, the Superior gave me a meaningful glance. 'I would like to talk to you.'

We went to a room furnished with only a prayer altar, a straw mattress and a cross on the wall. As soon as we entered, the Superior unleashed a look of perplexity which he had been concealing all evening.

'We have done everything we could for you. But Viceroy Acuña still hasn't consented to an audience with the envoys.'

In response to the letter I had entrusted to the Acapulco fortress commander, the Superior had appealed to senators and influential parties in Mexico City to see to it that the Japanese envoys were treated with due respect. The Viceroy, however, was still reluctant to grant them a formal audience.

The Superior sighed heavily. 'It's because there are some who oppose your plan.'

'I am aware of that.'

I knew without asking who was working against me. There are aristocrats and trade barons here who have business dealings with the Spanish merchants in Manila. They are afraid that their own profits will decline if Japan begins to trade directly with Nueva España without going through Manila. But behind it all, as the Superior was well aware, are the Jesuits.

'They are saying that the petition you submitted is . . . full of lies.'

'In what respect?'

'You wrote that the Japanese king would gladly welcome more missionaries. But reports from Manila say that the Japanese are hostile towards Christianity, and that you have distorted the truth . . .'

'There is no denying that the political situation in Japan is unstable,' I said, speaking more loudly than I had intended. 'There is still a power-struggle taking place; the family of the ruler who invaded Korea has fallen, and now a new Shōgun is solidifying his hold on the country. Nevertheless we surely could not have made this voyage and come to Mexico City without the endorsement of the Shōgun?'

'You understand Japan better than us.' The Superior smiled faintly, as if to console me. 'If you say that is the situation . . . we shall believe you.'

The only concern of this goodly Superior was that I might become a laughing stock and the object of mockery. His timid face reminded me of Father Diego. I wondered if that red-eyed priest was still in Edo.

I left the Superior's office and returned to the room which had been provided for me. There I lit a candle and bound my wrists to avoid the temptations of the flesh. I had anticipated these machinations by my enemies. I had never assumed that everything would proceed smoothly from the outset. It is true, as the Jesuits say, that the Christians in Japan are undergoing persecution, and that the Naifu and the Shōgun are not pleased with the missionary work there. But that is no reason for us to retreat and abandon that nation to Satan and to heathen religions. Missionary work is like diplomacy. Indeed it resembles the conquest of a foreign land. In missionary work, as in diplomacy, one must have recourse to subterfuge and strategy, threatening at times, compromising at others – if such tactics serve to advance the spreading of God's word, I do not regard them as despicable or loathsome. At times one has to close one's eyes to certain things for the sake of sharing the gospel. The conqueror Cortez landed here in Nueva España in 1519, and with only a handful of soldiers he captured and killed multitudes of Indians. In light of God's teachings, no one could call such an act proper. But we must not forget that as a result of that sacrifice, today countless Indians have come into contact with the word of our Lord, and have thereby been saved from their savage ways and begun to walk the paths of righteousness. None can lightly judge whether it would have been better to leave the Indians to their devilish ways, or to close our eyes to a degree of evil and bring them the word of God.

If the Viceroy suspects the contents of my petition and is hesitant to grant the Japanese envoys an audience, then I will have to employ a certain stratagem to put his mind at ease. I prepared my trump card aboard ship. . . .

I have carried out my strategy. For the past three days, I have taken the envoys to call on people of influence here in Mexico City. We seemed much like beggars asking for alms. The Archbishop, a man grown fat on lavish living, welcomed us amiably at first and stared curiously at the four envoys, who stared silently back with the stern expressions peculiar to the Japanese. The Archbishop had a weak heart, and sometimes pressed his pudgy hand against his chest as he asked some perfunctory questions about Japan. It was clear, however, that he had no interest in this Asian nation.

Acting almost as a spokesman for the Japanese, I stressed how beneficial trade with Japan would be for Nueva España. For instance, the ship fittings, gunpowder, nails, iron and copper which are transported to Acapulco each year from Sevilla could be obtained at a much lower price from Japan, while the Japanese are eager to buy raw silk, velvet and wool, which can be had cheaply in Nueva España. I also pointed out that the tin needed in Nueva España could be had in large quantities from the Japanese regions of Nagasaki, Hirado and Satsuma, and I emphasized the disadvantages if trade negotiations between España and Japan collapsed, since trade with Japan would be monopolized by Holland or England.

The Archbishop erased the smile from his face and pressed his hand against his chest. 'But Japan began persecuting the Christians seventeen years ago. I understand that the persecutions are still going on. Is it possible to dispatch Spanish missionaries to such a country?'

I knew that news of the execution of twenty-six martyrs in Nagasaki in 1597 had reached even as far as Nueva España.

'The situation is improving,' I explained. 'The new rulers of Japan have realized that trade and missionary work are inseparable, and they have given orders to the Lord of these envoys permitting the recognition of Christianity in his domain alone. If trade flourishes in his domain, I'm certain the other nobles will follow suit and welcome the missionaries. In fact, the Japanese merchants who made the voyage with me have come forward of their own accord and are giving ear to the word of God.'

I paused and watched breathlessly for the Archbishop's response.

'Do they plan to be baptized?' His interest aroused for the first time by the trump card I set before him, the Archbishop rose from his chair.

'I believe they will be baptized.'

'When? Where?'

'Here in Mexico City. Soon.'

Unable to understand our conversation, the four envoys stood stiffly, their expressionless faces unchanged. It was a godsend to me that they could not understand Spanish.

'Please give your blessing to these envoys.'

The Archbishop lifted his plump hand and gave the Japanese a blessing, and the unsuspecting envoys received it. My intention was that this overfed Archbishop should immediately inform the people of influence in Mexico City that some of the Japanese were going to be baptized. As the story spread, the bad reputation of the Japanese would surely be mitigated.

Concluding our visit, we returned to the monastery. There I called the merchants together.

'The cargo you brought to Acapulco should reach Mexico City soon.'

As they congratulated themselves, I told them in no uncertain terms that they would have great difficulty selling their goods. I explained that word of the Japanese persecution of Christians had reached here, and that as a result the authorities did not feel kindly disposed towards them. With that, I turned my back upon the agitated group and returned to my room.

The merchants consulted together after I left. I knew what they would be conferring about. Prayerfully – yes, prayerfully – I awaited their answer. Before long that yellow-toothed merchant – the fellow on the ship who had implored me to give him special trading privileges in Nueva España – came creeping to my room with several of his comrades.

'Padre,' the yellow-toothed fellow grinned fawningly. 'Padre, all the men say they want to become Christians.'

'For what reason?' My voice was icy.

'Because we've realized the value of the Christian teachings.'

He stammered on tediously, explaining how he and the others felt. It had turned out just as I thought it would. I know many righteous Christians will be critical of this tactic of mine. But commonplace methods are of no avail in fashioning Japan into a nation of God. Even if these merchants intend to use baptism and indeed the Lord Himself for the sake of riches and commerce, God will not abandon them once they have received baptism. The Lord will never forsake someone who has uttered His name even once. That is what I want to believe.

As I anticipated – or rather, as I planned – the news that a group of Japanese were to be baptized passed from the Archbishop to the people with influence, from the mouth of one monk to another, and spread throughout the city. Everyone I have met in the last few days has questioned me about this matter. I am waiting now, like a spider waits for its prey to fall into its web, for the rumour to reach the ears of the Viceroy. Then, amidst the curiosity and satisfaction of the citizens of Mexico City, the Japanese will receive a glorious baptism.

And when that happens they will have to admit that I, who showed forth this great achievement to the people, am worthy to become Bishop of Japan.

'O Lord, are these actions I have taken contemptible? I have uttered these lies and plotted these stratagems so that some day hymns praising Thy name will flow throughout Japan, and the flowers of faith blossom there in profusion. The soil in Japan is so hard and barren that I had no choice but to employ such strategies so that Thy seeds may sprout therein. Someone had to soil their hands. Since there was no other, I did not hesitate to smear myself with mud for Thy sake. Yet why am I so attached to that land and its people? There are many nations in this world where missionary work is more easily accomplished. Ah, Japan. The more unyielding you are, the more my fighting spirit is inflamed. I am drawn to you, Japan, until it seems there is no other country in the world.'

'Therefore seek ye the kingdom of God and His righteousness.' On Saint Michael's Sabbath, in the chapel of the Franciscan monastery here in Mexico City, thirty-eight Japanese were baptized by Father Superior Guadalcázar. At ten o'clock the bell in the church tower rang forth, its peal echoing through the blue skies, and people flocked to witness the ordinance. The Japanese lined up in two rows, each holding a candle in his hand. As they stood before the Superior, he asked, 'Do you believe in our Lord, and in His Church, and in life everlasting?' Each lifted his voice and vowed, 'I believe.'

When the throng assembled in the chapel heard those words, some of them knelt, others wept, and all praised the Lord and gave thanks for the love God had showered upon these foreigners. The church bell rang out again. As I served as assistant to the Superior, a feeling of gratitude washed over me. Even if these thirty-eight Japanese merchants were motivated only by the prospect of wealth and trade, surely the sacrament of baptism can overcome their greed? One by one the Japanese knelt before the Superior. When he had sprinkled the baptismal water upon their foreheads, they returned to their seats with curious looks on their faces. I prayed fervently for them.

For their benefit, Father Superior Guadalcázar delivered a sermon to the following effect. In Nueva España today many Indians under Spanish protection have abandoned their barbaric customs and heretical beliefs and now tread the path of God. In the same manner, these thirty-eight Japanese have discarded their pagan beliefs and been welcomed into the fold of the righteous. He asked the whole congregation to join him in praying that Japan would soon become a land of God. He crossed himself, and the stir in the chapel was silenced. All present knelt and bowed their heads.

From the altar I stole a glance at the envoys, who had been given seats in the third row from the front. Nishi was watching the progress of the ceremony with curiosity and interest, while Tanaka and Hasekura sat with folded arms, following my movements with their eyes. Only Matsuki's seat was empty, an obvious sign of his opposition to this ceremony.

After the service I spoke to Tanaka and Hasekura, pointing to the merchants who were surrounded by people and were being showered with bouquets of flowers.

'I suppose you think those merchants are despicable. But the people of Mexico City welcome them as friends now. No doubt their business negotiations will proceed very smoothly from now on.'

The two men were silent.

'That's not all. I suspect that today's ceremonies will not be without effect on the Viceroy's decision to permit trade with Japan.'

Tanaka averted his eyes at my irony. Hasekura looked most uncomfortable.

The baptism of the Japanese put the Archbishop in high spirits, and through his good offices a meeting between Viceroy Acuña and the envoys was arranged even sooner than I had imagined. The envoys were delighted when I brought them the news – even Tanaka managed a clumsy smile.

On the Monday of the audience the envoys boarded the carriage which the Viceroy had sent for them and equipped each of their retainers with spears. I rode with them from the monastery to the Viceroy's official residence. News of the baptism had spread throughout the city, and people walking along the streets waved and called out greetings to us. But the envoys were excessively apprehensive about the approaching audience, and not even the cheering voices of the crowd could soften their dour expressions.

Their nervousness mounted when our carriage passed through the gate of the Viceroy's residence, which is situated in the heart of Mexico City; as we advanced through a row of solemn guards and the carriage pulled to a stop at the carriage porch, I could feel young Nishi's kneecaps quivering slightly. The Viceroy, a tall, aristocratic-looking Spaniard, was waiting with two of his secretaries in a reception room decorated with gleaming armour and spears. He sported a moustache on his thin face. The envoys bowed to him in the Japanese manner, oblivious to the hand he had extended to them, and he shrugged his shoulders in embarrassment.

The contrast between this Japanese style of greeting and the Viceroy's bombastic welcoming speech, done in typical Spanish fashion, made an amusing spectacle. Although essentially these two nationalities are utterly dissimilar, they are alike in their respect for formality and in their exaggerated mannerisms. The Viceroy conveyed his gratitude to the Japanese king for the good will he had demonstrated in protecting the shipwrecked Spanish sailors and sending them home. He then congratulated the envoys on the safe arrival of the Japanese ship in Nueva España, and expressed his hope that Japan and España could prosper and flourish together. When he had finished his lengthy greeting, Hasekura reverently raised His Lordship's letter above his head and stepped towards the Viceroy. Both men performed with deadly seriousness, unaware of the absurd figures they cut.

The Viceroy, however, avoided giving any answer to the question of greatest concern, merely saying to me, 'We will do our best to see that the Japanese emissaries are able to rest and relax here in Mexico City.' As time passed the envoys began to show signs of exasperation, until the sharpwitted Matsuki, unable to endure it any longer, pressed me to ask for an answer to His Lordship's letter.

'Personally,' the Viceroy spluttered, 'I do not have the authority to reply to this letter. Of course I give you my firm promise that I will convey your request to Madrid. . . .'

The envoys looked at me in surprise. Worry filled their faces, and they looked just like children seeking aid from an adult.

'I'm sure the Japanese would like to know when to expect an answer from Madrid,' I asked on their behalf.

'Because of the problems involved in this matter, and taking into account the time needed for deliberation, I imagine it will take about half a year,' replied the Viceroy with a shrug. 'I'm sure you're aware of this, Father, but Spanish trade with the Far East is indissolubly linked with the missionary effort, so the views of the Pope will also have to be considered.'

Of course I knew that. I was also well aware that the Viceroy of Nueva España did not have the authority to grant permission for trade with Japan. I had come with the Japanese envoys for that very reason. But I pretended to be greatly surprised, as though this were the first I had heard of such a thing, then I explained the situation to the Japanese. My aim was to plunge them into confusion, leave them helpless, and then direct them exactly as I wished.

'The Viceroy says that an answer from España will take a year,' I lied.

'A year? We are supposed to wait a year?'

The envoys looked as though they had been bludgeoned. I ignored their reaction and turned to the Viceroy as though I were at my wit's end.

'The envoys say that six months is too long to wait. If that's the case, they say they would rather go to España themselves and convey the wishes of the Japanese king to the King of España.'

'That makes no difference to me, but . . .'

Realizing that what the Viceroy really wanted was to get these bothersome Japanese envoys far away from Mexico City, I poured a little priming water into the pump.

'Could we then prevail upon your kind offices so that they can make the journey to España?'

'I can hardly refuse if that is what the envoys desire. But please tell them that the journey from here to the eastern coast is beset with danger.'

'Danger? What do you mean?'

'Didn't you know? An Indian uprising has broken out near Veracruz. And we cannot spare any guards to accompany the Japanese envoys.'

This was the first I had heard of such a thing. In order to travel from Nueva España to España across the Atlantic Ocean, we first had to get to the port of Veracruz. And near Veracruz an Indian tribe was burning down villages, demolishing the mansions of the landlords, and even attacking clergymen.

'We cannot stay here for a year,' Tanaka, understanding nothing, pressed me. 'The Council of Elders ordered us to return by next winter.'

'Let me tell that to the Viceroy.'

Of course I did not translate Tanaka's remark for the Viceroy. I thought quickly. The purpose of this voyage is to give our Order, rather than the Jesuits, the sole right to proselytize in Japan, and to obtain the appointment of Bishop of Japan for myself. To achieve these goals I must travel to España, no matter what dangers I encounter. For only the Cardinal of España can appoint me Bishop.

'They recognize the dangers, but they still wish to go to Veracruz. They say they will accept full responsibility for themselves.' Now I was lying to the Viceroy, too. 'I would like to point out to you that, even though some people here oppose trade with Japan, commerce between Nueva España and Japan is in no sense pointless. Our enemies England and Holland are currently vying for trade agreements with Japan.'

I explained to the Viceroy the same things I had related to the

Archbishop – stressing that the Protestants in England and Holland
now had their eye on Japan, since they had learned that plentiful
supplies of tin and silver could be had there at extremely low cost;
that the King of Japan, however, wanted to trade with Nueva España
instead of the Spanish colony of Manila; and that since the Jesuits
were meddling in the trade relations with Manila, it would be beneficial hereafter for our Order to act as intermediaries.

'I would be grateful if you would send prompt word to España that
our Order here in Mexico City was responsible for baptizing a
number of Japanese.'

His cool eyes sparkled for the first time. 'My reports will do you
no damage.' He patted me softly on the shoulder. 'You seem to have
chosen the wrong profession, Father. You should have become
a diplomat instead of a missionary.'

I felt sorry for the envoys, who left the Viceroy's residence totally
deflated, but personally I was grateful to God and thoroughly
satisfied.

It was almost midday when we returned, and the passers-by on the
road again called out greetings as our carriage drove by.

'Since there is no other way,' I said to the envoys, 'I shall go to
España alone and try to bring back a favourable response.'

They said nothing. They were not angry, but simply at a loss what
to do. Step by step, they were moving precisely in the direction I
desired. . . .

From the Viceroy's official residence, the envoys returned despond-
ently to the monastery. As they alighted from the carriage, an Indian
stepped from the cheering crowd and tugged insistently at the
samurai's sleeve. His pigtail hung down his back, and his eyes shone
with a peculiar light. When the samurai halted in amazement, the man
quickly muttered something to him. Above the clamour of the crowd
the samurai could not understand what he said, so the man repeated
his words.

'I am . . . Japanese.'

The samurai was speechless with surprise. Although he had heard
that a Japanese was here, he had not imagined they would meet so
soon in such an unexpected place. The man clutched the samurai's
sleeve firmly and would not move, as if to sniff out the scent of Japan
from the samurai's face and clothing. Finally, something like a moan
escaped his lips, and tears welled in his eyes and trickled down his
cheeks.

'I am in the village of Tecali,' he said quickly. 'But please don't tell the padres about me. I used to be a monk, but I have abandoned Christianity.'

Then the man noticed Velasco approaching, and added hurriedly, 'The village of Tecali is near Puebla. The village of Tecali.'

With that he disappeared into the crowd. When the stunned samurai had recovered his composure, he searched among the onlookers for the man. The tear-stained face was peering at him and smiling from the middle of the throng.

Once they had returned to their room, the samurai told the other envoys what had happened. Nishi's eyes flashed.

'Let's go to Tecali! We might be able to use him as an interpreter.'

'Do you think we can go without Velasco finding out?' jeered Tanaka. 'We can't do anything without Velasco. Everything goes the way that bastard wants.'

'That's why we need an interpreter of our own.'

'We can't use him.' Matsuki shook his head too. 'Didn't he say not to tell the padres about him because he'd rejected Christianity?'

As always during such debates, the samurai stood silently in a corner of the room. He said nothing partly because he was not good at putting his feelings into words, but also because he had the characteristic timidity of people from the marshland. Constantly at work was the belief that one could only suffer by getting into an argument, or by harbouring unpleasant feelings towards another person. A man did not voice his own feelings or thoughts unless he had first considered them carefully. That was the nature of the peasants in the marshland, and the samurai was no different.

'Then are we going to sit on our hands and do just what Lord Velasco tells us?'

Neither Tanaka nor Matsuki had any reply to Nishi's question. None of them could decide what course of action to take.

'Are we going to stay here in Mexico City until then?'

Nishi repeated the question tauntingly, as if in retaliation for the constant chiding he received from Tanaka.

'Lord Velasco said he would go to España alone.'

'Velasco has no intention of going to España by himself,' Matsuki shook his head. 'Deep down, he thinks we'll follow along behind him.'

The other three turned their attention to Matsuki. Matsuki's sarcasm and his mocking way of speaking disturbed the samurai, but he had to admit that the man had a keen mind.

'How do you know that?' Tanaka asked.

'Put yourself in Velasco's place,' Matsuki replied. 'From his point of view, it's no doubt a good plan to lead the Japanese envoys to

España and make a grand entrance into the capital, displaying his achievement before all his superiors and comrades. You can guess what he has in mind if you remember how proudly he's strutted around here in Mexico City since he made Christians out of those merchants. España is Velasco's native land. In the capital city of his homeland, he will convert the Japanese envoys to Christianity and show us off to the King and the dignitaries and the Christian priests, and they'll fall down at his feet. That's his aim.'

'Then it would be better if we ignored Velasco's coaxing and didn't go to España.' Nishi gazed around at the others.

'But,' the samurai murmured as though to himself, 'if going to España would help establish relations between the Council of Elders and Nueva España . . .'

Tanaka, who stood with folded arms, nodded in agreement.

'What Hasekura says is true. No matter what Velasco has in mind, accomplishing our mission is our first priority.'

'I'm not so sure,' Matsuki smiled faintly. 'In the first place, the Council of Elders ordered us to complete our mission as quickly as possible and return to Japan. If we go to España, we'll be delaying our return a great deal.'

'Even if we are late in returning . . . even if it takes two years, our first duty is to accomplish our mission.'

'In that case, Lord Tanaka, if it will help our mission, will you follow Velasco's suggestion and become a Christian when you get to España?' Matsuki poured out the sarcasm liberally, knowing that Tanaka despised Christianity.

'Would that be so wrong?' Nishi interjected. 'The merchants became Christians to further their business. If it would aid our mission . . .'

'Don't talk drivel!' The ferocity in Matsuki's voice startled the others. The faint taunting smile vanished from his lips. 'Nishi, you must not become a Christian, even as a means to your goal!'

'Why not?'

'You don't know anything,' Matsuki stared pitifully at Nishi. 'You know nothing of the struggles within the Council of Elders. You've never even thought about why we lance-corporals came to be picked as envoys for this voyage.'

'I have no idea. Do you know, Lord Matsuki?'

Nishi and Tanaka stared at Matsuki, waiting for an answer.

'That's all I thought about on board ship. A number of reasons came to me.'

'What reasons?'

'One is that they want to put a stop to lance-corporals petitioning for the return of our former lands. If they send a few of us on this arduous journey and we vanish amidst the seaweed along the way, so much the better. Or if we are unable to carry out our impossible commission, they can then punish us in the name of disloyalty as a warning to the others.'

'Ridiculous!' Tanaka sprang from his bed. 'Didn't Lord Shiraishi tell me very plainly that they would consider returning my former lands if we fulfilled our duty as envoys?'

'Lord Shiraishi?' Once again Matsuki smiled mockingly. 'But Lord Shiraishi is not the only member of the Council. There are elder statesmen who do not think well of the actions of Lord Shiraishi's faction. I'm talking about Lord Ayugai's faction. Unlike Lord Shiraishi, Lord Ayugai detests Velasco and the Christians. From the beginning he was opposed to sending Velasco as our interpreter. Lord Ayugai feels that spreading Christianity throughout His Lordship's domain will prove to be the root of great evil in the future.'

'Then why did even the Naifu and the Shōgun give their permission for our voyage?'

'Lord Ayugai thinks it's a trap for His Lordship, set by the Shōgun's clan. His Lordship, like the *daimyōs* of the other great domains, holds formidable power, and Lord Ayugai is of the opinion that Edo intends to crush him. That's why Lord Ayugai's faction opposed the appointment of Velasco, who was thrown out of Edo. Lord Shiraishi's views finally prevailed, but after much debate the Council agreed to abandon the idea of sending elder statesmen as envoys. In their place, low-ranking lance-corporals were selected.'

Matsuki explained the course of events precisely, as though he had personally observed the discord within the Council of Elders. Neither the samurai, the tongue-tied Tanaka nor young Nishi could take issue with Matsuki's articulate logic. Yet in spite of the surprise they felt, something they could not suppress was throbbing in the throats of the three men.

Tanaka could no longer control himself. 'All this is just conjecture on your part, isn't it?'

'I suppose it is.'

'I don't believe any of it.'

'You're free to believe it or not,' Matsuki retorted. 'But I have something I must say to Lord Hasekura and Nishi. Don't be taken in by Velasco's intensity. If you fall for his tricks, even if it is for the sake of your mission, it could prove to be your ruin when you return to Japan. If Lord Shiraishi loses his influence in the Council before our return, and Lord Ayugai's faction takes control, there will be a change in the way we're treated. During our voyage we have to adapt ourselves to every tide of change in His Lordship's domain.'

His head ached. The debate between Matsuki and Tanaka dragged on. The samurai wanted to be alone. He slipped quietly out of the room. It was still siesta time, and the corridors of the monastery were silent. He went out into the courtyard. Opposite the pond an emaciated man hung upon a cross, his head drooping. Water sprayed from the fountain with a faint gurgle and trickled down. Flowers he had never seen in Japan blossomed like flames about the sculpted figure.

Having been brought up to believe that his own tiny patch of land was the sum total of the world, the political manoeuvres of which Matsuki spoke meant nothing to him. He had never considered the possibility that complex networks of veiled enmity totally beyond his comprehension might exist within the Council of Elders. He had simply made this journey in earnest response to Lord Shiraishi's directions.

He rubbed his eyelids with his fingers, then gazed listlessly at the brilliant flowers in the courtyard and listened to the trickle of the fountain.

'I may be going from Nueva España . . . to the distant land of España,' he muttered, thinking of Riku's face. 'All I can do is believe what Lord Shiraishi told me.'

But that was not all. In his heart he felt an urge to defy the all-knowing Matsuki. He felt compelled to resist Matsuki's conjectures about what the Council of Elders had in mind.

He heard footsteps behind him. Nishi was standing there. He gave a sigh.

'I'm exhausted.'

'Because of Matsuki?' The samurai nodded his agreement. 'He thinks the worst of everything. I don't like that about him.'

'Lord Matsuki says that one of us should return to Japan with the merchants and report the situation to the Council, and that the others should remain in Mexico City. He insists that by handing His Lordship's letter to the magistrate of Nueva España we have fulfilled our duty. He says that now we should just wait here for word from Velasco once he has reached España.'

'We have not fulfilled our duty. Lord Shiraishi told us to see it through to the end. I remember him saying that. I cannot support Matsuki's plan.'

'Then will you go to España? I want to go too. Our mission is one thing, of course, but now I'm fascinated by unknown lands and unfamiliar cities. I want to know how vast the world really is.'

The ocean, with its waves snapping at one another. The great ocean, without a single trace of land visible as far as the eye could see, flashed before the samurai's eyes. Young Nishi wanted to see more of that wide world. But to him the thought of entering that vastness was oppressive. He was weary. An intense yearning to return to his marshland suddenly clutched at his chest, and he gazed enviously at Nishi.

Tanaka appeared in the courtyard. He kicked a stone into the pond, an indication that his rage had not yet dissipated.

'The clever bastard. . . .' Tanaka heaped abuse on Matsuki. Nevertheless, he still seemed unable to make up his mind as he slumped in a chair in the courtyard. 'Hasekura, no matter what Matsuki says, we have no hope of advancement unless we complete our mission. I – I don't know anything about intrigues in the Council of Elders. . . . But as a lance-corporal I didn't have any choice but to go on this journey if I wanted to recover my old lands.'

Torment clouded Tanaka's downcast face, and his voice shook as though he were weeping.

That evening the samurai visited the quarters of Yozō and his other servants. 'Quarters' is an inappropriate term – instead of rooms, the merchants and attendants had been given straw mattresses in the corridors of the monastery.

The three men stood when they saw the samurai. They sensed something in his stiff expression, and waited quietly like dogs for their master to speak.

'We must continue our journey.' The samurai blinked his eyes. 'We are going to cross the sea again, and travel to another distant country.'

He could see that Ichisuke and Daisuke were trembling.

'It's been decided that Lord Matsuki and the merchants will remain here; they will board the great ship at the end of the year and return to Tsukinoura.' In one breath the samurai spat out the words he knew would be most painful for his attendants: 'We and the other two envoys are setting out for España.'

Although Yozō merely stared at him in silence, the samurai knew that, whatever became of Ichisuke and Daisuke, Yozō would never abandon him. He knew that, like himself, Yozō had never once defied the course of his fate.

Chapter 5

I have done all that had to be done. I leave Mexico City with no regrets. The Father Superior of my Order and the good-natured Archbishop have written a letter to Madrid detailing the missionary service I have rendered and reporting that under my tutelage many Japanese merchants have been baptized. And Viceroy Acuña has reported to the court advisers that trade with Japan would be of value in staving off incursions by the Protestant nations. These two letters will serve to stifle the manoeuvres of the Jesuits better than any letter of recommendation. I can say that my stay in Mexico City has been a success.

As the day of departure approaches, the weather is still clear. I recite Mass at the monastery and give Communion to the newly-baptized Japanese merchants. They have most definitely become Christians for the sake of profit, but whatever their motives, they have come into contact with God. Those who have encountered God cannot flee His presence. Thanks to their baptism, these Japanese merchants have been able to sell their wares to the traders here, and in turn they have purchased plentiful amounts of wool and fabrics. Four months from now they will load these goods onto the ship and go back to Japan to realize a healthy profit.

'When you return to our castle town, Padre,' the beaming merchants announced in gratitude, 'we will have a church built and waiting for you.'

A splendid proposition! That yellow-toothed fellow made it a point stealthily to take me aside and whisper in my ear. He told me that if I would arrange for him to have sole claim to the wool market in Nueva España, he would gladly donate a tenth of his profits to my Order. My designs have not gone amiss. It delights me to imagine what that castle town will look like when it is transformed into a Christian capital more resplendent than Nagasaki.

Still, not everything has gone as planned. As I assumed, the Japanese envoys have told me that they will follow me to far-off

España, but it turns out that Matsuki will stay in Mexico City by himself and return to Japan with the merchants. I assume that he has been breathing slanders about me into the ears of the other envoys, but it is incredible that he should part company with his comrades and give up his commission as envoy at midpoint. He must have some reason for daring to hurry back to his country, for this action will surely invite the censure of the Council of Elders. I sometimes wonder if Matsuki was sent on this journey not as a genuine emissary, but on orders from the Council to observe and report my movements to them. Such cunning would be just like the Japanese.

From another standpoint, however, Matsuki's withdrawal is opportune. It will be easier for me to have things my own way on the forthcoming voyage if I only have to deal with Hasekura, who is the very embodiment of loyalty; Tanaka, who swaggers like a cockerel but lacks Matsuki's cleverness; and Nishi, who is still a boy. For that reason, when I see Tanaka exploding at Matsuki, I do what I can to placate him.

It is not this matter that concerns me. I am anxious about the insurrection by the Huaxteca tribe which has broken out on our path to Veracruz. This insurrection is the fault of the stupid *encomenderos*. From the outset the King permitted the Spanish *encomenderos* who migrated to Nueva España to have private ownership of the farm lands and pastures as if they were of the aristocracy. But they took advantage of this privilege to force the Indians into merciless labour as tenant farmers. They even cheated the peons out of what little land was left them. Our Order has continuously opposed these *encomenderos*, and this new uprising has resulted from their tyranny. The Huaxtecans were originally a docile tribe, their weapons little more than stones. Yet now I am told they have obtained guns.

Fools like these may be found in every subjugated land. Here the landowners did not have the wisdom to insure their own profits by providing appropriate incentives for the Indians. It is perhaps not going too far to say that the situation here closely resembles the failure of the ministry in Japan. The flaws in our missionary endeavours – pressing for our own aims alone, and ignoring the position and feelings of the Japanese – appear here in Nueva España in different guise as a conflict between the *encomenderos* and the Indians.

To my regret, our journey must take us through the region where the insurrection is taking place. I have not told the Japanese envoys about this disturbance, and I have asked the brothers at the monastery to remain silent on the matter. My plans would be confounded if the envoys wavered on account of the uprising.

For the past few days, I have been turning to Corinthians and pondering the tribulations of St Paul on his missionary journeys. 'In journeyings often, in perils of waters, in perils of robbers, in perils by mine own countrymen, in perils by the heathen, in perils in the wilderness, in perils in the sea,' the Apostle writes. All for the purpose of bringing the teachings of God to the heathen peoples. Like Paul, I begrudge not 'watchings often, hunger and thirst and cold.' Because for me there is Japan. Those tiny islands, shaped like a unicorn, are the lands which the Lord has given me to conquer, the battlefield where I must fight. That assurance has been strengthened each time I have prayed since our arrival in Nueva España.

Two nights before our departure, the good Superior invited the Japanese to a farewell banquet. Much like the feast at Cana, the merchants drank wine and sang songs. The Japanese melodies sounded monotone and tedious to our ears, but the brothers who shared our table remarked that they were very like Indian songs. At this banquet the Japanese, slightly drunk, finally confessed with a laugh that the thin air at the high elevations around Mexico City had been suffocating to them, and that the smell of the food and the olive oil they had been served had been nauseating. Tanaka was the heaviest drinker among the envoys, but he did not become in the least disorderly. The envoys maintained proper Japanese etiquette as they ate their food, much to the admiration of the brethren.

The banquet ended. As I left the dining-room with the monks and started to make my way to the chapel, my hands clasped for evening prayers, Matsuki drew me aside. Letting our faces betray nothing as we sought to read each other's mind, we exchanged words of farewell.

'Padre,' he said softly, 'we will not be meeting again.'

'Why not? When this mission is completed, I will return . . .'

'No. Don't come to Japan again.'

'Why not?' I spoke firmly, shaking my head.

'Padre.' Matsuki looked up at me almost pleadingly. 'Why do you want to disrupt our domain?'

'Disrupt it? I don't understand.'

'We . . . no, it isn't just us. All of Japan has lived in peace until now. Why have you padres come to disturb our peace?'

'We did not come to disturb. We came to share true happiness with you.'

'True happiness?' Matsuki's lips twisted into a tormented smile. 'Your brand of true happiness is too intense for Japan. A strong medicine turns to poison in the bodies of some. The happiness you padres preach is poison to Japan. That has been very clear to me since we arrived in Nueva España. This country would have lived in peace if the Spanish ships had not come. Your version of happiness has disrupted this country.'

'This country. . . .' I recognized what Matsuki was trying to say. 'I'm not denying that much blood has been spilled here. But we have atoned for that. The Indians have learned many things. . . . Most important of all, they have learned the way that leads to happiness.'

'Then do you intend to treat Japan just as you have treated Nueva España?'

'Me? I am not that foolish. I simply want to provide advantages for Japan and in return receive permission to spread the teachings of Christ.'

'Japan will gladly learn superior knowledge and skills from your countries. But we need nothing else.'

'What good will it do you simply to copy our skills? What will it profit you to obtain mere knowledge? Those skills and that knowledge were created by human hearts seeking after the happiness that comes from the Lord.'

'The happiness you talk of,' Matsuki repeated, 'is a nuisance for our little islands.'

Neither of us would yield our position. Finally Matsuki fell silent, fixed a look of loathing upon me, then turned and walked away. I felt then, as he had said, that we would not be meeting again.

On the day of their departure the weather was clear.

The merchants clustered at the gate of the monastery to bid farewell to the group and to wish them a safe journey. The three envoys entrusted them with letters and gifts for their families. The previous evening the samurai had written to his uncle and elder son.

'I will write only briefly,' he told Kanzaburō. 'Things are tolerably well here. No harm has come to Yozō, Ichisuke or Daisuke. Unfortunately Seihachi died aboard ship. Be obedient and courteous to your mother. I should give you many more details, but I can write only the essentials in this hurried letter.'

The samurai despised this letter – it did not convey even a thousandth part of all he felt in his heart. He thought of Riku's pained face as she read these words over and over again.

The envoys and Velasco rode on horses, while the attendants led donkeys loaded with baggage. The Superior and the monks waved from among the crowd of merchants. The bright sun beat down. As the samurai placed his foot in the stirrup, Matsuki Chūsaku unexpectedly ran to his side.

'Listen.' He clutched the samurai's trousers. 'Take care of yourself. Remember to take care of your health.' The samurai was startled, but Matsuki continued, 'The Council of Elders won't protect or defend a lance-corporal. From the moment we became envoys, we were sucked into the whirlpool of politics. Once you're caught up in that whirlpool, you can depend on no one but yourself.'

The samurai balked at this cunning little speech. 'I believe the Council of Elders,' he thought of shouting, but gulped back the words.

From his saddle the samurai nodded to the monks and merchants who were waving farewell. Matsuki stood among them with his arms folded. Envy stabbed at the samurai's chest as he reflected that these men would be returning to Japan before him. But in the marshland the samurai had been always obedient, and at this moment too he was prepared to accept the fate that had been handed to him. Behind him Yozō, Ichisuke and Daisuke followed in silence, leading their donkeys.

Once more, as on the road from Acapulco to Mexico City, a wilderness dotted with maguey and cactus spread out before the travellers. As they descended down to the plains, the heat became intense. Indians working in the fields ceased their labours, and children chasing sheep and goats stopped in their tracks to stare endlessly at the peculiar procession.

In the harsh light of the sun, the shimmering sky was not blue, but more the colour of mica. A solitary bird – the first bald eagle the Japanese had seen – floated slowly on the air currents. The wilderness gave way to lean fields of corn and groves of olives. These lingered for a while, only to turn back into a desert of cacti. Where there were fields, the Indians had built huts, with roofs thatched from leaves and branches and walls made of mud. On the roofs bald eagles were perching.

The Japanese passed through the ruins of several villages, their stone walls tucked away in corners of the granite-strewn hills. Deserted plazas still remained, through which a dry wind was almost invariably rattling. Listening to the sound of the wind, the samurai remembered the words that Matsuki had shouted almost defiantly: 'Once you're caught up in the whirlpool of politics, you can depend on no one but yourself.'

Tanaka asked whether the villages had fallen to ruin as a result of famine.

'It wasn't famine,' said Velasco. 'Our ancestor Cortez carved up the Indian lands with less than a hundred soldiers.' He seemed almost proud of his answer.

'What good is it to speculate?' the samurai asked himself as he
swayed in his saddle. 'A witless fellow like me has to think only of
accomplishing his mission. I'm sure that's what my father would say
if he were alive.'

They came to a river. There was not a drop of water. A bald
mountain splattered with granite appeared. When they reached its
summit, another enormous mountain capped with white snow
towered majestically on the horizon. The mountain was incompar-
ably taller and grander than any in His Lordship's domain.

'Is it taller than Fuji?' Nishi cried in amazement.

Velasco turned to the young man and smiled sympathetically. 'Of
course it is. This mountain is called Popocatepetl.'

Overcome with emotion, Nishi uttered the same words he had
spoken earlier. 'The world truly is . . . vast.'

The towering mountain remained constantly in view as they
descended the hill like a column of ants. It drew no nearer, no matter
how long they walked, but seemed to stare down in silence at the
world of men. As the samurai gazed up at it, Matsuki's opinions
began to seem trivial. He was setting out now into a world Matsuki
could know nothing about.

On the evening of the fifth day, the exhausted, sweat-soaked
Japanese staggered into a town they had first seen far in the distance.
As they neared the town wall the air finally cooled, blending the
aroma of trees, the fragrance of flowers and the smells of human life.
Having tramped so long through sun-baked, deserted wastelands,
the envoys inhaled these smells deep into their lungs, as though they
were gulping water.

'This town is called Puebla.'

When they caught sight of the Japanese the soldiers guarding the
town gate hurriedly disappeared inside. Velasco raised his hand and
halted the procession, then dismounted from his horse to show the
soldiers their pass from the Viceroy. He did not notice the three
envoys exchanging glances. Puebla. They had heard the name
before. It was the one mentioned by that Japanese who had looked so
much like an Indian. 'The village of Tecali is near Puebla. The village
of Tecali.'

The group finally obtained permission to enter and passed through
the gate. Within, a market-place like the one in Mexico City had been
erected. The pigtailed Indians who sat on the ground hugging their
knees looked like stone statues. They had set out fruit and vegetables,
pottery called *talavera*, long sarapes and broad-brimmed sombreros
for sale. Flocks of goats scrambled between these wares, the tiny bells
around their necks jangling. The Indians exhibited no surprise at

seeing the Japanese, thinking perhaps that they were a tribe from some mountain region. A sharp surge of longing for the marshland stabbed unexpectedly at the samurai's chest. He wondered what his wife and children were doing at this moment. Perhaps the pain came from having journeyed so long through an uninhabited wilderness and now finally arriving at a place filled with the smells of humanity.

Velasco led the Japanese to the Franciscan monastery in Puebla. Knowing the correct procedure after their experiences in Mexico City, the Japanese shook hands with the monks who came out to welcome them, and smiled and nodded even though they could not understand what their hosts were saying. They were furnished with a large room. The aroma of flowers floated in through the open windows.

'What are you going to do?' Nishi whispered to the samurai as he removed his dirt-stained trousers. 'Are you going to visit that Japanese?'

'I'd like to, but I have a mission to carry out.' The samurai lowered his voice too, so that Tanaka would not hear. 'But he must know that we have arrived in Puebla. I have a feeling he'll show up again.'

Night came. When they lay down on their beds after dinner they heard the peal of bells, just as they had in Mexico City. This bell chimed from the great cathedral erected thirty years earlier in the town plaza. As they listened to the bell the Japanese, weary from their journey across the desert, fell into a deep sleep. Soon there were footsteps in the corridor and Velasco, carrying a candle, peered into their room. After determining that all were sleeping peacefully, he slipped softly away.

In his dreams the samurai was back in the marshland again. A low, leaden sky that seemed about to release a swirl of powdery snowflakes hung over the swamp. He and Yozō, their bodies wrapped in straw coats and their feet covered with straw boots, waited with bated breath at the edge of the marsh. It was still sprinkled with frozen snow. From behind a clump of dried reeds, they could see a flock of ducklings clustered on the black surface of the marsh. Yozō tapped the samurai's shoulder and pointed out a single white swan, its long neck thrust into the water, beneath a tree deep within the marsh.

The samurai nodded and listened as Yozō puffed away at the coals in the fire. He wondered vaguely where the bird had migrated from. Each year flocks of these swans came soaring through the winter skies to visit the marshland. They crossed the ocean, from some distant, unfamiliar land.

At a signal from Yozō the samurai hurriedly stuffed his fingers into his ears. The report of the musket was thunderous. Scores of ducklings soared into the air. The white swan leaped up, then splashed into the water. It glided away, flapping its wings. The report of the gun spread out through the chilly air like the ripples that formed on the surface of the water. I'm glad we missed, the samurai thought. The reverberation of the shot lingered in his ears, and the smell of the gunpowder clung persistently in his nostrils. . . .

The samurai's conjecture proved correct. When the Japanese envoys and their attendants visited an Indian market-place near the monastery the following evening, the Japanese man was watching them from near by.

Some of the Indians at the market aped the Spaniards by wearing sombreros and leather sandals, but most were naked to the waist, with their long hair falling down around their broad bare shoulders. The Japanese were fascinated by the wares which the Indians had strewn on the ground, and by their peculiar chatter as they packed up their bundles and prepared to leave. When Daisuke jestingly propped a sombrero on his head and made everyone laugh, the samurai looked up and noticed the Japanese man watching them enviously from beside a large, dusty sycamore tree a short distance away.

'Hello!' The samurai scurried over to the man. 'So you've come after all. Why didn't you come to our lodgings?'

'I can't go there. I've been waiting here for you since early afternoon.'

Tanaka and Nishi also came over to talk to the renegade monk. 'Is Tecali near here?'

'It's by the marsh on the outskirts of town.'

His eyes closed as if he was remembering something, the man stroked at their clothes as he had done before.

The bell of the church began to ring. It was the bell of Angelus, but to the Japanese it was also a signal that dinner was ready. Velasco had instructed them to return to the monastery when it tolled.

'We have to go back,' Tanaka ordered them. 'If we're late, people will say we have no manners.'

'Please tell me about Japan. When do you leave here?'

'Tomorrow. Just after noon, I hear.'

'Tecali is very near. Early tomorrow morning I'll have an Indian guide wait for you here in the plaza.'

'We can't do that.' Unyielding, Tanaka shook his head. 'We've come to this country to perform a mission. If we went out of bounds and something happened to us, it could hinder our mission.'

The renegade monk nodded forlornly. He stood beside the sycamore tree and watched as the Japanese returned to the monastery.

The cold awoke him. In the light of the moon he saw Nishi wrapping his leggings around his shins, taking care not to arouse anyone. Then, sensing the samurai's gaze upon him, the young man bared his white teeth in embarrassment. That grin made it evident to the samurai where he was going.

'I won't cause you any trouble. I'll be back before morning.'

The samurai glanced quickly towards Tanaka, who was fast asleep. 'You don't understand the language. How will you manage?'

'He said he would send a guide.'

The samurai pictured the renegade monk, stroking their clothes and begging them to tell him news of Japan. Still, he could understand Tanaka's insistence that their mission was more important than anything else.

'Please let me go.' Nishi quietly stood up.

The samurai envied Nishi's fervent curiosity and his youthful, resolute personality. He and Tanaka, whose only hope was that no troubles would befall their mission, were lacking in those traits.

'Are you set on going?'

'Yes.'

'Wait.' The samurai sat up and peered at the snoring Tanaka. He was seized by a desire to rebel against Tanaka and against something within himself.

'Let's go,' he said, getting to his feet.

He dressed quickly, and the two men tiptoed from the room. Neither had a candle, but the moonlight shining through the windows in the corridor guided them to the door leading to the courtyard. As the monastery slept, the courtyard was bathed in the pale light and scented with the heavy aroma of the tropical flowers.

The town was still in a dead sleep as the two men slipped unobserved from the monastery. At the base of a tree where donkeys were tied several Indians lay sprawled out like a heap of rags. One of them opened his eyes and started to say something incomprehensible.

'Tecali,' Nishi repeated, offering the man a medicine case as a gift. 'Tecali.'

The man took the medicine case, sniffed at it, and said, '*Vamos!*' as he untied the reins of three of the donkeys from the tree. They passed through the sleeping town and out through the high black wall.

As the donkeys crossed a dried-up river, the darkness of night finally began to break, and the horizon was dyed a rosy pink. As that pink line gradually grew wider, the men came to a marsh. Its surface was as red as blood, and here and there water-birds rustled their wings as they flew up from the reeds. Beyond the marsh rose a range of mountains basking in the golden sun.

'*Para aquí.*' The Indian reined in his donkey, which was panting white gusts of breath. '*Tecali.*'

The morning sun illuminated a cluster of ten or so huts with reed-thatched roofs. In one of the doorways a pigtailed, pug-nosed Indian woman was washing herself with water from a bucket. When Nishi called out '*Japoneses*' in a loud voice, she turned her head towards them. '*Japoneses!*' But the woman, who seemed like a relic from ancient days, stared blankly and gave no answer. The sun began to beat down upon the fields of scrawny sugarcane and corn, presaging the coming heat of the day. Here and there, Indians naked to the waist appeared from the huts. One of them let out a cry. It was the renegade monk.

'Thank you for coming. Thank you for coming!' he gasped, scurrying up to the envoys. As he spoke, the saliva collected in his mouth, but he talked on and on, like a man forbidden to speak for many long years who has finally been given permission to talk.

He told them he had been born in Yokoseura, in Hizen Province. In his youth he had lost his father and mother in a war; he had been picked up by a Christian priest who was proselytizing in the area and had become the priest's servant. Together they had travelled all over the island of Kyushu. When the Christian persecutions began and the missionaries decided to go underground, with the help of a colleague this priest found the young man passage on a boat to Manila so that he could study at the seminary there. Although he had qualified as a monk, he had begun to feel disaffected with the clergy. At the urging of a sailor acquaintance, he boarded a ship bound for Nueva España, convinced that he would be going to an entirely new world. After a long, difficult voyage he arrived in Mexico City, where for a time he did odd jobs at the monastery. Here too, however, he found it impossible to feel close to the fathers, and he grew disenchanted with everything. He fled and joined this group of Indians and now lived with them in this settlement.

'Won't you ever return to your home in Japan?' the samurai asked.

The renegade monk smiled sadly. 'I have no relatives. Even if I returned, there would be no one to welcome me. And Christians are . . .'

'But you've abandoned Christianity, haven't you?'

'No, no, I am still a Christian. It's just that . . .' He stopped. Then a look of resignation came into his eyes, suggesting that he could not convey his feelings in words. 'It's just that . . . I don't believe in the Christianity the padres preach.'

'Why not?'

'Atrocious things happened here in Nueva España before the padres came. The foreigners snatched away the lands of these Indians and drove them from their homes. Many were brutally murdered; the survivors were sold into slavery. Everywhere you look there are villages these people had to abandon. Nobody lives in them now – only the stone houses and stone walls still stand.'

The two envoys remembered the ruins they had seen in the desert between Acapulco and Mexico City, and on the journey from Mexico City to Puebla. Buried under sand and overgrown with weeds, the plazas of those ruined villages were visited only by the mournful wailing of the wind.

'But war is like that,' the samurai muttered. 'It's the same in any defeated country.'

'I'm not talking about a war.' The man made a grimace. 'It's just that the padres who came to this country later on have forgotten the many sufferings of the Indian people. . . . No, they haven't forgotten. They pretend that nothing ever happened. They feign ignorance, and in seemingly sincere tones preach God's mercy and God's love. That's what disgusted me. Only words of beauty come from the lips of the padres in this country. They never soil their hands in the mire.'

'Is that why you abandoned Christianity?'

'No, no!' The renegade monk glanced behind him. Several Indians were standing in front of the hut to the rear, staring at the Japanese.

'No matter what the padres might say, I believe in my own Jesus. My Jesus in not to be found in the palatial cathedrals. He lives among these miserable Indians. . . . That is what I believe.'

In one breath the renegade monk spewed out everything he had held inside for so many years. The samurai studied the man as though he were peering at something far off in the distance. It seemed almost as if he had heard nothing but talk of Christianity from the day they left Tsukinoura. Since their arrival in Nueva España, everywhere they went they had seen men and women kneeling in the churches, and images of a loathsome, emaciated man illuminated by the flames of many candles. The very life of this vast world seemed to centre on whether one believed in this loathsome man or not. But as a Japanese raised in a tiny marshland, he could feel no interest or concern for this man called Jesus. Such a religion was alien to him and would remain so as long as he lived.

The man stopped talking and fingered Nishi's clothes. He stroked them again and again and cried, 'Ah, these smell of Japan!'

'Why don't you go back?'

The samurai felt pity for the man, no longer distinguishable as either a Japanese or an Indian.

'The merchants who came with us are taking a ship back to Japan at the end of the year. Wouldn't you like to go with them?'

'I'm too old to return.' The renegade monk lowered his eyes to the ground. 'I . . . wherever the Indians go, I shall go; where they stay, I shall stay. They need someone like me to wipe off their sweat when they are ill, to hold their hands at the moment of death. The Indians and I – we are both without a home.'

'Then we won't see you again?'

'These Indians won't stay here forever. When the land here loses its richness, they will move to another place. But if it is the Lord's will, perhaps we shall meet again.'

Then he asked the samurai and Nishi where they were making for.

'Veracruz,' said Nishi. 'From there, I understand we board another ship.'

'Veracruz?' The man looked puzzled. 'That's very dangerous!'

'Dangerous . . .?'

'Didn't you know that the Huaxteca tribe in that region has risen up? They are burning Spanish villages and setting fire to houses.'

'A rebellion?'

'When they have been trodden upon to such a degree . . . even docile Indians finally can bear it no longer.'

Velasco had told them nothing. This was the first they had heard of the uprising. The samurai gazed at Nishi's bewildered face and clenched his sweaty hands. Since their departure from Mexico City, Velasco had chattered confidently from his saddle, constantly smiling his supercilious smile.

'Are you sure?'

'Everyone knows about it – that the Huaxtecans are using guns and gunpowder. You'd better think again about going to Veracruz.'

'We have to go.'

The samurai repeated the words forcefully to bolster himself. 'We have to go!' Surprisingly, he had absolutely no desire to return to Mexico City. His mind, which had often vacillated because of Matsuki Chūsaku's remarks, was now firmly made up.

'Do you want to go back, Nishi?'

'If you are going on, Lord Hasekura, I have no objection.'

The renegade monk accompanied them to the edge of the fields. The dusty corn stalks swayed languidly in the breeze that blew from the marsh. A carved wooden image of a man on a cross stood at the edge of the fields like the guardian deity of this settlement. The emaciated man on the crucifix had pigtails and a pug nose, and eyes filled with dark endurance just like those of the Indians who had been sold into bondage by the Spanish. At his feet lay a pool of melted wax, like tears shed by the man himself.

'In the evening the Indians come here to pray,' said the former monk. 'They tell this Jesus their sorrows and their trials.'

He thrust his hand into his soiled shirt and pulled out a rosary made from seeds and a tiny sheaf of paper worn around the edges.

'I don't have anything to give you. Please take this. It's a life of the Saviour I have written.'

There was no reason to refuse the gift. Beside the marsh reeds the man who had guided them here was waiting patiently with the donkeys. Somehow the eyes of the donkeys seemed to resemble those of the renegade monk. In a language the Japanese could not understand their compatriot gave the Indian instructions.

The sun was already up when they returned to Puebla. Several Indians standing in the road noticed them and stared as the two men dismounted from their donkeys. They quietly entered the courtyard of the monastery and peeked into their room. Tanaka was glumly polishing the scabbard of his sword.

'Did you go to Tecali? After I told you not to?' He scowled accusingly at his fellow envoys.

Nishi told him about the Indian uprising which they had learned about from the Japanese man. 'I wonder if Lord Velasco thought we would be afraid?'

This remark enraged Tanaka.

'Did he think we'd shrink back like the Indians? I'm going to go see what Velasco has to say about this!' He put his sword down and stood up.

'Don't.' The samurai shook his head. 'Velasco will just make clever excuses for himself. No matter what he has to say, this is a journey we have to make.'

Once again the samurai had the feeling that he was defying his own destiny by going on this journey. When he had known nothing but the marshland, he had never thought of anything except his life there. But now he realized that he had changed. The tiny marshland, his uncle, his uncle's tedious complaints beside the hearth, orders from the Council of Elders – for the first time since their departure from Mexico City, the samurai felt a desire to rebel against those unyielding elements of fate that had been thrust upon him.

The Japanese advanced like ants carrying food. They seemed to be making scarcely any progress, but merely inching slowly across a vast, never-changing plateau. Velasco and the three envoys rode horses, encircling the donkeys laden with several saddlebags each. The attendants shuffled along in silence. To the north they could see a range of mountains; overhead a bald eagle circled, floating on the air currents.

Velasco and the three envoys knew that they were still a great distance from the site of the Indian revolt. Hills spattered with white boulders, patches of earth baked and cracked by the sun, river beds where withered trees lay like bleached bones – once they left these parched landscapes behind, fields of corn appeared, blanketed with a layer of dust. None of these scenes resembled the soft, gentle landscapes of Japan. The samurai thought longingly of the marshland, the cool water of the rice fields and the water-wheels turning.

Similar memories were no doubt being savoured by each of the other envoys and their attendants, but no one expressed these thoughts aloud or on his face. Heat and exhaustion had rendered all of them silent and sullen.

But when they struggled to the top of a small granite hill on the afternoon of the fifth day since their departure from Puebla, an unexpected landscape stretched out below them. The first pine grove they had seen since their arrival in this country surrounded a group of Indian mud huts, and well-cultivated fields fanned out alongside the grove. Unlike the Japanese pine, these trees were a variety with soft needles, but a pine was after all a pine.

'Oh!' the Japanese cried out with one voice. They raced to the trees, plucking off the needles and greedily drinking in the aroma. Some clutched the needles in their sweaty hands and relished the touch. The pines bore the unmistakable scent of Japan.

'At home,' Ichisuke called to Daisuke, 'it must be about *mushiokuri* time.'

The samurai's eyes grew distant as he heard those words. *Mushiokuri* was a festival held to drive plagues from the marshland. According to custom, in the dead of night the men, carrying torches, would parade through the villages from west to east.

'I want to go home,' Daisuke murmured to Ichisuke. 'I want to go back now!'

Yozō overheard and reprimanded Daisuke. 'Idiot . . .!' But the samurai went over to the man and shook his head.

'I know you want to go back. Even I don't know when we'll be able to return, or what kind of country we will find when we reach España. But I will see to it that your trials are not for nothing.'

As the samurai spoke these words, his three attendants peered into his sunken eyes and nodded dejectedly. Like stone statues, they stood looking at each other. Suddenly tears welled up in Yozō's eyes, but he averted his head so that the others would not see.

On the seventh day they approached the first real settlement they had encountered on this stage of their journey – Córdoba. They arrived just in the wake of an evening shower, and in the shade of the Spanish-style houses and their white fences, flamelike flowers shivered in the cool breeze, while clouds the colour of straw drifted slowly across the sky. At shouts from the children, the townspeople congregated at the entrance of the town.

When the group of Japanese reached the tiny plaza, they were met by the mayor and the chief local dignitaries. The mayor, one of the landowners in this region, shook hands with Velasco and then examined the dust-covered Japanese much as he would inspect sheep that an Indian had brought to sell. For good measure, however, he voiced words of welcome accompanied by exaggerated Spanish gestures.

'Padre,' the mayor enquired, keeping his eyes riveted on the Japanese, 'if you wouldn't mind telling us why these Orientals have come here . . . .?'

'You must have had word from the Viceroy in Mexico City,' Velasco blustered as though he himself had been slighted. 'These men are diplomatic envoys from Japan, and naturally I assume that they will be treated here as elsewhere like foreign ambassadors.'

Yet somehow the Japanese looked too wretched to be ambassadors. Their clothing and leggings were coated with dust from the long journey, and they maintained a rigid silence, their faces sour and betraying not the slightest degree of affability.

'We should like to invite them to dinner tonight,' the mayor announced after a hushed deliberation with his influential colleagues, not one of whom had any idea where Japan was situated or what manner of country it might be.

The samurai and the other envoys were much more desirous of sleep than of food. Neither the samurai nor Tanaka had any appetite for Spanish food, though Nishi was an exception. But Velasco ignored their feelings and replied, 'I'm sure the ambassadors will be pleased to join you.'

The attendants were escorted to the town meeting hall which was
to serve as their lodgings for the night. The three envoys and Velasco
walked with the major to his residence. Then, in a state of total
exhaustion, the envoys were made to listen to an interminable
salutation they could not understand, after which the food was
brought out.

'Japanese do not eat meat.'

At Velasco's explanation, the mayor and the dignitaries once again
eyed the Japanese as though assessing the worth of some domestic
animals.

After dinner the mayor had a servant bring in a globe from his
study. He wanted to ask Velasco where the country called Japan was
to be found. On the globe, which was shaped like an ostrich egg, only
the outlines of India and China had been crudely sketched in. Japan
was pictured as a peninsula, oozing out from the eastern edge of the
Chinese continent like a tiny droplet of water.

'This is not correct.' No longer able to endure the ignorance of his
fellow countrymen and the crudeness of the globe, Velasco shrugged
his shoulders in exasperation. To see Japan belittled was to have the
object on which he had staked his life subjected to ridicule. 'This is
not Japan!'

'How large is it, Padre?'

'It's a tiny island nation. It's probably less than one-fifth the size of
Nueva España.'

'Then it's one-fiftieth the size of the Spanish empire?' one of the
dignitaries chuckled. 'Why doesn't the Viceroy of the Philippines
just take over the islands? That would make your missionary work
much easier, Padre. And we could create new estates there.'

'Japan is small, but they are inferior to no nation in battle. You
wouldn't be able to trample them into submission the way you have
the Indians here.'

Unable to understand the language, the envoys were excluded
from the conversation, and they stifled yawns as they stared at the
globe. One of the dignitaries, still listening dubiously to Velasco's
comments about Japan, pointed out to them España and its many
colonies.

'*España. Sí, España.*' He repeated himself as though he were
instructing children. Finally he pointed at the tiny droplet dangling
from the Chinese continent.

'Japan,' he said softly.

'You don't understand.' Velasco turned his piercing eyes on the
man. 'With a port of call in Japan a nation can rule the Pacific. That's
why the Protestants in England and Holland are at this very moment

doing everything they can to establish friendly relations with Japan. España must make the first move. For just this reason, Viceroy Acuña of Mexico City has requested that His Majesty the King grant these ambassadors an audience.'

At these words, silence engulfed the dining-hall. Velasco of course had fabricated the idea that the Viceroy in Mexico City had petitioned for an audience with the King, but the remark had its effect. The *encomenderos* of Nueva España were duly impressed by the word 'king'.

With a triumphant look Velasco gazed at the weary Japanese and spoke slowly and gently. 'These fools are amazed to hear that you will be meeting the King of España.'

'King . . .? What do you mean by "king?"' Tanaka asked.

'A king is the supreme ruler. In Japan, for instance, the Naifu is the king.'

'Are we going to meet this King of España?'

'Why not?' Velasco flashed his usual confident smile. 'You are ambassadors of Japan, after all. . . .'

Drained by the weariness of the journey, the three envoys seemed almost stunned by this unexpected piece of news. Lance-corporals who were not even allowed an audience with His Lordship, they were now to meet the King of España.

'Is this true?'

'Please leave everything to me.' At some point Velasco had begun to believe that his lie was no lie at all, but something that would become a reality. No, it was not a lie. It was a goal, an aspiration which he must bring to pass.

'The ambassadors are tired.' He paid lip-service to the mayor's hospitality. 'They are grateful for your kindness.'

Anxiously, the mayor drew Velasco aside.

'Padre, are you leaving tomorrow?'

'That is our plan.'

'Are you aware that the way to Veracruz is dangerous?'

'The Huaxtecans may harbour antagonism towards you Spanish *encomenderos*,' Velasco gazed ironically at the mayor, 'but I doubt whether they will feel any hatred towards ambassadors from an island nation which seems so small and distant to you.'

When they returned to their lodgings in the town hall, the envoys were physically depleted, but their excitement had not abated. They were to have an audience with a king, something they had never anticipated.

After the candles had been extinguished, Nishi's excited voice echoed in the darkness. 'Now that we're meeting the King, we've as good as finished our mission.'

'That's if we do in fact have a direct audience with the King,' the samurai replied, turning over in bed to face Nishi. 'But . . . we don't know if what Velasco says is true.'

'I agree with Hasekura.'

Tanaka's voice came from the direction of the open window. Thereafter the three men were silent, plunged in thought as they lay with open eyes in the darkness. Although they still distrusted Velasco, they could not help picturing themselves being received by a king. Men no better than petty rural samurai could cross the sea and have an audience with the king of a whole country! It was inconceivable, the equivalent of travelling to Edo and being granted an audience with the Naifu or the Shōgun. Elation spread like ripples from the bottoms of their hearts to every corner of their bodies. It was almost enough to dispel all the doubts and suspicions they had about Velasco. Finally the weariness of the day herded them into a deep sleep.

When the group set out from a cloudless Córdoba the next morning, surrounded by donkeys and attendants, elation lightened their steps. Concern about the Indian rebellion had all but vanished from their thoughts. As the envoys pressed their horses forward, it was Velasco who occasionally peered through a spyglass at the range of hills in the distance. Thunderheads rimmed in gold hovered over the hills, which seemed to be coated with a fine powder.

They came to a plain strewn with rubble. Shadows of the clouds floated slowly across their path. Cacti stood sternly like ill-tempered old men scrutinizing the group, and buzzing bird lice grazed their sweat-bathed faces.

As he stared at the dazzling horizon of this broad plain, the samurai thought of the ocean that lay beyond it. And he thought about the country called España which lay at the farthest extremity of that ocean. Oceans and countries he had never seen before. A destiny he had never considered for himself, but which he now felt impelled to accept without complaint.

Here and there they discovered the ruins of altars abandoned by the Indians. Velasco explained that, like the Japanese, the Indians in this region had long worshipped the sun. Pedestals made from red volcanic rock, and stone pillars, now lying in rubble on the ground, had been carved with strange markings. Lizards, their backs shimmering in the sun, scurried about between the inscriptions.

In the afternoon the group rested for a time amid some of these ruins. Languidly they drank the water they carried in bamboo tubes and swatted at the bird lice.

They stared absently at the undulating plain, still dotted with the shadows of clouds. They planned to cross it by nightfall and reach an estate where they could spend the night. On the far side of the plain a cloud of sand like a waterspout slowly swirled up into the sky. Eventually their tired eyes realized that what they were watching was not sand, but a pillar of yellow smoke.

'It looks like a smoke signal. . . .' Tanaka jumped up from the stone pillar on which he had been sitting and shaded his eyes with his hand.

'No, I don't think it is,' Nishi shook his head. The Japanese recalled the Indian smoke signal which had spiralled over the bald mountain outside Iguala many days earlier. This smoke was too thick to be a signal, and there were no other signals in response.

'I can see flames.' Standing apart from the others, Velasco was holding the spyglass up to his eye. The three envoys stared at him, waiting for his report.

'They must be burning a grove at one of the estates. In this country,' he nonchalantly lowered the glass from his eye, 'they often burn a grove of trees to make way for a field.'

'Lord Velasco.' Tanaka's voice was filled with anger. 'There's no reason to hide anything now. We know all about it.'

Caught off guard, Velasco's face reddened, and he stammered as he tried to explain himself.

'Lord Tanaka, I didn't keep anything from you out of spite.'

'It doesn't matter.' Tanaka shook his head sullenly. 'Your unnecessary concern for us is more a nuisance than anything else. We aren't women or children. It's nothing more than a peasant revolt, after all. What did you see?'

'They're burning the estates.'

The only way to reach Veracruz was to proceed directly across this sun-soaked plain; if they made a detour around the mountain range, their journey would be lengthened by many days. Velasco insisted that they set up camp outdoors that evening and move on the following morning, but Tanaka shook his head more persistently.

'The Indians have no grudge against the Japanese. This rising has nothing to do with us.'

'We have to avoid unnecessary mishaps as we pass through. Your mission is your most important concern, isn't it?'

'We know more about fighting than you, Lord Velasco. From now on leave everything to us.' Tanaka smiled loftily. 'Any objections, Hasekura and Nishi?'

Tanaka's juvenile bravado made the samurai feel uneasy. If

Matsuki Chūsaku were here, he thought.

'I have no objections, but I don't think there's any need for us to strike the first blow,' the samurai chided his colleague. 'There is something in what Lord Velasco says. Our mission comes first.'

The baggage on the donkeys' backs contained only twenty muskets. They got them out and formed a ring to protect Velasco and the donkey team, then sent their attendants ahead to act as scouts. Tanaka gave all the orders.

In the distance the smoke stained the sky an egg-yolk yellow. As they moved forward, within the smoke they could make out orange flames flapping faintly like moth's wings. Occasionally there was a distant sound like beans popping.

'Is that gunfire?'

Tanaka raised his hands to halt the group and listened intently for a few moments. Then like a true leader he nodded solemnly and said, 'No need to fear. It isn't gunfire. That's the sound of the fire crackling.' Unlike the samurai and Nishi, Tanaka spoke from experience – in his youth he had fought in His Lordship's wars.

They entered a belt of cultivated land. The fields of corn had been ruthlessly trampled down, and half the thatched huts among the banana groves had been burned.

Smoke trailed from one of the banana groves like a thin mist. There was a smell of burning. The Japanese could not see through the smoke to determine whether any Indians were hiding there, so Tanaka dismounted and, taking a gun from one of the attendants, strutted alone into the cloud of smoke, as if to demonstrate his daring to everyone. The others heard him coughing. Finally his voice echoed from the smoke. 'There's nothing to worry about. It's just a barn on fire.'

A large barn was burning. The interior had been reduced to ashes. Now the flames had formed a line and were scampering along the scorched uprights and roof beams like a troupe of dancing midgets. From time to time the sound of the beams collapsing added a measure of desolation to the scene.

Studying the ground closely like a seasoned warrior, Tanaka found a jumble of footprints.

'The natives have already passed through here,' he announced to the samurai and Nishi. Then he turned to Velasco, who was still clutching the reins of his horse and staring distractedly at the scene. 'What's the matter? Are you frightened, Lord Velasco?' he taunted. Velasco forced a smile. It was the first indication of weakness they had ever seen in the missionary.

'Well,' Tanaka rallied the group, as though to indicate that now he and not Velasco was giving the orders, 'let's get going. It will be dark soon.'

With the burning barn crackling behind them, the Japanese set out. They picked their way through the gloomy banana grove, their ears alert to every sound. Between the white trunks of the trees they caught glimpses of the sweltering sky and hills hunched like sleeping cats and blanketed with olive trees. When they emerged from the grove the sun beat against their foreheads. A tattered human smudge started to flee from beneath the shade of an olive tree. It was a pigtailed Indian woman with three children.

'I'm a padre,' Velasco called out. 'I'm a padre. There's no need to run!'

The woman and children turned towards Velasco with animal-like fear in their eyes.

'Don't you understand Spanish?'

The woman shouted something in a piercing, bird-like voice, but Velasco could not understand what she said.

'Quiet!' Tanaka pricked up his ears and silenced Velasco. He had heard something the others had not. The group stood motionless amid the heat and silence, staring fixedly at the hills.

Faintly they heard the sound of footsteps trampling the weeds. A single black head cautiously appeared. Blood flowed down the sunburned face. At the same time a group of armed Spaniards stood up from amongst the grass. When they noticed the Japanese they gawked at them in astonishment. Finally they spotted Velasco.

'I am a priest.' Velasco raised his hand and approached them, winding his way between the olive trees. After talking with the man whose cheeks were stained with a patch of blood like a flower petal, Velasco turned back to the Japanese.

'There's nothing to worry about. This is an *encomendero* and his servants who have come out to escort us.' He questioned the man about what had happened. 'Have the Huaxtecans got this far?'

'No, Padre,' the *encomendero* shook his head. 'The Indians around here heard of the rebellion, and now they are making trouble all over the place and burning barns. They set fire to the fields, and now they're hiding somewhere around here.'

'We have to get to Veracruz. . . .'

'We will go with you. Can the Japanese use muskets?'

'I imagine they can shoot a gun better than you. They're a people steeped in war.'

The *encomendero* and his men gave Velasco a dubious look but said nothing. The Indian woman who had been crouching beneath the olive tree drew her children to her with both arms, looked up, and called out something in her shrill, bird-like voice. The *encomendero* exploded at her.

'What is she saying?'

'She says we shot her brother . . . and that now he's dying.' The *encomendero* shrugged his shoulders. 'What difference does that make? But she says if you're a padre, she'd like you to offer extreme unction and a prayer for her brother.'

He spat on the ground and wiped at the blood that clung to his cheek like a decoration for valour.

'They fight against us, but when things go badly for them, they come begging to us. That's typical of the Indians. Don't bother with them.'

'Where is the dying man?'

'Don't be foolish. If you go, they'll take you hostage or kill you. It's an old trick of theirs. They use their women and children to throw you off guard, then they take you by surprise.'

'I am a priest,' Velasco answered softly. 'If you're a Christian you must understand. A priest has certain duties he must perform. Even if the recipient is an Indian. . . .'

'You can't feel sorry for them. Padre, you just can't trust these Indians.'

'I am a priest.' Velasco's face and neck suddenly flushed crimson. This always happened when he tried to suppress anger or a violent emotion.

'Padre, stop!'

As if to shake himself free of the man's words, Velasco started up the hill. When the Indian woman saw him, she left her children behind and ran barefoot after him, like a beast in pursuit of prey. The envoys, not knowing what was happening, began to follow them.

'Please wait there,' Velasco shouted from halfway up the hill. 'I'm not going now as an interpreter. I'm going in my calling as a Christian padre.'

The woman and Velasco entered a dark banana grove. The stench of rotting leaves filled the air. Somewhere a bird cried. To Velasco the sound seemed like the eerie shriek of a vulture feasting on carrion. The woman darted nimbly between the trees, turning from time to time to glance back at the slower missionary. Strangely he did not feel the slightest fear or apprehension. A pug-nosed, half-naked Indian stood with smouldering eyes in the shade of the thick growth of banana trees. At a word from the woman, he allowed Velasco to pass through the grove.

A young, bare-chested Indian lay panting in a small depression in the ground. A young woman sat beside him in a state of abstraction.

From a glance at the man's trousers, it was obvious that he too was a peon who worked on the farms. There was a clearly-defined bullet wound in his neck, caked with dirt and bood.

'Can you speak Spanish?' Velasco asked, but the man only went on panting heavily from his gaping mouth. His open eyes had ceased to focus, as though a thin veil had been drawn across them. Like gathering darkness death was setting into the body of this young Indian.

'*Habeas requiem aeternam,*' Velasco murmured, taking the young man's muddy, blood-stained hand. For that moment he ceased to be a missionary possessed by a burning ambition to convert Japan. He was now no different from a priest in a tiny village who holds vigil as an aged woman breathes her last.

'*Requiescat in pace.*'

As if he were shutting the last gateway of life, Velasco reached out and closed the eyes that seemed to be frozen open. Gazing at the wretched face, he thought of the Japanese Christian who had come to him at the lumber yard in Ogatsu to seek remission of his sins. That man dressed in tatters, with chips of wood still clinging to his shoulders. And that Japanese face. . . .

The wind swept through Veracruz, bouncing clumps of dead grass like balls along the walls of the stucco houses and the grey road, and dyeing the rough water out to sea a murky brown.

It was the windy season in Veracruz. The procession of exhausted Japanese staggered against the wind as they entered the city. Just as when they had arrived in Mexico City and Puebla, two cowled monks with folded arms stood waiting like bronze images at the entrance to the town. One of the envoys had a broken leg and was barely able to stay on his horse, and one of the attendants lay in a cart pulled by a donkey. They had been attacked by Indians along the way.

From the windows of their room in the monastery the envoys could see the turbulent sea baring its white fangs. Although different from the great ocean they had crossed for more than two months, the envoys were aware that this ocean was just as vast, and that when they had crossed it they would be setting foot on the continent of Europe, where such countries as España, Portugal, England and Holland were located.

As he gazed at the rough sea, the samurai thought, 'Compared to this world, His Lordship's domain where I lived was so tiny! The marshland and the tract of land at Kurokawa were like a single grain of sand. And yet my family has gone into battle, fought, and lived until this day for the sake of that one grain of sand.'

The day they had set sail from Tsukinoura, with the sound of creaking halyards and the shrill calls of seagulls echoing all around them, the samurai had felt he was being swept forward by a new destiny. At sea, and again in Nueva España, he had sensed an intangible change taking place within his heart. What that change might be he could not put into words; all he could be certain of was that he was no longer the person he had been in the marshland. And he was somehow afraid, wondering where this destiny would lead him, how it would finally change him.

The wind rattled the windows of the monastery all that night. At midnight rain began to fall.

The seasonal winds were blowing as we arrived in Veracruz. We are now staying in the Franciscan monastery here.

I can't help feeling that we were somehow able to survive the attack by the Huaxteca tribe because the Lord protected us for the sake of the work in Japan which I struggle so earnestly to accomplish. For the Lord granted me an unexpected opportunity to escape danger.

The day we set out from Córdoba, near one of the estates I administered the last rites and offered the final prayers for an Indian peon who had taken part in the riots with the Huaxtecans. The young Indian had sustained a mortal wound from the bullets of the Spanish *encomenderos*. I held his hand as he died in a little hollow amid a grove of banana trees. May the Lord grant him eternal life. I did only what I had to do as a priest.

Out of gratitude, two Indian peons, who saw what I did for the dead man, escorted us to the outskirts of Veracruz. They were our staunchest allies, and indeed it was because of them that we were able to survive a dangerous attack by the Huaxtecans.

It was the day before we were to reach Veracruz. We had taken a detour to avoid the estates which were the focal point of the attacks.

As ever the sun was merciless, and both men and horses were weary. We marched in single file between the crags that looked as if they had been sprinkled with salt. With our fuzzy perception we sometimes mistook the clusters of cactus trees for swarms of human beings.

We rested for a while. I was absently watching the movements of a vulture circling over the hills. The valley was so silent I began to feel somewhat uneasy.

Suddenly something black leaped out from a hill off to one side. At first I thought it was a bird. But it was no bird. Nearly a dozen pigtailed Huaxtecans carrying nets appeared on top of the crag. They had seen us from a distance and had lain in wait for us. They began hurling nets filled with stones at us.

I had heard before that Indians threw stones wrapped in netting. They had fought back with such weapons when our ancestors conquered Nueva España. I struggled to calm my rearing horse while the Japanese, at a sharp command from Tanaka, scurried to conceal themselves behind the cactus trees.

One of the men wasn't quick enough and tumbled to the ground. He was one of Tanaka's attendants. Tanaka rushed out from behind the cactus where he was concealed to rescue his attendant. Against the sun I saw a tall Huaxtecan aiming his stone net at the two men. I had a clear view of his pug nose, his white teeth and the pigtails that fell to his shoulders. And I watched as a white stone the size of a man's head plummeted towards the two Japanese.

The two Indians we had brought with us raced towards Tanaka. The next stone fell beside them. In pleading tones they shouted to the Huaxtecans on the crag. They must have told them that this was a group of Japanese, not Spaniards. Then miraculously, as if they had evaporated, our attackers disappeared from the crags.

It was all like a dream. The valley grew silent once again, and the sun smouldered whitely. The Japanese and I hurried from behind the cactus trees and gathered round the injured man. Tanaka's right leg was broken, but his attendant's knee had been split open like a pomegranate, and blood flowing from the wound was staining his leg a bright crimson. His joint might have been crushed. He tried to stand on his feet, but could not. After we placed him in a donkey-cart he continued to cry out in pain, and from time to time he called, 'I'm sorry,' to his master. 'Please take me with you,' he moaned. 'Even if you have to tie a rope around my neck and drag me. I must go back home!'

Enduring his own pain without a murmur, Tanaka repeatedly consoled his retainer. 'Yes, we'll take you with us. We'll take you with us.'

The relationship between the Japanese samurai and their attendants is exactly like that between noblemen and slaves in ancient Rome, but there are bonds in this relationship that go beyond mere personal interest, and an almost familial sense of love. In Japan I often felt that I must serve God the way these Japanese retainers serve their lords.

Now that I think of it, we were able to escape from the Huaxtecan ambush with only these few injuries thanks to those two Indian peons. I can't but feel that the Lord lent us His strength in that moment, too. We were a piteous sight when we entered Veracruz, but all my apprehensions had dissipated.

Veracruz is a harbour town sometimes swept by seasonal winds. Two days after our arrival Hasekura, Nishi and I had a taste of the winds when we went to call on the commandant of the fortress of San Juan de Ulúa, situated in what might be called the outer port of the city. We hoped to apply for passage on one of the vessels of the Spanish fleet which occasionally anchor here to prepare for their ocean voyages, and to request that a good army doctor provide medical treatment for Tanaka and his attendant. I knew there would be no problems with the former, since I had with me orders from the Viceroy in Mexico City.

When we arrived at San Juan de Ulúa, the winds were howling so strongly we could scarcely catch our breath. The sea was clouded a muddy brown, and three ships huddled fearfully behind the jetty. The fortress, which resembled the one in Acapulco, was surrounded by a dull grey wall, and the rotund, balding commandant greeted us in high spirits. He had already been notified of our coming by the Viceroy, and he merely glanced over our orders before putting them in a drawer of his desk.

'Padre, there's a letter for you here from your uncle,' he said, and as if in response to our orders, at once took a letter from the same drawer. 'I am acquainted with your uncle.'

I had not imagined that my good uncle Don Diego Caballero Molina would reply so quickly to the letter I had sent hastily from Acapulco. I placed the letter in its waterproof envelope carefully in my pocket.

The commandant was as delighted as a child with the Japanese sword the envoys gave him, and he granted us permission to take passage on the *Santa Veronica*, which is due to set sail as soon as these fierce winds die down. He then apologized to Hasekura and Nishi for the trials the Japanese had undergone.

We returned to the monastery, and that evening I finally had a chance to open my uncle's letter. He wrote that he had received my letter in Sevilla, and that the entire family would do all they could to help me achieve my desires.

'But you must be prepared to meet with formidable obstacles. That such obstacles will arise is clear from reading a petition to the King from the Jesuits, which we were able to obtain by certain means. I am enclosing a copy with this letter. It is filled with slanders and censures directed at you by the Jesuits.

'Also – and this too is based on information which the family has obtained – it appears that the Jesuits have been planning for some time to call a Council of Bishops after your arrival in Madrid to see to it that the purposes of the Japanese ambassadors are brought to naught. At the Council of Bishops, you will likely be matched against the famous Father Valente, who lived in Japan for thirty years. I know I needn't explain this to you, but Father Valente is a close friend and confidant of Father Valignano, who was the Provincial; he is also a scholar of history and a man respected here by both the high officials and the aristocracy. For this reason, you must make all necessary preparations for a confrontation with him.'

In the evening the strong winds continued to pound against the window of my room. I stood up and pressed my forehead against the glass, peering down into the courtyard beside the monastery. It was deserted. The only objects in sight were a few clumps of withered grass scattered here and there by the wind. The petition from the Society of Jesus which my uncle enclosed with his letter reads as follows:

'We have already submitted a report to Your Majesty concerning the journey of the Japanese ambassadors to Nueva España. If we may begin by expressing our conclusions on this matter, we feel that an attitude of caution is necessary in dealing with their request for mutual trade. According to reports from Jesuit fathers residing in Japan, Father Velasco of the Franciscans who accompanies the ambassadors is an imprudent man whose actions far exceed what is necessary. In Japan the king continues to persecute the Christians, and we of the Society of Jesus feel there is little possibility that freedom to proselytize will be allowed, as Velasco claims. This is not all – we should add that the Japanese are using freedom to proselytize as bait, when in fact their only purpose is to secure profits for themselves through trade. Furthermore, without consulting any of our missionaries in Japan, Father Velasco on his own initiative persuaded a Japanese feudal lord to construct a ship and send out the previously mentioned ambassadors to plead for the dispatch of missionaries to his domain. If their mission is successful, it will inevitably bring calamity upon the few missionaries and Christians who remain in Japan, and the end result will be tragic. His exaggerated, overblown designs are all a mass of falsehoods, and we therefore desire that Your Majesty respond to them with the appropriate discretion.'

The wind filtering in through cracks along the window extinguished the flame of my stubby candle. I made no move to relight it, but sat in the darkness for a long while, supporting my head with both hands as I tried to imagine how Father Valente, whom I would soon confront face to face, might look. His name is known to every missionary who has ever been to Japan. He is the author of *A History of Proselytization in Japan*, a missionary whose labours covered every region in Kyushu and Kamigata, and a man respected by Hideyoshi and his retainers such as Konishi Yukinaga and Takayama Ukon.* If that had been the sum total of the matter, however, I would not have been so lost in thought. But he is no common priest – I had long heard that he is a debater possessed of a shrewd mind and subtle skill. As my uncle said, I would have to prepare myself well. Like a soldier who is braced for the enemy's attack no matter what form it takes or whence it comes, I would have to prepare impenetrable defences against the doubts he would thrust at me, the questions he would fire at me. In the darkness, I dropped off to sleep with my head propped upon my desk. . . .

---

* Konishi Yukinaga (1558?-1600) and Takayama Ukon (1552-1615) were influential Kyushu *daimyōs* who converted to Christianity. After the expulsion edict, Takayama died in exile in Manila; Konishi, who sided against the Tokugawas in the decisive battle of Sekigahara, was executed by the victors. Both died faithful Christians.

Chapter 6

Our ship is now sailing up the Guadalquivir River towards Coria.

Our voyage across the Atlantic took so long because the *Santa Veronica* met with strong winds and suffered considerable damage; she had to lie in the harbour at Havana for six months while repairs were being made. In Havana Tanaka Tarozaemon's poor retainer died. This was the man who sustained critical wounds in his knee. Tanaka's despondency even after the man's burial has been pitiful to behold. I often saw the haughty fellow staring glumly at the Caribbean Sea, as if he had lost his own brother. Thereafter we encountered two further storms spawned by the seasonal winds. It was ten months after we set out from Veracruz that we at last sighted the port of San Lucar in my homeland of España.

Not for a moment during our voyage did my thoughts turn from the words of caution my uncle had written to me from Madrid. The figure of Father Valente, with whom I would soon have to debate before a group of bishops, floated constantly before my eyes.

In my imagination Father Valente was a tall, thin man with sunken cheeks like an ascetic. The sharpness of his mind seemed to emanate from the light that flashed in his eyes. I felt as though his low voice clawed at the weakest parts of my arguments and spread open those gaping wounds for all to see. If I relaxed for even a moment, he would be sure to pounce on me with a barrage of questions, or set a trap for me with his words and lie in wait until a discrepancy appeared in my line of reasoning.

I tried to anticipate each of the questions with which he might assail me. He would surely ask in what capacity these envoys were dispatched. And no doubt he would lay bare the contradiction in the fact that on the one hand the Naifu was persecuting the Christians and on the other sending out ambassadors. And he would certainly criticize me for covering up the nearly desperate state of missionary work in Japan, not only covering it up but insisting that there are grounds for optimism in the future.

As I conjured up all the questions I could think of, I tried to put my answers into words, like a seminary student before an examination. But as I did so, a feeling that was somehow at once angry and at the same time sad surged within me. Why should clergymen professing the same faith as mine try to frustrate my attempts to make Japan into a nation of the Lord? Why should they try to interfere?

I thought then of Paul, who was pitted against the Apostles at Jerusalem because he took the gospel to the Gentiles. Even Paul was hindered, reviled and abused by other Christians. The Christians at the Church headquarters in Jerusalem gave it out that Paul was unqualified to be an apostle, and they even criticized his missionary labours because he tried to carry the word of the Lord beyond national borders and without respect to race. In the same manner the Jesuits consider me a priest unworthy to proselytize in Japan.

As I try to contain the anger welling within me, an indescribable sadness consumes my breast. Though we believe in the same God, worship the same Lord Jesus, and share the same desire to make Japan a nation of God, we feud and fight amongst ourselves. Why must men always be so ugly and selfish? Instead of becoming purer within the structure of our religious societies, at times we become uglier than any layman. We seem at this point to be far removed from the obedience, the long-suffering and the limitless meekness which the saints possessed.

Last night a heavy shower pelted our ship as it moved upstream. I awoke to the fierce drumming of the rain. Much to my shame, I had experienced a wet dream. I bound my wrists tightly precisely that I might not commit sin at times like this. This was how I had to fight through the night against the powerful lusts of my flesh, though they are not as violent now as in my youth. I knelt and prayed. How loathsome this physical body is. As I prayed, I was suddenly overcome by a terrifying sense of despair. Drop by drop I tasted the poison seeping through my soul, and I felt as though I had just discovered my own ugly face in a mirror. The lusts of my flesh, my hatred for the Jesuits, my almost arrogant confidence in my work in Japan, my thirst for conquest – one after another they surged up from the depths of my soul, to the point that I could no longer feel that the Lord would listen to my prayers and my petitions. I felt as if He were pointing a finger at me, showing me the abominable ugliness of the selfish ambition that lurked behind my prayers and my aspirations.

'No, it's not true!' I protested frantically. 'I have limitless love for Japan and the Japanese people. It's because of that love that I want to arouse them from their lukewarm stupor. As a priest I would have no regrets were I to devote my entire life to that purpose. All I do is for Thy sake.'

But the tiny crucifix on my desk – from that crucifix the Lord looked at me sadly, and listened sadly to my protests.

'Then, Lord. would you have me abandon Japan? Should I leave the Japanese, so blessed with superior talents and strengths, in their torpor? Somehow these people seem determined to defend as a peculiar part of themselves these feelings which are "neither cold nor hot", as the Bible describes them. What I want to give them is that warmth which seeks after Thee.'

Only one way to prevail against Father Valente. To see to it that the envoys become Christians in Madrid. Just as I had the Japanese merchants baptized in Mexico City. If that happens, the bishops will believe that what I say is true. Just as the Viceroy of Mexico City acceded to my views because of those glorious baptisms.

The envoys travelled up the Guadalquivir River and at last set foot on European soil. They landed in the Spanish city of Sevilla. A year and a half earlier, they had never even heard the name of this town, much less realized that such a place existed.

It was the beginning of autumn. Beyond fields bathed in soft sunlight, white houses stretched as far as the eye could see. Cathedral spires thrusting into the clear sky were visible in every direction. Many ships made their way up and down the river, and on the banks a profusion of flowers bloomed freshly beneath the sun. Every corner of the town smelt of flowers, pots adorned the white window-sills of every house, and through the elaborately decorated gates they could see tiled courtyards lined with sculptures and flower pots. The interiors of the houses were enclosed by walls decorated with an intricate ultramarine pattern, and a dark and peculiar odour emanated from within.

The first Spanish town they had ever seen. Until they set out on this voyage, these three lance-corporals had never seen beyond His Lordship's fief, knew nothing even of Kyoto or Edo, so everything in this grand city was a source of surprise to them. Velasco explained that in former days Sevilla, before it was conquered by Spanish Christians, had been inhabited by Arabs. But the envoys had no idea where the country of Arabia was located, or what traces the Arabs had left behind in this city. They gasped at the grandeur of palaces like El Alcazar, and they were awed and rendered speechless by the towering cathedral buildings.

Each day brought a flurry of activity unlike anything they had experienced in Mexico City. With the assistance of Velasco's family, who were natives of the city, the envoys rode in a carriage to meet the mayor, paid calls on councillors, and received invitations from members of the aristocracy and high-ranking clergymen. They were engulfed in a maelstrom of incomprehensible words, forced down a variety of unfamiliar foods, and struggled with all their might to hold out to the end.

'*This* is Europe!'

From the top of a towering cathedral one afternoon they looked out over Sevilla, and Velasco pointed out each of the many spires, identifying one as the Church of San Stephano, another as the Cathedral of San Pedro. Then in a sardonic tone he said, 'This is the España that everyone in Japan talks about.' He laughed aloud. 'On this voyage you've gained some idea of how huge the world is. It's no exaggeration to say that España is the wealthiest nation in all that vast world. . . . And now you are in that very nation. You are in the land of the foreigners!'

Tanaka kept his arms folded and lowered his eyes to keep his excitement from showing on his face. Nishi was the only one who took out a writing case and zealously copied down names of all the buildings and churches Velasco pointed out.

'But Sevilla cannot begin to compare in size with Madrid, the capital of España. In Madrid you will be meeting the King of España.'

Velasco was aware that Tanaka and the samurai were trembling.

'Yet there is another person before whom even the King of España humbly kneels. Do you know who that is?'

The three envoys had no answer.

'That person is the king of the Christians, who is known as the Pope. If we compare the situation to Japan, the Naifu might be like the King of España, and the Emperor in Kyoto might be like the Pope. But the Pope has infinitely greater power than your Emperor. Still, even the Pope is no more than a servant to one other person.' With a smile Velasco peered into the faces of the envoys. 'I think you know without my saying it who that Person is. . . . You have seen His image in every part of Nueva España. And not only in Nueva España. Nor only here in España. Every nation in Europe adores Him, and worships Him, and bows down before Him.'

With a definite purpose in mind, Velasco took the three envoys to the Cathedral of San Francisco the following Sunday. On that day Bishop Lerma was to say a special Mass for the Japanese ambassadors. From early morning wheels squeaked along the paved roads as the carriages funnelled one after another into the entrance of the great cathedral. Lavishly dressed nobles and merchants crowded round the stone columns, flames from a multitude of candlesticks illuminated the golden altar, and the strains of the organ reverberated against the stone walls of the chapel. From the pulpit, decorated with spiralling ornaments, Bishop Lerma blessed the people and proclaimed, 'Today, in the company of Father Velasco, a native of Sevilla, emissaries who have crossed the thousands of leagues of ocean from the Oriental nation of Japan have joined with us to celebrate the Mass. For this reason, we would like to offer this Mass for the benefit of those emissaries and for all the Japanese people. Just as over the years our ancestors have erected churches in many foreign lands and moulded them into nations of God, let us pray that someday the land of these emissaries will also praise the Lord.'

The multitudes jamming the chapel all knelt, and the choir sang a hymn.

> *Sanctus, sanctus, sanctus*
> *Dominus Deus Sabaoth*
> *Pleni sunt coeli et terra.*

Velasco buried his face in his hands and gave way to the emotions rising up within him. 'O Japan, Japan,' he called out from the depths of his heart. 'Hear these voices. Japan, Japan. However much you ignore the Lord, however many priests you slaughter, however much of the blood of the faithful you shed, one day you will serve the Lord.' He bowed his head and prayed. 'O Lord, to that end . . . let me win the battle. Help me to prevail over Father Valente.'

When the Mass ended, the crowd, still ecstatic, swarmed around the envoys and like a torrent of water swept them out of the cathedral. They mobbed the Japanese, patting their shoulders and shaking their hands, and they made no move to leave until Bishop Lerma escorted Velasco and the emissaries to shelter in a subterranean room beneath the cathedral.

'Well, my son.' When they reached the dark, musty, underground room away from the cheering voices of the congregation, Bishop Lerma looked at Velasco with concern. 'The ceremonies have ended. Now we must return to reality. You must not be deceived by all this furore. The situation does not bode well for you. A Council of Bishops is being assembled for you in Madrid, but such a council will by no means look with favour on your ideas.'

'I am aware of that,' Velasco nodded, glancing quickly over at the envoys. 'But just now Your Lordship said you would like to offer up the Mass today for the benefit of the emissaries and the Japanese people. You asked with all of us that someday Japan will become a nation that praises the Lord.'

'It's true that I said "someday". But that day is not now. Even at this distance, we know how much the Japanese have hated the missionaries and persecuted the faithful for the past twenty years.'

'The situation is changing.' Velasco made the same speech he had delivered to the Archbishop in Mexico City. 'If that were not so, Japan would not have sent these emissaries to España.'

'My son. Our brethren of the Society of Jesus report that the situation grows worse each day. They tell us that these emissaries are not official representatives of the King of Japan, but merely knights in the service of a single Japanese lord. . . . We do not want any more priests to shed their blood in that land.'

'I believe that missionary work is like a battle. I'm fighting a battle with Japan. A missionary is like a warrior who must not be afraid of dying for the Lord. The Apostle Paul surely did not grudge spilling his own blood for the sake of the Gentiles. Missionary work is not the same as sitting cosily in the sunshine or in a monastery and talking of God's love.'

'Yes.' Velasco's irony did not escape the Bishop's notice. 'I agree with you that missionary work is like a battle. And just as every warrior must obey his leader, you too must be obedient.'

'There are times when the leader is far removed from the field of battle and knows nothing of the true nature of the fighting.'

'My son,' the Bishop looked steadily into Velasco's face, 'you are too impassioned. You must examine your heart to be sure that in the future your passion does not do damage to your soul.'

Velasco flushed and gave no answer. It was just as the Bishop said. The fervour of his character had occasioned words of caution from his superiors throughout his long period of religious training. 'Yet without that fervour,' Velasco thought, 'I would never have gone to Japan. To do battle there, I have to be impassioned.'

'We are going to Madrid from here. I have a request I would like to make directly to the Archbishop. . . .'

'What is it?'

'I would like the King to grant an audience to the Japanese ambassadors. . . .'

Bishop Lerma gave Velasco a look of pity and extended his hand to accept a kiss. 'I pray that the Archbishop will grant your request.' Then in a despairing tone he repeated, 'But you are too impassioned. Take care that your fervour does not destroy your soul.'

When the crowds had dispersed and Bishop Lerma had disappeared into the diocesan offices, and when the Japanese had returned in a carriage to their lodgings at the monastery, Velasco knelt alone at the altar of the great cathedral. Except for the few shafts of sunlight shining through the stained-glass windows, the spacious chapel was dark and silent. The eucharist candlesticks on the altar burned redly, and beside them the glorified Christ gazed down at Velasco with one hand raised. This was how He had looked when He told His disciples, 'Go ye into all the world, and preach the gospel to every creature.'

'O Lord,' Velasco pleaded, his hands clasped as he peered into the eyes of the Christ. 'You commanded us to preach the gospel to the ends of the earth. I have devoted my life to those words and journeyed to Japan. Do you intend now to withdraw Your hand from there?

'O Lord, please answer me. Japan is about to be cast away from Thy voice. The Church which Thou hast established is about to forsake Japan. The archbishops, the bishops and the cardinals fear Japan; they abhor the thought of any more priests spilling their blood in that land, and they would desert the saints who still remain there. O Lord, please answer me. Must I too submit to the orders of that Church?

'O Lord, command me to fight. I am alone. Please tell me to fight those who hinder me and envy me. I cannot abandon Japan. That tiny Asian nation is the one country I must conquer with the power of Thy gospel.'

Sweat coursed down Velasco's forehead, streaming into his eyes as he held his head high to stare into the face of Christ. A multitude of Japanese faces flashed through his mind. Their thin smiles mocked Velasco. They were like the faces on the Buddhist statues he had once seen in the sanctuary of a Kyoto temple. With one voice they murmured, 'Japan does not want the Christian fathers to come. Japan does not want churches to be built. Japan can survive without Jesus. Japan. . . .'

'Go.' Suddenly a voice sounded in Velasco's ears. 'Behold, I send you forth as sheep in the midst of wolves; be ye therefore wise as serpents, and harmless as doves. And ye shall be hated of all men for my name's sake; but he that endureth to the end shall be saved. Be ye wise as serpents.'

These were the words Jesus spoke to His disciples when He sent them forth into the villages of Judaea. 'Be ye therefore wise as serpents.' For a long while Velasco was motionless, his face buried in his hands. He felt as though his own future and everything he must do hereafter were contained within those words. 'I will be hated of all men. By the brethren of the Society of Jesus. By the bishops here. But I will go to Madrid, and there confront the Jesuits and the Council of Bishops. To achieve victory in that encounter I must show wisdom like a serpent's. My weapons are words and the Japanese I have brought here. I must make the bishops believe that my words are the words of the Japanese, that my wishes are the wishes of the Japanese. To do that . . .'

Velasco returned to the monastery and went to the envoys' room. The envoys and their attendants had congregated on the sunlit balcony to watch the streams of people and the traffic of carriages making their way past the tower of Giralda, the pride of the citizens of Sevilla. The Guadalquivir River was jammed with ships, and they could hear the voices of merchants selling their cargo.

When the attendants noticed Velasco, they bowed and quietly withdrew. The missionary stood beside the three envoys on the balcony, pointing out the boats that moved up and down the Guadalquivir beneath the gentle autumn sun, and explaining that many ships set out from this port for a host of nations.

'Two days from now we will leave for Madrid, which is the capital of España. There you will have your audience.'

'Then have we actually been granted an audience with the King?' Tanaka's voice trembled with excitement.

'I have to be honest with you. . . . An unexpected obstacle has presented itself.' Velasco hesitated for a moment, then went on, 'There are some in Madrid who do not think well of us.'

The envoys looked at one another and waited for Velasco to explain. As the missionary spoke, Tanaka stared glumly off into space, while the samurai blinked his eyes and volunteered not a single word. It was impossible to determine from their rustic faces what they were thinking, but young Nishi alternately folded his arms and wrung his hands in apprehension. Somehow the three envoys seemed to be able to comprehend what Velasco told them about the situation in the Church and the history of the conflict between the two brotherhoods concerning missionary work in Japan.

'And so I must go the Council to debate. High-ranking ecclesiastics will attend the debates and judge whether my words or the claims of those who slander me are correct.'

Velasco paused. Then, as though speaking to himself he muttered, 'I . . . I must win.'

The envoys were motionless, as if their bodies had frozen stiff.

'Those who slander me . . . they say that Christianity has been proscribed throughout all Japan, and they are spreading rumours that the letters from His Lordship welcoming the padres are a fraud. To dispel these doubts . . . if even one of you were to become a Christian. . . .'

At those words, a look of child-like astonishment raced across the normally expressionless faces of Tanaka and the samurai. Velasco pressed on, hoping to stifle that astonishment.

'If that were to happen, the ecclesiastics here would believe what I say. They would accept His Lordship's promise that the Christians will not be abused, and that the padres will be welcomed with open arms. At this moment the Church authorities here accept without question the reports of those who say that the Japanese are slaughtering Christians and torturing the padres.'

The samurai scowled at Velasco. For the first time Velasco saw anger on the face of this normally docile man.

'Padre.' The samurai's voice quavered. 'Why didn't you tell us this in Nueva España? You must have known all this in Nueva España.'

'To tell the truth, I had no idea that the slanders had spread this far abroad. No, actually, while we were still in Nueva España, they were sending frequent letters from Japan to España in an attempt to impede our journey.'

'I . . .,' the samurai announced in a voice that was almost a groan, 'I will not become a Christian.'

'Why not?'

'I do not like Christianity.'

'If you know nothing of the teachings of Christianity, you can't either like or dislike it.'

'Even if I studied them, I would not believe.'

'You cannot believe if you do not study.'

Velasco's face and neck became increasingly flushed. At this moment, he was no longer a schemer, but a missionary expounding his beliefs to those who had no understanding.

'In Mexico City the Japanese merchants converted to Christianity, but it was not from their hearts. They did it for profit. But I accepted that. Because I believed that those who accept the name of the Lord even once will eventually become His captives.'

A voice sounded in Velasco's ears. 'What you are trying to do now? To baptize men who do not believe in the Lord, for your own benefit, is a blasphemy and a profanation. It is an act of arrogance, and through the sacrament of baptism you heap the sins of unbelievers upon the Lord.'

Velasco struggled to exorcize the voice. He took one of Christ's statements as his shield. When John had raged at discovering unbelievers healing the sick in the name of Jesus, the Lord had said, 'He that is not against us is for us.'

The samurai remained stubbornly silent. The timid man grew obstinate in such circumstances precisely because of his timidity. Tanaka stared as usual at a spot in the air, while Nishi, also characteristically, waited in apprehension for his seniors to respond before forming his own opinion. Finally the samurai answered in a firm voice, like a heavy, immovable boulder.

'No. I cannot. I cannot become a Christian.'

After Velasco had left the room, the three envoys sat down in their chairs and remained motionless for some time. Noises of activity at the Toriana Gate streamed through the open window. In the afternoon Sevilla quietened down for a while. The residents shut themselves up in their houses and took a leisurely siesta.

Nishi glanced sheepishly at the weary faces of his companions. 'Lord Shiraishi told us we were to follow Lord Velasco's instructions in all matters during our voyage.'

'But, Nishi,' the samurai sighed, 'how many times has Lord Velasco deceived us since we left Japan? It's just as Matsuki said. First Velasco told us that if we went to Nueva España, we could complete our mission at once. But when we got to Nueva España, he said we wouldn't be able to get a definite answer unless we continued on to España. . . . And now today he tells us that things are not going well. That if we want our mission to succeed we ought to become Christians. I don't believe anything he says any more. Don't you agree, Nishi?'

This was the first time the samurai had revealed his own feelings to such a degree. Because he was a man of few words, each and every word he spoke carried weight, and when he finished speaking both his companions remained silent.

'But we can't do anything without Lord Velasco's help.'

'That's what Lord Velasco is capitalizing on. All he really wants is to force us to become Christians.'

'But we could become Christians, as a formality to help further our mission. It would be simple.'

'Yes,' the samurai looked up and sighed. 'When the fiefs were reorganized, the Hasekura family was given a barren marshland. We get hardly any rice or wheat from the land. But we have moved the graves of our ancestors and the grave of my father to that land rimmed with hills. I can't be the only one in my family to convert to a foreign religion that my father and my ancestors never knew.'

The samurai blinked his eyes. He sensed the blood of many generations of the Hasekura family flowing through his own body, their ways permeating his own life. He could not wilfully alter that blood or those ways by himself.

'Besides that . . .,' he continued, 'remember what Matsuki said to us in Mexico City. That Velasco is too passionate. That we must not be caught up in Velasco's fervour and become Christians. Don't you remember that, Nishi?'

'I remember, but. . . .' Perhaps in fear of a reprimand, Nishi looked anxiously at his fellow envoys. 'The Council of Elders seems to think that the future of Japan lies not in battles, but in trade with India and the countries of Europe. And they know very well that, whatever the case may be in India, trade with the nations of Europe will not be possible if we ignore Christianity. So long as that is their policy, they will surely understand that, if we become Christians, we did so only as a means of accomplishing our mission.'

'Are you intending to become a Christian?' Tanaka asked sharply.

'I don't know. I'll have to give it a lot of thought as we travel to Madrid. But on this journey I've realized how huge the world is. I've learned that the nations of Europe surpass Japan in wealth and grandeur. That's why I'd like to learn their languages. I don't think we can simply close our eyes to the beliefs of all of the people in this vast world.'

As ever, the samurai envied Nishi his vibrant youth. Unlike himself or Tanaka, this young man was effortlessly drinking in, almost inhaling, everything that was new and surprising in these foreign lands. Nevertheless, although the samurai had resolved to surrender to his new destiny, in the final analysis his attachments to the marshland and to his family, attachments from which he could not separate himself any more easily than a snail could tear itself from its shell, prevented him from doing so.

'What do you think, Lord Tanaka?' As the samurai gazed at Tanaka's thick arms and broad back, he sensed the same blood flowing through his comrade's veins. The blood of a rural samurai – that blood which stubbornly sought to defend the lands and customs their forebears had protected for so many years.

'I . . . I don't like the Christians either.' Tanaka emitted a feeble sigh. 'But, Hasekura, I didn't take on this mission because I was ordered to by the Council of Elders. I took it because I wanted to get back our old fief at Nihonmatsu. It's because I want those lands back that I've put up with those miserable sea voyages, with the heat and with that disgusting foreign food. . . .'

The samurai was no different. If what Lord Shiraishi and Lord

Ishida said were true, the lands at Kurokawa might be returned to the Hasekura family as a reward for his making this difficult journey.

'If we don't get our lands back,' Tanaka muttered tearfully, 'I shall be disgraced. I shall be unable to face my family with honour. I don't like the Christians. But to get back our lands . . . if they told me to eat dirt, I would eat dirt.'

'It's for the sake of the mission,' Nishi added.

'Matsuki told me not to become a Christian.' The samurai shook his head obstinately. 'I don't like Matsuki . . . but I can't become a Christian.'

They resumed their long journey; their destination was now Madrid. In single file, the Japanese, their carriages and horse carts advanced across the Andalusian Plain.

Hills and olive groves appeared one after another like waves upon the sea. The hills were reddish-brown and the silver olive leaves glittered like the blades of myriad swords as they fluttered in the wind. At the approach of evening the ground chilled swiftly.

Occasionally they caught glimpses of the same white villages, looking rather like piles of salt, that they had seen in Nueva España. Some of these villages clung to the sides of the hills as if they had been fastened there with glue. An ancient fortress towered menacingly on top of one of the hills.

Once the olive groves and patches of red earth had run their course, wheat-fields stretched out in a bow-like curve as far as the horizon. At the furthest edge of the horizon the party sighted something that looked like a tiny needle. As they drew nearer, they realized that the needle was the spire of a church. Its tip stabbed at the blue sky and was swallowed up within it.

'*This* is Europe!' Velasco reined in his horse and pointed proudly. 'The earth has its own labours to perform. As a symbol of those labours, this spire reaches up into the skies in search of the Lord.'

Since their departure from Sevilla, he had not pressed the envoys again for their co-operation. He had not tried even indirectly to make them convert. Yet he smiled confidently from his horse, as though everything had already been decided. In their usual manner the envoys made no mention of the subject, as though it were something to be dreaded.

At the point where the colours of the Tajo River changed and water tinged with brown flowed across the fields, the group entered the ancient capital of Toledo. Here too the spire of the great cathedral built upon a hill could be seen from far off. The large evening sun was setting in the golden sky, and the cross on top of the cathedral sparkled dazzlingly in its reflected rays. The sweat-soaked Japanese silently climbed the sloping stone-paved path towards the cathedral, conscious as ever of the curious stares of the townspeople.

'*Japoneses!*' called someone from the crowd lining the slope. '*Me han encontrado con Japoneses antes.*' He was a beaming, snaggletoothed man. At the voice, Velasco stopped his horse in surprise and spoke to the man.

'This man,' Velasco told the envoys, 'says that when he was a child, he saw a group of Japanese youths who visited this town.'

'Japanese . . .?'

'He says that about thirty years ago, some young men from Kyushu, perhaps thirteen or fourteen years old, came to España as Christian emissaries, just like you. Have you heard anything about this?'

They had not. They had blithely assumed that they themselves were the first Japanese to visit these foreign lands. But this townsman claimed that a group of Japanese, led by four youths and accompanied by a missionary, had come to Toledo and Madrid some thirty years before, and had even had an audience with the Pope in Rome.

Velasco turned back to the man. He was smiling proudly, apparently delighted that everyone around him was listening to what he said.

'The Japanese youths visited the home of an old man of the village, the watchmaker Toriano. They were very pleased with their visit. This man says he was working as an apprentice in the old man's house then.'

The middle-aged man bared his yellowed teeth, pointed to his own face, and nodded over and over. The envoys also learned that one of the Japanese youths had been stricken with a high fever here, but thanks to the careful nursing and prayers of the townspeople he had recovered, and finally he and his comrades had set out for Madrid in a fleet of four carriages.

The Japanese gazed around at the stone pathways and the houses illuminated by the declining sun. A feeling of wonder came over them as they realized that their own countrymen had climbed this same slope before them, looking at these same foreign houses dyed pink in the setting sun.

'Children thirteen or fourteen years old . . .!' Tanaka gasped. The other Japanese also thought of their own long, painful journey and could scarcely believe that a group of young men had undergone a similar ordeal.

'Did those children return safely to Japan?' Nishi asked Velasco.

'Yes, they did,' Velasco nodded broadly. 'Just as one day each of you will.'

At Velasco's reply, a profound silence fell over the Japanese. Would they really be able to return home safely someday? They all shared the same thought. Eventually a faint, almost tearful smile flickered across each man's face.

On the day the group finally reached Madrid, rain was falling. The rain moistened the Plaza de Castilla and fell softly on Calle de Alcalá. Against the mist-clouded sky the Palace of El Escorial hovered like a grey mirage. Carriages filled the paved roads, splashing mud and water in all directions.

At the Franciscan monastery the Japanese slept like stones for an entire day. Now that they had reached their final destination, the physical and mental fatigue that had been accumulating since their arrival in España came over them in a rush. Aware of the situation, the monks at the monastery kept their distance from the building where the Japanese were sleeping and refrained from ringing the bell which usually tolled the hour.

In his dreams the samurai saw scenes from the day of his departure. Horses whinnied; the village elders were lined up before the gate of his residence; Yozō carried the samurai's spear; Seihachi, Ichisuke and Daisuke led three horses laden with baggage. When the samurai mounted his horse, he bowed his head to his uncle. Riku stood behind, struggling to keep back her tears. He smiled at his elder son Kanzaburō, and at his younger son Gonshirō, cradled in a servant girl's arms. Then for some reason Lord Ishida was waiting on his horse outside the gate. The samurai could not understand why Lord Ishida had come all the way to the marshland to meet him.

'Listen now,' Lord Ishida smiled and nodded. 'We will give you just one more chance to carry out your mission. Next time for sure, I will see to it that you get your lands in Kurokawa.' Then do I have to repeat this dreadful journey? The thought all but suffocated the samurai. But he realized that it was his destiny, and he had no choice but to obey. Endurance and submission – like the peasants in the marshland, over the long years these traits had become a part of him. . . .

After he opened his eyes, it took him a while to realize that this was not Japan, but a monastery in a strange country. Rain was streaming down the window of an unfamiliar building in a foreign town. It was quiet. The samurai felt so alone he could almost have wept.

Quietly, so as not to awake Nishi, he put on his clothes and crept out into the hallway. He peered into his attendants' room. Yozō was sitting distractedly on the edge of his bed. Beside him Ichisuke and

Daisuke were fast asleep.

'Are you awake?' the samurai whispered to Yozō. 'I . . . dreamed about the marshland.'

'They must be starting to cut firewood about now.'

'I suppose so.'

Nearly a year and a half had passed since they had set out on this journey. The samurai thought of the days he had spent about this time two years before, working alongside the peasants in the thicket to cut timber for firewood. As their axes hacked at the trees, the sounds echoed sharply through the silent grove where the leaves had just begun to fall. Kanzaburō and his younger brother gathered mushrooms in that grove.

'We just have to hold on a little longer,' the samurai muttered, glancing at the window misted with rain. 'Once our mission is accomplished here in the capital . . . all that is left is to return to the marshland.'

Yozō nodded, resting his hands on his knees.

'But that's if everything goes smoothly. . . . Lord Velasco says for that to happen we must become Christians.'

Yozō looked up in surprise. The samurai asked, 'What . . . what will you do?'

'Ever since Seihachi died . . .,' Yozō started to say, but he caught himself and answered, 'No, I will do whatever Your Lordship orders.'

'What I order?' The samurai smiled forlornly. 'Nothing like this has ever happened in the Hasekura family. My uncle would never permit such a thing.'

The samurai mulled over his dream of the marshland. The marshland, crammed with farmhouses that seemed squashed together. But in that marshland, everyone shared in the lives of everyone else, with the samurai's family as the nucleus. Their lives, their very way of living, were all in harmony. Each family tended its fields in the same manner, planted its seeds in the same manner, and observed its festivals in the same manner. When someone died, everyone participated in the funeral rites. The samurai thought of the hymn of praise to Amida Buddha that his uncle often chanted as he massaged his wounded leg beside the sunken hearth.

> Ten eons have passed
> Since Amida entered into Nirvana.
> The halo emanating from the Buddha's sublime body
> Illumines every corner of this hell of darkness.

When he had finished chanting the hymn, his uncle would always repeat, 'Praise to the Amida Buddha. Praise to the Amida Buddha,' over and over again in a low voice, and a look of relief would appear on his face. The samurai could almost hear his voice now. Yes, in the marshland everything was as one. The samurai did not intone such hymns himself, but he could not abandon the faith revered by his father and his uncle. That would be tantamount to betraying his own flesh and blood, betraying the marshland.

I set out in a carriage for the home of my cousin Don Luis. His father Don Diego Caballero Molina, who is staying with him, is a former mayor of Sevilla, and even now the elderly gentleman wields considerable influence in the Church and the court. Don Luis is President of the Inquisition Court.

When I arrived at my cousin's house, it appeared that word of my visit had been sent before me, for a swarm of men, women and children came hurrying down the staircase to greet me. The children sprang upon me. The women embraced me in a typically exaggerated fashion, and the men gave me all the handshakes their dignity would allow. They surrounded me, this relative who had returned from a strange Asian country, and were eager to hear me recount my experiences. In the drawing-room and again in the dining-room they hung upon my words as if they were hearing tales of how our conquering ancestors had overrun continents and chains of uncharted islands.

When we finished with supper and with our small-talk in the drawing-room, my uncle Molina signalled to me with his eyes. He led me into his study, together with his son Luis. It appeared that the others had been told what would happen, for they compliantly bade me farewell.

We talked for some time about our strategy for the impending debate. My tall, thin uncle paced about the room as he informed me that my prospects in the Council of Bishops looked dim. Luis stood stiffly like a sentinel, listening to our conversation.

'You say that missionary work is like a battle, but there are moments in battle when one must retreat. At the present time the bishops here want to retreat from Japan. If the Council of Bishops does not come out in your favour, the family will be able to obtain you a position as Father Superior . . . not in Japan, but in Manila.'

My uncle explained that they intended to exhaust every effort in order to obtain for me the position of Superior at the Franciscan monastery in Manila.

'Your chances seem very good. I seriously doubt whether the cardinals or the bishops will oppose you.'

The sound of his pacing footsteps ceased, and my uncle sat down in a chair and clasped his hands, peering at me to see what reaction I would have to his words.

'I'm not sure I quite understand what you mean. . . .'

'No one wants you to be exposed to danger, even if it is in the Lord's cause. I'm sure there will be even greater opportunity for you to cultivate your talents as the Superior at the Manila monastery.'

I closed my eyes and thought of the beggarly hut in Edo where Diego and I had lived. That hospital where we took in lepers had only three rooms. Cockroaches and rats scurried about every corner of the building, and a filthy sewer flowed outside our door. At the monastery in Manila, instead of vermin, there would be birds singing in the trees of the garden, and no need to eat spoiled fish and foul-smelling rice.

'I am a missionary,' I murmured, still smiling. 'I'm sure I must have been born to be a missionary. My work is not to pray in safe, resplendent cathedrals. My work is to preach the word of God in lands where persecution continues to rage.'

My uncle shrugged his shoulders and sighed. His gesture was precisely like that of the Bishop in Sevilla when he heard my reply.

'You've been like this ever since you were a child. When you were just a little boy, you were fascinated by sailors like Columbus. . . .'

'If Mother hadn't put me in the minor seminary, I'm sure I would have become a soldier or a seaman,' I laughed.

'Your mother sent you to the seminary to subdue some of your fervour.'

'Well, after all, the blood of my ancestors the conquerors flows through my veins. . . .'

My uncle and cousin had never seen Japan and knew nothing of the country; it was difficult to make them understand how I felt. And my cousin, standing there like a sentinel, looked at me with apprehension in his eyes. He was afraid that by getting embroiled in my schemes, he and his family would be inviting the scorn of the nobility and the clergy of Madrid.

'I would like to see the Archbishop. If His Majesty the King will grant an audience to the emissaries. . . .'

'We have already been in touch with the Archbishop's secretary,' my uncle shook his head in consternation. 'The answer came back that everything would depend on the outcome of the Council of Bishops. The Archbishop can't just step in and arrange an audience for the Japanese without considering the opinions of the bishops. It's not just a question of trade. . . . This is a problem that relates to the missionary effort in Asia. But we'll do what we can for you.'

I sensed from my uncle's words that the Archbishop was trying to avoid the troublesome problem I presented. I shook hands with my uncle and cousin. They escorted me out to the porch, where I boarded my carriage.

A cold rain was falling. I returned along the stone road to the monastery. The light from the street lanterns illuminated images of the Holy Mother affixed to walls and along the roadside, but otherwise the city was dark and quiet. With the clatter of the horses' hooves in my ears, I closed my eyes and once again conjured up an image of Father Valente, a man I had yet to meet. I tried to imagine how this priest would rebut my arguments and assail me. From a window somewhere I heard the loud laughter of a woman.

I opened the door to the lodging hall and lit a candle in the hallway. As I started down the long corridor to my room, I saw some Japanese figures standing in front of my bedroom door.

'Who is it?'

The flame from my candle illuminated the faces and robes of the three envoys. I noticed drops of rain glistening on my own clothing.

'Haven't you gone to bed yet?'

'Lord Velasco.' Hasekura's voice was taut. 'When will you have word about our audience with the King?'

'Why do you ask me that? I am doing everything within my power. In another month. . . .'

The Council of Bishops was to be convened in the middle of January. At that council I would confront the Jesuits. Holding the candle in one hand, I explained this to the envoys. Their attendants were already asleep, and it was cold inside the building. I explained to the three envoys, who listened with stiff expressions, the enormous influence which decisions of the clergy in this country had upon the foreign policy formulated by the court.

'Then if your debate goes well . . .'

'I hope that it will. The result will determine whether you have an audience with the King.'

'Will you win the debate?'

'That I do not know.' I smiled. 'But as samurai, I'm sure that each of you would take the field in battle even if there was no hope of victory. I am the same.'

'Lord Velasco.' Nishi took a step forward. 'If it will help you . . . I am willing to become a Christian.'

In the light of my candle, I could see that the customary confidence had drained from Tanaka's face.

'Do Lord Tanaka and Lord Hasekura feel the same way?' I asked.

Neither Tanaka nor Hasekura gave an answer. But I sensed that neither was as obstinate as they had been when we discussed the matter in Sevilla.

Rain fell again on the day the Council of Bishops was convened. It splashed from the roof of the Inquisition courthouse, forming black puddles in the courtyard. Carriages entered the courtyard one after another, spraying mud and water in their wake. As the guards opened the carriage doors, bishops in fluttering cloaks crouched beneath the proffered umbrellas and disappeared into the courthouse.

Two men in black uniforms stood in front of the heavy door to guide each bishop to his seat. Velasco sat facing those seats, with Father Valente beside him.

'So this . . . is Father Valente.' With mild surprise, Velasco glanced at the dwarfish old man who was sitting in a chair a few feet away with his hands folded on his lap. This old man in shabby robes, this old man with his eyes clenched shut and a weary look on his face, was Father Valente.

Since his uncle's letter had arrived in Veracruz, Velasco had spent almost every moment trying to imagine how his opponent would look. In his daydreams Father Valente wore a look of searing intelligence and occasionally flashed a sardonic smile. He was nothing like this shrivelled old man whose shoulders drooped as though they had been wasted away by life. Instead of being relieved at the appearance of his adversary, Velasco felt affronted. It seemed almost inexcusable that he had been tormented for so long on account of such a feeble old man.

As though he sensed Velasco's piercing gaze upon him, Father Valente opened his eyes and looked in Velasco's direction. Then he nodded slightly, giving a smile full of sympathy.

A uniformed man rang a bell. This was the signal for the debate to begin. The bishops, who reminded Velasco of a flock of vultures, took their seats in a single row opposite Velasco and Father Valente, gave several solemn coughs, and put their heads together to deliberate.

The bishop who served as president of the Council got up and began to read from a paper. His statement declared their intention to debate, in their capacity as the Council of Bishops of Madrid, the discord between the Jesuits and the Franciscans concerning the methods of proselytizing in Japan, and their desire to determine the qualifications of the Japanese emissaries who had arrived in Madrid.

As his soft voice seeped into every corner of the silent room, the other bishops were motionless, staring at Velasco and Father Valente with eyes like those of dead men.

'To summarize the problem at hand. . . .' The presiding bishop, having finished his recitation, addressed his colleagues. 'Fifteen years ago, His Holiness Pope Clement VIII issued the Apostolic Constitution "*Onerosa Pastoralis*", in which the right to proselytize in Japan, originally restricted only to the Society of Jesus, was granted to other Orders. The Franciscans at once sent eleven missionaries to Japan. Father Velasco here is one of that group. He believes that the deterioration of the missionary effort in Japan since the arrival of Francisco Xavier in 1549 is the result of errors by the Jesuits; he desires an improvement in the situation, and claims sufficient grounds for optimism. The Jesuits, on the other hand, assert that the abrupt changes in the leadership of Japan have hampered the missionary work, and insist that the present problems result not from a failing in the methods of proselytizing, but from other causes. For this reason, we propose to hear detailed reports of the situation from both sides in the dispute.'

The bishops conferred in soft voices with their neighbours on either side and then agreed to this proposal. As they deliberated, Velasco gazed at them with his usual confidence. Father Valente of the Society of Jesus remained motionless, his hands clasped on his lap.

Velasco rose when his name was called. He deliberately fixed a smile upon his lips. Respectfully he expressed his gratitude for the honour afforded him of describing his feelings and experiences relating to the missionary endeavour in Japan.

'For half a century missionary work in Japan went forward smoothly, unquestionably because of the dedication of our brethren in the Society of Jesus. In this respect, I have the profoundest respect for the labours and sacrifices of the Society of Jesus.'

There was something pleasurable in praising those who had slandered him. He knew that such an approach would give objectivity to his remarks. He spared no panegyrics as he enumerated the achievements of the Jesuits. When at last a flicker of curiosity stirred in the eyes of the bishops, he interjected, 'However!'

'However . . . without even realizing what they were doing, the Jesuits committed a grave error. They did not anticipate the serious setbacks their errors would inflict upon the missionary effort.'

With these words, Velasco shifted his gaze to Father Valente. But the old priest sat motionless, his eyes closed as though from weariness, and it was impsssible to determine whether he had even been listening to Velasco's pronouncements.

'The error of the Jesuits was that they took Japan to be the same as any other country. But Japan is not like any of the other nations which our ancestors conquered. Japan has been protected by a great ocean, the Pacific, and though its people have been ignorant of Christianity, they have been able to maintain enviable order and equip themselves with a powerful army. Unlike the slothful races, the Japanese are clever and cunning and filled with pride, and whenever they or their nation have been insulted, they have swarmed together like bees and retaliated. In a country like that, we must adopt methods of proselytizing suitable to that country. We must not insult them. We must not incense them. Yet the actions of the Society of Jesus have done precisely that.'

At this point Velasco paused. Once he had ascertained traces of interest and concern in the faces of the bishops who initially had stared at him with lifeless eyes, Velasco lowered his head and asked, 'May I be permitted to describe those actions in detail?'

'That is why we are here,' one of the bishops nodded.

'For example, the Jesuits obtained a totally unnecessary tract of land in the harbour town of Nagasaki. To them it was a source of revenues to carry on their missionary labours, but to the heathen Japanese it was apparently a source of uneasiness and distrust. The Japanese cannot allow any part of their narrow islands to be turned into a foreign-owned colony. That is not all. Some of the brethren of the Society of Jesus, in an excess of missionary zeal, set fire to the Buddhist statues which many of the Japanese worship. It is true that in Nueva España they were able to burn the altars of the Indians without it becoming a hindrance to their proselytizing. But when the same thing is done in Japan, it simply arouses needless animosity in the hearts of those who might one day become children of God. This is shown by the fact that when the Taikō, the ruler of Japan, learned what the missionaries were doing, he abandoned his earlier magnanimous attitude and instituted a policy of persecution. The persecutions were in fact caused by the errors of the missionaries. The Jesuits cannot escape responsibility for that. Yet they close their eyes to these facts and report to Rome and to you in Madrid that they have done all that they could, but that missionary work has become extremely difficult.'

Velasco charged through this indictment in one breath, and when it was finished he again bowed his head reverently and was silent. The pause was deliberate, intended to inflame the curiosity of his listeners. 'However!' Velasco continued forcefully.

'However . . . there is still hope for missionary work in Japan. . . . It is true that the present situation is unfavourable, but this can be

remedied. I am convinced of that. This hope is not, as the Jesuits have
claimed, a vain dream detached from reality. Were it so, I would not
have come all this way, bringing with me Japanese ambassadors who
bear a letter from their ruler.'

At this point Father Valente raised his head from his chest. Velasco
saw a thin smile spread slowly across his lips. It was like the pitying
smile of an adult watching a clumsy jester. Velasco stifled his
mounting anger and continued his speech.

'The ambassadors – no, the Japanese people themselves – are eager
to profit from trade with Nueva España. Japan is a small and
impoverished land. For that reason the Japanese will do anything at
all for the sake of profit. That willingness is their greatest strength as
well as their greatest weakness. The Church cannot possibly suffer
by granting them minimal profits in exchange for the freedom to
perform missionary work. If we do not humiliate them, if we do not
arouse their ire, if instead we offer them profits for their recognition
of our proselytizing labours, I am certain that the persecutions will
come to an end.'

The sound of the rain was still audible in the room. The bishops
listened in silence to Velasco's propositions.

'The Japanese will give anything to get profits,' Velasco repeated.
'They may even give us their hearts.'

The sound of the rain was still audible. The samurai sat down on his
bed and looked uncomfortably about the room. It was just like all the
many monastery rooms they had slept in ever since their arrival in
Nueva España. A single plain bed, and a single plain desk, holding a
porcelain water pitcher and a wash-basin of arabesque design. On the
bare wall an emaciated man with both hands nailed to a cross hung
with drooping head.

'A man like this. . . .' Once again, the samurai experienced the
same incomprehension. 'Why do they worship him?'

He remembered that he had once seen a prisoner in a similar
condition. Riding bareback, he had been paraded about with both his
hands lashed to a pole. Like this man on the crucifix, the prisoner was
ugly and filthy. His ribs protruded, and his stomach had caved in as
though he had not eaten for a long while; he wore only a cloth about
his loins, and he supported himself on the horse with spindly legs. The
more he looked at it, the more the image on the wall reminded the
samurai of that prisoner.

'What would the people in the marshland think . . . if I worshipped
someone like this?'

He pictured himself worshipping this man, and an unbearable feeling of shame swept over him. He did not believe wholeheartedly in the buddhas in the way his uncle did, but when he made a pilgrimage to a temple, his head automatically wanted to bow down before the magnificent idols, and when he stood before a shrine where pure waters were flowing, he felt an urge to clap his hands in supplication. But he could detect nothing sublime or holy in a man as wretched and powerless as this.

'Those merchants . . .'

Surely the merchants he had left behind in Nueva España had really felt the same? Yet they had knelt in the cathedral and received baptism from the foreigners of their own volition in order to guarantee trade relations with Nueva España. Watching them, the samurai had felt a confused mixture of contempt and envy. He was contemptuous of the baseness which allowed the merchants blithely to sell their souls for the sake of profit, and envious of the audacity that enabled them to undertake anything at all in the name of profit. Yet now Nishi Kyūsuke claimed he was planning to be baptized as a formality in order to carry out his mission as an emissary. Such an act was certainly no more than a formality, and not something that came from his heart. The samurai knew that he too should engage in every available form of deception on His Lordship's behalf and in order to achieve his mission. He realized that, but he could not do it.

'I cannot . . .'

To become a Christian was to betray the marshland. The marshland was not made up merely of those who lived there now. The ancestors and relatives of all the living silently kept watch over the marshland. So long as the Hasekura house continued, the samurai's deceased father and grandfather would be a part of the marshland. Those dead souls would not permit him to become a Christian.

Father Valente of the Society of Jesus rose slowly from his chair. He too bowed his head to the bishops, then entwined his fingers and held his hands across his chest. In a slightly hoarse voice, he began to speak.

'For thirty years I lived in Japan, and with my own eyes I have witnessed what Father Velasco claims are the errors of the Jesuits. Because of that experience, I will not now deny what he has related. It is true that our Society was overzealous. Because of our excess of zeal, at times we pushed matters too far. But not all the persecutions in Japan are the result of these excesses alone. There is ingenious exaggeration in Father Velasco's words. And an element of wishful thinking in his hopes for the future.'

Velasco clenched the fists that rested on his knees, but he forced himself to smile. In the presence of the bishops he had to demonstrate complete composure.

'I must tell you that the ambassadors Father Velasco has brought with him are not representatives of the Japanese king, who is known as the Shōgun. Their master, who rules over a domain in the eastern part of Japan, is only one of many noblemen. Even supposing that this delegation has the authorization of the Japanese king, they can hardly be said to be official emissaries representing the nation as a whole.'

Father Valente put his hand to his mouth and coughed feebly. He did not speak forcefully or try to enthral the bishops with dramatic pauses as Velasco had, but was content to describe the situation in a tedious sing-song voice. Yet from the very outset he was thrusting at Velasco's most vulnerable spot.

'Father Velasco has just told you how formidable he considers the Japanese people. He says that they are so wise and cunning and eager for profit that they must not be treated like the peoples of other nations. We agree with him. Because we agree, we would like your excellencies to consider the following. Since the Japanese ambassadors who accompanied Father Velasco here are not official emissaries, no matter how alluring the promises about missionary work in the letter they bear may be, at some point in time the Japanese will be able to say, "Those were not the promises of the king. Those were nothing more than promises from a single nobleman. Those were not official ambassadors. They were merely private envoys."'

Father Valente paused and gave another weak cough. 'From my many years of experience, I can tell you that this is a tactic the Japanese often employ. They prepare their excuses well in advance so that they can slip out of what they have said whenever it suits them – that is the Japanese way of doing things. When a battle commences, for instance, if a Japanese noble is not certain which side will be victorious, he often makes his brothers ally with either side. No matter which side wins, the nobleman's family can vindicate themselves before the victor by claiming, "Our family is not responsible for our brother siding with the enemy. He did it of his own accord." It was with the same cunning that the Japanese sent these envoys to Nueva España. What I am saying is that the Japanese are not interested in missionary work. They are merely dangling the promise of freedom to proselytize as bait before us, while their real aim lies elsewhere.'

'Then what is it that they want?' asked one of the bishops, his chin cradled in his hands. He reminded Velasco of a vulture. 'What do the Japanese want besides trade with Nueva España?'

'They are out to steal our sea routes across the Pacific and to poach our skills in navigation. No doubt they have managed to pilfer all that knowledge on their present voyage.'

There was a stir of alarm among the bishops. When the clamour subsided, their gaze shifted from Father Valente to Velasco, whose face had stiffened as he sat listening in his chair. Velasco raised one hand slightly to request permission to speak. When one of the bishops nodded, he began to speak in a wavering voice, his face flushed.

'There is something your excellencies should understand. Without the permission of the King, no Japanese nobleman has the authority to release Spaniards who have been detained in Japan. We travelled to Nueva España together with a group of Spanish sailors who had been held in custody. This is proof that the ambassadors who have come from Japan do so with the authorization of their king. It is further evident from the letter which the King of Japan sent directly to the Philippines ten years ago that he himself is eager to trade with Nueva España. And while we are on the subject, it is common knowledge that thirty years ago the Society of Jesus to which Father Valente belongs tried to pass off four Japanese children no better than beggars as children of distinguished *daimyōs*, and sent them to España and Rome under the pretence that they were official ambassadors.'

When Velasco had taken his seat, Father Valente rose slowly from his squeaky chair. Again he placed his arms on his chest and gave two or three dry coughs.

'It is a fact that the King of Japan once desired trade with Nueva España. But even then, their plan was to allow trade and prohibit missionary work, and in fact many Christians were burned at the stake in their capital, and the missionaries were expelled from all their domains. It is obvious that in due course these ambassadors will also have to submit to that policy. For that reason, even if the lord of these ambassadors promises to protect the missionaries and to allow freedom to proselytize, that does not make it a promise from the King of Japan.'

'You . . .,' Velasco interrupted from his seat, 'you and the entire Society of Jesus seem to have given up all hope of ending the persecutions. But I . . . I believe that we can extinguish the animosity towards Christianity which you have aroused in the Japanese.'

Velasco raised his voice to a shout, forgetting that the bishops were looking on. Seeing Velasco's crimson face, Father Valente smiled at him pitifully.

'Can you extinguish it? I doubt whether it will be so easy.'
'Why?'
'Because I believe – and I say this after many years of living among them – that of all the people in the world the Japanese are the least receptive to our religion.'

The sardonic smile vanished from the priest's face, and now he looked at Velasco with sorrow in his eyes.

'The Japanese basically lack a sensitivity to anything that is absolute, to anything that transcends the human level, to the existence of anything beyond the realm of Nature: what we would call the supernatural. I finally realized that after thirty years there as a missionary. It was a simple matter to teach them that this life is transitory. They have always been sensitive to that aspect of life. The frightening thing is that the Japanese also have a capacity to accept and even relish the evanescence of life. This capacity is so profound that they actually revel in that knowledge, and have written many verses inspired by that emotion. Yet the Japanese make no attempt to leap beyond that knowledge. They have no desire at all to progress beyond it. They abhor the idea of making clear distinctions between man and God. To them, even if there should be something greater than man, it is something which man himself can one day become. Their Buddha, for instance, is a being which man can become once he abandons his illusions. Even Nature, which for us is something totally detached from man, to them is an entity which envelops mankind. We . . . we failed in our attempts to rectify these attitudes of theirs.'

The bishops received these unexpected remarks from Father Valente with a ponderous silence. Of all the missionaries who had been sent forth to distant lands, none had ever spoken with such despair.

'Their sensibilities are firmly grounded within the sphere of Nature and never take flight to a higher realm. Within the realm of Nature their sensibilities are remarkably delicate and subtle, but those sensibilities are unable to grasp anything on a higher plane. That is why the Japanese cannot conceive of our God, who dwells on a separate plane from man.'

'Then . . .,' one of the bishops shook his head, as though he could not accept Valente's argument, 'then the Japanese Christians, who once numbered four hundred thousand . . . what did they believe in?'

Father Valente replied softly, his eyes fixed upon the ground.

'I do not know.' Painfully, he closed his eyes. 'When the King banned Christianity, half of them disappeared like a mist.'

'Disappeared?'

'Yes. A seemingly endless stream of Japanese we considered among the best of believers renounced their faith the moment the persecution began. When a feudal lord abjured Christianity, his entire family and his knights followed suit, and when a village chief apostatized, nearly all the villagers also left the Church. And to our astonishment, from their faces one could not tell that anything at all had happened.'

'They felt no pangs of remorse for having abandoned God?'

'When I used to look at a map,' Father Valente muttered, his eyes still closed, 'the shape of Japan sometimes reminded me of a lizard. Much later it occurred to me that the true nature of the Japanese was much the same. We missionaries were like children who delight in cutting off a lizard's tail. The lizard went on living even without its tail, and finally its tail grew back as it had been originally. Despite sixty years of proselytizing by our Society, the Japanese did not change at all. They returned to the way they originally were.'

'The way they originally were . . .? Explain what you mean, Father Valente.'

'The Japanese never live their lives as individuals. We European missionaries were not aware of that fact. Suppose we have a single Japanese here. We try to convert him. But there was never a single individual we could call "him" in Japan. He has a village behind him. A family. And more. There are also his dead parents and ancestors. That village, that family, those parents and ancestors are bound to him tightly, as though they were living beings. That is why he is not an isolated human being. He is an aggregate who must shoulder the burden of village, family, parents, ancestors. When I say that he went back to the way he originally was, I mean that he returned to that world to which he is so firmly bound.'

'You are not making yourself very clear, Father Valente.'

'Then please allow me to give you an example. When the first missionary to Japan, Francisco Xavier, began his labours in the southern provinces, this was the most formidable obstacle he encountered. The Japanese said, "I believe the Christian teachings are good. But I would be betraying my ancestors if I went to a Paradise where they cannot dwell. Our ties to our parents and our ancestors are very firm." Let me point out that this is not a simple matter of ancestor-worship. It is a compelling faith. Sixty years were not sufficient for us to obliterate that faith.'

'Your reverend excellencies!' Velasco shouted, cutting Father Valente short. 'What this father has just said is a gross exaggeration. There are also martyrs in Japan who have given their lives for the teachings of Christ. How can he say that the Japanese people have not believed in our Lord? Hope for the missionary effort in Japan has by no means been extinguished!'

He then laid down the trump card which he hoped would verify his claim.

'This is evident from the fact that thirty-eight of the Japanese merchants I brought to Nueva España were baptized at the Cathedral of San Francisco in Mexico City. And at this very moment, one of the three Japanese emissaries who is patiently awaiting a just decision from your excellencies has come forward and promised me that he will become a child of the Church.'

As he listened to the rain, the samurai stretched out on his bed; linking his fingers behind his head, he stared at the naked man suspended from the wall. There was no one in the room but the samurai and this man.

The door opened and Tanaka came in. Raindrops glistened like dew on his garments.

'You must be tired. Did Nishi come back with you?'

The samurai sat up and crossed his legs. Though both men held the same rank, he remained deferential to the older Tanaka.

'He's still out walking around the city in the rain. I got tired of everyone watching me and came back,' Tanaka said irritably. He removed his sword from his waist and wiped the damp leather scabbard-cover with a cloth. People had stared at them when they walked the streets of Nueva España, but here in España it was even more annoying. The crowds that trailed after them pawed curiously at their clothing and swords and chattered at them. There were even children who begged for money. The adults competed to snatch up the tissue paper which the Japanese discarded on the streets after wiping their noses. At first the Japanese had laughed at such behaviour, but eventually the impertinent stares and questions had become irksome.

'I suppose Velasco's debate must be over?' Tanaka mumbled to himself as he pulled off his rain-soaked boots. The samurai, Nishi, and their attendants had bought similar leather boots in Sevilla.

'I don't think it's over yet.'

'I'm worried.'

The samurai nodded. Tanaka sat down on his own bed and crossed his legs.

'Hasekura, what will happen to us if Velasco loses the debate . . .? Do we crawl meekly back to Japan?'

The samurai blinked and said nothing. He did not know how to reply. Velasco had told them that the audience with the King and the presentation of His Lordship's letter all depended upon the outcome of that day's debate. Since that morning, when Velasco left in a carriage, the three envoys had been on edge. The samurai could understand why Nishi was out walking in the rain.

'Are we supposed to be content with that?' Tanaka stared fiercely at the samurai. 'I can't do it. I would be shamed before my entire family. My relatives have all looked forward to getting our old lands back for a long time. I wouldn't be able to hold my head up in front of them.'

The samurai was in exactly the same position. He turned to look at the rain trickling down the window.

'Listen, Hasekura,' Tanaka declared. 'Like Nishi, I'm thinking of becoming a Christian. I hate the Christians. But with things the way they are now . . . there's no other choice. I thought – in battle sometimes you get down on your hands and knees and bow your head in submission, but it's only to deceive the enemy. You don't put your heart into it. Last night I convinced myself of that.'

'Matsuki Chūsaku said. . . .'

'What good is it now to believe what Matsuki said? Matsuki claimed the Council of Elders sent us on this journey to silence the petitions from the lance-corporals to have our lands returned. But I don't want to believe that. Throughout this entire journey all I've been able to hold onto is that promise from Lord Shiraishi. I think Matsuki must have the support of Lord Shiraishi's enemies on the Council. . . . What do you reckon, Hasekura?'

'To become a Christian . . . even if it's just an expedient . . . I feel as though I would be turning my back on the Hasekura family and my ancestors.'

'I feel the same. I don't want to give up the religion my ancestors followed. But I won't be giving it up in my heart. The greater impiety would be not to get back the lands I inherited from my ancestors.'

The samurai struggled for a handhold as he felt his heart beginning to crumble inside him. The sound of the rain suddenly called up memories of the rainy season in the marshland. The rainy season in the marshland – shut up inside day after day by the rain, an array of odours trapped within the house, withered branches sputtering in the sunken hearth, children coughing. The earth crumbling beneath the rain. . . .

'Think about it, Hasekura.'

The samurai looked at the image on the wall. Every day on their voyage, the merchants had listened to Velasco's stories about this man. 'This Man died with the sins of mankind upon Him,' Velasco had explained with a smile. 'A *daimyō* defeated in battle willingly takes his own life to save the lives of his retainers. And this Man died that He might ask God to forgive all men who had rebelled against Him. Then had this Man joined hands with all the others to rebel against God? No, that is not the case. This Man committed no sin whatsoever. Not once did He ever turn against God. Yet He died a sacrifice for all.'

Although the merchants had not believed this absurd tale for one moment, they had nodded their heads for Velasco's benefit. To them a man like this was no different from a stone on the roadside which they might use in place of a hammer. Once it has served its purpose, that stone can be discarded. If clasping their hands before this man would help them to do business with the foreigners, they would pretend to worship him and then later discard him. That was how the merchants had really felt.

'How am I . . .,' the samurai thought, batting his eyes, 'any different from those merchants?'

This ugly, emaciated man. This man devoid of majesty, bereft of outward beauty, so wretchedly miserable. A man who exists only to be discarded after he has been used. A man born in a land I have never seen, and who died in the distant past. He has nothing to do with me, thought the samurai.

'I do not deny the fact that those baptisms took place.'

Father Valente sighed and got up from his chair. He was panting heavily, his shoulders shaking, as though it was physically painful to have to refute Velasco.

'Yet at the same time, I question whether they were sincere in their request for baptism.'

'What do you mean?' the same bishop asked.

'I have already told you. When the persecutions began, half the Japanese faithful disappeared like a mist. If the persecution grows any more fierce, no doubt the remaining half will abandon the teachings of Christ just as if it meant nothing at all to them. Instead of conferring baptism, we should be considering how to help them defend their faith. Instead of making temporary converts in the midst of persecution, we . . .'

'Your reverend excellencies,' Velasco interrupted impatiently. 'The honour of the thirty-eight Japanese and of the emissary who is in fact joyously preparing to join the faithful demands that I object to Father Valente's humiliating remarks. It is lamentable that such words could come from the lips of a clergyman. With those words he also belittles the many Japanese saints whom he baptized with his own hands.'

'I am belittling no one. I am merely telling you the facts . . .'

'Even if what you say is true,' Velasco shouted, 'you seem to forget that the sacrament of baptism transcends the will of man and bestows the grace of God upon the recipient. Yes, even if by some chance there were such impure motives in their baptism, from that day forward the Lord will surely not ignore them. Even if they used the Lord then to their own advantage, the Lord will never abandon them. And . . .,' he paused, 'and I think now of the words of the Lord recorded in the Bible as he admonished John. When John sought to criticize a man who used the Lord's name to heal the sick, the Lord said, "He that is not against us is for us. . . ."'

For a fleeting instant, Velasco felt a searing pain in his chest, as though it had been pierced by a sharp sword. He knew that the Japanese merchants had not believed his sermons. He recognized they had merely used their baptism as a means to pursue the profits of trade. Though he realized this, he had shut his eyes to everything.

A bishop seated at one end raised his hand and declared, 'This Council of Bishops was not convened to hear theological debates on baptism. Our task is to determine whether these emissaries are official ambassadors of Japan or private envoys of a single nobleman. But first we have to know whether the persecution in Japan is a temporary phenomenon, or whether it will continue for a long while.'

'I do not consider the persecutions in Japan either temporary or permanent.' Velasco directed his attention to the enquiring bishop. 'It is a fact that in Edo, where the present ruler's great castle is situated, and in the regions under his influence, the Christians have been persecuted. The Jesuits contend that this persecution and suppression will continue indefinitely, but we do not concur. This ruler most assuredly despises Christianity, but at the same time he is not fool enough to be blind to the escalating profits that are accruing from trade with Manila and Macao. It is our considered opinion that he will in fact gladly relax the persecutions if Nueva España offers him wealth exceeding that of Manila and Macao. I have said this over and over again. In my opinion, by offering their ruler wealth, we can make him authorize our freedom to proselytize, even if there are a few restrictions placed upon us. The persecution is neither temporary nor permanent. It is something which we ourselves can put a stop to.'

The bishop nodded at Velasco's remarks and then turned to Father Valente, who sat with clasped hands, staring at the floor. 'We would like to hear Father Valente's opinion.'

The priest coughed again, and answered languidly in a voice thick with phlegm. 'The persecution will likely continue. The prohibitions which are now applied only partially will probably be extended throughout Japan. If this were fifteen years ago, there would still be a glimmer of hope, because at that time the ruler whom Father Velasco has mentioned had a powerful adversary named Toyotomi. But the Toyotomi clan has gradually dwindled in power until now they are isolated in a town called Osaka, and soon they will surely be annihilated. There is not a single nobleman left in Japan who can oppose the present ruler. He is of course seeking profits from trade, but he has begun to think it better to approach the Protestant nations. The Protestants have promised him that they are interested only in trade, not in spreading Christianity.'

'So then,' Velasco called out loudly, 'are we to sit back and yield Japan to the Protestants? This is a question that will also affect the Spanish advance into the Orient. . . .'

The debate went on interminably. Outside darkness had already enveloped the courthouse. The bishops were drained, as evidenced by the way they smothered their yawns and stretched their shoulders. Velasco felt utterly exhausted. He closed his eyes and muttered to himself the last words Christ had uttered before He gave up the ghost. 'Father, Thy will be done. I have finished the work which Thou gavest me to do. Into Thy hands I commend my spirit.'

As he descended the stairs, which exuded a musty odour peculiar to old monasteries, he heard a raspy monotone voice singing:

> O God of the fields: welcome! Please, sit down.
> Well have you finished your work and come –

The samurai knew the song well. It was a tune the women hummed at planting time in His Lordship's domain as they thrust the tender shoots of rice into the flooded ground. The samurai paused for a moment on the landing and listened to this clumsy rendition of the song. The singer, a man leaning against the grey wall, hurriedly cut short his song, bowed and disappeared into his room. He was one of Nishi Kyūsuke's attendants.

An angry voice echoed from the end of the corridor. Yozō was lashing out at Ichisuke and Daisuke.

'We all want to go home! You know the master himself is trying to complete his mission as fast as he can. . . . You selfish bastards!'

The shouting was followed by the whack of a flat palm smacking against flesh and the murmurs of a tearful apology.

The samurai stood in the darkness, blinking his eyes and listening to the commotion. Doubtless Yozō had overheard Ichisuke and Daisuke complaining that they wanted to return to the marshland. The samurai was painfully sympathetic to his attendants' desire to go home, yet at the same time equally understanding of the feelings that drove Yozō to upbraid them.

'What are you holding back for?' He felt as though he were hearing another voice beside him. 'It's your stubbornness that's keeping your attendants from returning to the marshland. To help your mission, and to help your friends, why can't you become a Christian just for appearance's sake?'

'Selfish bastard!' There was the sound of another whack, like the slap of a wet cloth.

'Enough. Enough! I am weary,' the samurai murmured to himself. 'It isn't Ichisuke or Daisuke who are selfish. It's me.'

'Yozō,' he called softly. Three grey figures turned towards him and lowered their heads remorsefully. 'That's enough. It's only natural that Ichisuke and Daisuke feel homesick. I feel the same. These days all I dream about is the marshland. . . . Yozō, I've decided to go along with Lord Tanaka and Nishi and become a Christian.'

When he had finished speaking, the three dark figures seemed to tremble.

'It will help . . . help us to complete our mission in this country . . . and help get you back home to the marshland.'

For a few moments Yozō looked sympathetically into his master's face. 'I . . .,' he said in an almost inaudible voice, 'I too will become a Christian. . . .'

While the bishops were arriving at a decision in a separate chamber, Velasco sat on a hard chair in a tiny anteroom, muttering over and over to himself, 'Lord, Thy will be done.'

'Lord, Thy will be done. If Thou wilt not cast Japan out of Thy presence – if Thou bore the cross for Japan too – then Lord, Thy will be done.

'Japan. Scheming Japan. Japan the epitome of cunning. Japan so skilled at staging battles. Everything is just as Father Valente said. In that country there is not the slightest desire to seek after the eternal, after that which transcends the human level. It's true. Not a single ear in that land listens to Thy word. It's true. Japan nods, pretending to listen, but inwardly her mind pursues other thoughts. It's true. A lizard that grows back the way it was even if you sever its tail. At times I have hated that lizard-like island, but I've been driven less by hatred than by a violent urge to conquer precisely because it is that sort of country. The more difficult a nation she is to manage, the more I have wanted to fight with Japan.' The door to the anteroom creaked. In the doorway Velasco's cousin Don Luis, holding a wide-brimmed hat, stood still dripping from the rain. He toyed with the brim of his hat as he looked compassionately at his cousin.

'The bishops have just left.'

'Is there a chance we'll win?' Velasco removed his hands from his face and sighed wearily.

'I don't know. Bishop Seron and his group are strongly antagonistic, but Bishop Salvatierra says that even if the Japanese ambassadors are not official, they ought to be treated with courtesy.'

'Does that mean he will recommend an audience with the King?'

Luis shrugged his shoulders, unable to answer with certainty.

'At any rate, something has to happen if you are to win. Something to sway the hearts of the bishops.'

'Do you think the bishops' hearts will be swayed if the Japanese are baptized?'

'I don't know. We have to try every means at our disposal. We'll do everything we can to help you.'

Chapter 7

Seated in the front row facing the altar were Tanaka Tarozaemon, the samurai and Nishi Kyūsuke. Behind them sat the attendants who were to be baptized together with their masters. To either side of the altar were Velasco's uncle and cousins, who were acting as godfathers for the baptismal candidates, and a row of monks garbed in brown habits with sashes about their waists. Since the general congregation had been given permission to attend, the seats were jammed almost to the entrance, but a majority of those present were either members of Velasco's family or guests they had invited.

Tanaka's eyes were closed. Nishi was staring at the flames of the many candles flickering on the altar. Occasionally they could hear sniffles or coughs from Yozō and the other retainers behind them. The samurai wondered what each man was feeling as he sat here in this chapel.

The samurai himself felt that he must be dreaming. In the marshland the powdery snows had pelted against his face as he had worked beside the peasants, chopping wood to lay up against the winter. Beside the sunken hearth he had nodded in acquiescence at his uncle's long tirades. Now that all seemed like part of the distant past. Never could he have imagined then that he would be coming to a strange, distant country, or that he would be sitting in a Christian cathedral surrounded by foreigners and preparing to be baptized. He wondered what sort of shock his uncle or his wife Riku would feel if they could see him now. But he could not even visualize their faces.

A youth wearing scarlet robes under a white tunic stepped forward carrying a candle. Then the bishop of this Franciscan church, followed by Velasco and another priest, knelt before the altar. At a signal from their godfathers the Japanese, as they had been instructed earlier, knelt upon the old, cracked marble floor.

An incomprehensible and apparently endless prayer was recited in Latin. The samurai fixed his eyes upon the massive crucifix behind the altar, coming face to face with the emaciated man nailed to it.

172

'I . . . I have no desire to worship you,' he murmured almost apologetically. 'I can't even understand why the foreigners respect you. They say you died bearing the sins of mankind, but I can't see that our lives have become any easier as a result. I know what wretched lives the peasants lead in the marshland. Nothing has changed just because you died.'

He thought of winters in the marshland when the winds swirled through the houses. He remembered stories of the famine, when the peasants ate all that was to be had and then left the village to scavenge for food. Velasco claimed that this beggarly man would save all mankind, but the samurai could not understand what that salvation meant.

For several days now, from dawn to dusk, Velasco had been preparing the envoys for this ceremony. At each session Velasco had told them stories about this emaciated man. The stories seemed remote and unbelievable to the Japanese. Many of them smothered yawns, while others lowered their heads and dozed. Signs of anger flashed across Velasco's face when he noticed the men who were napping, but he would force a smile to cover up his rage.

To the samurai, the life of Jesus seemed bizarre. Without ever knowing a man, his mother had given birth to him in a stable, and when it was all finished she had quietly become the wife of a carpenter. Yet from the time of his birth Jesus had been appointed as the king who would save men and nations, and answering the call of Heaven he had abandoned his native land and practised the ascetic life under a priest named John. At length Jesus returned to his own country, acquired many disciples, showed forth wondrous works before the multitudes and taught them how to live. Because of his great following, he was hated by the Church and the priests, endured much tribulation, and was falsely sentenced to death and executed. Jesus recognized this as the appointed way of Heaven, and submitted to these indignities without resistance. Then, three days later, he was restored to life in the tomb and ascended to Heaven.

The samurai could not understand how a man like Velasco could believe a story so palpably absurd. Nor could he comprehend why all the other foreigners considered this story to be true. Equally strange was the fact that there were people in Japan who adhered to these ridiculous teachings.

'You all know how difficult it is for man to avoid sin. The question is whether man can be saved from sin by his own efforts, or saved by this Man called Jesus. The priests of Jerusalem who hated Jesus believed falsely that they could save themselves. But Christians believe that they can go to the true Pure Land only with the help of

Jesus. For Jesus took upon Himself our irredeemable sins, and willingly submitted Himself to tribulation and agony.'

As he listened absently to Velasco's words, the samurai stole a glance at Tanaka, who sat with his eyes closed, then at Nishi. 'This is all for the sake of our mission,' Tanaka's words echoed in the samurai's ears. To live again after death – how could anyone believe such a thing?

'You all fear death. And you lament the impermanence of this world. The priests of Japan preach the transmigration of souls after death, which they call eternal metempsychosis. But in Christianity we teach that we, like Jesus, will be resurrected in the Pure exalted Land. This, too, comes to us only through the intercession of Jesus. With strength and conviction Jesus taught us of the power that enables us to crawl up from the mire of sin, and of the hope that allows us to escape death. For this reason we may call Jesus the King who leads us all.'

Here Velasco suddenly lowered his voice and spoke softly, trying to captivate his listeners.

'Do you want to live in this world accepting the principle of reincarnation through metempsychosis, or do you hope for resurrection in a paradise overflowing with rich rewards? Do you believe that the practice of the foundation of goodness as taught by the Japanese priests is the way to salvation, or do you recognize the limitations of your own power and rely upon the mercy of Jesus? If you ponder which is the wise path and which the foolish path, the answer will be clear.'

But how could Velasco say that Heaven had bestowed this strange, miraculous power upon Jesus? Velasco had explained that Jesus had received it before His birth, and that the word of God had been bestowed upon Him.

'This is for the sake of our mission,' the samurai repeated to himself. 'All for the sake of our mission.'

The three godfathers stood up from among the people seated on either side of the altar. By gestures they indicated that Tanaka, the samurai and Nishi were to advance to the altar. The three priests stepped towards them, Velasco on one side of the bishop carrying a basin, the other priest holding a silver pitcher.

The lips of the ruddy, well-fed bishop fluttered faintly, and he asked something in Latin which the envoys could not understand. Velasco quickly translated his question into Japanese and whispered to them that they were to respond, 'I believe.'

'Do you believe in the Lord Jesus Christ?' the bishop asked.

'I believe.'

'Do you believe in the resurrection of the Lord Jesus Christ, and in life everlasting?'

'I believe.'

Each time Velasco prodded them, like ignorant parrots Tanaka, the samurai and Nishi repeated in chorus, 'I believe.' As they spoke, a feeling of remorse surged within the samurai's breast. This is not from my heart – it is for the sake of my mission, he repeated to himself, but a twinge of bitterness stabbed at him, accompanied by the tormented sensation that in this moment he had betrayed his father, his uncle and Riku. He felt a loathing like a woman must when she is forced to sleep with a man she neither loves nor trusts.

When the three men bent their heads, the bishop took the silver pitcher from the priest and sprinkled their foreheads with water. The water trickled down the samurai's eyes and nose and dripped into the basin held by Velasco. That was baptism. A mere formality to the envoys, an irrevocable sacrament to the Church.

> *Jesus Deus, amor meus*
> *Cordis aestum imprime*
> *Urat ignis urat amor*

At that moment a low rumble of voices surged forward from the entrance of the chapel. To celebrate the submission of the Japanese envoys before the glory of God, the congregation lifted their voices as one and chanted prayers of thanksgiving. The bishop handed the three envoys candles with flickering flames and sent them back to their seats, with Velasco's relatives, who had served as their godfathers, flanking them on both sides. As he started back to his seat, the samurai noticed Velasco standing next to him, looking from the supplicant congregation to the envoys with the customary smile on his face.

'It's only a formality,' the samurai bitterly repeated to himself as he clasped his hands. 'I didn't speak from my heart when I said I believe. Eventually I'll forget all about this day. About everything. . . .'

Following after their masters, the attendants thrust their foreheads over the basin.

When the congregation stood, Tanaka, the samurai and Nishi also stood; when the congregation knelt, Tanaka, the samurai and Nishi also knelt. The service of baptism gave way to Mass, and the bishop spread his hands out before the altar and read from the Gospels, then bowed his head before the bread and the chalice. To the three envoys, who knew nothing of the intent or substance of the sacrament, the bishop's actions seemed strange and unaccountable.

Velasco, kneeling beside them, explained in a low voice.

'That bread itself is the body of the Lord. Watch what I do, and do reverence to the bread and chalice which the Bishop offers you.'

A profound silence enveloped the chapel. With both hands the bishop held out small, thin white wafers as he mouthed a prayer. The monks and the congregation knelt and bowed their heads reverently. The envoys could not grasp the meaning of any of this, but they did realize that it was a moment of great solemnity for them.

'This is only a formality,' were the words the samurai muttered to himself in place of a prayer. 'I don't have any intention of worshipping that miserable man.'

A bell rang. Amid the silence the bishop set the wafers down and picked up a chalice of pure gold, which he raised up over his head. That was the moment in which the wine became the blood of Christ.

'This is only a formality,' the samurai repeated as he imitated the others and bowed his head. 'I don't believe any of this.'

The samurai could not understand why he had become so obsessed with that emaciated man with both hands nailed to a cross. If this truly was a mere formality, there was no need to keep repeating the same words to himself over and over again. There was no reason why emotions as bitter as gall should swell up inside him. There was no reason he should feel remorse, as if he had betrayed his father, his uncle and Riku.

The samurai blinked his eyes and shook his head, taking care that Velasco and the godfathers did not observe him. He tried to drive these apprehensions from his mind. 'Soon you will forget. There is no need to worry.' Over and over again he sought to reassure himself.

Thus the long baptismal ceremony ended. The bishop, Velasco and Velasco's uncle, who had served as a godfather, extended their hands and grasped those of the three envoys, and for a long while they would not let go, eager to let the congregation drink in the scene. As the Japanese started for the door, several bouquets of flowers were tossed to them from the surrounding pews. Velasco translated the words of congratulation shouted from the crowd.

'May your land of Japan become a nation of God. . . .'

Every day after the baptism the stone-paved slopes of Madrid were soaked by drizzling rain. The three envoys went with Velasco to call upon various dignitaries and nobles. Inside the carriage, Velasco explained to them repeatedly how vital the support of such people was.

Though he was fully aware that he was acting only for the sake of their mission, it was a trial for the samurai to bow down before these dignitaries and utter florid speeches of gratitude. Especially arduous was the unrelieved tension they endured when they were invited to dinner or supper and had to preserve their dignity amidst a barrage of incomprehensible words.

The anxiety of social calls and the nervous strain of mealtimes aside, most difficult of all to tolerate were the ignorant questions which the dignitaries and clergymen asked about Japan. The envoys were humiliated when they realized that their hosts grouped the Japanese together with the Indians of Nueva España.

'We are delighted to have a visit from Japanese who have cast off the superstition of Buddhism and the pagan gods and come to believe in our Lord.'

When the clergymen uttered such greetings with a condescending air, the samurai sensed in them some of the pride of a rich man bestowing a favour upon a beggar. Somehow he did not enjoy having the Buddha whom his father and uncle and wife had worshipped over the years reviled in such a manner. 'I am not a Christian!' he told himself. 'I will never worship the Christ these men bow down before.'

Since they had publicly accepted baptism, however, the Japanese were obliged to attend the masses which were performed each morning at the monastery where they lodged. In the cold morning air, before dawn had even broken, a bell rang out and the Japanese delegation fell in line behind the monks holding candles and proceeded down the long corridor into the chapel. At the altar, illuminated only by the flames of the candles, that emaciated man stretched forth his arms. The bishop intoned the Latin liturgy of the Mass in a low voice, eventually lifting the bread and chalice above his head. At each service, the samurai thought of the marshland. He remembered how he had visited the graves of his father and his relatives in the surrounding hills. 'This is not me. This is not how I really feel inside,' he said to himself.

After one such Mass, the samurai whispered furtively to Nishi, 'Doesn't it worry you that you had to become Christian?'

Nishi laughed nonchalantly.

'Everything is so novel – the Mass and the hymns and the organ. When I hear the hymns or the melody of the organ, sometimes I feel almost intoxicated. I see now why it's impossible to understand the West without understanding Christianity.'

'Then . . . have you started worshipping that man?'

'I don't feel like worshipping him. But . . . there's certainly nothing wrong with the Mass. There's nothing like it in the shrines or temples at home.'

Velasco was beside himself. The bishops had been favourably impressed by the baptism of the Japanese, and with each new day the voices clamouring to recognize the envoys as official ambassadors grew in volume. As a result, Velasco told the envoys, the court would undoubtedly be notifying them soon of a date for a formal audience with the King. Then the letter from His Lordship which the envoys carried could be accepted, and the requests contained within it would be given due consideration.

If this was true, then soon they would be able to return home. At that thought, the hearts of the envoys overflowed with elation, with a joy like that felt by the peasants in the marshland at the coming of the long-awaited spring thaw in the wake of a long winter.

'Your baptism has been rewarded,' said Velasco, smiling. 'The Lord never fails to give some reward to all those who enter at the gate of His Church.'

When the clerics of Madrid learned that a group of Japanese visiting their land from the furthest reaches of the globe had been converted to Christianity, they at once cast off their obdurate prejudices. Each day we visit high-ranking clergymen and receive their blessings. Now everything is working in our favour.

The decision of the Council of Bishops will be made public in a few days. My uncle and my cousin feel that most of the bishops are leaning towards recognizing the envoys as official Japanese ambassadors, treating them as such, and requesting an audience with the King. For some reason Father Valente and the Jesuits remain silent. I don't know yet whether to interpret this as an indication of defeat.

'They have lost! Even I take my hat off to you!' My uncle was in high spirits. 'Our family has always fought more stubbornly the greater the obstacles before us, but you seem to have inherited a particularly strong dose of the family blood. Sometimes I think you should have been a politician!'

When he threw his arm around my shoulders, I allowed my feelings to rise to the surface. 'Perhaps I am like James, the disciple of the Lord who was known as Thunder. James, whose fervour even the Lord could not control. . . .'

Today, after concluding some consultations concerning the decision of the Council of Bishops, I left my carriage behind at my cousin's house and walked back to the monastery. Not far from my destination, I was climbing the stone-paved hill; it was still wet from the rain, and I looked up at the clouds floating overhead. At the edge of the path several carriage drivers were seated on barrels, talking together. There was no one else in sight. I groped for the rosary in my pocket, as I always did when I wanted to offer thanks to the Lord.

It was then that it happened. I felt as though somewhere I heard a voice laughing. It was the laughter of a woman who seemed to be choking on something. I looked behind me, but I could no longer see the drivers, and the street was deserted.

For an instant I was seized by the gnawing, hollow feeling that everything I had done was crashing down around me like an avalanche. I felt as though I were seeing before my very eyes all my labours come to naught, all my plans stripped of meaning, and everything I had believed in turning out to be solely for the sake of self-gratification. Again I heard the laughing voice. Raucous laughter even louder than before echoed around me.

I could not move. My eyes were riveted on the grey clouds trailing across the sky. In that sky I caught a glimpse of something I had never seen before. It was my own fall.

I wondered if the Lord no longer loved me, if in fact He had abandoned me. 'Lead us not into temptation!' I prayed. 'Now or in the hour of death. . . .'

> O God of the fields: welcome! Please, sit down.
> Well have you finished your work and come.
> To bring you here sooner still
> We will hasten the tempo of our song.

Tanaka, the samurai and Nishi sat in chairs, listening to the singing of one of their attendants. They hadn't been so happy since the day their journey began. Until today their expressions had been weary and resigned. Now looks of elation glistened upon their faces. This morning, as he had boarded a carriage bound for the Inquisition courthouse, Velasco had confidently informed the group that their mission would soon be successfully completed; now they could start thinking about returning to Japan.

'Right about now they'll be holding the festival of exorcism in my village.' Tanaka's customarily glum expression was gone, and he smiled at Nishi. 'We call it "ink-painting". We wait for people who are supposed to have a bad year to come along, and we paint their faces with ink. They say by doing that their bad luck will vanish.'

'We have a similar custom in our village,' Nishi nodded. 'The young people burn straw ropes and mix the ashes with snow. Then they go about from house to house, smearing it on everybody's faces.

All the single girls run around trying to get away. When it's over, everyone shouts, "The flowers have borne fruit! This will be a bountiful year!" And then the revelry begins.'

'I wonder if we'll be home by this time next year?' Tanaka cocked his head, counting on his fingers. 'If so, it will be just about the time of the exorcism festival. That's if all goes well, like Velasco says.'

'I'm sure it will turn out well.' Nishi turned to the samurai. 'Somehow, now that there's a chance we'll be going home soon, I feel sorry to leave this country. To be honest, I'd like to stay here and learn the language, and see and hear all there is to do, and then go back home after I've studied all that.'

'I envy your youth,' the samurai smiled. 'Lord Tanaka and I can hardly wait to get home and taste rice and *miso* soup again. In my dreams, these days, that's what I picture myself doing.'

In the great hall of Inquisition Court, Velasco had the same seat beside Father Valente. Facing them, the black-robed bishops were lined up in the same stately manner. The bell rang, and the proceedings commenced.

The bishop in the centre stood and, holding an ivory-coloured sheet of paper, read out the decision of the Council of Bishops.

'After studying the recent reports of Father Lope de Valente, Inspector of Asia for the Society of Jesus, and Father Vrais Luis Velasco of the Order of St Francis, on this thirtieth day of January, by the authority vested in the Council of Bishops of Madrid, we submit the following reply to the parties concerned and to His Majesty's Council for Religious Inquiry. The Council of Bishops proposes to accept the contention of Father Vrais Luis Velasco, to recognize the Japanese envoys as official ambassadors of Japan, to afford them the reception due their qualifications, agrees to pay their living expenses during their stay, and declares its intention to take every necessary precaution to guarantee their safe return to Japan. Furthermore, the Council will recommend to His Majesty that he grant these Japanese ambassadors an audience, and proposes that all due consideration be given to the letter they bear.'

Stumbling over the words, the bishop read the resolution. Father Valente, as he had done before, stared at the floor and coughed from time to time. For some reason he looked on abstractedly, as if he were hearing words that had nothing to do with himself. Velasco wanted to turn around and look behind him. His uncle, his cousin and other relatives were listening from the public seats to his rear.

'O Lord, I thank Thee.' He clasped the hands that rested upon his knees. 'All Thy works are indeed good. Thou hast had need of me after all.' Yet strangely a feeling of elation did not gush forth within him. Instead it lapped slowly at the folds of his heart like ripples lapping at the shore. He felt as though this judgement had been determined long before, and that he himself had always expected it.

'Before the Bishops reaffirm this decision, they will hear any formal objections to the judgement from Father Velasco and Father Valente.'

The bishop looked down at the two men as he rolled up the ivory-coloured paper. Although it was the accepted custom to ask for objections, it was uncommon for any to be raised once a decision or judgement had been read. Velasco shook his head.

Father Valente rose slowly from his chair. The bishops watched suspiciously as the priest took a single folded sheet of paper from his dilapidated habit. He put his hand to his mouth and gave a dry cough, then began to speak in a weak voice.

'Before I respectfully submit to the decision of the Council of Bishops, I would like to request that you read an urgent letter from Father de Vivero of the Society of Jesus in Macao, received by the Jesuit headquarters in Madrid one week ago.'

The bishop seated in the centre took the letter and, spreading it out on the bench, began to read it silently to himself. Father Valente sat down again, then lowered his head and closed his eyes.

The bishop in the centre passed the letter to his neighbour. When he had finished reading, the two discussed what to do in hushed voices.

'I ask permission to read this letter aloud to all the bishops assembled here.' The bishop in the centre looked to his right and left. 'We feel that this letter has considerable bearing on this case.'

He got to his feet and, stammering again, slowly began to read.

'There have been two new developments in the situation in Japan. First, although our enemies the English have often repeated slanders concerning our country to the King of Japan, the King has now given ear to these slanderers, and in preparation for severing trade with Luzon and Macao he has publicly recognized trade relations with England and given permission to the British to build a trading station in the south-west of Japan at Hirado. The other development is that a nobleman of the Tōhoku region, who until now has been comparatively tolerant towards our missionary activities – the same powerful *daimyō* who recently sent personal trade emissaries to Nueva España – has begun to persecute the Christians. According to reports we have received here, a small number of the faithful have already been martyred. We understand that this nobleman has done this in order to suppress the general rumour that he was planning to join forces with our nation to overthrow the Japanese King.'

Velasco heard laughter. It was the same laughter that he had heard several days before on the rain-soaked hill, the chortling, woman's laughter he had heard as he passed the carriage drivers. That laughter had pierced the grey clouds floating across the sky. Now it echoed in his ears.

> O God of the fields: welcome! Please, sit down.
> Well have you finished your work and come.
> To bring you here sooner still
> We will hasten the tempo of our song.

The laughter of the attendants ceased abruptly.

Velasco was standing in the doorway like a beggar drenched by the rain. The eyes of the Japanese were fixed upon him.

'Lord Velasco!' Nishi jumped up. 'We've all been waiting here for the good news.' He motioned Velasco to sit in the chair he had just vacated.

Velasco was smiling as usual. But now his smile was feeble and forlorn.

'My fellow ambassadors,' he replied weakly. 'Something has happened which I must tell you about.'

The samurai looked intently at Velasco. Struggling to dispel the ominous premonition that had welled up within him, he turned towards his attendants, who were kneeling in formal posture. They all sensed that something was amiss and were looking up anxiously at Velasco.

'What happened, Lord Velasco?' the samurai asked in a quivering voice. Then, gesturing to Nishi to stay behind, he followed Velasco out of the room. Tanaka also rose to his feet. The three men walked wordlessly down the corridor, which basked in the pale winter sun of the afternoon, and went into Velasco's room. The tightly closed door seemed as though it would never open again. Sounds of laughter and singing no longer echoed from the attendants' room.

That evening the lamps at the monastery were extinguished early and the building where the Japanese lodged was thickly cloaked with darkness and silent as death itself. At eleven o'clock the night-watchman, wrapped in his large cape and carrying an iron lantern in one hand, made his way sluggishly up the frozen pavement of the hill, jangling the many keys he wore at his waist and clopping his wooden shoes. When he reached the street corner, he turned towards the sleeping houses as though he had remembered something, then called out, '*Han dado las once y sereno.*'

Chapter 8

A candle flickered on the desk. The dancing flame threw shadows on Velasco's haggard face. His customary look of confidence had vanished, replaced now by the dispirited expression of a defeated man.

'Our hopes . . .,' Velasco muttered hollowly, 'have all fled away.'

The three envoys stared lifelessly at the candle flame, which fluttered as though taking its final gasps. The flame writhed in desperation, like a moth which has exhausted all its energies and finally fades away.

'All we can do now is return to Japan.'

Somewhere inside his head the samurai could faintly hear the rice-planting song which his attendants had been singing earlier. The men had been intoxicated by the joyful prospect of their imminent return to the marshland. But now everything had changed. Japan had finally set in motion the total prohibition of Christianity. By venturing a ban on Christianity it was obvious that they had given up the idea of trade with Nueva España. That meant that the mission entrusted to them, their entire journey, had become futile, meaningless.

The long journey. The great wide ocean. The scorched plains of Nueva España. The white disc of the sun. The deserts, barren but for maguey and cactus. The wind-swept villages. Each scene fluttered up before his eyes, slipped past, and was gone. To what end? To what end? To what end? The words thundered in his ears – the same rhythm, the same refrain, like the pounding of a drum.

Nishi Kyūsuke was sobbing. The remorse and bitterness were more than he could endure, and his shoulders quivered pitifully.

'Have we lost every possible hope?' Tanaka asked feebly.

Velasco did not reply. The foreigner was still struggling against his personal torment.

'Do you think the things written in that letter are true?'

'I think they are. No padre would send a false report.'

'He might have been misinformed.'

183

'I thought of that too. But here in Madrid, so far from Japan, there is no way we can ascertain the truth of the matter. It's possible that other reports have reached the Pope in Rome, but . . .'

'Then I will go to Rome . . . or to the ends of the earth.' Tanaka spat the words out in one breath. Velasco lowered his hands from his face.

'You'll go to Rome . . .?'

'I don't know what Hasekura or Nishi intend to do. But I . . . I can't go back to Japan empty-handed. If all I'd wanted was to go back, I could have got on the boat with Matsuki in Nueva España.' Tanaka's voice was almost a moan. 'I endured this journey to España . . . only from a sincere desire to complete our mission. I can't return to Japan empty-handed. I will go . . . even to the ends of the earth.'

The samurai was startled. He knew how fiercely this man wanted to have his former lands returned to him, and that he had taken upon himself the expectations of his entire family by accepting this mission. But now he realized for the first time how impassioned, how compelling those hopes and those familial expectations actually were. Tanaka had declared that he would go to the ends of the earth. But what if success was not to be achieved no matter where they went, no matter how far they travelled? An unpleasant foreboding darted across the samurai's mind like a great bird skimming over a ravine. If they were unable to achieve success, there was only one thing Tanaka could do to make amends to his family. His integrity would not allow him to consider any alternative. He would apologize for the insufficiency of his efforts by committing suicide. Cutting open his belly. The samurai stared at Tanaka's profile and hurriedly tried to dispel this dark notion.

'What will you do, Lord Hasekura?'

'If Lord Tanaka goes . . .,' the samurai answered, 'I will go with him.'

For the first time Velasco managed a feeble smile.

'This all seems very strange. Before we set out, and throughout the entire journey, I felt as though I were walking a different path from each of you. To be honest, it seemed as if we never communicated with one another. But tonight for the first time I feel somehow that we have all been bound together by a single cord. From now on you and I will be pelted by the same rains, buffeted by the same winds, and we will walk side by side down the same path.'

The candle flame flickered, and a bell tolled to signal the end of the day. The samurai shut his eyes, wondering how to tell his unsuspecting attendants that they must continue their journey. Yozō was one matter; but he could not bear it when the other two men stared glumly at the floor. Fondly-recalled scenes from the marshland, the smell of the hearth, the faces of his wife and children – all receded from him like an ebb tide.

'Tomorrow I will have to tell them. Tonight I shall forget everything and go to sleep. I am weary.'

That night the samurai dreamed of the marshland again. In his dream he saw two of those white swans flying against the overcast winter sky. The swans rode the air currents, soaring freely as they glided slowly down towards the swamp. Yozō suddenly aimed his musket. The samurai had no time to stop him. The report of the gun was deafening, echoing through the withered forest. The birds of passage abruptly lost their equilibrium and tumbled like pebbles towards the waters of the swamp, describing black spirals as they fell. The samurai stared at Yozō through the acrid cloud of gunpowder smoke and for some reason felt faintly angry with him. A useless slaughter, he started to say, but he caught himself. Why did you shoot them? Those birds had to return to a distant land. Like us. . . .

The Japanese and I were like nomads wandering in search of a peaceful haven. Or like wayfarers seeking the lights of a human dwelling on a dark and rainy night. After we left Madrid, I thought every night of the Lord's remark, 'The Son of man hath not where to lay his head.'

Once the Council of Bishops had delivered its decision, in a twinkling people began to treat us coolly. We received no more invitations, and no one came to call on us. Even the Superior of the monastery where we were staying wrote a letter to his diocese complaining that the lives of the other monks would be disrupted by allowing the Japanese to stay any longer in one of their buildings.

Our only supporters are my uncle and his family. And surprisingly enough, a duke who had been apathetic towards us has become our ally. He was incensed that Spanish Christians – for whatever reason – would be inhospitable to Japanese who had converted to the same religion, and on our behalf he sought assistance from the influential Cardinal Borghese of Rome. As a result, my uncle had no choice but to prepare a felucca to take us from Barcelona to Italy, along with two thousand ducats for travelling expenses. He made the condition, however, that if the Vatican did not sanction the Japanese requests, I would give up the entire matter and live docilely in a monastery in Nueva España or the Philippines.

We set out from wintry Madrid, crossed the desolate plateaux of Guadalajara, and passed through such cities as Zaragoza and Cervera on our way to Barcelona.

The winds were sharp and the air chilly. As I watched the Japanese pressing ahead with their journey in silence, a mixture of unspeakable remorse and guilt stabbed at my breast. The lack of emotion on the faces of the Japanese only intensified my anguish. I began to think of myself as one of the false prophets of Israel, leading his people on a pointless, meandering journey. Even if we did go to Rome, I couldn't be sure that the Vatican would welcome us or grant our requests. The Japanese and I plodded on, placing our hopes in a miracle.

We were all disheartened. We were like a wandering tribe that trails day after day across the desert in search of an illusive spring of flowing waters. Though they would never say so in so many words, inwardly the Japanese grieved at the realization that they had been betrayed by their Lord and the Council of Elders in whom they had trusted. Likewise, the knowledge that the Lord had forsaken me and all my dreams made me suffer. It was as though a friendship had at last been forged between the betrayed and the forsaken – a mutual sympathy and a mutual licking of wounds. I felt an affinity with those Japanese that I cannot describe. It was as if a firm bond of solidarity that I had never felt before had formed between the envoys and myself. To be honest, I had employed many stratagems up until then, dragging them about by the nose to achieve my own private purposes and taking advantage of their weaknesses – whether it was their inability to speak the language or their ignorance even of our destination. For their part, they had shrewdly attempted to use me to accomplish their mission. That icy distance that once separated us seemed to exist no longer.

Yet has the Lord Jesus really deserted me? As I gazed at the leaden sky stretching overhead, I remembered the loneliness the Lord Himself had tasted when He was forsaken by God the Father. No, the life of the Lord Jesus was not in any sense a journey abounding in glory and blessings. The Lord walked about Trans-Jordan and wandered from Tyre to Sidon as an outcast, amid the misunderstandings and jeers of the people. 'Nevertheless I must walk,' the Lord had said in sorrow then, 'today, and tomorrow, and the day following'. In former days those piteous words of the Lord had not made a deep impression on me. But now, as I walked with the Japanese along the road to Barcelona, I thought of the anguish that must have been etched on the Lord's face as He uttered those words.

Nevertheless I must walk today, and tomorrow, and the day following. But how is it that the Japanese can endure such despair? Their fleeting joy now shattered to the core, they must set off again on their long journey and visit yet another unfamiliar country. It would come as no surprise if the Japanese were to be disillusioned with me, even if they were to hate and despise me. But they have never spoken such feelings aloud. The smiles are gone, and they have but little to say now. Watching them following me in silence, how often have I reproached myself! Such were our feelings as we boarded a small, crude barquentine in Barcelona harbour. An icy rain was falling.

Our second day at sea, a storm forced us to seek refuge in the French port of St Tropez. The residents of this tiny village gaped in amazement at the first Japanese they had ever set eyes upon, and warmly offered us the château of the local lord as lodgings. Neither the lord and his wife nor the villagers were able to contain their thoroughly affable curiosity, and all day long they gawked at every slightest movement of the Japanese. They fingered the envoys' clothes and asked to see their swords, which they said resembled the crescent-shaped scimitars of Turkey. Nishi Kyūsuke entertained the crowd by placing a thick sheet of paper on the blade of his sword and then cutting it by gently moving the sword, and every onlooker cried out in admiration. We waited for the storm to pass before we set sail from St Tropez, but the two days we spent there were sufficient to revive smiles as faint as the winter sun on the previously glum faces of the Japanese.

Yet when St Tropez passed out of view and the Mediterranean once again stretched before out eyes, melancholy expressions crept back over the faces of the Japanese who squatted on the deck. As I studied the face of Hasekura, who stood apart from the others gazing at the sea, I realized that he maintained little hope for success as he proceeded on this voyage. His face wore that look of total resignation and fatalism peculiar to the Japanese.

'No one knows what tomorrow will bring,' I told him. 'When we reach Rome, who is to say that everything may not change for the better, the way a ray of sun may suddenly shine through the rain? I have not lost hope. I shall not give up hope to the very end. We cannot discern what is in the mind of God.'

As I spoke these words I turned my eyes towards the horizon. It was almost as though I was trying to encourage not Hasekura, but my own dispirited heart. To be honest, I can no longer comprehend the mind of God. I can no longer determine whether God accepts or rejects my desire to plant the seed of His word in Japan. All I can hold onto now is the knowledge that man cannot deduce the fathomless will of God. What may appear to us as a setback may in fact, in God's reckoning of things, be a purposeful seed which has been planted, or a foundation stone upon which future results may be raised up. These days I repeat this to myself every night as I pray. But that alone is not enough to placate or satisfy my heart.

'O God,' I cry now from the depths of my heart. 'Please tell me. Was it Thy wish that I forsake Japan? Or art Thou telling me not to lose hope to the very end? That is all I want to know.'

But before me there is only gaping silence. In the thick darkness God is silent. At times all I can hear is that laughing voice. The mocking laughter of that woman's voice.

God is the centre point of all order, the standard of all history. Beneath the currents of human history, God maps out another history in accordance with His own will. I am well aware of that fact. But all I have done, all I have planned, all I have dreamed, and even Japan itself are not a part of that history conceived in the mind of God. Have I been an outsider, a hindrance?

Yet during His lifetime even the Lord Jesus experienced the despair I am now tasting. When on the cross He cried, 'Eloi, Eloi, lama sabachthani? My God, my God, why has Thou forsaken me?' Jesus must have been unable to discern the will of God, as I am unable to discern it now. But just before He gave up the ghost, Jesus conquered that despair. And He offered up to God the childlike words of trust, 'Into Thy hands I commend my spirit.' That much I know. And I would like to become such a person.

'Lord Velasco.'

Hasekura interrupted my musings. He spoke hesitantly, like a believer confessing the dark secrets of his heart to a priest.

'I've wanted to ask you this for some time. . . . If we reach Rome and our requests are still not granted, will you remain in España?'

'I . . . I shall return to Japan with all of you. I have no other country now. Japan seems to me more my own country than the land where I was born or the land where I was brought up.' I spoke the words 'my own country' with special emphasis. 'I will go with you to the end.'

'Lord Velasco, haven't you realized yet? If by some chance all our hopes prove to be empty in Rome,' with a burst Hasekura spat out what he had pent up in his heart, 'Lord Tanaka will . . . commit *seppuku*.'

Then, so that he would not have to say those words a second time, he shifted his eyes towards the grey ocean and said no more.

'For a Christian,' I replied, my voice trembling, 'it is not permitted to take away with one's own hand the life which God has given.'

'We did not convert to Christianity in earnest. We became Christians against our will just for the sake of our mission, and for His Lordship.'

Hasekura displayed a coldness he had never revealed before. It was almost as though he was retaliating against me.

'Why would he commit *seppuku*? It's so futile!'

'Lord Tanaka would lose face if he did not commit *seppuku*. He would not be able to face his relatives and friends with dignity.'

'What are face and dignity? I know how much you have suffered for the sake of your mission. As a witness to your journey, I will tell Lord Shiraishi and the Council of Elders everything.'

'Lord Velasco,' Hasekura sighed, 'you don't understand the Japanese.'

I remained on the deck after Hasekura had gone, my spirits darker than the colour of the sea. At the edge of the deck Tanaka stood talking with his attendants. Nothing about him betrayed even the slightest indication that Hasekura's assertions were correct.

On the afternoon of the second day after our departure from St Tropez, we finally caught a distant glimpse of the port of Genoa in the kingdom of Savona. A white city backed by yellowish-brown hills and bathed in a pale sunlight came into view. The turret of an old grey castle rose from its centre. I pointed out the turret and told the envoys and their attendants that a man named Christopher Columbus, who was born here, had traversed the ocean in quest of a golden country in Asia, and that the golden country he sought was none other than Japan.

The harbour town of Genoa, one corner brightly illuminated by the afternoon sun. I leaned back against the deck rail, and like Columbus I thought about the 'golden country'. To Columbus it was a strange Oriental land full of treasure to be plundered. To me that island nation was a land of treasure where the word of God must one day be planted. Columbus sought the golden country but could never find it, while I have been rejected by that golden country. 'Ah Japan. Such an arrogant land. A land which knows only how to take, but never how to give.'

For five days we sailed south along the coastline of Italy, making our way toward Civitavecchia, the outer port of Rome. We arrived there in the evening. A misty rain was falling. On the wharf, which was veiled in a haze and glistening in the rain, several men holding lanterns stood like spectres beside four carriages, patiently waiting for us. They had been sent to welcome us by Cardinal Borghese. From their attitude, which was proper but cool, I could surmise the degree of their discomfiture. The lodgings provided for us were in the fortress of Santa Severa, which is owned by Cardinal Borghese.

The treatment we received there was by no means that befitting foreign ambassadors.

It was clear then what sort of letters and what manner of instructions regarding us had already been sent out from Madrid. Each night I awoke and pondered our situation.

'The delegation of Japanese ambassadors was most quiet and reserved. They were all short in stature, with sun-tanned faces. Tanaka and Hasekura and Nishi each had a flat little nose, and the ends of their long hair were tied up with white ribbons. They told us that this was the mark of a Japanese knight. When the three went out of doors, they wore Japanese robes of deep purple, but on ordinary occasions they wore monks' habits with a little collar attached, with Spanish-style hats on their heads. The long and short swords they carried were exceedingly sharp and just slightly curved. At meal-times, they deftly manipulated two slender sticks to eat their food; they were particularly fond of cabbage and onion soup' (From the diary of the widow Costo of Genoa).

The same suspicious looks that greeted us in Madrid. The same questions repeated, the same replies. For the past few days I have been interrogated here in Civitavecchia by Father Cossudacudo, who is Cardinal Borghese's private secretary, and by Monsignore Don Pablo Alla Leone. From the outset my opinions have clashed with theirs on numerous occasions. They claim that missionary work is now hopeless in Japan, and that it is no longer possible to send missionaries there, while I continue to insist that there is still hope, that it lies in giving the Japanese profits from trade and demonstrating to them that we have no aggressive intentions. For their part, they assert that the Vatican has maintained a tradition of non-interference in other countries' internal political affairs, and they argue that the Pope himself has no authority to override the decisions of the King of España. In my usual fashion, I retorted that the problem concerned only missionary work, and that His Holiness would surely not plunge the Japanese Christians, now without either bishop or Church, into eternal isolation.

The envoys, unable to speak the language, of course did not participate in these debates. All they could do was listen to my reports of the progress of events in the chilly fortress at Santa Severa. Even the most optimistic predictions could no longer bring cheer to the sombre faces of Tanaka and Hasekura. That is understandable.

These Japanese have been disillusioned all too often. Nishi has developed a high fever. This man who made every effort to appear jovial, who of all the Japanese demonstrated the most youthful curiosity, could no longer subdue the weariness that overcame his mind and body. And I too am exhausted. As I gazed at Nishi's sleeping face, which looked even younger than his years, I no longer cared what happened.

We had to wait another two or three days for the announcement of Cardinal Borghese's decision. On the fifth day I was summoned to the Cardinal's villa in Palidoro. The thought of being interrogated by this famous Cardinal, the nephew of Pope Paul V and the most able man in the Vatican, all but paralysed me. Yet within my heart was kindled a faint hope that such a man might perhaps understand my fervour for Japan and the importance of the missionary effort there.

In the study of his villa, which overlooked a well-cultivated garden and a pond where ducks were swimming, the Cardinal, dressed in a cape and a red hat, remained seated as he welcomed me. I purposely arrived dressed in a habit which had faded over the course of our long journey. Of what should I be ashamed? Just as a mud-stained uniform signifies the gory battles in which a soldier has engaged, so I felt my humble robes themselves bore witness to the afflictions of missionary work in Japan which the high-ranking clerics of Rome had never experienced. And so, although I knelt before him and reverently kissed his ring, afterwards I lifted my head defiantly.

'My son. Arise.'

Cardinal Borghese pretended not to notice my posture. His eyes were fixed upon me as I stood up, but when he spoke his voice was soft, as though he was addressing himself.

'The Vatican makes every effort to see that its decisions are always fair and unbiased. We think we know how diligently you and your Order have struggled in Japan. At any rate, we have not taken at face value the personal slanders that have been heaped upon you.'

With a flutter of his cape he placed his large thick hand on my shoulder in a gesture of trust. He seemed to be watching intently to see what effect his action had upon me.

'You can have no idea how the Vatican has prayed that your efforts would bear fruit in Japan. More than anything else, the Vatican itself has prayed that the light of the Lord would shine upon the land of Japan.' There the Cardinal paused, staring intently at my face with his grape-coloured eyes. 'But I tell you now to be long-suffering. I urge you to be patient.'

Though only for a moment, I felt daunted; the Cardinal's eyes and voice were filled with the gentleness and compassion a father shows to his son. He seemed to be aware of the effect of his performance. But at once I saw that Cardinal Borghese was less a clergyman than a shrewd politician.

'You must understand,' the Cardinal admonished me, his hand still resting on my shoulder, 'that the Vatican can no longer countenance the dispatching of missionaries like yourself to a land of persecution. Just as there is no general who willingly sends his soldiers to a meaningless death on the battlefield when he knows he is defeated . . .'

'No.' I recovered my emotional equilibrium. 'Your Eminence, I do not believe Japan is a lost battleground. If our missionary endeavours have not made headway, the primitive tactics of the Jesuits are to blame.'

The Cardinal chuckled softly. It was like the pained smile an aged schoolmaster gives an irascible child.

'Your Eminence, a missionary is not like a soldier. The death of a soldier can sometimes be futile, but when a missionary dies amid persecution, seeds imperceptible to the human eye are sown. Seeds which manifest the glory of God. . . .'

'What you say is true. At the time of persecution in Rome, Peter, the first Pope, planted imperceptible seeds in the hearts of men by his martyrdom.'

'The Lord Himself did not fear death on the hill of Golgotha.'

'What you say is true.'

Time and again the Cardinal repeated, 'What you say is true.' Then the smile vanished abruptly from his lips, to be replaced by a look of sternness.

'But . . . we do not live in the age of the Lord and the Apostles, my son. We run a massive organization. We have a responsibility to the Christian nations and their peoples. And as an organization, we have certain policies. Even if they seem cowardly and tainted to you, it is because of those policies that the organization is sustained. Order is preserved, and the faithful in the Christian nations can maintain their faith in confidence.'

'But even though their numbers are few, some of the faithful are in Japan. Some have left their homes and abandoned their property, hiding in mines and in the hills so that they can maintain every particle of their faith amid the persecution.'

As I replied, I thought of the beggarly face of the man who had come seeking confession at the construction site in Ogatsu. I do not know whether he is alive or dead now. But for the sake of people like him, I had to say to the Cardinal the things that had to be said.

'Those believers . . . no longer have a Church. There are no more missionaries to encourage them, to bolster them, to set an example for them. If the Vatican is a splendid Mother who protects the faithful, don't they too have the right to be embraced in her gentle arms? Aren't they now like the one lamb separated from the flock of which the Bible speaks?'

'If in searching for the one lamb the other sheep are exposed to danger . . .,' the Cardinal said sadly, 'the shepherd has no choice but to abandon that lamb. It cannot be helped if one is to protect the organization.'

'That reminds me of the words of the High Priest Caiaphas when the Lord was killed. To save an entire nation, there is no choice but to sacrifice a single man. Those are the words Caiaphas spoke.'

Yes, the High Priest Caiaphas always valued order and safety. He sacrificed the Lord Jesus to preserve order and safety.

The Cardinal averted his head. He sat for a long while without uttering a word, wrapped in his large cloak.

I saw that my audacious remarks had angered this influential member of the Vatican hierarchy. But I no longer felt like shrinking away from him. The world has placed too much emphasis on the quest for order and safety.

'That is true.' When the Cardinal finally turned towards me, it was not anger but an indescribable blend of weariness and sorrow that was visible on his face. 'My son. I do not wish to concur with the High Priest Caiaphas's remarks. But at that time the Lord did not direct an organization, while Caiaphas did. Those who run organizations, like Caiaphas, will always say – to protect the majority, we have no choice but to abandon the one. Even we who believe in the Lord place ourselves in the same position as the High Priest Caiaphas from the moment we create religious orders and set up organizations. Even Saint Peter had to abandon his comrade Stephen to a death by stoning in order to preserve his religious order.'

I stood very still, listening to his words. I had never imagined that such a statement could come from the lips of the Cardinal himself. He avoided my eyes and murmured softly, almost to himself, 'This is a . . . a constant source of anguish to me.'

'Is that what you call the justice of an organization?'

'Yes.'

'Is this the way things are always carried out in the Vatican?'

'Even I don't know that. But so long as I am responsible, I have no choice but to adopt Caiaphas's attitude towards the faithful in Japan. Yet . . . I would not want you to think that my heart is devoid of sorrow and remorse. Someone must bear the burden of that torment.'

The Cardinal lifted his head. The face that shortly before had shone with confidence was now twisted in misery. At a loss for words, I was still suspicious of the Cardinal's true feelings. I had never thought it possible that a man who claimed to be a cardinal could confess his own anguish so directly and forthrightly.

'Of course I know that this all runs counter to the Lord's teachings about love. Perhaps other cardinals will denounce this policy of mine. But for now, I will not alter my opinion.'

'Why not? Why should you insist on maintaining something that goes against the Lord's teachings about love?'

In my excitement I came close to forgetting the rank of the man before me.

'Then for what reason did the Lord Jesus die on the cross? Your Eminence has just said it was for the sake of the organization. But until today I believed that the Vatican organization was not administered like a country. I always thought that it was an organization of love which transcended the limitations of all nations and peoples.'

Cardinal Borghese studied this raving man before him with a look of perplexity. He clutched at the cross he wore on his chest, debating whether to say something. Then he spoke up decisively.

'My son. Do you believe you can overcome the real world . . . with love alone?'

'But Jesus was a Man of Love.'

'And because of His love . . . he was murdered in the world of politics. And, sadly, our organization cannot flee this world of politics either. The Vatican cannot adopt any measures that would weaken the influence of the Catholic nations.'

'What does that have to do with the missionary work in Japan?'

'Protestant countries like England and Holland also have their sights set on Japan. For that very reason, we must do nothing to provoke further hatred of Catholic countries like España and Portugal over the question of missionary work in Japan. In my judgement it would be more profitable to both España and Portugal if they avoided goading the ruler of Japan any further, and sat back and watched the situation for a time. The Vatican is not an isolated entity. It has a responsibility as an organization to oppose the Protestant nations and to support the Catholic ones.'

The Man of Love was murdered in the world of politics because of His love. The Cardinal spoke the words as though he were spewing bitter poison from his mouth. I stared at his red hat and large cloak, the symbols of his office.

'My son. Please understand.'

This was the culmination of my long journey.

'Hereafter I will pray for you, and for Japan.'

I bowed deeply and left the room. The Cardinal remained in his chair, staring out of the window. I have no idea what he was thinking.

The ragtag company of Japanese emerged from the fortress of Santa Severa, which was soiled with pigeon droppings and debris from the recent storms. Like a protective force the group encircled Nishi Kyūsuke, who had just recovered from his illness, and sluggishly descended into the flatlands. The samurai, who rode beside Tanaka and Velasco at the head of the group, looked back anxiously at his young compatriot from time to time, and waited patiently for the lagging company to catch up. When they had travelled across Nueva España, despite the fierce glare of the sun their steps had still been light with hope and strength. But now that their hopes had been dashed, the Japanese trudged along, all but dragging their feet. Not one of the party had any illusions that matters would change for the better in the capital called Rome. Whether they went to Rome or to yet another country, each of them now knew that this journey of theirs was futile. All that remained was for them to add the finishing stroke to this pointless endeavour. If they did not add that final stroke, they would have no pretext for returning to Japan. This journey, which for so long had dragged them from one illusion to another, was now drawing to a close.

It was already spring. The pale pink blossom of the almond trees which splashed the fields with green was in full bloom, and a farmer was busily plying his hoe. He gazed at the peculiar procession with wide eyes. Dressed in long robes like Arabs, with *obi* about their waists and their hair tied up behind, to this farmer the Japanese appeared to be visitors from a tropical country. He threw down his hoe in the field and raced back to his house.

In the samurai, the white apple blossom and the call of the birds aroused no emotion whatsoever. He could no longer muster even any longing for the springtime in the marshland. He merely surrendered himself to the jostlings of his horse and followed behind Velasco. How many times, he wondered, had he been betrayed by this man? He had been instilled with hope, only to have those hopes crumble. Then he had embraced yet another illusion and gone on with his journey. But his weary soul lacked even the will to hate the missionary. To the samurai, Velasco was just a pitiful man like himself.

When they passed through a village, they were watched with frightened eyes by the people who lined the roads; occasionally someone would call out to them cheerfully, but the Japanese walked on without expression, as though they had not noticed. They were like a funeral procession following a coffin.

Spring rains fell in the evening. By the time the rains let up, they had reached the top of Torre Vecchia Hill. The Eternal City lay in a slight haze; the Tiber meandered drowsily; the Pincian Hill, cloaked by a light-green forest, was visible in the distance; brownish houses were stacked one on top of another; and the domes of innumerable cathedrals stabbed at the sky.

Velasco halted his horse on the hill and dutifully pointed out the Colosseum and the Roman Forum, but this time the Japanese did not even nod.

'That is the Vatican, where the Pope resides.'

A round white cupola peered out from among the brown houses, and people scurried like ants about the circular plaza. The Japanese were glumly silent, as though they were attending a wake.

At last they entered Rome. As they made their way along the rain-soaked roads, a group of children began to follow them. Soon they were joined by curious adults. The Japanese climbed the high stone staircase to the Campidoglio and disappeared inside the monastery of Ara Coeli. Once the doors closed behind them, they did not reappear. A rumour spread that these were ambassadors from Hungary, and the crowd departed.

For the space of a week, Rome waited through signs of a rainy spring for the arrival of Easter. In the cathedrals every altar was draped in purple cloth in mourning for the death of Jesus, the flames of the sacred candles were extinguished, and prayers were said for the resurrection. Only around the image of the Blessed Mary did a cluster of candles flicker, and in the evening groups of men and women gathered before them to chant the litany of the atonement. But not one of the supplicants could say that he had seen the Japanese emerge from the monastery of Ara Coeli.

On Easter morning, in the faint light of daybreak, shadowy figures began to congregate, one group after another forming into lines in St Peter's Square at the Vatican. Parties of monks and pilgrims who had come from afar, they camped before the great basilica and waited patiently. Beneath the milky mists, the crowd braced themselves against the morning chill, their soft voices endlessly intoning the litany. By the time the mist had gone, the square was almost packed with such pilgrims and monks. On the stone steps young military guards wearing silver helmets and red uniforms stood in single file, their lances poised diagonally.

At eight o'clock the first bell rang out. At this signal, the belfries of every cathedral throughout Rome echoed one after another. The Easter festival had begun. Soon the lavish carriages of the noblemen invited to the High Mass clogged the entrance to St Peter's Square. They threaded their way through the crowds and disappeared into the great basilica.

Just before nine o'clock the doors on either side of the basilica were opened. The monks and pilgrims who had gathered in front of the stone steps pushed their way through the doors. They would be allowed to receive a blessing from the Holy Father. The spear-carrying guards restrained the stampeding crowds and forced them into lines. Those who were left outside had to kneel on the ground where they were.

The great basilica, supported by marble columns, was packed to bursting. Cardinals, wearing their characteristic hats decorated with gold, sat on either side of the central altar, waiting in silence for the appearance of the Pope. The golden altar, which until the previous day had been draped with a purple cloth, was today adorned with a multitude of silver candlesticks. From a seat of honour among the clergy, Cardinal Borghese gazed down indifferently at the heads of the masses who knelt on the floor in reverent silence. Presently a stir arose near the entrance to the great basilica. The massive main door through which the Pope would pass had been opened. The organ blared out and the Vatican choir began to sing the Easter '*Vidi aquam.*'

'*Pontifice nostro, Pontifice nostro.*' The cry originated in one corner of the basilica, swept throughout the hall, spread to the masses assembled in the square, and soon became one great voice.

'*Pontifice nostro! Pontifice nostro!*'

At that moment the figure of Paul V suddenly soared into view, like the figurehead of a ship surging up between the waves. Seated on a palanquin borne by several priests, the Pope appeared in his white papal robes and high hat, one hand raised wearily. As he gave the sign of his blessing to the frenzied masses all about him, his palanquin slowly made its way through the sea of humanity towards St Peter's Basilica.

'*Oremus pro Pontifice nostro.*' In one corner of the sea of humanity stood a party of monks who lifted their voices in unison. The mud which stained their humble robes made it clear that they had travelled a long way to attend this Easter celebration.

'*Dominus conserveto eum.*'

The Pope looked towards the monks with satisfaction and made the sign of the cross in blessing. When the crowd saw this, the orderly ranks were thrown into chaos. Those who hoped to move even a single step closer to the palanquin and receive a similar blessing pushed against the people in front of them, thrusting their way through the crowd. But like a boat drifting on the sea, the Pope's palanquin left the pursuing masses in its wake and was swept toward the great basilica. As the palanquin laboriously climbed the stone steps, guards dressed in silver helmets and red uniforms formed a wall to restrain the jostling crowd of pilgrims. The palanquin was swallowed up by the main doorway to St Peter's Basilica.

The moment the palanquin entered the basilica, the voices of the waiting chorus echoed through the great hall like an avalanche. It was an Alleluia. The strong, thick male voices resounded from each wall and the high domed ceiling.

Alleluia, Alleluia
Confitemini Domino

As the palanquin passed by, the nobles, clergymen and pilgrims kneeling on all sides lifted their heads like stalks of wheat to observe the hand extending from the pure white papal robes to proffer a blessing. The heads then bowed as one. In the apse, twelve cardinals representing the Apostles stood to welcome the arrival of the palanquin, scores of candles flickered in silver candlesticks about the altar, and all was in readiness for the beginning of the High Mass to be offered by Pope Paul V.

Suddenly, from amid the throng in the north transept, several figures rose to their feet. They rushed towards the passing palanquin, and one of their number shouted out the first words which the jostling supplicants heard uttered in the basilica.

The Pope had brought his right hand up near his cheek and was about to etch a silent cross. But the urgency in the eyes of the three men standing below him stayed his gesture. The Pope noticed that the faces of the men were brown like Arabs', their noses small, and their hair tied up tightly behind.

They were Asians. But he could not tell what country they had come from. They each wore long robes reaching to their feet, which were clad in short white socks and peculiar sandals. The Pope could tell that one of the men was pleading for something, but he could not understand what he was saying.

'We are Japanese!' Tanaka cried frantically. 'We are envoys who have come across the sea from Japan.'

Three monks tugged forcefully at the foreigners, trying to pull them away from the palanquin. But the Japanese planted their feet firmly and refused to budge.

'Please!' The three men were at a loss for words. Once they had said this much, they could no longer suppress the emotions that swelled inside them, and they looked up into the face of Paul V. The words 'a petition' caught in their throats and would not come forth. Tears welled from the envoys' eyes and flowed down their sun-baked cheeks.

'Please . . .!'

When the three Asians bowed their heads deeply and reverently, the monks who held them from behind loosened their grip. They realized that these men were not mad or malicious.

The Pope looked out over the people kneeling behind the Asians, seeking some sort of assistance. He could sense that these men were pleading desperately for something, and wanted to hear their request.

When the Pope's glance fell upon him, Velasco did not move from among the crowd. He spoke not a word. Among all the multitudes crowded into the great basilica he alone understood Japanese. Only he knew what it was these men were trying to shout. Yet, as though some massive force were restraining him, Velasco did not move. All he could do was stare fixedly at the fat, tranquil Pope seated atop his palanquin. An old man dressed in white robes, barely raising the fingers laden with bejeweled rings. A voice whispered in Velasco's heart: 'None of you understands the sorrow of these Japanese. None of you understands my sorrow as I have battled with Japan.' An emotion much like revenge sealed his lips.

When he realized there was no one to tell him what these foreigners were seeking, a faint look of remorse flickered in the Pope's eyes. Believers all over the world were waiting for the Easter observances, and the Pope could not neglect to perform them simply because of these Asians. The many sheep of the flock could not be ignored for the sake of a single lamb. In a low voice he ordered the palanquin bearers to move on.

'Please . . .!' the Japanese pleaded for the last time. The cortège ignored them and moved forward. The Pope smiled again and gave his blessing to the nobles and clergymen on either side. As one the people raised and lowered their heads. And before the altar, Cardinal Borghese nodded broadly as he welcomed the palanquin. . . .

Velasco waited for the Cardinal in a chamber of St Peter's Basilica. He had not sought a meeting with the Cardinal, but rather had come at his summons.

The tiny chamber was quiet and cold and solitary. The floor was inlaid with marble, and the ceiling decorated with a fresco of Michael the Archangel bearing a spear, his great wings spread wide. But the painting was cracked, and it lacked the impact of a Michelangelo.

Velasco knew why he had been summoned by the Cardinal. By now all Rome knew that the Japanese had acted indecorously towards the Pope, and it was understandable that Velasco should be reprimanded for failing to subdue them.

'How could I have stopped them then . . .?'

Velasco knew better than anyone else the ordeals the Japanese had been through. For that reason he had been unable to restrain them when they darted out from the crowd and cried out in voices laden with sorrow. He had wanted to pour out his bitterness and all the thoughts of his heart. He had no excuses to offer, but even if he were to be reprimanded by Cardinal Borghese, in his heart he felt no pangs of remorse.

He heard footsteps in the distance. Cardinal Borghese, wearing the same red hat and large cloak, came wearily into the room and sat down in a chair. He was accompanied by a steadfast-looking young priest.

'I know why I was ordered to come here today.' Before the Cardinal had a chance to speak, Velasco bent over his proffered hand and started to apologize. 'I also realize that I am responsible for the error of the Japanese. But knowing how much they have suffered until now . . .'

'I did not call you here to condemn you,' the Cardinal interrupted. 'When the Holy Father heard all about the incident from me, he was filled with profound compassion for the envoys.'

Velasco looked down and said nothing. Compassion and pity required no compensation. He and the envoys had not traversed the world in order to be pitied and shown compassion.

'I called you here,' the Cardinal looked sadly at Velasco, 'to find out whether you still maintain even a speck of hope. If you do, you must abandon it.'

'I gave up hope when I spoke to you before.' Velasco sensed a tone of defiance in his own voice.

'No, you have not given up yet,' the Cardinal muttered, a sullen look clouding his face. 'Because you know nothing at all.'

At these words, the priest who served as secretary drew a sheet of paper from the folder he was holding in his hand.

'This is a letter from the Viceroy of the Philippines which the Vatican received two days ago. You would do well to read it.'

Velasco took the brownish, sun-parched paper and lowered his eyes to the letters that seemed to leap off the page at him. As he read, the Cardinal sat rubbing his hands together.

'You must give up. As the letter explains, the Japanese King is now enforcing the expulsion of all missionaries and monks from his country. He has further prohibited any more missionaries from setting foot in Japan hereafter. You and the Japanese envoys . . . must give up.'

The letter was an official document dated November 1614. The signature of Viceroy Juan de Silva leapt up like a dwarf on the final line of the letter. Velasco closed his eyes, maintaining an unusual state of composure. What passed before his eyes then was the scene of judgement by the bishops in Madrid. The scene in which the bishop with the vulture-like face had read aloud the letter from Macao in Velasco's presence.

'The Vatican can risk no further danger. We cannot encourage España or Portugal to trade with the Japanese when they utterly reject and persecute the Christians. You must appreciate that under these circumstances the ambassadors' letter is now meaningless.'

'O Lord, Thy will be done.' He struggled to remember the prayer. 'If this is God's will, then I shall obey. My designs were not a part of the history which God had mapped out. Now I see that clearly.' He heard laughter. He could hear a woman's laughing voice far, far in the distance.

'They will die.' The words suddenly tumbled from Velasco's lips like medicine trickling out of the mouth of an invalid. 'When they hear this news,' Velasco repeated to the Cardinal, who was looking at him suspiciously, 'they will have no recourse but to die.'

'Why?' The Cardinal's tone was more angry than surprised. 'Why would they do such a thing?'

'They are Japanese samurai. The samurai have been taught to die when their pride is wounded.'

'They have discharged their duty. And they are Christians, aren't they? They are not allowed to commit suicide!'

Velasco felt a touch of hatred for the uncomprehending face of this prelate. That hatred impelled him to intimidate his foe.

'In the last analysis, it is the Vatican that is murdering them, by forcing them to commit the grave sin of suicide.'

'Can't you stop them?'

'I . . . I no longer have any idea,' Velasco shook his head. 'If only the Vatican would . . . at least help them to hold onto their pride.'

'What is it you are asking?'

'For an audience with the Pope. To have him treat the Japanese as
ambassadors. . . .'

'Even if he grants the Japanese an audience, we cannot respond to
their requests. Our policy has already been determined.'

'I am not asking you to grant their requests. But the envoys are so
. . . pathetic. If only for the sake of their honour, their pride, an
audience with the Pope. . . .' A stream of tears trickled down his sun-
bleached habit. 'That is all . . . all I ask.'

It was the day on which the Pope of Rome was to receive the Japanese
envoys. After Mass and breakfast at the monastery, with the help of
their attendants the envoys for the first time put on the ceremonial
robes they had brought with them for formal audiences.

The carriage sent for them by the Cardinal was already waiting
outside the gate of the monastery. Since this was an unofficial
audience, no guards accompanied them, but three uniformed coach-
men rode on the ebony carriage decorated with gold markings. As
they bade farewell to the monks and their attendants, the samurai,
seated beside Tanaka, Nishi and Velasco, gazed out of the carriage
window and saw Yozō looking at him, his hands clasped as though in
supplication to the gods.

Yozō seemed to be encouraging the samurai not to give up hope to
the very end. He seemed to be saying he would follow his master
whatever happened. Yet the samurai had no illusions as he set out for
this perfunctory audience. It was no more than a ceremony to signify
the final ending of their long journey.

Still, Yozō's gesture moved the samurai to the point of tears. In his
present state of despair, forsaken and betrayed from all quarters, the
samurai felt that this servant who had attended him faithfully since
childhood was the only man he could trust. Blinking his eyes, he
nodded to Yozō.

The coach lurched forward. The clatter of the horses' hooves
echoed sharply and regularly from the paved roads. The three
envoys sat in silence. Two months earlier the prospect of meeting a
king, of having an audience with a pope, would have seemed like a
glorious dream. To rural samurai who had never even seen His
Lordship, it would have been an unimaginable, unprecedented event.

But now no surge of joy leapt up within them. They felt not the
slightest enthusiasm. The envoys knew that this audience had been
granted out of sympathy by a cardinal who had given way to
Velasco's entreaties. They realized it was an elaborate gesture

intended to persuade them to accept with resignation. Then their long journey would come to an end. Thereafter all that lay before them was the long, empty, futile road back home.

Umbrella pines lined both sides of the road. The clatter of the horses' hooves grew louder still. Far in the distance they could see the dome of St Peter's Basilica, a cloudy sky as its backdrop. The carriage passed from Palleone Street to Borgo Street and entered the square in front of the Vatican.

'When the Pope appears,' Velasco repeated once more, 'touch the floor three times with your right knee, and bring your face up to his feet.'

As they passed through the iron gate to the right of the great basilica, they were saluted by spear-bearing guards dressed in red uniforms. When the carriage halted, a man wearing a silver wig and long white stockings expressionlessly opened the door for them, then stared coldly at Velasco and the envoys who were dressed in their peculiar ceremonial robes.

They climbed the stone steps and walked down a corridor which had a floor of slickly shining marble. Black bronze statues lined one side of the corridor.

Two priests awaiting them at the end of the passageway wordlessly directed the four men to an antechamber. Frescoes covered the walls, and lavish chairs with golden armrests had been arranged on the plush carpet.

The four men waited for a bell to ring. They had been told to enter the audience chamber at a signal from the bell.

'I will go in first,' Velasco repeated carefully. 'Then you follow in single-file – first Lord Tanaka, then Lord Hasekura and Lord Nishi.'

It seemed to them that a long time passed. Tanaka and the samurai sat in their chairs and closed their eyes; Nishi readjusted his formal headdress. After the long, long wait, a bell finally sounded in the distance, and the door opened.

'Pull yourself together, Nishi,' Tanaka said softly. His voice was filled with compassion, quite unlike the usual Tanaka.

High-ranking clergymen stood along both sides of the cardinals' conference hall where the audience was to take place. With Velasco leading the way, the three men advanced through the profusion of red vestments and red hats. They sensed scores of eyes fixed on them from either side. In the distance the Pope sat in a tall chair; he alone wore a white hat.

The Pope was a short, chubby man who looked towards the ambassadors with gentle eyes steeped in affection. There was none of the august air of the King of Kings about this man, and it seemed that any moment he would get up from his chair and come towards them.

Velasco halted and dropped his right knee to the floor. The three Japanese tried to emulate his action, but Nishi staggered slightly, and the samurai moved quickly to steady him. Cardinal Borghese, standing beside the Pope, leaned over and made some comment in his ear.

'Read it . . . the letter from His Lordship,' Velasco hurriedly prompted Tanaka, who stood gawking like a simpleton. Tanaka took out the letter and unfolded it with both hands.

'We humbly come before the great Lord of all the earth, His Holiness Paulus V, Pope of Rome.'

Tanaka's voice caught in his throat, and even the samurai could see his hands trembling.

'Velasco, a monk of the Order of Saint Francis, has come to our land and expounded Christianity. He has visited our domain and taught me the mysteries of the Christian faith. As a result, I have been able to understand the purport of those teachings for the first time, and I have decided to embrace them without hesitation. . . . However, at the present time, extreme circumstances prevail. They have proven a hindrance to me . . . and I have not yet . . . been able to achieve my desire.'

Again Tanaka's voice faltered. Each time his colleague stumbled, a feeling of emptiness surged up in the samurai's breast. There was no possibility that the clerics assembled in this audience chamber could understand the language or the import of the letter which Tanaka was reading. It was comprehensible only to Velasco and the envoys.

'Therefore, in consequence of my love and respect for the monks of this church, I wish to erect cathedrals for them, and to exert all my efforts in the propagation of goodness. If there be anything which Your Holiness might consider necessary for the spreading of the holy laws of God, I will gladly make provision for it in my kingdom. I myself will furnish whatever funding and lands are required for cathedrals, so Your Holiness need have no apprehensions in that respect.'

Enough! The samurai restrained the word that had risen to his throat. Enough! He wanted to stop poor Tanaka from continuing this ridiculous farce. The meaningless words of this letter. This man in the white hat who listened in silence. This man, and Cardinal Borghese beside him, seemed to have no difficulty enduring this absurd farce.

'Although Nueva España is very distant from our land, I earnestly desire to enter into relations with that land, and therefore I beseech the influence of Your Holiness to assist me in attaining that ambition.'

When Tanaka had managed to stammer his way to the end of the letter, unsightly beads of perspiration trickled down his forehead. Velasco waited for Tanaka to present the letter, then took a step forward to offer a translation.

Unexpectedly the Pope rose to his feet. Such a gesture was not a part of the normal course of the ceremony and a mild stir arose in the audience chamber. The clerics all turned as one towards the throne.

'I . . .' Paul V bent down and addressed the envoys. His voice was filled with sorrow. 'I promise you that I will pray at each Mass for the next five days . . . for Japan and for each of you. I believe God will not forsake Japan.'

The Pope stepped down from the throne and stared intently at the envoys once again. Then, accompanied by Cardinal Borghese and three other cardinals, he lifted his hand in blessing to the entire assembly and disappeared into a separate chamber.

Under the watchful gaze of the clerics, the envoys and Velasco retired to the antechamber. After the thick door creaked shut, the four men collapsed into chairs. All four were absorbed in their private thoughts. In the heavy silence, Velasco rested his hands on his knees and let his head droop.

Chapter 9

I have not written in this journal for a long while. It was too painful for me to tell of the collapse of our hopes, and to describe our departure from Europe, with the continent disappearing in the distance as we crossed the rain-misted ocean.

Only one person – the priest who serves as Cardinal Borghese's private secretary – accompanied us to the wharf at Civitavecchia harbour. As a gesture of the Cardinal's goodwill, the priest gave each of the three envoys a certificate conferring Roman citizenship upon them. Since there is no possibility the envoys will ever visit Italy again, the certificates are worthless. We had presented a meaningless letter to the Pope, and in exchange the Cardinal sent these worthless scraps of paper.

In no time at all the Spanish government added insult to injury. We were forbidden to stop in Madrid and ordered to proceed directly to Sevilla. Even in Sevilla there was no one to welcome us but my family, and the Japanese, stripped of all privileges, were no better than miserable nomads. And in return for the 3,300 ducats in travel expenses provided for our empty purses by my Order and my family, I was forced to agree to labour in a monastery in Nueva España or Manila. In short, I have been defeated on all fronts.

I no longer understand what God wanted. For many years I was confident that He wished the gospel to be preached in Japan, and that He had given me life to that end. That conviction gave me the strength to endure every trial. But now my confidence has slipped away, and, even more frightening, I even feel at times as if God was toying with me. I had always thought that the history of man was bound up in the history mapped out by God. God's history, however, was a world apart from my own thoughts and ambitions.

One month from Civitavecchia to Sevilla. From Sevilla, another three months on the Atlantic Ocean, encountering two storms. I have passed each day of our voyage prostrated in humiliation. But the Japanese – though at first they stared at the sea with those blank eyes that never reveal emotion – are better equipped to accept misfortune than we Europeans, and they have quickly resigned themselves to their plight. Sometimes when they congregate on deck I can hear them laughing with one another. Perhaps it is their elation at being liberated at last from the long, bitter journey and the prospect of finally returning to their native land that prompts these occasional expressions of light-heartedness and good cheer.

The envoy Nishi Kyūsuke approaches the crew and bombards them with all sorts of questions, using broken Spanish and sign language, much as he did on our voyage across the Pacific. The young man has an extraordinary degree of curiosity about our civilization and technology, and in his notebook he carefully records everything he learns from the sailors.

Tanaka Tarozaemon no longer berates Nishi for his curiosity. He has in fact abandoned his usual obstinacy, and occasionally when the attendants are singing on the deck he will clap his hands in time to the music. As I watch him clapping his hands, it seems inconceivable that he would do the sort of thing Hasekura feared. He looks to me as though the thought that he has done all that could be done has brought a quiet resignation to his heart.

Most of the Japanese, however, do not attend the Masses I say each day aboard ship. Although I recognize that they did not receive baptism from their hearts and were baptized only for the sake of their mission, when I intone the words of the Mass in the dining-hall which serves as a chapel and see only one Japanese offering up prayers, I experience a feeling of humiliation I cannot describe.

'It is all . . . because of Thee. If Thou hadst not brought about such a result, our voyage home would have been filled with joy, and the ship would have rung with the voices of Japanese singing hymns to Thy praise. But Thou didst not desire that. Thou chosest to forsake Japan.'

Only one Japanese steals furtively to Mass. He appears midway through the service so as not to be noticed by his comrades, and he flees away as soon as he has received communion. His pitiful figure reminds me of the beggarly Christian I met beside the stacks of lumber at Ogatsu.

This Japanese is not one of the envoys. Tanaka, Hasekura and Nishi have not come to Mass even once since the day of the audience with the Pope in Rome. They have not said a single angry word to me directly, but by their absence they have clearly demonstrated what is in their hearts. The man who skulks into Mass is Hasekura's servant Yozō. When I look into his eyes, I am reminded of the eyes of a dog. Nervous, forlorn eyes. But he will not forsake the lord to whom he has sworn allegiance. I remember him constantly at Hasekura's side throughout our long journey. Perhaps now he will not forsake our Lord either. . . .

It has again been some time since I have taken up my pen. After encountering those two storms on the Atlantic, we finally docked in Veracruz. When we passed this way before, the seasonal winds were sweeping noisily through the city, but now the streets are almost deserted, and the place seems as desolate as our despairing hearts.

Nothing has changed. The monastery where we stayed is the same, and we can hear the same bell tolling every two hours from the tiny plaza near the monastery. When we went to pay our respects to the fortress commander at San Juan de Ulúa, we saw the same creases which his military cap had carved into his forehead, and he had proudly hung the Japanese sword he received on the wall of his office.

He invited us to supper. Officers and their wives were also in attendance at the party, and they greeted us warmly. This time the Japanese were more subdued as they drank the wine and ate the tasteless food. When the banquet came to an end after a long succession of trivial questions, Tanaka spoke for the entire group of Japanese and solemnly offered their thanks. Despite being unable to achieve their desired goal, they had had the pleasure of seeing many nations and various lands, and so they had no regrets, Tanaka candidly told their hosts.

When our returning carriage reached the plaza near the monastery, three fellows wearing sombreros and white outfits were playing music in a bar. As if to himself, Tanaka blurted out that the tune reminded him of a song he often heard back home.

The envoys retired to their rooms in the dark monastery. I lit a candle in my room and sat down at the desk to write two letters. One was to my uncle in Sevilla, the other to the Superior of the monastery in Mexico City. I asked the Superior to arrange for a boat bound for the Philippines to carry the Japanese back to their homeland, and reported that I would be accompanying the envoys to Manila where, in accordance with the orders from my superiors, I would spend the rest of my life working in the monastery.

When I finished writing the letters, my heart was strangely at ease. The realization that the flames of passion which had been my reason for living had now burned themselves out brought me a tranquillity I had not known since our departure from Rome. I set down my quill and, staring at the candle's flickering flame, I realized that my long attachment to Japan was now at an end.

Now that I think about it, the first time I ever heard that there was a country called Japan was in 1595, when I was at the San Diego Monastery in Sevilla. My superiors had been encouraging me to do missionary work in Nueva España, but somehow I had always been faintly uncomfortable with the idea. I suppose that was because of the personality I inherited from my family. I felt that my temperament was not cut out to perform missionary work among safe, docile Indians in an already peaceful country like Nueva España.

The yearning to go to a land of suppression and persecution and to fight as a soldier of the Lord throbbed ceaselessly in the depths of my heart. My superiors continually warned me that this nature of mine militated against the virtues of meekness and submissiveness.

Three years later, in 1598, the name and substance of Japan came to mean even more to me. The previous year a report had come in from the Society of Jesus in Japan that the 'Taikō', the ruler of Japan, had begun to persecute the Christians there. Twenty-six captured missionaries and Japanese Christians had been sent from the capital to Nagasaki on the island of Kyushu and burned at the stake. This event created a stir even in Sevilla, but at that moment I decided Japan was the country where I wanted to be buried when I died. The words of the Lord commanding His Apostles, 'Go ye into all the world and preach the gospel,' echoed in my ears.

In 1600, the Apostolic Constitution *'Onerosa Pastoralis'* was promulgated by Pope Clement VIII. For me it was a manifestation of the Lord's limitless grace. By means of that papal brief the proselytization of Japan, which previously had been restricted to the Jesuits, was now opened to all monastic orders. Our Order in the Philippines then summoned from España those who wished to work in Japan, and preparations were made to teach the Japanese language.

But my family did not support my desire to serve in Japan. The women in my family, especially my mother and my aunt, urged me to go to a safe monastery in Nueva España, and they even attempted to change my mind by taking steps to have me appointed to such a post.

That same year I joined a group of missionaries assembled by Juan de San Francisco and bound for the Philippines, and on the twelfth day of June I boarded a ship at Sevilla. That voyage was considerably more trying than my present journey with the Japanese – enduring storms, shortages of food and water, and plagues, I arrived in Manila a near-invalid. Yet my afflictions on that voyage could not begin to compare with the sufferings which the Lord bore on the cross.

The first Asian city I ever laid eyes on, Manila was filthy, vulgar and unbearably noisy. Spaniards, blacks, native Filipinos and Chinese jostled, shouted and scurried about amid a scorching heat that was like a smelting furnace. Our brethren had entirely despaired of doing missionary work among the many Chinese who lived there. Since at that time any Chinese who received baptism was exempted from paying taxes for a period of ten years, the number of Church members was great, but it was obvious that their conversion to Christianity was not sincere. Despite their baptism, they did not lead Christian lives, but indulged in the strange and eerie superstitions and rituals practised by their own people.

Compared to the twenty thousand Chinese in Manila, the Japanese were fewer in number – less than a tenth as many – and most of them were engaged in trade. Some two hundred of them were Christians.

I learned the Japanese language from those Japanese Christians, and from them I found out what sort of people the Japanese were. From my observations, the Japanese mind worked considerably faster than that of any other race, and they were richly blessed with curiosity and a desire for knowledge. They were possessed of a stronger sense of pride and decorum than even the Spanish. I marvelled that such a people had been able to live so long without a knowledge of God's grace.

During my two and half years in Manila, an image of the Japan I hoped one day to visit took shape in my mind like clouds on a summer's day. Just as Columbus had crossed the wide oceans in search of a golden country, in my dreams Japan became a golden country – an island to be conquered for God, a field upon which to do battle. The ruler of Japan had already died, and the Tokugawa Shōgun had assumed control. We heard that this king had also adopted a policy of persecution towards the Christians, and that the Jesuit missionaries had been banished to Kyushu, where their meagre missionary efforts struggled to survive. Yet as those reports reached Manila, one after another, instead of being disheartened, my fighting spirit was even more fervently aroused.

My opportunity came in June 1603. The Viceroy of the Philippines decided to send an embassy in response to the Japanese King's gesture of amity, and I was included in that group, not as a missionary but as an interpreter. Our ship sailed the tides northward, and after a month on the edge of the horizon I was finally able to see the country that had so attracted me. Birds danced over the waves. Scores of fishing boats plied their trade beneath the hot summer sun. Soon the soft, gently-sloping hills and the outlines of the islands came slowly into view at the furthest border of the sea. It was Japan. It was a Japan very different from the land of persecution and oppression I had imagined.

But when our ship entered the bay several skiffs suddenly appeared. An arrogant-looking leader boarded our ship, accompanied by several subordinates carrying guns. They forced us onto shore as if they were hauling prisoners about, and after making us wait for a long while on the hot beach, they finally conceded that we were emissaries of the Viceroy of the Philippines. We had landed in a bay called Ajiro, near Edo where the King resided.

The scenes which float before my eyes now as I stare at the candle flame are of the beautiful mountains and seas of Japan as I saw them for the first time. A Japan which at first glance in the sunlight seemed the very epitome of tranquillity. I felt then that this was indeed a land worthy of the Lord's beatification, 'Blessed are the meek.'

But the real Japan did not prove to be so meek. The scene before my eyes shifts to an inner chamber in Edo Castle, where I was taken to meet an old man sitting on a velvet-upholstered chair. Edo, a city no less orderly than any of the cities of the west. Long black fences marked off the residences of the *daimyōs* and warriors, and black canals surrounded the majestic, multi-layered castle which glowered at us menacingly. Unlike the opulent palace of Madrid, the interior of the castle to which we were led was a succession of treacherous, blackly glistening corridors and gold-leafed sliding doors misty with age. After passing through a maze of corridors, we had our first glimpse of an old man of average height, about sixty years old, sitting on a velvet chair. The old man was engaged in an audience with the most powerful lord in all Japan, and yet that lord grovelled on the floor like a slave and withdrew from the room bent over so low he seemed to be kissing the ground. The old man fixed his eyes upon us and scarcely spoke a word. All the questions were asked by a secretary who sat about fifty paces from the King. From the secretary's lips we learned that the King not only wanted to do business with the Philippines, but also sought trade with Nueva España and hoped to have Spanish miners sent to Japan. The delegation promised to discuss these matters with Manila.

After consulting several priests and monks of the Franciscan order who were already in Japan, I remained behind in Edo when the emissaries left. My pretext was that I needed to take care of some loose ends left by the delegation, and that I would serve as interpreter for any future foreign emissaries who visited Japan. Since the Japanese knew I was a Christian priest, the secretary sternly reminded me of the letter which the King had sent to Manila in 1602. In it, foreigners were given permission to reside in Japan, but they were prohibited from promulgating their religion.

I of course was undaunted, and I did not obey those orders. On the pretext that I was going to build a crude hospital in Asakusa for the benefit of reprobate lepers, I secretly commenced my missionary labours even while I cared for the sufferers with the help of two companions. The Japanese Christians who had gone into hiding soon began to contact me, providing me with my first activities. But these secret, forbidden acts were not sufficient to satisfy my ideals. In my heart I thought continually of the old man on his velvet chair in the inner chamber of that castle, fervently hoping to open trade relations with Nueva España.

I no longer struggle against that old man. The Japan which was my life has now receded far into the distance, beyond my grasp. In defeat I will go to Manila and live in a monastery surrounded by a white fence, with well-manicured flower-beds in the courtyard. Offering the monks inoffensive words of counsel, examining the account ledger, writing reports each day. The life of a meek superior, who blesses mothers and pats their children's heads. That is what the Lord has 'willed' for my life.

I knelt on the floor, lashed my wrists with rope, and prayed, 'Thy will be done.' As I prayed, I realized that my carelessly bound fists were damp with sweat. I struggled with all my might to suppress the violent emotions that surged up within me.

At that moment, I noticed someone standing in the doorway.

'What is it, Lord Hasekura?'

Standing very still, Hasekura replied softly, 'Lord Tanaka has taken his own life.'

Hasekura spoke the words as if he were announcing a departure time. 'Lord Tanaka has taken his own life.' I remained on my knees, staring at the flame of the candle he was holding. Above Hasekura's hand the flame flickered convulsively. 'Thy will be done.' Yet now that 'will' was more cruelly cold than ice.

Without a word Hasekura led me to Tanaka's bedroom. Our two shadows were reflected on the wall of the pitch-dark corridor, and both of us were silent. The only light came from a room at the end of the corridor, where Nishi was standing with several attendants outside the door. When we stepped into the room, we found Tanaka's body lying on a blood-soaked sheet with his head turned to the side. The short sword he had used to commit suicide was arranged neatly with its scabbard beside the bed. Two of Tanaka's attendants sat in formal posture by the candle stand, steadily watching their dead master's face as though awaiting a command.

When the attendants saw me they quietly made room for me; they were quite composed, as if they had already anticipated their master's suicide. I had the impression they were carrying out a predetermined ordinance. There was no sign that anyone other than the people on our floor was awake in the monastery, and in fact no one else had realized what had happened.

In death his face was at peace. The haughty, brusque expression he had often displayed during our journey was gone now, and his face was tranquil, as if by dying he had been released from all the trials that had tormented him on the journey. I felt almost as if death had granted him a calmer repose than the Lord had ever provided.

One of the attendants tried to place a tiny Buddhist idol at the bedside, but his action reminded me that Tanaka had been baptized and that I, for better or worse, was a priest.

'We do not need Buddhist images. Lord Tanaka was a Christian.'

The attendant gave me a spiteful look, but he took back the idol and rested it on his lap.

'*Habeas requiem aeternam.*'

Once, in a banana grove near Veracruz, I had grasped the hand of a wounded Indian and recited the same prayer. But unlike that Indian, Tanaka had committed suicide, a mode of death which the Church considers an unforgivable, mortal sin. The Church does not allow the sacrament for the dead to be performed for those who take their own lives. But at that moment I no longer cared about the regulations of the Church. I knew the anguish of Tanaka's journey. I knew what had been in the hearts of Tanaka and Hasekura and Nishi as they persevered with their hopeless mission. And I knew why Tanaka had had to cut his own belly open with his tiny sword. Just as I had not been able to abandon the young Indian man to death, I could not forsake Tanaka in death.

'*Requiescant in pace.*'

I closed Tanaka's staring eyes, as though I were shutting the final gateway of life. Throughout all this, neither the attendants nor Hasekura and Nishi standing in the doorway made any move to interrupt my prayers; they clustered in the corner of the room and stood there without moving.

At length the attendants cut off some of their master's hair and nails and put them in the bags which hung around their necks. Then, in place of the bloodstained sheet, they covered the body with a new silk cloth. Hasekura observed the proceedings and then spoke to me.

'Tomorrow morning I must apologize to the padres and monks here. Please help me.'

In keeping with Buddhist tradition, the Japanese kept vigil beside the dead body until daybreak. I remained with them all night beside the body covered with white silk.

The pale dawn came. With special permission from the monastery, we buried him beside an Indian graveyard that lay between the village and the port of San Juan de Ulúa. Not a single priest or monk from the monastery came to the burial. They had no wish to attend the funeral of a man who had committed the grievous sin of suicide. I fashioned a cross out of two dead branches and thrust it into the grave mound. The morning sun tinted the forest, and nearby a group of naked Indian children stood sucking their thumbs and watching us quizzically. Nishi crouched on the ground, while Hasekura stood stiffly erect with his eyes tightly closed.

After some time the fortress commander of San Juan de Ulúa arrived on horseback with his deputy.

'They're just like the Indians.' He dismounted from his horse and wiped the sweat from his face. 'The more inferior the people the more they want to kill themselves.'

'The Japanese consider it a virtue to choose death rather than endure shame,' I replied, staring fixedly at him. 'This Japanese envoy believed that he could not carry out his mission as an ambassador unless he died.'

'I'm afraid I don't understand,' the commander shrugged in amazement. 'But from what you say, Padre, it sounds as if you approve of suicide, which the Church forbids.'

Perplexity and wariness of me were concealed in his eyes. Perhaps letters from España had informed him that I was a traitor who had rebelled against the Church.

Yes, it is true that I am confused, that I have reached the brink of despair, that I can no longer grasp what the Lord's will might have been. But for all that, I am struck with an unutterable fear that my faith might waver.

My only aim in undertaking our journey was to make Japan into a nation of the Lord. Yet were there no elements of convenient self-justification and a selfish thirst for conquest concealed with that goal? Was there no ambition within my heart one day to become Bishop of Japan, and to manipulate the Church there with my own hands? Did the Lord discern the feelings of my heart and punish me for them?

'Certainly the Church does regard suicide as a mortal sin,' I murmured, gazing at the ground. 'But I don't want to believe that the Lord will forsake this particular Japanese who has committed suicide

. . . I don't want to believe that.'

The commander could not understand my hoarse mutterings. If anyone made Tanaka commit the mortal sin of suicide, it was I. My haughty schemes drove him to his death. If Tanaka is to be punished, I too must be punished. 'O Lord. Do not abandon his soul. Rather punish me for his sin.'

'I am come to send fire on the earth, and what will I, if it be already kindled?'

'But I have a baptism of death to be baptized with; and how am I pained till it be accomplished!'

'For even the Son of man came not to be ministered unto, but to minister, and to give his life a ransom for many.'

When the Lord spoke these words, He had certainly prepared Himself for death. In this life there are missions which can only be accomplished through death.

The journey from Veracruz to Córdoba. The mountain range was veiled with thunderheads, and from time to time bolts of lightning flashed. The wilderness where maguey and cactus grew like bizarre hieroglyphs. As I crossed this wasteland with the Japanese, I thought of the Lord, proceeding towards Jerusalem across a similar desert, resolved to die. The Lord had predicted His own death then, saying, 'But I have a baptism of death to be baptized with; and how am I pained till it be accomplished!' There are missions in this life which are accomplished only through death. The suicide of Tanaka Tarozaemon has taught me that. Yet in one regard the death of Tanaka and the death of the Lord are clearly different. The Japanese took his own life to atone for his inability to perform his mission as an envoy. But the Lord accepted death 'to minister for many'.

Lightning; and immediately after a clap of thunder heard in the distance. Lightning also flashes through my heart now. There are many people to whom I too must minister. A priest lives to serve others in this world, not for his own sake. I thought of the man at Ogatsu. It is to him that I must minister, and to other Japanese like him. 'I am come to minister unto many,' I told myself as I stumbled along the road, 'and to give them life.'

Nothing the Lord did was meaningless. Neither was Tanaka's death void of meaning, for it has taught me these things.

'What is going to happen to us now?' Nishi Kyūsuke sat down on his bed in the Córdoba public hall and stared at the window. They had been given the same room they had stayed in before after the rainstorm. But then Tanaka Tarozaemon had still been alive. Otherwise nothing had changed. On the wall that emaciated man with both hands nailed to a cross was revealed by the faint light from the candle.

'Now . . .?' the samurai asked wearily. He was more than physically tired; he was exhausted to the core of his soul. It was depressing and annoying to think of what lay ahead.

'After we return to Japan.'

'I have no idea. But I'm sure that His Lordship and the elder statesmen will understand all the suffering we have been through.'

'Even if we return empty-handed?'

The samurai recalled the fresh, youthful figure Nishi had once been. When he smiled, his white teeth flashing against his swarthy face, his eyes had sparkled with such curiosity that the samurai had occasionally been jealous. That sparkle was gone now; his complexion was as pasty as a invalid's, his zest a thing of the past.

'I wish I could have stayed in España and learned more about it,' Nishi said dully, turning towards the candlestick. 'And I thought how huge the world is. I never had the slightest idea we would be going back like this.' Listening to these words, the samurai suddenly had a clear picture of the moment their ship set sail from Tsukinoura. When the ship had moved out into the open sea – the halyards creaking unexpectedly, the waves beating against the hull, and seagulls skimming over the the edge of the ship with shrill cries – he had felt that the course of his destiny was about to be altered. It had never occurred to him then that the world was so huge. Now he had seen that world and all that remained was weariness. He was weary to the depths of his soul.

'Don't you think that even Lord Tanaka was afraid of what lies ahead of us?'

'What do you think he was afraid of?'

'That His Lordship and the elder statesmen would turn their backs on us.'

The samurai blinked his eyes. It pained and frightened him to think too deeply about Tanaka's death. By his death Tanaka had sought to preserve his dignity before his family and relatives. When the samurai thought of the hollow-cheeked face of his own uncle, eagerly awaiting his return beside the sunken hearth, he too wanted to die. He envied Tanaka that suicide. But he could not die himself. On behalf of Nishi and the attendants who had suffered so much, he had to tell the Council of Elders everything that had transpired on the journey. If someone had to assume the duties of spokesman, the samurai felt that someone was himself.

'There is no reason for them to abandon us,' the samurai said with uncharacteristic firmness. 'Sometimes even the greatest effort is not enough. We must tell the Council that.'

Yet even as he tried to convince himself, inwardly he was not so sure. He was afraid to think the matter out thoroughly. What good would it do to imagine that this or that might happen in the future? The samurai gulped down bitter feelings of resignation.

Night air poured through the open window. The smell of the earth reminded him of the marshland. Even if he couldn't get back the lands at Kurokawa, the samurai was satisfied having only the marshland. Unlike his father and uncle, his heart was bound less to Kurokawa than to the marshland.

'But won't the Council of Elders denounce us,' Nishi persisted, 'for not getting any reply from the King of España?'

'It doesn't matter. Thinking about it will resolve nothing. Since there's nothing we can do, it's better not to think.'

To end the conversation, the samurai stood up. Nishi was beginning to irritate him, and he wanted to go out into the courtyard and breathe in some of the night air that smelled of the earth.

The courtyard was so cold it made the heat of the day seem incredible. Three men were crouched down talking together. It was Yozō and his other attendants. Yozō was angrily berating the others.

'Can't you sleep?'

The three men stood up, embarrassed. They looked shamefacedly at their master, afraid that he might have overheard their conversation.

'The smells of the evening remind me of home.' The samurai smiled in an attempt to put the three men at their ease. 'The night in the marshland was filled with the same smells of earth and trees. Soon . . . we'll be able to breathe in those smells again.'

It was clear from their arguing voices that weariness and irritation were affecting not only Nishi, but his attendants as well. I alone must be strong, he told himself.

The following morning they left Córdoba. The blistering desert once again. At the edge of the wilderness, olive groves and Indian huts and the manor houses with Spanish-style roofs belonging to the *encomenderos*. The scenes they had observed on their outgoing journey were repeated. Now that they were hardened travellers, however, not a single glimmer of curiosity stirred in the eyes of the Japanese. Occasionally they remembered that each step they took brought them closer to Japan, but somehow the thought failed to move them.

The samurai glanced over at Velasco, who was riding beside him, and realized that he missed seeing the customary smile. To be honest, the foreigner's confident smile had made the samurai uncomfortable. Velasco had always fixed it on his face when he was trying to subject the Japanese to his will. Whenever the samurai saw that scheming smile, he was suspicious of Velasco's real motives. They had in fact been deceived on several occasions because of it. But since their departure from Rome, the haughty smile had disappeared from Velasco's face, to be replaced by a tormented, lonely expression.

'There's nothing we can do now.' From the back of his horse, the samurai started to speak to Velasco, but he stopped himself. The foreigner, who had caused them such anxiety, who had provoked in them rage and even hatred, lifted his eyes glumly towards the range of hills blanketed with rain clouds. The samurai felt sorry for the man. He knew that, since he had not been able to carry out the vows he had sworn to the elder statesmen, he would never be able to return to Japan.

It was on the evening of the tenth day that they passed through the grey wall surrounding the village of Puebla. As before, a market had been set up beside the wall, and pigtailed Indians had arranged pottery, woven goods and fruit on the ground; they sat silent as stone images, hugging their knees.

'Lord Hasekura, do you remember that Japanese man?'

'The one who had been a monk?'

Even before Nishi asked, the samurai had been thinking about their fellow countryman who had come to see them in Mexico City. That renegade monk who lived with an Indian woman in a hut with a reed-thatched roof, near the Tecali swamp that shimmered red as blood in the morning sun. He had said they would not be meeting again. If that were true, where was he now?

'I . . . I'm going to go back to that swamp,' Nishi whispered to the samurai, taking care that Velasco did not overhear.

'There's no point. He said the Indians never cultivate the same fields twice.'

'It doesn't matter even if I don't see him again.'

'Then why are you going?'

'That fellow . . .,' Nishi smiled sadly. 'Somehow I can understand now why he could never return to Japan.'

'Do you want to remain here too?'

'To someone who has seen the vastness of the world, Japan seems stifling. My heart is heavy when I think of the people born into lance-corporal or foot-soldier families in Japan; they have to live that way for the rest of their lives. But even I . . . I have people who are waiting for me to come home.'

They could not follow their own whims and wishes. There were people awaiting their return. The samurai knew how Nishi felt. An uncle, a family and peasants, who looked to him as head of the family for their support, were living in the marshland. He would return there and lead the same sort of life he had lived before. Never again would he leave his home and venture out into the wide world. This was all a dream. It would be best to think of it that way: as a dream that would soon be over.

The samurai and Nishi set out from the monastery before dawn the next morning, just as they had done before. They knew the road now. The heat of the day had not yet aroused the village from its cool, peaceful sleep when they passed through it. As they reached the forest, rose-coloured cracks had appeared in the sky. Small birds taunted them with their screeches. The horses kicked up spray as they crossed a clear mountain stream. Shafts of morning light shot like arrows through the trees. The swamp at Tecali was as quiet as ever, the reeds rustling faintly. Nishi dismounted and, putting his hand up to his mouth, called to the monk. Two or three bare-chested pigtailed Indian men poked their heads out the doorways of their huts. They remembered the samurai and Nishi and smiled, crinkling their squashed noses.

The former monk came hobbling out, leaning on the shoulders of his wife, who was as sturdy as a slab of meat. The ailing man squinted painfully into the morning sun, then at last noticed his visitors and cried out to them.

'It's good to see you again!' He stretched forth his hands, as though he were being reunited with relatives he had never expected to meet again during his lifetime. 'I never thought I would see you again. . . .' Suddenly he stopped speaking and he put his hand to his chest, gasping in pain.

'Don't worry. It will be over in a moment. In just a moment.'

But it took some time for the attack to subside. The morning sun had climbed the sky, its rays spreading languidly across the swamp, and the heat of the day set in. The Indians watched the three men curiously from a distance, but eventually they grew bored and disappeared.

'As soon as we find a ship bound for Luzon we are returning to Japan. If there's anything you'd like to send to your friends at home. . . .'

'There is nothing,' the renegade monk smiled forlornly. 'If anyone found out that you had kept company with a Christian monk, it would only make trouble for you.'

'We had to become Christians ourselves.' The samurai stared at the ground in embarrassment. 'We weren't sincere about it, but . . .'

'You still don't believe in it?'

'No. We did it for the sake of our mission. And what about you? Do you actually believe in that man called Jesus?'

'Yes, I do. I told you that before. But the Jesus I believe in is not the one preached by the Church or the padres. I cannot ally myself with the padres who invoke the name of the Lord when they burn the altars of the Indians, and drive them from their villages, claiming that they do it in order to spread the Lord's word.'

'How can you revere such a miserable, wretched fellow? How can you worship someone so ugly and emaciated? I can't understand it. . . .'

For the first time the samurai asked the question in earnest. Nishi gazed up at the renegade monk from a crouched position, waiting to hear his reply. From the swamp they could hear the strange voices of women doing their washing.

'In the old days,' the man nodded, 'I had the same doubts. But I can believe in Him now because the life He lived in this world was more wretched than any other man's. Because He was ugly and emaciated. He knew all there was to know about the sorrows of this world. He could not close His eyes to the grief and agony of mankind. That is what made Him emaciated and ugly. Had He lived an exalted, powerful life beyond our grasp, I would not feel like this about Him.'

The samurai could not understand what the renegade monk was saying.

'He understands the hearts of the wretched, because His entire life was wretched. He knows the agonies of those who die a miserable death, because He died in misery. He was not in the least powerful. He was not beautiful.'

'But look at the Church. Look at the city of Rome,' Nishi countered. 'The cathedrals we saw were all like golden palaces, and not even the people of Mexico City could imagine the grandeur of the mansion where the Pope lives.'

'Do you think that is what He would have wished?' the man shook his head angrily. 'Do you think He is to be found within those garish cathedrals? He does not dwell there. He lives . . . not within such buildings. I think He lives in the wretched homes of these Indians.'

'Why?'

'That is how He spent His life,' replied the renegade monk in a voice filled with assurance, then he lowered his eyes to the ground and repeated the same words to himself. 'That is how he lived His life. He never visited the houses of those who were puffed up or contented. He sought out only the ugly, the wretched, the miserable and the sorrowful. But now even the bishops and priests here are complacent and swollen with pride. They are no longer the sort of people He sought after.'

He blurted out these words in a single breath, then suddenly clutched his chest. The samurai and Nishi watched wordlessly until the attack subsided.

'Because of my condition, the Indians have been good enough to stay behind here in the swamp. Otherwise,' he smiled embarrassedly, 'I would have moved far from Tecali. Sometimes I discover Jesus among these Indians.'

It was obvious from the man's swollen face and murky complexion that he did not have long to live. He would die here beside this sweltering swamp. And he would be buried at the edge of a corn-field.

'No matter what I do,' the samurai muttered apologetically, 'I can't think of that man the way you do.'

'Even if you care nothing about Him . . . He will always care about you.'

'I can get by without thinking about him.'

'Do you really think so?'

The renegade monk stared sympathetically at the samurai and began to shred a husk of corn. The sunlight had become even more intense, and in the reeds of the swamp insects began their sultry chirping.

'If people can live all alone, why do cries of grief fill every corner of the world? You have travelled through many countries. You have crossed the ocean and circled the globe. Surely all along the way you must have seen that those who lament and those who weep are seeking after something.'

What he said was true. In every land, every village, and every home they visited, the samurai had seen an image of that ugly, emaciated man, his head bowed and both his arms extended.

'Those who weep seek someone to weep with them. Those who grieve yearn for someone to lend an ear to their lamentations. No matter how much the world changes, those who weep and those who lament will always seek Him. That is His purpose in living.'

'I don't understand.'

'Someday you will understand. Someday you will understand this.'

The samurai and Nishi took up the reins of their horses and bade farewell to the ailing man, knowing they would not be seeing him again.

'Don't you have anything you would like us to say to your family back home?'

'Nothing. I have finally been able to grasp an image of Him that conforms to my own heart.'

The swamp glimmered in the sunlight. The horses plodded slowly along its banks. The two Japanese glanced back from their saddles. The Indians were huddled together like a mound of earth, still watching as the Japanese departed. Among them the envoys could see the tattered, motionless figure of the renegade monk leaning against his wife.

November 3, Chalco. Passed through the same wilderness as before on our way to Mexico City.

November 4, stayed on the outskirts of Mexico City. Sent a messenger requesting permission to enter Mexico City.

From the outskirts, we could see the city streets in the distance, surrounded by the white walls and with the spires of the churches towering over them. Among those spires piercing the azure sky was the steeple of the Franciscan Cathedral where the Japanese had been baptized, and the spire of the monastery where we had lodged.

We received orders from the Viceroy that we were not to pass through Mexico City, but were to proceed directly to the port of Acapulco. He claimed that they were not in a position to welcome the Japanese in Mexico City, but I knew of course that this was an excuse for him to avoid us. No doubt everything was done in accordance with instructions from Madrid. Still, the Superior of our Order in Mexico City took pity on us and sent wine and food to our inn here. The two monks who brought the provisions in saddlebags on the backs of donkeys handed me a letter from the Superior. A copy of reports sent from a Franciscan monastery in Manila, it contained considerably more detail about the situation in Japan than I had heard in Rome.

I knew that the suppression of Christianity on a national scale had commenced in the February following our departure from Japan, just at the time our ship was waiting to sail from Havana. At that moment, in Japan, the old man in the velvet chair unexpectedly sent out an edict declaring that all the missionaries as well as the leading Japanese Christians were to be banished, and prohibiting the practice of Christianity in every region of the country.

The envoys and I had known nothing. We had been totally

ignorant of everything as we struggled towards España in pursuit of a single dream. But that dream had been a castle rising up out of a mirage.

According to the report from Manila, after the edict was sent forth all the missionaries from every part of Japan were herded like cattle to Nagasaki. Father Diego, awaiting my return in that Edo hovel, must have been among them. I could almost see my colleague – the good fellow whose eyes were always as red as if he had just finished crying – helplessly and timorously leaving Edo.

The missionaries and Japanese monks were massed together in Fukuda near Nagasaki and forced to live for nearly eight months in thatched huts no better than cattle sheds. Nagasaki was the scene of unprecedented chaos, with the people dividing into camps of apostates and those who sought to go into hiding. They write that our Brotherhood, together with the Dominicans and the Augustinians, held a two-day prayer meeting and then paraded through the streets on Easter Sunday chanting 'Martyrdom!'

The report goes on to say that on a rainy November 7th, eighty-eight of the missionaries and Japanese monks who had been held in confinement were crammed into five junks and sent from Japan to Macao. On the 8th, thirty priests, monks and faithful set out for Manila in a tiny decrepit ship. All were condemned to perpetual exile, and such powerful Christian warriors as Lord Ukon Takayama and Lord Juan Naitō* were among those aboard the ships bound for Manila.

As I read the copied missive, I thought about that old man in his velvet chair. That plump, Chinese-looking monarch may have conquered us Christians in the political arena, just as Nero defeated the Apostles, but we shall triumph in the world of the spirit. That old man probably does not yet know that, in spite of his thoroughgoing policy of expulsion, forty-two missionaries have in fact gone into hiding on the islands with the secret assistance of the Japanese faithful.

It's all an exact replica of the circumstances at the time of the Lord's passion. In the political arena presided over by the High Priest Caiaphas, the Lord was spitefully used and then tossed aside, and finally hung upon a cross on the hill of Golgotha. But our defeated Lord achieved His victory among the souls of mankind. In that same struggle I do not concede defeat.

O Lord, please show me what it is Thou desirest of me.

O Lord, Thy will be done.

---

* Naitō (d. 1626) was another of the leading Christians exiled to Manila.

O Lord, if this seed which has begun to sprout within my heart truly be Thy will, please make that known to me.

Acapulco. The galleon that will carry us to Manila is anchored in the grey harbour. The promontories encircling the harbour and the islets within are all blanketed with olive trees. It is hot here compared to Mexico City.

The Japanese are staying in a barracks at the fortress. They sleep throughout the day as if they were dead. They do not so much as set foot outdoors, as though the strain and fatigue of their long journey had swept over them all at once. It is quiet at the barracks, only the shrill cries of seagulls from the harbour occasionally breaking the silence.

The ship is due to set sail in a month's time. We will go back across the Pacific, enduring the raging waves, weathering the storms and – God willing – arrive in Manila at the beginning of spring. There I shall remain, while the Japanese return home with the ship and its crew. Once they have gone, I shall follow the orders of my uncle and my superiors and make my home in a pure white monastery with a well-cultivated flower garden.

Or else . . .

O Lord, please show me what it is Thou desirest of me.

O Lord, Thy will be done.

O Lord, if this seed which has begun to sprout within my heart truly be Thy will . . .

Chapter 10

Just before dawn, he was shaken from his sleep. Yozō's face slowly came into focus before his misty eyes. Yozō was smiling like a mother gazing down at her child, and from his expression the samurai knew what he was about to say.

'Oh!'

He sprang from his bed and shook Nishi Kyūsuke, who was still asleep in the next bed.

'It's Rikuzen . . .!' The samurai infused the word with a flood of emotions.

The Japanese scrambled head over heels onto the deck. The sun shone on the glassy surface of the sea, colouring it orange. Close at hand they could see a familiar island. Beyond the island was Mount Kinka, veiled in a pink mist. Familiar trees grew in profusion on the mountain and boats were pulled up on the familiar beach.

For a long while everyone was silent, gazing at the island, the beach, the boats.

Their elation was somehow muted. Not a single tear spilled forth. Though they had thought about this moment for so long, it was almost as if the scene was still part of their dreams. They had seen it there time and time again on their journey.

From the mast a Chinese sailor pointed to an island and shouted something. Perhaps he was saying they had arrived. Perhaps he was telling them that this was Tsukinoura.

All the men were silent, motionless. Each looked abstractedly at the view of their homeland that moved slowly before his eyes, savouring his own particular memories and feelings. The only sound was the dull slap of the waves against the ship. The waves glimmered like fragments of glass, then disappeared. Seagulls skimmed over the white caps and swirled upwards like leaves in the wind.

From all his memories of the journey, it was the hour of their departure that came to the samurai now. The halyards had creaked, waves had slapped against the hull of the ship, and seagulls had

225

skirted the edge of the ship and flown away, as they had just now. He had sensed that an unseen destiny was about to begin for him, and now he had fulfilled it: he had come home. Why was it that weariness and a sense of emptiness – not joy – were all that remained? Had he seen too much of too many things, until it was as if he had seen nothing at all? Had he experienced too much, until it was as though he had experienced nothing at all?

'Officers!' someone cried. A boat flying bunting embossed with the domainial crest appeared from the opposite side of the harbour. Between gaps in the bunting a diminutive officer was peering towards the ship. Two skiffs rowed by boatmen followed behind. The officer shaded his eyes with his hand and quickly studied the face of each of the Japanese who stared down at him. After a brief exchange of words between the two vessels, the officer finally grasped the entire situation.

The samurai and several others were put aboard the skiffs, and they gradually gained a closer view of the bay of Tsukinoura. Here and there on the promontories at either side of the bay stretched rows of tottering thatched houses. To the rear of the houses, they caught a glimpse of a small red torii gate with a vermilion streamer rising above it. Children ran down the roads. This was unmistakably Japan, a uniquely Japanese scene.

'We're home . . .!'

For the first time, the samurai was gripped by intense elation. Instinctively he looked into Nishi's face. He looked into the faces of Yozō, of Ichisuke, of Daisuke.

'The shores . . . of Japan . . .!' Nishi took a deep breath and could say no more.

As they set foot on the beach littered with black seaweed, a clear rippling wave crept up and quietly soaked the feet of the Japanese. For a long while they stood with their eyes closed, as if to savour the sensation of the water lapping at their feet. The officers who appeared from the guardhouse halted in their tracks and looked on suspiciously. Then one of them cried out.

'Oh!' The man scampered across the beach, kicking up sand behind him. 'Have you come home?' He clutched the hands of the samurai and Nishi and would not release them. 'Have you come home?'

The officers had received no notification of the envoys' return. Since there were no ships returning to Japan, Nishi and the samurai had remained in Luzon for over a year, and the letters they had sent by way of Macao had apparently never reached Japan. The officers were stunned by their unexpected arrival, and had no idea what to do.

Compared to the spectacular day of their departure, everything was quiet. The only welcome that the samurai and Nishi received came from the officers, the children watching them from a distance, and the sound of the waves washing languidly onto the beach. The samurai looked out at the sea, where the great fortress of a ship that was to carry them away had floated that day. Now only the glimmering surface stretched before him. Scores of tiny boats laden with cargo had been moored on this beach, and labourers had been scurrying about. All of that was gone now.

Accompanied by the officers, they set out for the temple where they had spent the night before their departure. Nothing there had changed. The chief priest remembered them and showed them to a room. When the samurai looked at the straw mats baked reddish-brown in the sun, he suddenly thought of Tanaka Tarozaemon. He and Nishi had spent a night on these mats with Tanaka and Matsuki. Tanaka and Matsuki were no longer with them. Tanaka's miserable grave in a thicket near Veracruz. They had brought a lock of his hair and some clippings from his nails back to Japan.

In quick succession the officers filed in and out of their room. They had not a moment to themselves to rest. A messenger on a swift horse had already set out from Tsukinoura to inform the Council of Elders of their return. The samurai and Nishi were prepared to leave for the castle the following day should the Council summon them.

Literally everything brought back cherished memories. The smell of a Japanese room, the furnishings in the room, the low dining tray set before them – these were things they had long dreamt about. In a separate room, some of the attendants wept as they stroked the wooden pillars.

The chief priest and officers listened with looks of disbelief on their faces as Nishi described what he had seen in foreign lands. He told them of buildings made of stone piled layer upon layer, and of cathedrals that pierced the sky, but it was difficult to make them understand. He tried to describe the deserts of Nueva España, so vast that one could walk and walk and see nothing but maguey and cactus. But it was no use.

'The world . . .,' Nishi gave a smile of resignation, 'is larger than you can ever imagine here in Japan.'

When Nishi finished his account, it was the turn of the chief priest and the officers to tell of the events that had transpired in the domain since their departure. About the time the envoys were leaving Rome, the last great battle had taken place in Japan. The retired Shōgun had annihilated the Toyotomi clan. Fortunately His Lordship had only sent troops as a rearguard to the capital, and had not become involved in the fighting at Osaka. The elder statesman Lord Ishikawa had been killed. It was about that time that the merchants and seamen who had accompanied the envoys returned to Nagasaki by way of Luzon. They had left the great ship in Luzon and come back on another foreign vessel.

'Lord Matsuki too?'

The officer nodded. He told the envoys that Matsuki had been appointed an Assistant Inspector to the Council of Elders after his return to Japan. This was a real distinction for a lance-corporal.

What about the ban on Christianity? the samurai wanted to ask. And he wanted to know whether Lord Shiraishi and the others who had sent them to Nueva España still wielded power in the Council of Elders. But the question only rose as far as his throat, and neither he nor Nishi could spit it out. They sensed that somehow such a question should be avoided, and the chief priest and officers told them nothing on that subject.

Night came. He lay down beside Nishi, but his emotions were tightly strung and he could not sleep. The only sound was the roar of the waves in the distance. This was his first night in Japan in four years. At this thought, the samurai saw a vivid image of how the marshland would look when he returned there in five or six days' time. The wrinkled face of his uncle, who would probably cry; the face of Riku, who would stare at him without a word; the faces of his children as they flew into his arms. He thought of the letter he had just written: 'This is written in haste. We have arrived in Tsukinoura. All are well. When our work is finished, we will hurry home. I should give you many more details, but . . .'

Nishi tossed in his bed, also apparently unable to sleep. When the samurai coughed softly, Nishi whispered, 'I still can't believe that we're home.'

'Neither can I.' The samurai's answer was as much a gasp as a sigh.

On the afternoon of the following day the post horse returned. It brought orders from the Council of Elders.

The envoys sat in formal posture and listened to their instructions. The officer reported that they were to remain in Tsukinoura until the elder statesmen arrived; they were not to meet or correspond with their families until then.

'Who gave these orders?' the samurai asked, his face somewhat flushed.

'Lord Tsumura Kageyasu.'

Lord Tsumura, like Lord Shiraishi, Lord Ayugai and Lord Watari, was one of the elder statesmen. If the orders came from Lord Tsumura, they had no choice but to obey them.

'Don't let it worry you,' the officer quickly consoled the two envoys. 'The merchants and ship's hands who came back underwent the same investigation.'

It was beyond all understanding. Everyone knew that they had travelled to distant countries as His Lordship's envoys. The elder statesmen were certainly aware of that fact. It was mortifying to get the same treatment as the merchants and seamen.

Furthermore, overnight the attitude of the officers changed completely; they no longer visited the envoys' room. From their behaviour it was obvious that they had been ordered not to fraternize with the envoys.

'This is just like being in prison!' Anger tinged Nishi's eyes as he looked out from the veranda.

As he sat in his room, warmed by the setting sun, the samurai had time to ponder why they were being dealt with in this manner. Was it because they had not accomplished their mission as envoys? But if they explained that they had not fulfilled their mission because they could not, surely the Council of Elders would be satisfied?

They passed three days without setting foot outside the temple. On the morning of the third day, one of the officers who had stopped coming to see them burst into their room to announce, 'Lord Tsumura is coming today!'

That afternoon, the samurai lined up with Nishi and their attendants in front of the temple to await the arrival of Lord Tsumura's entourage. Soon they heard the neighing of horses and the sound of footsteps climbing the sloping path leading from the beach to the temple. The bamboo hats of Lord Tsumura and five or six of his retainers came into view. The samurai and Nishi bowed their heads, but the elder statesman passed without a word and disappeared into the temple.

They were kept waiting for a long time. Lord Tsumura was probably reviewing the details of the group's return, their numbers, and the names of each individual. Eventually an officer came out to summon them, and the two envoys went in to be interrogated.

When they entered the room where Lord Tsumura was seated, the elder statesman fixed his gaze upon them. The flash of his eyes, tempered through many battles, was sharp and piercing. Among the three retainers in attendance at his side, the samurai discovered the lean figure of Matsuki Chūsaku, whom he had not seen since Mexico City. At once surprised and wistful, the samurai stared at Matsuki, but for some reason his former colleague kept his face turned towards the veranda, avoiding the samurai's gaze.

'You have done well on your long journey. I'm sure you want to return to your homes as soon as possible.' Lord Tsumura began by expressing his appreciation to the two envoys. 'But, since last year, the Shōgun has ordered that the domain must interrogate everyone returning from abroad. Please understand that this is part of my duty.'

Lord Tsumura went on to ask why the envoys' ship had come directly to Tsukinoura without calling at Nagasaki or Sakai. The samurai replied that the ship had unloaded cargo at an island off the coast of China called Taiwan and then headed north on its way back to Nueva España.

Was there anyone on the ship who seemed like a missionary or a monk? Was there any indication that someone might have stolen into Japan along the way?

'No.'

Lord Tsumura asked one question after another, and gradually the elder statesman's expression and the tone of his remarks impressed upon the samurai the severity of the anti-Christian edicts which the domain had promulgated during his long absence. He began to feel uneasy, wondering whether he should openly admit that he and Nishi had become Christians in España.

'What happened to Velasco?'

'We parted with him in Manila.'

'What was Velasco doing in Manila? Did he say whether he was coming back to Japan?'

The samurai shook his head firmly. He of course remembered very clearly the declarations Velasco had made in Mexico City and Manila, but he felt that he ought not to mention them at this point.

'The domain has no more use for Velasco. Edo has forbidden the practice of Christianity throughout every corner of Japan. His Lordship will not allow anyone who would spread the Christian teachings into our domain. Velasco is no exception.'

Perspiration was trickling down the samurai's forehead. He could feel Nishi's knees twitching spasmodically beside him.

'Did any of your attendants convert to Christianity?'

'No.' The samurai's voice was shrill.

'You're sure, aren't you?'

The samurai looked down and said nothing.

'That will be all.' Lord Tsumura smiled for the first time. 'I understand that the merchants who accompanied you on the voyage converted to Christianity there. But since they did so out of expediency, to enhance their profits, they were forgiven after they wrote vows of recantation. But you are samurai. That's why I was particularly concerned about your affiliations.'

Matsuki, who was sitting beside Lord Tsumura, still kept his eyes averted, but somehow the samurai was conscious of his stinging gaze. He recalled with loathing the words Matsuki had uttered when they left Mexico City.

'You must recognize,' Lord Tsumura continued, 'that His Lordship's views and the stance of the Council of Elders have changed. The domain no longer welcomes foreign ships or seeks their profits. We have abandoned our desire to trade with Nueva España.'

'Then . . .,' ventured the samurai in a strangled voice, 'the circumstances under which we were chosen as emissaries have also . . .'

'Times have changed. I know that your long journey must have been a bitter experience. But the Council of Elders no longer has any use for Nueva España. We do not need great ships to cross the ocean.'

'Then . . . our mission . . .'

'You no longer have a mission.'

The samurai tried to keep his own knees from trembling. He swallowed the shout of anger that rose to his throat and stifled his feelings of chagrin and sorrow. What Lord Tsumura was saying with such indifference was that their journey had been utterly without meaning, that it had served no purpose whatsoever. Then to what end had they crossed the limitless deserts of Nueva España, travelled across España, and ventured as far as Rome? And Tanaka Tarozaemon, buried all alone in a thicket near Veracruz. Tanaka's death – what had it been for?

'I . . .' the samurai still stared at the floor. 'Nishi Kyūsuke and I . . . never imagined such a thing.'

'There is no way you could have known. The Council of Elders had no way of informing you.'

If no one else had been present, the samurai would have laughed out loud at the futility of all their efforts. Nishi, who sat like the samurai with his head down and his fists pressed against his knees, suddenly cried out. His face was ashen.

'We were stupid!'

'It isn't your fault,' Lord Tsumura said sympathetically. 'The Shōgun's orders banning Christianity have changed everything.'

'I became a Christian!'

At Nishi's exclamation, Lord Tsumura looked up abruptly. A chill spread through the room. In the silence, Matsuki turned his eyes towards the envoys for the first time.

At length Lord Tsumura asked softly, 'Is that true? That is . . .'

'It wasn't done in earnest,' blurted the samurai, desperate to forestall Nishi, who seemed ready to shout something more. 'We thought it would help us to carry out our mission.'

'Did you convert too, Hasekura?'

'Yes. But like the merchants, we weren't sincere about it.'

Lord Tsumura stared silently at the samurai and Nishi with his piercing eyes. Finally he motioned to his retainers and one of them slipped out of the room. Lord Tsumura stood up, and the others followed suit. Their robes rustled dryly. Matsuki was the last to leave. He stopped on his way out, glanced quickly at the samurai, and was gone.

Left to themselves, the samurai and Nishi remained seated in the formal position, their hands still resting on their knees. It was quiet in the room, and the sunlight spilled from the veranda onto the wooden floor.

'I . . .' Tears gathered in Nishi's eyes. 'I said something I never should have said.'

'It's all right. The Council of Elders would have found out eventually.'

I understand why you said it, the samurai started to tell Nishi, but he decided against it and said nothing. He too wanted to fling his own unspeakable chagrin and hatred at Lord Tsumura, and at the Council of Elders behind Lord Tsumura, and at the great powers behind the Council of Elders.

'What will happen to us now?'

'I don't know. That is for Lord Tsumura to decide.'

'Is this . . .' Nishi smiled tearfully, 'the reward we receive?'

No, this was our destiny, something within the samurai muttered. That destiny had already been determined when their ship set sail from Tsukinoura. The samurai felt he had known that for a long time.

Leaving Yozō and the other attendants at Tsukinoura, the samurai and Nishi set out with Lord Tsumura's entourage to report the course of their journey to the Council of Elders, and to submit a written oath disavowing Christianity to the Religious Inspector. All this was in accordance with orders from Lord Tsumura.

His Lordship's castle had been enlarged during their absence. A new white corner turret had been erected beside the moat, and a main gate said to have been brought from Nagoya Castle in Kyushu barred the entrance to the castle. When they passed through the gate, a series of stone walls curved like sword blades and barricades with ominous gunports obstructed their path. The samurai and Nishi were left by themselves in one of the buildings.

The room, which had a wooden floor, glistened blackly. Although it was midday, it was dark and not a sound could be heard. The room was empty but for a nearly perpendicular staircase at the far end.

'This darkness,' Nishi mumbled, 'is difficult for me to endure now.'

'What do you mean?'

'The buildings in Nueva España and España were all brightly lit by the sun. They weren't anything like this castle. Everybody smiled when they talked. But here we can't talk as we want or smile as we want. We don't even know where His Lordship is.' Nishi gave a deep sigh. 'So long as we are alive, there is no escaping this darkness. Within it, an elder statesman lives as an elder statesman, a general as a general, a Patron as a Patron, and a lance-corporal like me will live his whole life as a lance-corporal.'

'Perhaps we have seen . . . things we should not have seen.'

This was indeed Japan. A wall with windows no larger than gunports, windows to keep an eye on those coming in, not to look out upon the wide world. The samurai wished he could talk to Lord Shiraishi. Lord Shiraishi or Lord Ishida would not stare at them mercilessly the way Lord Tsumura did. They would understand why the envoys had not been able to accomplish their mission, and they would offer warm words of gratitude.

But the approaching footsteps did not belong to Lord Shiraishi or to Lord Ishida. The two men who entered the room were the Religious Inspector, Lord Ōtsuka, and an officer. The aged Inspector, who was as gaunt as the samurai's uncle, asked the two men once again why they had converted to Christianity.

'Because our mission in Nueva España and España would have come to a standstill if we hadn't become Christians,' the samurai explained precisely. When he had finished telling about Velasco and the death of Tanaka, he appealed, 'It was all for the sake of our mission. We only became Christians as a formality. It was the same with our attendants.'

'And you have not the slightest belief in it now?'

'We never believed it from the beginning.'

'You had better write that in your oath of recantation. Put that in writing.' Lord Ōtsuka gazed pityingly at the two men and repeated, 'Put that in writing.' The officer placed a small stand, paper and brush in front of the two men and had them write their oaths of recantation.

As he wrote, the samurai thought of that ugly, emaciated man hanging on his cross. That man they had been forced to look at every day and every night in each and every village, in each and every monastery they visited on their long journey. He had never believed in that man. He had never had any desire to worship that man. Yet all the unpleasantness he was being subjected to now was on account of that man. That man was trying to alter the samurai's destiny.

When they had finished writing the oaths of recantation, they left the building and were taken to another where the Council of Elders met. But not a single elder statesman was present. Here three officials listened perfunctorily to what the samurai and Nishi had to say about their journey. No indications of sympathy, no expressions of gratitude came from their mouths. Apparently the Council of Elders had instructed them to treat the two envoys in this manner.

'Has there been any word from Lord Shiraishi or Lord Ishida?' the samurai asked, unable to hold back any longer. One of the officials reported coldly that he knew of no message, and that there was no need for an audience with such men. Then he added, 'For the time being the two of you will not be permitted to see each other.' He informed them that this was an order from the Council of Elders.

'Why should they forbid him to associate with me?' Nishi clenched his fists and stepped closer to the official.

'The domain has decided that those who have once converted to Christianity – for whatever reason – will not be allowed to associate with one another,' the officer declared, even managing a faint smile on his lips. He told the two that they were free to go back to their inn and then return to their homes.

It was evident from the official's words and from the treatment they had received that the entire castle regarded their homecoming as a nuisance that needed to be passed over in silence. And they were convinced that the elder statesmen were avoiding an audience with them. Not a single person accompanied them to the main gate. Discarded like worthless pebbles, the samurai and Nishi left the building. Sunlight filtering through the trees fell upon the gravel path, and the gunports stared unflinchingly at the two men. They had no idea whereabouts in the castle His Lordship resided. Perhaps he did not even know of their return.

As they quietly descended the deserted slope leading to the main gate, the samurai suddenly muttered to himself, 'The land in Kurokawa . . .!' Lord Ishida had promised to give consideration to the Kurokawa fief when their mission was successfully completed. Lord Shiraishi and Lord Ishida must know of their return by now. Why would they not grant an audience?

Even after they had returned to their inn beside the black waters of the castle moat, the two men scarcely had the strength to discuss their situation. They no longer understood anything. Tomorrow they would go back to Tsukinoura, where they would collect their attendants and return to their fiefs.

'So we won't be able to see each other for a while,' said the samurai, blinking his eyes. 'It's an order, so we'll have to obey it. I'm sure they'll come to their senses eventually.'

'I can't understand it. The treatment we've received from the Council of Elders is deplorable.'

Young Nishi went on uttering wasted words and futile complaints until night fell.

Night came. After supper Nishi remained crouched on the floor hugging his knees. Beside him the samurai wrote in his travel journal by the light from the candle. With each character he sketched, a rush of memories came back to him, and various scenes with their distinctive colours and smells came to life again. Each character and line in his journal was saturated with deep emotions and sorrows he could not fully express. The flame of the candle flickered, giving a small dry crackle from time to time.

A visitor arrived. His bird-like shadow moved along the wall, which was stained by rain that had leaked through the roof. It was Matsuki Chūsaku.

'I came to, er, say goodbye.' Matsuki leaned against the wall, avoiding their eyes as he had earlier. They could not tell whether he kept his eyes averted because he felt guilty that he had not shared the same fate as his two comrades, or whether he simply could not bear to look at them in their present state.

When neither the samurai nor Nishi said anything, Matsuki went on apologetically, 'From now on you must act as though the journey never took place.'

'I can't!' Nishi's eyes were filled with resentment. 'I understand you've become an Assistant Inspector for the Council of Elders. That's quite a step up for you. We can't hope to get on in the world as skilfully as you have, Lord Matsuki.'

'Nishi, watch your tongue. I told you this many times on the ship. I warned you time and time again that the Council members had differing views about the journey, and that Lord Shiraishi did not agree with Lord Ayugai. You're the one who wouldn't listen to me.'

'What has happened to Lord Shiraishi?' the samurai interjected, trying to mollify the two men. 'Is he still the senior member of the Council?'

'He has left the Council. The domain is now run by Lord Ayugai and his faction.'

Nishi grimaced and launched another assault. 'Is that why we're being treated like this? We didn't get a single word of thanks from the Council.'

Matsuki looked at Nishi with chilly disregard in his eyes. 'That's what Government is all about.'

' "Government"? And just what is "Government"?'

'The new Council of Elders, you see, is obliged to renounce all the policies of Lord Shiraishi and his faction. Everything Lord Shiraishi planned must be summarily eliminated. And sadly enough . . . those who were the symbols of those plans are judged and rejected, even if they have been given no warning at all. That is the world of Government.'

'I'm a lance-corporal . . . I don't know anything about Government. All I did was follow the orders I was given to become an envoy. . . .' Nishi lowered his eyes, and his shoulders began to quiver. Matsuki turned his head aside so that he would not have to look at his former colleague.

'Listen, Nishi,' he murmured almost consolingly. 'Do you still think that you were an envoy? Haven't you realized yet that you were nothing more than a decoy dressed up to look like an envoy?'

'What do you mean, a decoy?' Overcome by surprise, the samurai spoke more loudly than he intended.

Matsuki flinched. 'Edo and our domain never had trade with Nueva España as their main object. I've realized that since I returned to Japan . . .'

'What are you talking about?'

'Listen to me! They had absolutely no intention of inviting Christian missionaries in. Edo used our domain to find out how to build and sail the great ships. And the waterways the great ships navigate – that's why they stuck a lot of sailors in with the merchants on the voyage. We and the merchants were decoys to allay the foreigners' suspicions. That's why they didn't choose qualified people as envoys. Instead they appointed low-ranking lance-corporals who could die or rot anywhere along the way and no one would care.'

'And that is Government?' Nishi dementedly pounded his knees with his fists. 'Is that what you call the noble way of Government?'

'That's how Government works. I realize that now. Something that was good four years ago has to be judged evil if it has no use today. That is the noble way of Government. At one time Lord Shiraishi's plan to bring prosperity to the domain was proper for our domain. But now that the Shōgun no longer wants any one particular domain to prosper, Lord Shiraishi's ideas have become evil. Lord Shiraishi was expelled from the Council of Elders and his fiefdom

was reduced. That's to be expected. That's what the noble way of
Government is all about.'

Like Nishi, the samurai clutched his fists and glared at the candle
flame. Unless he clenched his fists until the nails bit into his flesh, he
would not be able to endure this mortification. Lord Ishida's
compassionate words. Lord Ishida's gentle smile.

'Even lance-corporals are human beings.' The samurai broke his
silence and groaned like a wounded beast. 'We are human beings.
Even lance-corporals!'

'Government is as fierce as a battle. Wars can't be fought if a
general has to worry about the private grief of his lance-corporals.'

'Does His Lordship . . . also feel that way?'

No matter how the Council of Elders and the elder statesmen felt,
he could not bring himself to believe that His Lordship was of the
same persuasion. The samurai had only seen His Lordship from afar.
His Lordship was in a position far beyond the reach of a mere lance-
corporal. But the samurai's family, his father, and his uncle had given
their all to fight for His Lordship. Some members of his family had
even died for him. In no sense was His Lordship helpless like that
miserable emaciated man with both arms outstretched. His Lordship
should be aware of all this.

'His Lordship?' Matsuki muttered sympathetically. 'His Lordship
is the Government.'

Unbroken cloud blanketed the sky, and now and then the forest
shivered and let fall a drop of rain. A single peasant wearing a straw
raincoat was lopping branches in the forest.

Beside the sunken hearth, the samurai was also snapping dried
branches. Next to him, his uncle was staring intently at the fire. The
dead branches broke in his hands with a dull crack. He tossed them
into the hearth. Tiny tongues of flame lapped them up.

'You must act as though the journey never took place.'

He still had a vivid recollection of the words Matsuki Chūsaku had
spoken out of sympathy. To forget, to believe that none of it ever
happened. Certainly nothing else could restore his sagging spirits. It
was pointless now even to reflect on the fact that they had not been
esteemed envoys, but nothing more than decoys sent to deceive the
foreign nations. Now the samurai understood what Matsuki had
meant when he said there was discord in the Council of Elders
between Lord Shiraishi and the other elder statesmen, that Lord
Shiraishi had fallen from power, and that this was the nature of
Government. There was nothing he could do about it.

Yet when he looked at the glum face of his uncle, who had placed all his hopes in his nephew's merits – that was painful for the samurai. His wife Riku just smiled sadly. She asked him nothing about the outcome of his interrogation in the castle, or of what lay in the future. She was good enough to act as though nothing at all had happened. But at times her very tenderness tore at his heart.

'Lord Ishida . . .' One evening his uncle, seated beside the samurai as he snapped branches, could remain silent no longer and asked, 'Haven't you had any word from Lord Ishida?'

'They're harvesting in Nunozawa now. When their work is finished, I'm sure he'll summon me.'

His Patron had sent no word to him since his return. It looked as though he was avoiding any association with the Hasekura family. The samurai had sent Yozō with greetings and a request for an audience, but the only answer that came back was that Lord Ishida would contact him at the right opportunity. He did not want to believe that even Lord Ishida was avoiding him.

'The world was very wide. But I can no longer believe in people.' That is what Nishi Kyūsuke had said when the two men parted after returning to Tsukinoura from the castle. As he spoke, Nishi had clutched the reins of his horse tightly in both hands to suppress his mounting resentment. Those angry words echoed sometimes in the samurai's ears. The two men had indeed been sent out into the wide world without knowing or realizing anything. Edo had tried to use the domain, the domain had tried to exploit Velasco, Velasco had tried to deceive the domain, the Jesuits had waged ugly contests with the Franciscans – and in the midst of this deception and strife the two men had pressed ahead with their long journey.

'I wonder if even Lord Ishida has forsaken our family,' his uncle muttered weakly.

In former days his uncle had never spoken in such a feeble voice. He sat constantly beside the hearth now, staring hollowly at the flames that crept lethargically like insects in late autumn. His body had shrivelled too. In desperation the samurai uttered words he did not believe himself in an effort to appease his ageing relative. Riku sat to the side, her eyes lowered as she listened to the two men talking. Sometimes she would get up and leave, as if she could not bear to hear her husband have to tell such lies knowing full well that they were lies. But the samurai had to go on lying to keep his rapidly deteriorating uncle alive for even one more day. The old man's only wish, which clung to him like a chronic disease, was to return to the lands in Kurokawa, the lands handed down by his ancestors, and to die there.

On days when he could not bear to face his uncle, the samurai joined the peasants and laboured with his body from dawn till dark, emptying his head of all thoughts. He would take up the firewood stacked around the house like a fence and pile it on his back until it seemed about to snap. Then, enduring the pain in his shoulders, he would carry it up the mountain path to the charcoal-burner's hut. Such tasks were his only means of escape. Yozō, also dressed in trousers, shouldered his own pile of firewood and followed word-lessly behind his master. Since their return the samurai had never questioned Yozō about his feelings. But when they sat down to rest in a hollow where a warm gold sun shone down on the grass and mountain chestnuts littered the ground, even without asking the samurai understood everything by looking into Yozō's eyes as his attendant stared silently into space.

'Yozō and the others,' the samurai thought as he plucked a mushroom with his fingers, 'are even more pathetic than me.'

The samurai could offer no recompense to Yozō or Ichisuke or Daisuke for the hardships they had endured on their journey. The council of Elders had not granted a single reward to the Hasekura family. Perhaps Yozō and the others were envious of the dead Seihachi. He had obtained his own kind of freedom. But Yozō and the others, like the samurai, would have to live out their lives content with the fate that had governed them in former days.

As the autumn gradually deepened, a messenger came at last from Lord Ishida. The orders required the samurai to come in secret, as Lord Ishida had various things to discuss with him.

He set out for Nunozawa, accompanied only by Yozō. The water in the moat surrounding Lord Ishida's mansion was murky, and rotting lotus leaves and water weeds clogged its surface. The wretched despair of having fallen from power in the Council of Elders was evident in the faded brown colour of the decomposing plants.

'Thank you for coming.' Lord Ishida coughed as he looked down at the prostrate samurai. When the samurai lifted his head, he realized that his Patron, like his uncle, had aged considerably, and that his once sturdy frame had withered.

'I know . . .' After a moment of silence, Lord Ishida said wearily, 'I know . . . how hard this is for you.'

The samurai struggled to contain his emotions. These were the first words of gentle compassion he had heard since his return. He felt like weeping aloud. Stifling the impulse, he rested both hands on his knees and bowed his head.

'But . . . there is nothing we can do. While you were gone, all the decisions of the domain were overturned, and His Lordship discarded all his dreams. You . . . you will have to forget about the lands in Kurokawa.'

The samurai had been prepared for this, but when he heard the pronouncement from Lord Ishida, the toothless face of his uncle flashed before his eyes.

'You must not even think of registering a protest. You had best make that very clear to your uncle. You must consider yourselves fortunate that the family of someone who became a Christian even briefly has been allowed to survive.'

'That was . . . for the sake of our mission.'

I did not believe in Christianity. I never thought to believe in it. The samurai tried to make his tear-clouded eyes tell Lord Ishida that it had all been in aid of his mission.

'You must realize that even the families of Lord Senmatsu and Lord Kawamura had their lands confiscated because they were Christians.'

'Lord Senmatsu and Lord Kawamura . . . ?'

This was the first he had heard of any such thing. The Senmatsu and Kawamura families were of far more prestigious lineage than the Hasekuras. Lord Kawamura Magobei of the Kawamura clan in particular had distinguished himself in the irrigation and afforestation of the domain, and he had been rewarded with an increase of over three thousand *koku* in Sarusawa, Hayamata and Ōkagi.

'You must accept this,' Lord Ishida admonished him. 'From today forward, you must live unobtrusively.'

'Unobtrusively . . . ?'

'Yes, without attracting any attention. You must not for a moment allow yourself to be suspected of being Christian. I can no longer protect you. In the old days His Lordship called upon the Ishida house to plan battle strategy. But now that times have changed, he has cast us aside like so many pebbles. I don't speak out of resentment. His Lordship is most adept at the ways of Government.' Lord Ishida laughed scornfully at his own words, his voice clouded with phlegm. 'Nothing's really changed for you, has it? Just a few years ago you were chosen as an envoy to the foreign lands even though you were only a lance-corporal. But now you are forced to live without attracting any attention. The relationship between one person and another is equally cold and heartless. Think about it. I called you here today because I wanted to tell you that.'

With downcast eyes the samurai listened to the melancholy voice of his Patron. Lord Ishida seemed to be talking not so much to the samurai as in an attempt to suppress his own sorrow and anger.

He left Nunozawa at nightfall with Lord Ishida's grating voice still ringing in his ears. Yozō plodded wearily behind his horse. To live in the marshland unobtrusively, without attracting any attention – that was the life that lay ahead for the samurai.

When he returned home that night, he told his unsuspecting uncle that he had discussed only the foreign countries with Lord Ishida. In reality Lord Ishida had not asked a single question about those countries or about the progress of their journey. Lord Ishida and everyone else in the domain had lost all interest in faraway lands.

'Then if he didn't mention the lands at Kurokawa,' his uncle shut his eyes, perhaps in resignation, 'didn't he say anything at all about a reward?'

'There's nothing he can do at this point. He told me to wait for the right opportunity.'

The samurai could not sever the only ropes that kept his uncle alive. He had to talk as though a faint hope still remained. The lie was bitter on his tongue, but the samurai spoke the words in a toneless voice. At a time like this it helped to have a face that betrayed no emotion.

After everyone had fallen asleep around the sunken hearth, he opened up the letter box which he had brought back with him from the journey. The box had been drenched in sea-water many times, and baked in the hot sun of Nueva España. In accordance with Lord Ishida's advice, he must burn everything that had the slightest scent of Christianity. The box contained scraps of paper on which the priests and monks at each monastery they visited had inscribed their names or prayers for a safe journey, and some of the tiny sacred pictures they kept in their prayer books. He had not thrown these worthless objects away, thinking that after his return the women and children would be surprised and delighted with them.

The samurai tore them up and tossed them into the ashes. The Council of Elders might be suspicious of these scraps and use them as evidence. The papers curled at the edges, turned chestnut brown, and were soon swallowed up by tiny flames.

Nights in the marshland were deep. No one who had never experienced a night in the marshland could know the true meaning of darkness or the silence of that darkness. Stillness was not the absence of sound. Stillness was the rustle of leaves in the grove at the back, the occasional shrill call of a bird, and the shadow of a man staring at tiny flames in a sunken hearth. As he stared at the ashes the samurai pondered Nishi's words. 'The world was very wide. But I can no longer believe in people.' He also thought of what Lord Ishida had said. 'From today forward, you must live unobtrusively.' Now, on this night, he could almost picture Nishi and Lord Ishida – both of them sitting silently with their heads bowed, as he himself sat.

From the bottom of the letter box he pulled out a small sheaf of tattered papers. It was something which that Japanese man had handed him silently as they parted beside the Tecali swamp in Nueva España. Had that man with his hair braided in pigtails left with the Indians and moved elsewhere? Or had he died by the banks of that sweltering bog? The world was wide, but in that wide world just as here in the marshland, people were crushed under the weight of their sorrow.

> He is always besides us.
> He listens to our agony and our grief.
> He weeps with us.
> And He says to us,
> 'Blessed are they who weep in this life, for
>   in the kingdom of heaven they shall smile.'

'He' was that man with the drooping head, that man as scrawny as a pin, that man whose arms stretched lifelessly out, nailed to a cross. Again the samurai closed his eyes and pictured the man who had peered down at him each night from the walls of his rooms in Nueva España and España. For some reason he did not feel the same contempt for him he had felt before. In fact it seemed as though that wretched man was much like himself as he sat abstractedly beside the hearth.

> When He was in the world, He undertook many journeys, but He never called upon the lofty or the powerful. He visited only the poor and the afflicted, and talked with no others. On nights when death visited the afflicted He sat beside them, clutching their hands until the dawn, weeping with the survivors . . . saying that He came into the world to minister unto men. . . .
> And behold, there was a woman who for many years had made her living selling her own body. When she heard that He had come across the sea, she ran to the place where He was. And she went to His side and spoke not a word, but only wept, and her tears did bathe His feet. And He saith unto her, with these tears all is satisfied, your Father which is in Heaven knows your misery and your sorrows. Therefore be not afraid.

Somewhere a bird shrieked frenziedly once, then twice. He broke a dried branch and tossed it into the hearth, and the tiny flames languidly sat up and began to munch the withered leaves.

The samurai imagined the pigtailed man putting these words to paper in his hut at Tecali. Nights in the swamp at Tecali were probably as dark and deep as those here in the marshland. The samurai felt he had a vague idea now why the pigtailed man had been impelled to write these words. He had wanted an image of 'that man' which was all his own. He had wanted not the Christ whom the affluent priests preached in the cathedrals of Nueva España, but a man who would be at his side, and beside the Indians, each of them forsaken by others. 'He is always beside us. he listens to our agony and our grief. He weeps with us. . . .' The samurai could almost see the face of the man who had scribbled these clumsy letters.

The first winter since his return was approaching. Each day, in the grove surrounding his house, withered leaves were scattered like powdery snow. One day he realized that the grove was totally stripped of foliage, and that the bare silver branches were twined together like the mesh of a net.

As usual the samurai went to the hills with Yozō and his other servants to cut wood. The felled trees were either chopped into firewood and piled up like an earthwork around the house or burned to produce charcoal. Wearing the same tight-sleeved *hangiri* and trousers as the other men, he worked all day, hacking off dead branches with a hatchet and cutting down tree trunks with a saw. He found that physical labour stopped him from thinking about anything. Loading the mountain of cut branches onto his back, he started towards the house with his men, mumbling Lord Ishida's words with each step he took: 'Unobtrusively, attracting no attention. Unobtrusively, attracting no attention.'

Sometimes as he worked the samurai would remember something and glance at Yozō, who laboured in silence. Like all the other men of the marshland, Yozō never exhibited any emotion, so when his eyes met those of his master, he merely returned the look without expression. But the samurai knew that a resignation like his own had sunk deep into Yozō's eyes.

Since their return the samurai had never once discussed the treatment he had received or his resentment with his loyal retainer. And Yozō had asked no questions. Yet the samurai felt that better than anyone else – even better than his wife Riku – Yozō understood his sorrow. However slightly, he felt consoled to have at his side a man like Yozō who had shared in the trials of the long journey.

By now the millet and *daikon* were already harvested, and the sheaves of hay that would be used for litter in the stables had been propped up in the bare fields like paper dolls. Once the hay was taken in, except for the charcoal burning there were no other major tasks until New Year's.

On the day which they called 'the end of autumn', when those final tasks were completed, the samurai saw white shapes against the sky over the marshland.

His son Gonshirō called out, 'White swans!'

'Yes, they are,' the samurai nodded. He had often dreamed of them on his journey.

The following day the samurai took Yozō and climbed up the mountain path to the swamp at the base of the hill where a castle had once stood. As they approached the swamp, four or five ducklings took flight.

It was precisely the scene he had viewed in his dreams. On the surface of the water, illuminated by a faint sun, the ducklings had clustered, calling out in their whistle-like voices, brushing their beaks against one another and parting, then forming a line and swimming towards the shore. A short distance from the ducklings was a flock of mallard ducks with dark green necks. Unlike the ducklings, the mallards took to the air one at a time.

Away from these lesser birds, the swans swam leisurely by themselves deep within the swamp. As they swam, they twisted their long necks from side to side and plunged them into the water. When they lifted their heads, tiny silver fish glimmered in their yellow beaks. When they tired of swimming, they spread their wings broadly on the shore and preened themselves.

The samurai had no idea where these birds had come from, or why they had chosen this tiny swamp as their home for the long winter. Doubtless some had weakened and died of starvation during their journey.

'These birds too,' the samurai muttered, blinking his eyes, 'must have crossed a wide ocean and seen many countries.'

Yozō was sitting with both hands clasped on his lap, staring at the water.

'It was truly . . . a long journey.'

The conversation broke off there. Once he had spoken these words, the samurai felt there was nothing more he needed to say to Yozō. It was not just the journey that had been painful. The samurai wanted to say that his own past, and Yozō's past, had been a succession of similarly painful experiences.

When the wind got up and tiny ripples skidded across the surface of the sunlit swamp, the ducks and swans shifted course and moved silently away. Lowering his head, Yozō shut his eyes tightly. The samurai knew that he was struggling against a flood of emotions. The samurai was suddenly struck by the impression that his loyal servant's profile resembled that man's. That man, like Yozō, had hung his head as though enduring all things. 'He is always beside us. He listens to our agony and our grief. . . .' Yozō had never abandoned his master – not now or ever in the past. He had followed the samurai like a shadow. And he had never spoken a word in the midst of his master's sufferings.

'I've always believed that I became a Christian as a mere formality. That feeling hasn't changed at all. But since I've learned something about Government, sometimes I find myself thinking about that man. I think I understand why every house in those countries has a pathetic statue of that man. I suppose that somewhere in the hearts of men, there's a yearning for someone who will be with you throughout your life, someone who will never betray you, never leave you – even if that someone is just a sick, mangy dog. That man became just such a miserable dog for the sake of mankind.' The samurai repeated the words almost to himself. 'Yes. That man became a dog who remains beside us. That's what that Japanese fellow at the Tecali swamp wrote. That when he was on the earth, he said to his disciples that he came into the world to minister unto men.'

Yozō looked up for the first time. He shifted his eyes towards the swamp as if to ponder what his master had just said.

'Do you believe in Christianity?' the samurai asked quietly.

'Yes,' Yozō answered.

'Tell no one.'

Yozō nodded.

The samurai laughed, deliberately, in an attempt to change the subject. 'When spring comes, the birds of passage leave this place. But we can never leave the marshland as long as we live. The marshland is our home.'

They had walked through many countries. They had crossed the great oceans. But in the end their point of return was this region of sterile soil and impoverished villages. That realization welled up even more forcefully within the samurai now. That was as it should be, he felt. The wide world, the many countries, the great oceans. Yet no matter where they went, people were the same. Contention raged everywhere and manipulation and intrigue were at work. That was the case in both the castle of His Lordship and the sectarian world of Velasco. What the samurai had seen was not the many lands, the many nations, the many cities, but the desperate karma of man. And above the karma of man hung that ugly, emaciated figure with his arms

246 THE SAMURAI

and legs nailed to a cross, and his head dangling limply down. 'We weep in the valley of sorrow and cry unto Thee.' The monk at Tecali had written those words at the end of his manuscript. How was this wretched marshland any different from the wide world? The samurai wanted to tell Yozō that the marshland was the world, was they themselves – but he could not find words to express what he felt.

'Japan. The storms of persecution have raged, and you exhibit only enmity towards God. Then why am I drawn to you? Why do I seek to return to you?'

On the twelfth of June I boarded a Chinese junk and left Luzon, where I had lived for a year. Several of the Japanese Christians who had been exiled to Manila secretly raised the necessary money for me. With those funds I was able to buy this termite-ridden junk, hire some crewmen, and set out from Luzon.

I do not know what the Lord Jesus must think of my reckless act. By now I cannot even decide whether it was the will of the Lord to keep me in that position as Superior of the monastery in Manila, or to have me go to Japan and do battle again. Of one thing, however, I am certain – that in time the Lord will clearly manifest His answer to me. And when the Lord gives me an answer, I shall meekly submit in all things.

I wrote that my act is reckless. I am returning again to Japan, where Christians are being persecuted and oppressed. In the eyes of others, that must indeed seem foolhardy. When the exiled Japanese in Manila first heard of my plan, they shook their heads and labelled my scheme reckless. They told me such an action would be foolish, that if I landed and were immediately apprehended, it would serve no purpose whatsoever.

But if my act is reckless and foolish, then was not the Lord Jesus's journey to Jerusalem also reckless? The Lord left the wilderness of Judaea and led His disciples into Jerusalem, knowing full well that He would be killed by the High Priest Caiaphas and the others. For the Lord knew then that the blood He shed would be efficacious for mankind. 'Greater love hath no man than this, that a man lay down his life for his friends.'

I think of His words now. The friends for whom I must lay down my life are not my fellow monks praying silently in the monastery at Manila. My friends are the Japanese faithful, like the man who came to me on the beach at Ogatsu. 'Let your heart be at ease. Soon the day will come when no one will laugh at your beliefs,' I had told him. Where is that man living now? I lied to him. The day when

Christians in Japan could proudly proclaim their faith never came. But I have not forgotten that man. Because of him, I cannot remain in the monastery at Manila, complacently reciting the Mass and delivering beautiful sermons.

Our uneventful voyage continues. Each day I pray for Japan. I pray for the Japanese envoys, whom I have not seen since they left Luzon. I pray for the man in the tattered working clothes. Half my life has been devoted to that barren land. I tried to plant a vineyard of God there, but I failed. Yet that land is my land. It is the land which I must subdue for God. I am drawn to Japan because its land is barren.

Rugged craggy islands dot the horizon to the east. The waves toss spray high against the crags, then turn into mist and scatter. Many years ago I passed by this place. It is the southern tip of Taiwan. Soon we will skirt the Ryūkyū Islands, go past the Shichitō Islands – known to be a precarious passage – and approach the southern extremity of Satsuma in Japan.

Our voyage still proceeds without incident. For several days now, I have been reflecting upon the last sea voyage of St Paul as recorded in Acts. On his final journey, did Paul have a premonition of his own martyrdom in Rome? Did he set out for the tyrant Nero's kingdom resolved to die? The book of Acts makes no mention of such a premonition, but reading between the lines I cannot help but feel that Paul foresaw his own suffering and wretched death.

From my youth, I was somehow drawn much less to the twelve Apostles – less to Peter, for example, whom the Lord loved – than to Paul. For this saint possessed a passionate nature, a passionate desire to conquer, and a passionate fervour like my own. He even had precisely the same faults as I. Because of his power and his passion, he wounded many people, including Peter. He did not hesitate to contend with the twelve Apostles to defend his own beliefs. When I ponder his life, I often seem to discover there strengths and weaknesses that are the very image of my own. Moreover, in the depths of his heart Paul refused to accept the overcautiousness and prudent indecisiveness of the twelve Apostles. Just as I cannot forgive the Jesuits their utter cowardice when it comes to the proselytizing of Japan. The associates of the twelve Apostles heaped insidious slanders upon Paul, a reflection of the attitude which the Jesuits have adopted towards me. Yet in the end it was because of Paul's efforts and his remarkable missionary labours to the Gentiles that the influence of the Church was able to reach out beyond Judaea. Similarly, no matter how much the members of the Jesuit Society try to repress me, who can say that I have not benefited the missionary effort in Japan?

Today as I stood on deck, facing the wind, I repeated over and over Paul's sermon which is recorded at the end of Acts, particularly the beautiful passage he quotes from Isaiah.

> 'Go unto this people, and say,
> Hearing ye shall hear, and shall not understand;
> and seeing ye shall see, and not perceive.
>
> For . . . their ears are dull of hearing,
> and their eyes they have closed;
> . . . lest they should hear with their ears
> and understand with their heart,
> and should be converted, and I should heal them.'

Yesterday we were pursued by a storm. The waves churned and bared their white fangs, the winds made the rigging creak loudly, and the entire sky was a leaden grey without a single break in the clouds. The Chinese jabbered that we would likely be caught up in this storm near the Shichitō Islands. To prepare for that eventuality, I wrapped my essential belongings – my breviary, these notes, and the bread and wine for the Mass – in a small bundle, wishing to hold onto this much at least.

In the afternoon the sea grew rougher, so the Chinese decided to take refuge at Kuchinoshima in the Shichitō Islands, and they shifted the course of the junk in that direction. Around three in the afternoon, ferocious rain and winds began to beat down on us. Our mast was blown away, and no sooner was our junk lifted high up on the waves than it plunged into the next deep chasm. Lashed to one another with ropes to avoid being hurled into the sea, we struggled against the waves that enveloped the deck.

When, after four hours, the storm had finished toying with our junk, it turned towards Japan and fled. The rudder no longer worked and we floated helplessly on the dark sea until daybreak. With the coming of a quiet dawn in total contrast to the previous day, we finally spotted Kuchinoshima on the horizon of the ocean which glittered in the morning sun. Soon several Japanese fishermen came rowing out in a tiny boat to assist us.

I am now in the hut of those fishermen. Thinking me a merchant headed for Bōnotsu, they have given me food and lent me clothes to wear.

After the storm the blue sky looks as though it has been wiped clean. This island was formed from an extinct volcano, and a gigantic mountain divided into three peaks towers before my eyes. On the one tiny beach composed of volcanic ash there are some thirty fishing huts, and their residents are the only inhabitants of the island. There are no Japanese officers here. According to the islanders, officers come here once a year from Satsuma, but they soon set out on a tour of inspection to the Ryūkyūs.

The unsuspecting islanders told us they would take us to Bōnotsu in their own boats once we feel better, but the Chinese say the rudder of our junk can be repaired.

I have come back. It is four days since we left Kuchinoshima, and Japan is now just before my eyes. The Japan I must conquer in the name of the Lord. . . .

A short while ago conical mountains appeared to the east. They were like tiny versions of Mount Fuji. I don't know what they are called. The sea reflects the hot sun, and the beach is white and deserted. The area beyond the beach is thick with vegetation like a jungle.

The junk sailed west along the coast until we came to a row of ten or so squalid fishing huts in the shadow of a promontory. Three boats were beached on the shore. To the left were a stone walkway made of black lava and a landing dock. Here too not a soul could be seen. It was almost as if a plague or some similar scourge had broken out and all the residents had fled.

The Chinese encouraged me to disembark here, but I hesitated. Somehow the atmosphere of this silent colony made me feel uneasy. I felt as though someone was lurking in the black shadows of the fishing huts, watching our every move. I managed to convince myself that whoever it was had made their way unseen to notify the authorities of our arrival. I knew how cunning and shrewd the Japanese were at times like this.

A considerable space of time elapsed. During that period nothing moved, as though everything had been solidified in this interval of heat and silence. Finally I determined to go ashore and announced my resolution to the Chinese. Our boat glided slowly towards the dock, and with my small bundle (the one containing the items which I could not bear to part with that afternoon of the storm), I stepped onto the edge of the boat. Just then a vessel appeared unexpectedly from behind the promontory to the east. Its flag was emblazoned with the crest of the local *daimyō*, and I could make out the forms of two officers standing up and looking in our direction.

They had obviously been aware of our movements for some time. My bundle contained items they must not see – my breviary, the bottle of wine for the Mass – so I flung it into the sea. I must tell them that I am a merchant en route to Bōnotsu, but that our ship was wrecked along the way and we drifted here.

Their ship approaches now. Soon the Lord will reveal the fate which He has prepared for me. The Lord's will be done. The heavens and the earth shout hosannas to God. Praise the glory of His name, glory and praises unto God. . . .

Now that I know what God wishes of me, I commend myself into His hands. This is not feeble resignation, but the absolute trust which the Lord Jesus demonstrated with His entire being upon the cross.

I was apprehended. The officers at Bōnotsu were not stupid enough to be taken in by us. Though they pretended to believe my assertion that I was a merchant, they placed me in gaol, claiming it was only until they had completed their investigation. Several Christians had been put into the same cell, and the officers secretly listened in on our conversations. One ailing old man quietly asked me to perform the extreme unction for him. That was how the officers found out everything.

I was removed from the gaol at Bōnotsu and taken to Kagoshima. There I was interrogated until winter, and at New Year's I was transported by boat to the office of the Nagasaki magistrate. At this moment I am in a place called Ōmura near Nagasaki. From here I can see the tranquil ocean.

Among the many Christians incarcerated here are a Dominican named Father Vasquez and a Japanese monk, Luis Sasada. The cell in which we are kept is sixteen *palmo* wide by twenty-four *palmo* long and built of logs, the gaps between them barely wide enough to thrust two fingers through. In one corner is a door through which the officers come and go. The door is kept locked, of course.

I noticed when I was taken out for questioning that the area outside our cell is surrounded with two rows of sharpened stakes, with thorns placed between each stake – all arranged so that no one can approach from outside. Beyond this fence lies the guardhouse, the head guard's residence and a kitchen.

Although they have a kitchen, our only meal each day is rice with a single bowl of greens, raw or pickled *daikon* or sometimes pickled sardines. Since we are not permitted either to cut our hair or shave our beards, we look much like hermits. We are not allowed to leave our cell to wash, so we are the epitome of filthiness, and, most distressing of all, we are forced to relieve ourselves inside the cell. As a result we live each day amid a foul smell that can hardly be endured. At night they will not give us a single candlestick.

From Father Vasquez and Brother Sasada I learned how the persecution of the missionaries has progressed since my arrest. Ten missionaries had been in hiding in the same region as Father Vasquez. Though their numbers were few, they continued their labours in accordance with instructions from their superiors, just as they had done before the expulsion edict. Most of them hid in caves, and even on the rare occasions when they spent a night in the home of a Christian, they hid inside a double wall that had been made for them.

'I spent many nights inside those double walls myself,' Father Vasquez told me. 'We would sleep until night and then move on to the next house. But I had decided not to spend more than one night under one roof. When we were summoned to a house, first we would hear confessions from the sick. When the faithful gathered furtively together, we would encourage them and forgive their sins. This would continue until the hour when all the doors of the village had to be shut.'

Yet despite all their vigilance, the magistrate of Nagasaki was not sitting idly back. Just as the High Priest Caiaphas gave Judas a reward for betraying the Lord, those who revealed the whereabouts of priests or monks in hiding were given a reward, while people who provided rooms or hiding places for the fugitives or gave them any form of assistance were subjected to extreme punishments. Dreadful tortures were inflicted on those found to be Christians, not only to force them to renounce their faith, but also to compel them to reveal where the missionaries were hiding.

'That was the worst thing about it,' said Father Vasquez. 'We could no longer trust even the Japanese faithful we had taught ourselves. We never knew when someone we thought we could trust would apostatize. So I didn't even tell the faithful where I was. Some priests revealed their hiding-places and were arrested by magistrate's officers the very next day. Living each day unable to trust anyone – that was sheer hell.'

I enquired after my former companion, Father Diego. I had not forgotten Diego – an ineffectual man though the very epitome of virtue.

'Father Diego died of an illness,' Luis Sasada told me. 'It was when we were all brought to Fukuda near Nagasaki to be banished from the country. He has no grave. The officers burned his body and threw it into the sea. The Japanese authorities reduce everyone who was a Christian to ashes so that no trace of them will remain, then toss the ashes into the waves.'

'I suppose that soon we too will be turned to ashes and cast into the sea.'

I shall calmly accept this fate which God has ordained, just as a fruit absorbs the mellow light of autumn. I no longer consider my own imminent death a defeat. I fought with Japan, and I was beaten by Japan. . . . I think again of the plump old man in the velvet chair. He may think he has vanquished me, but he will never understand that, although the Lord Jesus was defeated in the political world of the High Priest Caiaphas and slaughtered upon the cross, through His death He reversed everything. Doubtless the old man will believe he has taken care of everything if he annihilates me and reduces me to ashes that are tossed into the sea. But everything will begin from that point. Just as everything commenced and was set in motion with the death of Lord Jesus on the cross. I will become a single stepping-stone in the swampland that is Japan. Soon another missionary will stand on the stepping-stone that is me, and he will become the next stepping-stone.

In the darkness I pray for Hasekura and Nishi, from whom I parted in Luzon, and for the dead Tanaka. I have no idea where Hasekura or Nishi are at this moment, or what they are doing. Nor do I know whether they possessed even a particle of faith in Christianity. But with each new day, I grow more eager to have them forgive me for the many errors – albeit a result of my good intentions – which I committed against them during our journey. It is true that I bullied and cajoled and appeased and manipulated them. Perhaps I even made them become Christians so that I could use them. In any event, they have come in contact with the Lord. They have come in contact with the Lord – that alone is my greatest consolation now. Though I feel deep remorse for what I did to them, at the same time I am glad that it happened. For the Lord will never forsake those who have once been associated with Him.

'O Lord, please do not forsake Hasekura and Nishi and Tanaka. Rather take my life as a punishment for my sin of using those people, and to bring to pass their true salvation. And if it be possible, help them to understand that my schemes were meant solely to bring light to their country of Japan.'

Father Vasquez has fallen ill. Earlier he had complained that the foul smells and wretched food had upset his system, but three days ago he began vomiting up his food and could no longer sit up. We pleaded for some medicine, but the guards brought us only an earthen pot filled with boiled tree roots, and they make no move to summon a physician. Left with no recourse, Luis Sasada and I have placed a rag moistened with muddy water on Father Vasquez's forehead to calm his fever.

If the day of our execution is delayed, sooner or later we will surely fall victim to the same illness. Though I try to accept that fate, at times the fear of death jabs at my breast like a sharp sword. Desperately I remind myself that the Lord spent similar hours enduring the anxiety of approaching death. Of late I have been wondering how Jesus felt at that time. I wonder when it was that Jesus foresaw His own death, and how he lived with that realization.

The Lord forewarned His disciples of His death. 'But I have a baptism of death to be baptized with; and how am I pained till it be accomplished!'

'And how am I pained till it be accomplished!' Those words demonstrate that the Lord Himself experienced the same feelings we have now. That knowledge has been a great comfort to me.

But by passing through death the Lord created a new order for this world. He created an eternal order which lies behind the world of man. I too will follow the Lord's example, and by giving my life for Japan, by pouring my blood out upon Japan, I will become a part of that order.

'I am come to send fire on the earth.' These are also the Lord's words. 'Japan. I too am come to Japan to send fire. Japan, which up until the present day has sought only the gains of this world and the happiness of this life. No other nation on earth is as disinterested and apathetic about anything beyond that realm as you are. Your cunning and wisdom are directed only towards the profits of this world. You move swiftly, like a lizard pouncing upon its prey.

'Japan. I am come to Japan to send fire. For the present, you will not understand why I gave up everything and boarded a ship to return to you. For the present, you will think that, having failed in everything, I come to you again only to die, but you will not understand the reason. For the present, you cannot comprehend why the Lord Jesus, that He might send fire, showed Himself in Jerusalem where His enemies lay in wait, and died upon the hill of Golgotha.'

But the Lord will never forsake those who have once come in contact with Him. 'O Lord, please do not forsake Japan. Rather, to punish me for my sin of using this country, and to bring true salvation to this land, take my life.'

The fear of death. In the daylight, as I care for Father Vasquez, I feel I can accept any fate. But, in truth, when night comes and the guards will not grant us a single candle, in that darkness filled with the stench of excrement, as I listen to Father Vasquez groan, the fear of death stabs at my breast, claws with sharp nails at my chest. I am soaked with sweat. Sweat like drops of blood. 'Father, if Thou be willing,' I moan, 'remove this cup of death from me.'

The fear of death. During the night Father Vasquez died. It was a wretched, miserable death unbecoming a man who came to Japan as an eminent Dominican missionary and unflaggingly preached the word of God. Brother Luis Sasada and I listened as he bellowed and howled like a wild beast. Those were his final words of parting as he left this earth for all eternity. I fumbled in the darkness and closed his eyes (I am grateful it was too dark to see; I had the feeling that his eyes were open wide with resentment) and recited a prayer. The same prayer I had offered up for the Indian youth and for Tanaka. . . .

At daybreak the guards wrapped the priest's body in a straw mat and took it away. His arms and legs, which poked out from the mat, were as spindly as needles, covered with dirt and caked in mud. As I watched the scene with Luis Sasada, I had a flash like a revelation from Heaven. This was reality. No matter how much we try to camouflage or idealize it, the real world is as wretched as the dirt-stained, mud-caked corpse of Father Vasquez. And the Lord did not avoid this miserable reality. For even the Lord died covered in sweat and dirt. And through His death, He cast a sudden light upon the realities of this world.

As I think back on it now, I feel as though the Lord gave me all those setbacks so that He could force me to look this reality in the face. It is as though my vanity, my pride, my haughtiness, and my thirst for conquest all existed for the purpose of shattering everything that I had idealized, so that I could see the true state of the world. But, as the Lord's death pierced that reality with light, in order that my death may someday pierce Japan . . .

Father Vasquez's body will be burned and reduced to ashes, and those ashes will be cast into the sea. That is what the Japanese have done with many missionaries.

Today there was another interrogation. Actually they can hardly be called interrogations. An official from the Nagasaki Bureau of Religious Inspection merely goes through the motions of encouraging us to apostatize (the Japanese refer to it as 'falling'). But he doesn't for a moment think that we will, and we simply shake our heads. Today, however, he began questioning me about a separate matter. He asked me whether Hasekura and Nishi had been in earnest when they converted to Christianity in Europe. Thinking of their safety, I answered:

'They were converted for the sake of their mission.'

'Then,' the official stared fixedly at me, 'you could not say they are Christians?'

I said nothing. When an individual receives baptism, no matter what the circumstances, the power of that sacrament supersedes his own will. The official looked at me and wrote something on his paper.

'Listen . . . don't you think this whole thing is ridiculous?' On his way out, the official peered sympathetically into my face. 'You might have done some good for the Christians and other people if you'd just stayed quietly in Luzon. . . . It's almost as though you came to Japan simply so you could be arrested and meaninglessly killed. That's just plain lunacy.'

'It is not lunacy.' I replied with a smile. 'It happened because of the way I am. It's very much like what your Buddhist priests call karma. Yes, this was my karma. That's how it seems to me. But I believe now that God has made use of my karma to benefit Japan.'

'How do you think your God made use of it to benefit Japan?' the official asked, even more puzzled than before.

'Your question itself is the answer,' I asserted. I spoke with determination, not only so that he might understand, but also to reaffirm my own feelings. 'You have said that what I did was ridiculous. I understand that. But why did I knowingly perform such a ridiculous act? Why did I deliberately do something that seems so lunatic? Why did I come to Japan knowing I would die? Think about that sometime. If I can die and leave you and Japan to deal with that question, my life in this world will have had meaning.'

'I don't understand.'

'I have lived. . . . Whatever else may be, I have lived. I have no regrets.'

The official left without another word. On the way back to my cell, I asked the guard if I could have a glimpse of the ocean, and he consented. Standing beside the spiked fence surrounding the cell, I gazed out at the wintry sea.

The ocean shimmered in the afternoon sun. Several circular islands dotted the sea. Not a ship could be seen, and all was calm. This was Father Vasquez's grave, and the grave of many other missionaries. And soon this spot will become my grave. . . .

When the first snows fell, it was the custom in the marshland to make unsalted dumplings. Three leaves of cogon grass were inserted into each dumpling, and they were presented as an offering to the Buddha. The consecrated dumpling was then boiled in a pot of water and eaten by the family. It was said that the first person to pick the dumpling out of the pot would have good fortune. In the samurai's house Riku had the women servants hang a large pot over the sunken hearth. Their younger son Gonshirō managed to pluck out the dumpling, and laughter swirled about the hearth for the first time in some while.

The following day, however, a messenger came from Lord Ishida with word that the samurai was to remain dutifully at home, since orders were on their way from the Council of Elders. Orders from the castle were never dispatched directly to lance-corporals, but instead were sent via their Patrons.

His uncle, who had lain sick in bed since the end of autumn, insisted repeatedly that this might have something to do with the lands in Kurokawa. Or thinking that perhaps this was news of a reward from His Lordship for the samurai's strenuous journey, his uncle sent out servants to make persistent enquiries. But somehow the samurai could not bring himself to believe that the news was good.

Two officers arrived several days later. They entered the immaculately swept house and disappeared into a separate room to change their clothes. Riku helped the samurai change into his crested formal robes; he then seated himself in formal position at the edge of the straw mats and waited.

The two officers entered and sat in the place of honour. One said quietly, 'Orders from the Council of Elders,' and began to read a letter announcing the Council's decision.

'Inasmuch as Hasekura Rokuemon in foreign lands was converted to the Christian religion in violation of the law, he should be severely punished, but as a result of exceptional consideration by the Council, Hasekura is ordered to be confined to his own house.'

The samurai listened to these words with both his hands pressed to the floor and his head bowed down to the ground. As he listened he felt that he was falling into an empty void. He was so weary he no longer felt even remorse. Blinking his sunken eyes as he often did, he listened as the officer added a verbal explanation. Because of the clemency of Lord Ayugai and Lord Tsumura, his confinement meant only that he was never to leave the marshland. The officer added that he was also to submit an oath of recantation from Christianity to the Council of Elders once each year.

'I can imagine how you feel.' Once they had discharged their duties the officers felt obliged to express their condolences. Before they mounted their horses, one of the officers took the samurai aside. 'This is confidential,' he said. 'I have a message for you from Matsuki Chūsaku. The Council of Elders has received a report from Edo that Velasco has been captured in Satsuma. It's on account of that report that your punishment was so severe.'

'Lord Velasco?' Even now the samurai could only bat his eyes.

'I hear he was sent to the Nagasaki Bureau of Religious Inspection, and that now he's in prison in Ōmura with some other priests. I understand he hasn't apostatized yet.'

When the officers had gone, the samurai sat down, still dressed in his crested robes. Darkness was beginning to creep over the cold, unheated *tatami* room. Thinking of what the officer had said, he was convinced that the proud, arrogant foreigner would never apostatize, that such a man would never betray himself, whatever ordeals and tortures he had to endure.

'So he's come back to Japan. . . .'

He had known this would happen ever since he parted from Velasco in Luzon. There had been no reason to believe that the foreigner's violently passionate nature would be able to tolerate a calm, uneventful life. Many times over during their journey that passionate nature had hurt the samurai and his fellow envoys. On their journey the samurai had always thought of Velasco as a foreigner totally alien to the Japanese, and for a long while he had not been able to feel close to him.

He was aware of a faint stir. He turned his head and discovered Riku sitting in the corridor. Riku's shoulders quivered in the darkness as she fought to control her emotions.

'Don't worry,' he said gently to his wife. 'We should be grateful that the Hasekura family has not been obliterated, and that Yozō and the others were not punished.'

From that day on, there were many times after everyone else had gone to sleep when the samurai would sit alone staring at the flames that darted after the withered branches. What had become of Nishi? He had probably received the same orders, but of course they had no way of communicating. When he closed his eyes, the scenes of Nueva España, as he rode his horse alongside Nishi and the others, passed one by one before him. The sun like a smouldering disc, the desert where maguey and cactus grew, the herds of goats, the fields tended by pigtailed Indians. Had he actually witnessed such scenes? Had it all been a dream? Was he still dreaming? On the walls of the monasteries where he stayed, that ugly emaciated man had always hung with outstretched arms and drooping head.

As he snapped the dry branches, the samurai thought, 'I crossed two great oceans and went all the way to España to meet a king. But I never met a king. All I ever saw was that man.'

It occurred to the samurai that in foreign lands that man was called 'Lord', but he had never been able to understand why. All he knew was that destiny had brought him together not with any king of this world, but only with a man who was much like the vagabonds who sometimes came begging in the marshland. . . .

Even though he had been confined to his house, at the beginning of the year the family celebrated New Year's. In the marshland every family thrust chopsticks into riceballs, which were arranged in a basket and placed before the Buddhist altar. In the samurai's house, it had also been the custom for generations to offer up rice cakes to the god of the year and to decorate the entranceway with *otategi*, firewood bound up in a faggot with a young pine branch inserted in the middle.

By tradition too, the members of the branch families and cadet families came to the samurai's house to offer New Year's greetings to him as patriarch of the head family, but because of the circumstances this year the practice was abandoned. Normally his uncle would always drop by, but he did not come because of his illness. The samurai's only solace was his son Kanzaburō, who came to his father dressed in robes signifying the attainment of manhood and offered his New Year's salutations like an adult.

Still, New Year's was New Year's. Drops of water fell with a cheerful splash from the snow on the roof and the icicles on the eaves, and the family could hear Gonshirō playing on his stick horse beside the stable.

From time to time the report of a musket echoed through the marshland from the distance. The domain permitted the shooting of birds of passage only during New Year's, and Kanzaburō had apparently taken some peasants with him and gone hunting by the swamp. The echo of the shots lingered endlessly over the marshland.

The peasants came back carrying the ducks they had shot. Among the several ducks set down in the entranceway, there was one white swan.

The samurai summoned Kanzaburō and scolded him. 'I told you not to shoot the white swans.' He thought of the times on his journey when the swans and himself had merged into one in his dreams.

The body of the swan was already stiff and had begun to smell. When he picked it up two, then three of the white feathers from its breast floated to the ground like flakes of snow. Its long neck, stained with dark red blood and mud, dangled lifelessly from the samurai's arms like the head of that man. A grey film veiled its eyes. For some reason the samurai thought again of his own ill fate.

His uncle died at the end of January. The samurai hurried over to the branch family's house. His uncle's body had shrivelled up like a child's and the flesh of his cheeks had been hollowed away, but he was at peace. Even the old man's attachment to the lands at Kurokawa had utterly vanished, or so it seemed to the samurai.

With the coffin – which the local people called a *gambako* – at the centre, the funeral procession made its way along the snow-covered roads of Shirata towards the base of a mountain. The *gambako* was interred in the graveyard where the samurai's father was buried, and black earth mixed with snow and mud was piled over it. The samurai sent a messenger to his Patron Lord Ishida with news of his uncle's death.

Night after night the winds wailed over the frozen snows of the marshland. Then suddenly a messenger arrived from Lord Ishida. Perhaps out of deference to the Council of Elders, Lord Ishida had not offered a single word of condolence when the samurai's uncle died. Riku suggested that this unexpected message from their Patron might mean that the samurai's confinement had been lifted, and the samurai himself was persuaded of that possibility. After all, despite the declaration by the Council of Elders that the samurai was not to leave the marshland, Lord Ishida had specifically directed him to come to Nunozawa with one of his attendants.

Again he took Yozō and set out for Nunozawa. It was cold along the road, and though a faint sun occasionally broke through the grey snowy sky, the wind stirred up flakes of powdery snow from the forest and blew them repeatedly against the faces of the two men. As they pressed their horses along beside the river frozen over with a thick sheet of ice, the samurai wondered how many times he had made his way back and forth along this road. The times he had received orders for corvée labour, the times he had submitted

petitions for the return of the lands at Kurokawa, the times he had
been told to despair of those lands and had returned home with a heavy
heart. It was a path steeped in memories. And on each occasion, Yozō
had accompanied him.

From time to time the samurai turned in his saddle and looked back
at his servant, following silently behind. Yozō was wearing a
raincoat which the local people called *kakumaki*. Now, just as on their
journey, Yozō never left his master's side. 'It's cold, isn't it?' the
samurai called sympathetically to his servant.

It was still windy when they arrived at Nunozawa, but the sky had
cleared. Beneath the cloudless sky a range of white mountains
stretched out into the distance, and as far as the eye could see the fields
were blanketed with frozen snow. Unlike the marshland, the arable
land here was broad and easy to irrigate.

The moat around Lord Ishida's mansion was frozen. The straw
roof was weighed down with snow, and icicles dangled from the
eaves like white fangs. The samurai left Yozō in the garden and
waited for a long while on the wooden floor of the reception room.

'Roku?' Lord Ishida called in a raspy voice as he sat down on the
upper dais. 'You've had many difficult times. When I have the
opportunity, I would like to visit his grave. But you should at least be
happy that the Hasekura family was not wiped out.'

What did I do wrong? The words rose to the samurai's throat, but
he held them back. There was no point in saying them.

'None of this is your fault. Your luck was bad. The domain . . .'
Lord Ishida hesitated for a moment. 'If the domain hadn't treated you
this way . . . they wouldn't have been able to vindicate themselves,'
Lord Ishida wheezed.

'Vindicate . . .?' Confused, the samurai lifted his head and looked
ruefully at his Patron. 'What do you mean, "vindicate"?'

'Vindicate themselves to Edo. At this moment Edo is looking for
any excuse to crush the powerful domains one after another. After all
this time Edo has denounced His Lordship because for so many years
he sheltered the Christians who fled from Kantō, and because he gave
in to Velasco's wishes and wrote a letter to Nueva España saying that
he would welcome Christian priests. The domain has to come up
with some positive vindication.'

The samurai knelt with his hands pressed against the cold floor and
said nothing. A single large teardrop fell to the floor.

'You had the ill fortune to be caught up in the shifting tides of
Government.' Lord Ishida sighed. 'I know how painful this is for
you. This old man here understands your pain better than anyone
else.'

The samurai raised his head and stared into Lord Ishida's face. In that seemingly gentle voice, that seemingly gentle face, he sensed a lie. There were still more lies in the old man's expression, in his wheezing nasal voice and in his deliberate sighs. This man understood none of his resentment, none of his remorse. He merely pretended to understand.

'But, Roku, I won't let the Hasekura family be wiped out. That is as much as the Council of Elders and Lord Ayugai will allow.' Lord Ishida repeated his earlier remark in a firm tone. 'I will do . . . everything I can to look after Kanzaburō . . .'

The samurai was puzzled. What did the old man mean by this unexpected remark?

'Don't be resentful.'

'I am not . . . resentful.'

'There are new orders from the Council.' Lord Ishida spat out this information in a single breath, as though he were hurling away a heavy burden, then staggered to his feet and disappeared. There were footsteps. The same officers who had come to the marshland stepped into the room.

'Orders from the Council of Elders.'

The samurai bowed to the ground and listened to the officer's words.

'Because Hasekura Rokuemon converted to a heathen religion, after renewed inquiry he is ordered to appear at once before the Council of Elders.'

The samurai realized that several men were waiting breathlessly outside the closed doors to the corridor. They were waiting to arrest him should he grasp the implications of these orders and frantically try to resist.

When he had finished writing to his wife and Kanzaburō, he cut off a lock of his hair and placed it with the letter. Then he asked Lord Ishida's steward, who was waiting at his side, 'Please summon my servant Yozō.'

When the steward had left the room, the samurai placed his hands on his knees and closed his eyes. Doubtless Lord Ishida and the officers from the Council of Elders were in an inner chamber. But within the mansion all was silent.

Now and then he heard the sound of snow sliding off the straw-thatched roof, no longer able to resist its own weight. When the dull sound subsided, the silence grew even more intense.

'You had the ill fortune to be caught up in the shifting tides of Government.' Lord Ishida's words still rang in his ears. 'I know how painful this is for you. This old man here understands your pain better than anyone else.'

When he had finished, the officer, just as before, had added, 'This is difficult for me, even if it is my duty.'

The samurai sat motionless. Inside the mansion it was strangely quiet. His own heart had lost the strength to summon forth any emotion whatsoever. Renewed inquiry. That was nothing but an excuse. He had already explained and apologized to Lord Tsumura and Lord Ōtsuka time after time. 'If the domain hadn't treated you this way . . . they wouldn't have been able to vindicate themselves.' Lord Ishida's words came back to him. Everything had been decided from the outset; he was simply running along predetermined tracks. Falling into a dark, empty void.

Snow creaked on the roof and slipped to the ground. The sound reminded the samurai of the creak of the halyards. In a single moment the halyards creaked, the white seagulls flew over with a shrill call, the waves beat against the hull, and the ship moved out into the great ocean – and from that moment it was decided that this would be his fate. His long journey was now bringing him to this final destination.

When he looked up, outside the open door he could see Yozō sitting in the snowy garden with his head bowed. Undoubtedly the steward had told him everything. Batting his eyes, the samurai stared at his faithful servant for a few moments. 'All the trials you've gone through . . .' The words caught in his throat.

Yozō could not make out whether his master had muttered his gratitude for all those trials or his resentment because of them. He kept his head bowed, but he could tell that his master and the steward had stood up to leave.

Beyond the roof the samurai could see snow falling. The swirling flakes seemed like the white swans of the marshland. Birds of passage which came to the marshland from a distant country and then departed for a distant country. Birds which had seen many countries, many cities. They were he himself. And now, he was setting off for another unknown land. . . .

'From now on . . . He will be beside you.'

Suddenly he heard Yozō's strained voice behind him.

'From now on . . . He will attend you.'

The samurai stopped, looked back, and nodded his head emphatically. Then he set off down the cold, glistening corridor towards the end of his journey.

A day for the execution was decided upon. The day before the execution Velasco and the monk Luis Sasada were given special permission to bathe their bodies under scrutiny of the guards and to change into new prison robes. In the words of the guard, this was a result of 'exceptional consideration' on the part of the magistrate's office. Their filthy bodies were emaciated, and their ribs protruded. Their meal on the last evening – again through the exceptional consideration of their hosts – included one nearly spoiled fish with the usual bowl of greens. The guard explained that this would be the last meal they would get, since it was a rule that prisoners were not given any breakfast on the morning of their execution. Some prisoners were so terrified that they vomited up everything in their stomachs at the execution ground.

'Have you any requests?'

Velasco and Luis Sasada asked to be given some clean paper. Both wished to write a final testament. In the faint sunlight seeping through the cell bars, Velasco wrote to his comrades in the monastery at Luzon.

'With each passing moment now I sense my final hour pressing in upon me. Blessed be God, who sends the rains of love upon this rocky, barren land. I hope that each of you will also forgive me my sins. I committed many errors in the course of my life. Like an ineffectual man who tries to resolve everything with one single effort, I now await my martyrdom. May God's will be done in the trackless lands of Japan just as His will is done in Heaven. Please forgive me for not being able to carry out to the fullest the calling as priest which God granted me. Please overlook the many times I hurt you with my pride and arrogance. May each of you have success as goodly labourers in the Lord's wheatfields, and may He bring us all together within the glory of our Heavenly Lord.'

As he wrote his final testament, Velasco genuinely felt that his own pride and arrogance had wounded countless people over the years, and that he would have to endure tomorrow's agony as punishment for that.

By the time he handed the testament to the guard, the usual chill darkness had gradually crept over the cell. It occurred to him that at this hour tomorrow they would no longer be here, but that the same darkness would sweep over their deserted cell, and Velasco suddenly felt insulted.

As he was praying with Luis Sasada, unexpected footsteps sounded from the far end of the prison, and the barred door to their cell was thrown open. The face of the guard, as flat as that of a fish, flickered in the shadows of the candle flame.

'Inside.'

At the guard's order, a large crouching shadow slipped clumsily into their cell. It spoke to the two men in Latin, whispering, '*Pax Domini*.'

In the dark they could not make out the face or the form of this prisoner, but he gave off the same foul odour as themselves.

'Are you a priest?'

In a gravelly voice, he told them that he was Father Carvalho of the Society of Jesus.

'I was in the prison at Suzuda. I am to be executed tomorrow with both of you.'

He had been in hiding near Nagasaki, he told them, but he had been captured at the end of the previous year, and transported here from the prison in Suzuda – situated between Ōmura and Nagasaki – in order to be executed on the morrow.

In the darkness Velasco smiled. It was not his usual condescending smile. He smiled at the sudden realization that he had felt not the slightest resentment or anger at learning that this newcomer was a Jesuit, a member of the Order that had employed every possible slander to entrap him and obstruct his plans during his journey. Although the man standing before him was a priest of that Society, he felt not hatred, but even a twinge of nostalgia. Perhaps the knowledge that they would be sharing death the next morning had washed everything away. Certainly hatred and anger were trivial matters compared to the enormity of death that would come tomorrow. 'I . . .' he introduced himself, 'am Father Velasco.'

Father Carvalho said nothing. It was obvious from his silence that he had heard of Velasco's name and his activities.

'Do not worry,' Velasco said with gentle concern. 'I no longer have any such thoughts. Tomorrow we will be together in the same country.'

He asked whether it would be possible for Father Carvalho to hear his confession. He knelt beside the foul-smelling body before him. He knew that his voice could be heard distinctly by Luis Sasada, but that no longer bothered him.

'My haughtiness and pride have misled and wounded many people. I sought to satisfy my own pride by taking the name of God in vain.

'I confused my own will with the will of God.

'There have been times when I have hated God. Because God's will was not in accordance with my will.

'I have even denied God. Because God ignored my wishes.

'I was not aware of my own pride and my lust for conquest. I flattered myself that they were all for the sake of God.'

Spewing foul breath from his lips, Father Carvalho intoned the words of remonstrance in a rasping voice, then he crossed himself.

'Be at ease now. Go in peace.'

When he heard those words, Velasco thought of the man whose confession he had heard at Ogatsu. He had no idea where that man was or what he was doing now, but he was going to his death having lied to that man. He must die as a punishment for that lie too. Though his confession was complete, his heart was not at peace.

During the night Luis Sasada suddenly began to sob. Not for the first time, he was racked by the fear of death. As always Velasco clutched Sasada's slender hand and fervently begged God to pour out all this agony upon himself. Father Carvalho also knelt beside Sasada and prayed for the weeping, shuddering young man. Before long a white light slowly began to steal into the cell. The day of the execution had dawned.

Dawn.

The sky was clear, but the wind was strong. When the condemned men were taken from their cell, foot-soldiers carrying spears and muskets had already lined up in the prison garden, and bunting bearing the crest of the Ōmura domain flapped in the wind. Several clansmen were seated on stools in front of the bunting, among them the official from the magistrate's office who had interrogated the prisoners.

This official rose from his stool and ordered the three men to state their names. Then he stooped and muttered something to a man who appeared to be his superior. The stout old man unrolled a paper containing the sentence of death and read it aloud.

The wind was brisk. In the distance the foaming sea looked cold. When the sentence had been read out, the guards surrounded the three men and bound their hands. Ropes were also placed around their necks, but these were not tightened.

The procession set out. They made their way down a path that threaded through groves of mandarin orange trees, the officers on horseback, the prisoners, guards and soldiers on foot. Farm women ceased their labours and watched in surprise.

'*Crucifixus etiam pro nobis.*'

As they staggered down the sloping path, Father Carvalho suddenly began to sing.

'*Crucem passus.*'

The officers and guards did not attempt to interrupt his singing.

When they had descended through the orange groves, they entered the town of Ōmura. The road was lined with thatched houses, and on either side men shouldering baskets and women carrying children watched transfixed as the procession passed by. Velasco tried to encourage Luis Sasada, who occasionally reeled and fell against him.

'Soon . . . very soon, it will all be over. The Lord awaits us.'

The lines of spectators stretched right to the end of the street.

'Father, forgive them.' With this verse Father Carvalho concluded his hymn. 'For they know not what they do.'

A bamboo palisade came into view in the distance. Another platoon of foot-soldiers with muskets was lined up beside it. This area, called Hokonbaru, was the execution ground of the Ōmura domain.

As he walked along the beach, which was littered with shells and seaweed, Velasco stared at the sea. The wind slapped against his forehead. Far out in the harbour, the gentle orchid-coloured hills of Hario Island could be seen. The waves on this side of the tiny island swirled and drenched the rocks with a misty spray. The sun had reserved its brightest rays for the stretches of open sea. This was the last view of Japan that Velasco and the other prisoners would ever see.

The soldiers opened the bamboo palisade. The procession halted. The faces of the condemned prisoners, exposed to the sea winds, were pale all the way to their lips. In the centre of the palisade three new stakes had been driven into the ground, and straw and firewood had been heaped around them. The stakes stood straight and still, like tall executioners.

As the guards adjusted the bonds on the hands of the three men, the official from the magistrate's office approached.

'Come now, don't you feel like apostatizing yet? This is your last chance.'

The two missionaries firmly shook their heads. After a few moments of silence, Luis Sasada also declined.

The officer nodded and stepped back two or three paces. Then as if he had suddenly remembered something, he came back to Velasco and with a steady gaze reported, 'This is confidential information, but . . . Hasekura and Nishi, who went with you to the foreign lands, were executed because they were Christians.'

A smile of delight appeared on Velasco's blanched lips.

'Ah!' A cry escaped his throat, and he turned to Father Carvalho and shouted, 'Now I can join them!'

The three men recited the Lord's Prayer in unison as they walked in single file towards the stakes. The three stakes peered at them from a distance, waiting patiently for their arrival. The guards pushed each of them in front of the stakes and lashed their bodies tightly to them. The sound of the wind was deafening.

When the guards had finished binding the prisoners, they shouted, 'May you be reborn in Paradise!' and dispersed in all directions. The officers had meanwhile taken shelter from the wind, and observed these preparations from beside the bamboo palisade.

A foot-soldier holding a torch set fire to each of the piles of firewood and straw at the base of the stakes. Fanned by the wind, the flames swept up violently and spewed out smoke. From within the billowing smoke, the prayers of each man could be heard clearly and distinctly.

> *Libera me, Domine,*
> *De morte aeterna.*

As the flames grew fiercer, the voices first of Luis Sasada, then of Father Carvalho, were abruptly silenced. Only the wind and the sound of collapsing firewood could be heard. Finally from within the white smoke which enveloped Velasco's stake, a single cry rang out.

'I . . . have lived . . .!'

The officials and guards stood shivering some distance away until the force of the flames at last died down. Even after the flames had subsided the three stakes, robbed of their prisoners and bent over like bows, continued to smoulder. A guard collected the bones and ashes and placed them on a rush mat, then loaded the mat with rocks and went to cast it into the sea.

The frothy waves which swept onto the beach swallowed up the rush mat, collided, and retreated. Those movements were repeated several times, and then the winter sun beat down upon the long beach as though nothing had happened, and the ocean stretched out beneath the sound of the wind. The officers and guards no longer stood within the bamboo palisade.

POSTSCRIPT: Fact and Truth in *The Samurai*

Van C. Gessel

The Historical Background

When Hasekura Rokuemon (1571–1622) set sail from Tsukinoura on the twenty-eighth day of October 1613, he began keeping a journal account of his experiences abroad. After his death the diary was held for a time by his domain in north-eastern Japan, but like almost everything associated with this journey, this was either misplaced or destroyed by the feudal authorities. This is a great loss to us, since it may have been the only reliable source to shed light on the many mysteries surrounding the voyage of 1613.

In fact, so little is known about this embassy that both Japanese and Western historians have all but ignored it. Although secondary documents abound in Madrid and Rome, the crucial questions about the motives for the journey remain unanswered. It is true that Scipione Amati, an Italian archivist who travelled with the group as interpreter between August 1615 and January 1616, penned an account of the journey titled *Historia del Regno di Voxu*. But Amati's reports cannot be trusted unless they deal with something he witnessed with his own eyes. The details of events leading up to the journey and the first two years of its progress were related to Amati by an ambitious Franciscan priest from Seville, who had somewhat more than an explication of truth in mind when he dictated his recollections of the voyage to his scribe.

Father Luis Sotelo (1574–1624), the model for Velasco in the novel, seems to have been every bit the scheming zealot described by Endō. The exaggerated report which Sotelo gave Amati of his own proselytizing efforts in Japan makes him seem a far more persuasive and successful evangelist than the Man he claimed to represent. Since Sotelo cannot be taken literally, we are left to our own devices to determine why the embassy was ever organized in the first place, what the ruler Ieyasu and Hasekura's lord Date Masamune truly wished to gain, and why Hasekura was chosen as the chief envoy.

In this regard Endō's novel, besides being a superbly crafted piece of fiction, is a valuable work of speculation. *The Samurai* is meticulously faithful to history in a way that the author's earlier *Silence* did not attempt to be. Virtually everything about Hasekura in the novel (with the exception of the statement that he had never participated in a battle) is true; the sad fact is that we know so little else about him. Thanks to the painstaking work of Japanese historians like Matsuda Kiichi, we can verify that Hasekura was a member of the gun corps under Date, and that he was master over a relatively insignificant estate in the north-east of Japan. But we find no further mention of him until he appears on the deck of the *San Juan Baptista*, joined by upwards of one hundred Japanese and some forty Spanish sailors.

This ship docked in Acapulco on 28 January, 1614 – ironically, almost the same day that Ieyasu promulgated the notorious Christian expulsion edict which marked the beginning of the end for the missionary effort in Japan. The activities of Hasekura and his entourage remain cloudy even after they reach Nueva España. Amati conveys in glowing terms Sotelo's report that seventy-eight Japanese were baptized in Mexico City; but the extant church records there make no mention of such an event. The *History* goes on to describe the enthusiastic reception which the embassy enjoyed along its trek through Nueva España; but Sotelo, the perpetrator of this ecstatic official account, was simultaneously dispatching letters to the King of Spain complaining of the frigid treatment they were receiving from all quarters.

The group of twenty or so Japanese who sailed from Veracruz on 10 June, 1614 were probably the first of their countrymen to make the journey across the Atlantic Ocean. Only after they reach Europe does the documentation become fairly reliable. The envoys were in fact warmly welcomed in Sotelo's hometown of Seville; they did have an audience with Philip III of Spain (at which Hasekura, with typical Japanese deference, announced that he considered himself 'the most honoured of all my people' to be able to leave a land of darkness and bask in the light of a Christian nation); Hasekura was baptized on the seventeenth of February by the King's personal chaplain, and he was made a Roman patrician and senator when he arrived in the Eternal City. The Spanish government, however, in receipt of angry reports from the Jesuits questioning the true motives of the embassy, could not settle upon a reasonable response to the envoys' requests, and the group languished in Spain for nearly ten months.

Sotelo eventually concluded that the Pope was his only recourse. The audience with Paul V on 3 November, 1615, although elaborate, produced little concrete result. Sotelo was unable to get himself appointed Bishop of Japan, and the question of trade relations between Nueva España and Japan was skilfully deflected. Although the Pope agreed to send additional Franciscans to Japan, news of the violent turn of events there soon rendered that promise hollow.

Endō telescopes the final stages of the journey for dramatic effect. In reality, the envoys remained in Europe until the summer of 1617, although it is unclear exactly what they were doing. When their ship arrived in Manila in July 1618, the envoys were ordered by the Japanese government to remain there until further notice. In 1620 the Catholic Council of the Indies instructed Sotelo to return to Nueva España and pursue his missionary labours there. That same year, Hasekura was finally allowed to return to his homeland. He found a Japan dramatically different from the country he had left behind. Christianity was being systematically and bloodily strangled out of existence, and within a few short years the shōgunate would ban trade with most foreign nations and prohibit any Japanese citizen from leaving the country. The goals of Hasekura's mission had been completely abandoned in his absence. The Christianity he had embraced in order to serve his lord more diligently had come to be regarded as a dangerous heresy. And Hasekura himself was an irritating anomaly in the hostile, isolationist society of seventeenth-century Japan.

After noting that Hasekura had returned to his domain, the Japanese official records fall silent. Traditional accounts of his last years vary. Some say that he willingly abandoned the Christianity which he had assumed only as an expediency. Others insist that he clung to his new faith and was therefore ordered to die; still others that he publicly disavowed the foreign religion but continued to practise it in secret. Though we have no way of determining which of these accounts is true, a letter supposedly written by Hasekura's grandson must have aroused Endō's curiosity. This letter claims that in 1640 the Tokugawa authorities discovered that Hasekura's son Gonshirō was furtively observing the rituals of the illegal religion; for allowing this to take place, the eldest son Kanzaburō was commanded to disembowel himself.

Whether the letter is authentic or not, its intriguing suggestion makes Endō's reconstruction of history all the more interesting. In 1622, the year of Hasekura's death, Sotelo disguised himself and made his way back to Japan. His martyrdom on 25 August, 1624 took place precisely as the novel describes. The deaths of these two men, like their lives, affirm Endō's fundamental thesis that the essence of Christianity is determined not by bureaucratic fiat, but by the private yearnings of each and every believer.

The Novel

When *The Samurai* was published in Japan in the spring of 1980, it met with universal acclaim from the critics and attracted a wide reading audience. Endō received one of the most important literary awards in Japan, the Noma Prize, for the novel. Yet, reading what the reviewers have had to say about the book, one cannot help but feel that many Japanese consider it a gripping historical adventure tale and nothing more.

It seems to me that readers and critics alike have missed the mark. Endō, as he states in his introductory note to the Western reader, is not interested in historical facts *per se* in *The Samurai*. Facts, after all, have never attracted him as much as the less substantive 'truth' about individuals and events. Just as the story of Rodrigues in *Silence*, though not strictly factual, is unquestionably 'true' in a broader sense, so Endō's version of Hasekura's life is a true record of the spiritual voyage that is undertaken within one man's heart. Readers who expect the novel to deal only with a temporal journey are, if you will, all at sea.

Endō's primary concern in the novel is adequately demonstrated by the working title he had in mind when he began to write. The book was originally to be called *A Man Who Met a King*. That title is most appropriate, for the Hasekura of both fact and fiction had the opportunity to come face to face with several kings of the earth. These meetings, however, all proved to be hollow, defeating. Hasekura and his warrior comrades are bested in the arena of the flesh and return to Japan humiliated and unsuccessful. But when Hasekura stands before an abyss of despair and likely death, he encounters yet another King, one who seeks only to salve his wounds, one who has also been 'despised and rejected of men'. It is when Hasekura meets and embraces this pathetic King that his own sorrows become endurable.

This image of a miserable but sympathetic Christ is a familiar one in Endō's literature: it is the same forgiving Christ who urged Rodrigues to trample on the *fumie*. What is significantly different about *The Samurai* is that Endō does not bring Velasco's concepts of Christianity into direct conflict with the samurai's. In *Silence*, the Western priests had to be stripped of the cultural trappings of their faith before they could grasp the true nature of Christ. In the present novel, however, Endō is less dogmatic about the questions of faith and culture. Here Velasco, once he has cast off his pride, is allowed to worship and serve a glorified Christ with a rational and aggressive faith, and his martyr's death is an undiluted reflection of his dynamic Western beliefs. In contrast, Hasekura accepts the companionship of Jesus in an almost passive way. His faith is primarily non-rational and thoroughly internalized, and the vague, blurred outlines of his death are a fitting symbol of a conviction different from – but no less valid than – that of Velasco. Endō in this novel grants both men a place in the eternal mansions of heaven.

If Hasekura's defeats and eventual awakening to faith are yet another type of the rejection and final triumph of Jesus, they also represent something much more personal to Endō. In an interview published at the time of the book's appearance in Japan, Endō remarked:

> *The Samurai* is in some ways an autobiographical novel. I was the first Japanese to study abroad after the war, the first to travel to Europe. The thirty-five-day ocean voyage was absolutely agonizing. The descriptions of the ocean in this novel are based on my experiences then, and in the life of Hasekura and the manner of his death I have expressed my present state of mind. . . . (*Nami*, April 1980)

The novel is autobiographical in more than just the externals of a sea voyage to Europe. The feelings of incomprehension and even revulsion which Hasekura experiences as he gazes at the crucifixes that seem to pursue him around the globe are not unlike the emotions which Endō has attributed to himself in his younger days. The scene in *The Samurai* in which Hasekura is baptized in Madrid is an eerily accurate reproduction of the ceremony in which Endō participated at the age of eleven. Like Hasekura, Endō did not choose Christianity of his own volition, but initially had it thrust upon him, and for some time he felt very distant from it. Only when the trials of his life's voyage brought him to a point where he could 'meet a King' did he, like his novel's protagonist, come to terms with a religion no longer foreign, but intensely personal. On one level, this novel is the story of that journey towards faith.

It is Endō's sense of affinity with Hasekura, and the ways in which the lives of author and character intermingle and mesh with that of Jesus, that breathe ultimate life into *The Samurai*. The novel is in many ways just what its author hoped it would be – a symphonic piece that offers up many rich melodies, bringing together East and West, faith and unbelief, fervour and passivity. And though the players in this musical work come from dissimilar traditions and play upon completely different instruments, the concluding refrain sounds out clearly and, most important, harmoniously.

えいぶんばん さむらい
英文版 侍
THE SAMURAI
_____

1996 年10月 1 日　第 1 刷発行
2003 年 2 月 7 日　第 3 刷発行

著　者　遠藤 周作
　　　　えんどう しゅうさく
訳　者　バン・ゲッセル
発行者　畑野文夫
発行所　講談社インターナショナル株式会社
　　　　〒112-8652 東京都文京区音羽 1-17-14
　　　　電話　03-3944-6493（編集部）
　　　　　　　03-3944-6492（営業部・業務部）
　　　　ホームページ　http://www.kodansha-intl.co.jp

印刷所　株式会社 平河工業社
製本所　株式会社 フォーネット社

Japan's Modern Writers

TUN-HUANG   A Novel
Yasushi Inoue
Translated by Jean Oda Moy

An intriguing explanation of one of the great mysteries of western China—how the sacred scrolls of the Sung dynasty were saved from the barbarian tribes of the Hsi-hsia.

PB, ISBN 0-87011-576-6, 216 pages

INTO A BLACK SUN
Takeshi Kaiko
Translated by Cecilia Segawa Seigle

"No other account of Vietnam has been so vivid, so intimate or so moral."   —Edmund White, *The New York Times*

PB: ISBN 0-87011-609-6   224 pages, 110 x 182 mm

HOUSE OF SLEEPING BEAUTIES
And Other Stories

Yasunari Kawabata
Translated by Edward Seidensticker
Introduction by Yukio Mishima

Three short stories which center on a lonely protagonist and his peculiar eroticism. Kawabata explores the interplay of fantasy and reality at work on a mind in solitude.

PB, ISBN 0-87011-426-3, 152 pages

THE LAKE
Yasunari Kawabata
Translated by Reiko Tsukimura

By Japan's first nobel laureate for literature. "Seizes the reader's imagination from the first page."   —*Village Voice*

PB, ISBN 0-87011-365-8, 168 pages

MONKEY BRAIN SUSHI   New Tastes in Japanese Fiction
Edited by Alfred Birnbaum

Fresh, irreverent, and post-Zen, an astounding collection of the brightest and boldest voices in contemporary Japanese fiction.

PB, ISBN 4-7700-1688-3, 312 pages